sinister societies

SINISTER SOCIETIES

EDITED BY

LINDA HARTLEY

RUADÁN
BOOKS

BOSTON, MA

For Jim

" The very word "secrecy" is repugnant in a free and open society; and we are as a people inherently and historically opposed to secret societies, to secret oaths and to secret proceedings. We decided long ago that the dangers of excessive and unwarranted concealment of pertinent facts far outweighed the dangers which are cited to justify it."

PRESIDENT JOHN F. KENNEDY

ADDRESS BEFORE THE
AMERICAN NEWSPAPER PUBLISHERS ASSOCIATION
APRIL 27, 1961

TABLE OF CONTENTS

Introduction:
The Secrets We Dare To Share,
A Not-So-Furtive Foreword
John Skipp xi

Cult of Least Resistance
Cindy O'Quinn 1

Agent Josephine Baker Against the Island of Horrors
Errick Nunnally 75

The Witches of Paradise
Mercedes M. Yardley 143

Vengeful Spirits
Michael Burke 233

Tunnel 17
Tom Deady 319

Cult of the Rat King
Sarah Read 427

Afterword
Linda Hartley 485

JOHN SKIPP

John Skipp's 2021 Splatterpunk Lifetime Achievement Award encapsulates his long, weird, colorful career as a Rondo award-winning filmmaker (*Tales of Halloween*), Stoker Award-winning anthologist (*Demons, Mondo Zombie*), and New York Times bestselling author (*The Light at the End, The Scream*), whose books have sold millions of copies in a dozen languages worldwide.

His first anthology, *Book of the Dead*, laid the foundation in 1989 for modern zombie literature. He also co-wrote one of the gnarliest episodes of Shudder's *Creepshow* Season One. From splatterpunk founding father to bizarro elder statesman, Skipp has influenced a generation of horror and counterculture artists worldwide.

In 2022, Skipp announced his official retirement from writing fiction, dedicating the rest of his life to making movies and scoring them. Until now, his supposedly "last" book is a collection of short stories, short screenplays, and essays called *Don't Push the Button*. His two newest albums—in which he wrote, performed, recorded, mixed, and produced all the music—are *Cry Me a Rainbow* and *The Antidote to Fear*. And his most recent film—Skipp's solo feature debut as writer, producer, director, composer, editor, and actor—is a darkly satirical class-warfare comedy called The Great Divide.

We *all have secrets*. It's just a fact.

You think you know a person? You might be right. But probably not half-as-right as you think.

Truth is, we all have complicated, puzzle-shaped lives, with private pieces we keep hidden from the world, either because we are trying to protect you, or because we're afraid of what you'll do if you find out.

Sometimes, a secret is shared or held in common. When a secret is shared, a society forms. Together, you build a wall around that knowledge. Be it two people or a trillion, it's you and them against the world.

Sometimes it's personal. Sometimes it's business. Sometimes it's kisses. And sometimes it's blood. Most times, we don't find out until the mask comes off. Sometimes, not even then.

Point being, we all have secrets. Let's take that as a given.

But some of them are worse than others.

FOR EXAMPLE:

I once bought a house—the only house I've ever owned—from a guy named George, who was a friend of the family.

I'd just become a first-time father, living in New York City with now not-just-one-but-TWO gorgeous young women, sharing a tiny apartment in Chelsea. I'd also just become a soon-to-be New York Times bestselling author (which is to say, I'd just gotten paid for my first book deal), but that money wasn't gonna last long in Manhattan. It was time for us to get the fuck outta Dodge. And George had a place for sale.

So I went back to York, Pennsylvania, the last town I'd escaped from, where my super-kind mom and her boyfriend still lived. Their friend George's house was a nice little two-story on a tree-lined street in an unassuming neighborhood, with a sweet backyard sizable enough for a bunch of kids to run around in, and a big ol' round above-ground swimming pool large enough for a party of eight.

My lady and I checked it out, and found it good. I had the cash for the down payment. So George and I made the deal. In the process of paperwork and planning, there were a couple of nights where I wound up crashing on the couch of my new house, hanging out with George and talking till the wee hours.

The fact that we both smoked like chimneys and drank like inebriated fish had more than a little to do with it.

Plus, George was wicked smart. Surprisingly well-read. A very interesting cat. Sicilian. About 6'3". No wife or kids, at least so far as I could tell. Former Special Forces, so he'd been around and done some shit. Seen big chunks of the world. Was a formidable man. Dangerous. Also funny as fuck. And not afraid to theorize or philosophize at length.

It was not uncommon, on those nights, to smoke a pack of cigarettes and drink a dozen beers apiece. He'd also bring out the whiskey, but that wasn't my thing. (I'd sneak out back and smoke a little weed whenever he left to take a leak. Not really a secret. Just being polite and discreet.)

So anyway, we finally closed the deal. And on the night he signed the deed over to me, he made just the two of us a big old dinner—he was an excellent chef—and then we just stayed in the kitchen for-fucking-ever, celebrating with three packs of Marlboro Reds and a case-anna-half of Rolling Rock. Just talking and talking and talking.

It was about 3:30 in the morning when I finally agreed to take a shot, roughly ten beers in. He'd just gone on a long riff of his Vietnam war experiences, and I was talking about all the death I'd seen as a child in Argentina. The reality of violence. The matter-of-factness of it. Which was something I was urgently trying to convey in my not-yet-called-splatterpunk fiction. (*The Light at the End* was published two years before that funny word was even conceived, and completed a year-anna-half before that, after having spent another two years writing it.)

And it was right about that point—as we toasted and downed our shots—that George decided to tell me his secret.

Now, George had always been a little bit cryptic about what he did for a living. Said it was sales or something. Did not care to elaborate, nor did he make evasiveness a big deal. Just never brought it up, and deftly deflected whenever someone else did. Liked to play his cards close to the vest.

Clearly, the dude had cash. Was not short on amenities. Drove a very nice, roomy sedan. Hadn't sold me the house out of fiscal emergency. Just said it was time to go.

But now, on this night—as he prepared to leave town, the two of us loosened up by booze and confessional candor—I guess he just decided that it was time to tell somebody. Guess he thought I would understand. Or was just too drunk to care.

And I wish to God I could quote this conversation verbatim. But I can't, because I was drunk, too. If I tried to recount it, I'd just be making shit up. So I'd rather just tell you what I know for a fact.

What George told me was that there's not a whole lot of use for Special Forces experience in the civilized world. That being a trained killer brought with it a set of skills not commonly applied in the civilian marketplace. Once out of the military, his main choices were bullshit jobs, security, law enforcement, or crime.

He had no patience for bullshit jobs. That would be beneath him. That would be slumming. He was fucking Special Forces, goddamit! He was the best of the best. And he was proud. And he was smart. It was just not going to happen.

He was also profoundly contemptuous of authority figures, which was something we very much shared in common. This quality had been well-established over our last nights of drunken gab. So there was no way on Earth that he was gonna be a cop. And wanted as far away from the FBI and CIA as he could possibly get.

This left security and crime, which generally wound up working hand-in-hand. People who needed paid protection were generally up to something. And that something was generally nothing good.

In other words, it was less a slippery slope than a dark continuum.

Which is to say, his main profession was the disposing of human bodies.

And for that, he often had to kill them first.

Now, I was sitting toward the end of the enormous kitchen counter, right next to the phone on the wall. To my left was the doorway to the living room, leading straight to the front door. To my right, the counter was an island bisecting the kitchen, stretching all the way to the oven, the open back door.

On the other side of the counter, George stood by the fridge, the sink full of dishes beside him. We were sharing an ashtray that was squarely between us. He was looking me in the eye as he told me these things. And I just sat there, listening close and nodding my head.

I was not surprised to learn that George was a professional killer. I mean, what part of "Special Forces" did I not understand? He totally looked the part. For all his wit and charm, he radiated easy predator calm.

Fact is, we recognized each other's shadows. I was not a killer, but I knew what it meant. I was not judging him, as he knew I wouldn't. I was just listening. Bearing witness, as is eternally my job.

George didn't go into the gory details. There was no bragging, no attempts to impress. Nor was he guiltily confessing his crimes. He wasn't talking out of shame. He wasn't talking out of pride. He just wanted me to know. I think it felt good to tell.

Then he said—and this I recall very clearly—"Thing is, it's just not that hard. You just do it. Then it's done. And that's it."

I don't remember where the long, serrated carving knife came from. If it was on the counter, or in the sink, or in a drawer. But suddenly, he had it in his massive right hand.

Then he said, "Here. Let me show you."

As around the island he came.

Now, if I'd had any inclination to run, that would have been the time to do it. It was summer, so the front door was wide open, and I knew for a fact the screen door wasn't locked. But he was calm, and I was calm, and our eyes remained locked as he rounded the bend. Walking toward me. Weaving ever so slightly. The knife still in his hand.

I still had about an inch on my cigarette left. I thought about last cigarettes: a ritual for the condemned.

Then he came up to me. Stepped behind my bar stool.

Brought the knife to my throat.

And held it there.

I think he started talking then. I don't think it was to me.

He was definitely not spitting out threats, or mocking me, or insulting, or unleashing any of the thug-like verbal cliches we expect from cartoon villains, be they real or imagined.

And weirdly, I wasn't scared. I was just *sooooo deeply, sooooo terribly sad*. Thinking about my daughter. Her mom. My mom. How quickly this could end. How little I could do to stop it.

How easily I would fit into the trunk of that sedan.

I don't think I made any noise at all. I'm pretty sure I wasn't breathing. All I could feel were the warm, thick tears, running down my cheeks. And the gentle prick of that cold, serrated blade.

Then I guess he was done, because he pulled the blade away— and without another word, walked back around the island counter.

I took a deep breath. He got more beer out of the fridge. And we stayed up talking till the sun came up. About what? I have no idea. But I remember we laughed a lot, before finally staggering off to our respective quarters.

That week, George left town. I moved my family down. A couple months later, I heard George had died of cancer. And that, as they say, was the end of that.

I never told my mom or her boyfriend. I didn't think they needed to know. They remembered him as a good dinner buddy, a fun guy to drink and converse and play cards with. They loved him a lot. He loved them, too. I knew he never would have hurt them. It would have never even come up.

Like I said, everybody has secrets. Some are just worse than others.

And most, we'll never know.

WHICH BRINGS US to this book, and the wonderful stories you're about to read. Six novellas, kaleidoscopic in range. Three women. Three men. All carrying secrets, which they happily share.

Inside, you'll find spies, stars, sex cults, secret families, Nazis, demons, giant spiders, and the king of the rats himself. You'll find witches and crime lords and miners and monsters. Books that kill. Flowers with teeth. And moons that devour the sky.

You'll also meet people both brave and tragic, some of whom you may come to love. Not all of them will survive, alas. (But if it's any consolation, a whooooole lotta assholes die!)

Mostly, you'll meet these six talented writers, taking you inside their cunning puzzle-piece worlds.

With "Cult of Least Resistance," Cindy O'Quinn brings her warm, soulful, authentic and chilling Appalachian folk horror voice to this fraught, tightly-wound but brutally untangling web of haunted mothers, sisters and brothers, betrayal, psychosis, and a love so strong it might even prevail. It's a dark yet beautiful story, and a truly great way to begin.

"Agent Josephine Baker Against the Island of Horrors" is a super-fun pulp adventure, set to Errick Nunnally's zippy, vintage 1940's jazz score. It's playfully nostalgic and crisply textured, as fresh and full of surprises as our intrepid heroine, rollicking and replete with old-school anti-fascist thrills.

Mercedes M. Yardley brings her breathtaking vision of a natural world both insane and profound to her mindblowing fantasy, "The Witches of Paradise." It is, to me, the book's most shocking and unsettling piece. But there's a measure of the miraculous flowing through it that resonates hard in the collective unconscious. Which is to say, this crazy motherfucker runs deep.

Mike Burke is next with "Vengeful Spirits," a perkily-brooding Prohibition-era puzzle box that twistily mixes noir and the occult. It's a mystery packed with double-crossing mayhem, and impossible visions grounded in rich, vivid period detail, bringing us back down to earth with all cylinders firing.

Take a deep breath, and before you know it, you're waaaay the hell down in "Tunnel 17," Tom Deady's creepily atmospheric deep-dive into the nightmare pit. This is a piece that benefits mightily from Deady's dedication to getting the details right, juxtaposing supernatural horror with the economic horror of murderous union busters and unsurvivable working conditions.

Finally, we come face-to-face with Sarah Read's freakily ingenious "Cult of the Rat King," where a destitute young thief pickpockets far more than she bargained for. This fascinating mind-bender ping-pongs easily between photo-realism and total surrealism, bringing the book's wild adventures to a perfect flesh-shredding punch-in-the-nose conclusion.

What the whole thing underscores is how lucky we are to belong to this society of the creative and strange. It is a society that spans the globe, through books and film and music and dance and every art form the human race has yet deciphered.

Sharing our darkness, our light, and our dreams.

It's easy to forget just how deeply we're connected, like the root structures of forests nestled far beneath the soil. From the Lascaux Caves to the latest stolen scrapings in some upstart AI cyber-brain now struggling to be born, our dreams and visions are an infinite parade of gnosis in motion. A trail of breadcrumbs that goes on forever, all pointed toward meaning. Or the absence thereof.

The purpose of art is to remind us that we are not alone on this journey. That everyone is on it, whether they recognize it or not. That each of us is a piece of that macro-puzzle. That each of us carries at least one clue.

That we all have our secrets. And that's a good one, indeed.

I had a blast reading these stories, and suspect that you will, too. Which makes this a great time to get out of your way.

Thank you for joining this secret society of strange storytellers and story-lovers. Please allow me to assure you, there ain't no place I'd rather be.

And that, my friend, is the world's most open secret.

Yer pal in the trenches,

Skipp

CINDY O'QUINN

Cindy O'Quinn is an Appalachian writer. She grew up in the beautiful mountains of West Virginia. She writes fiction, nonfiction, and speculative poetry, which all lean heavily into the horror genre. She is the author of *Dark Cloud on Naked Creek*. It was Cindy's fifth Bram Stoker Award® nomination that garnered her the prestigious award. Her poetry has been nominated for the Elgin, Rhysling, and Dwarf Star awards.

Cult of Least Resistance

S ilence filled the old Buick as we passed the rural views on our way out of Lynchburg. All I could hear was the tired exhaust rattling underneath us as we drove along the dirt road. It was my fourth move in as many years—to yet another foster home—but that had come as no surprise, considering that terrible night. All I remembered was seeing flashing blue and red lights as a man carried me to safety. Truth be told, I was happy to leave the city behind.

My caseworker tried to reassure me. "You're going to love the Ramseys. They are nice people. I've known them for quite some time now."

I liked Eliza. As caseworkers went, she seemed to be a good one. Despite her confidence, I doubted the placement was going to be any better than the previous ones. I only hoped it wouldn't be worse.

Charlie Hartless. That's my name: the name bestowed on me at birth. Sometimes, I questioned that. It felt too made-up. Memories of my parents were vague, or maybe I'd filled in the blanks with what I reckoned belonged there. Something made me wonder if they had been fans of Charles Manson. Throwing Hartless into the mix only added fuel to the fire, as if people couldn't find enough shit to say about me. People never called me just Charlie, always Charlie Hartless, or worse still, Hartless. And I'm talking children and teachers alike. Wasn't all that surprised by kids, they were always cruel. But my teachers should have known better. I was sick of hearing *Charlie Hartless doesn't apply herself in class. Hartless is late for class. Hartless has another black eye. Charlie Hartless is being placed with another foster family.* I wanted people to call me Char, but it never stuck.

I kept myself busy with journaling. Writing was my only outlet. I'd been doing it for as long as I could remember. Unfortunately, several of my notebooks had been left behind when I was rushed away from one of many terrible foster homes. From then on, I started keeping my journals on me, or at least within reach. If I was moved in a hurry, my stories came with me. Writing was my way of feeling any semblance of being normal. At least what I considered normal. If I ever even knew what that was.

Sitting in the back seat, I watched the landscape change. It went from city buildings and row after row of houses to lush green fields, forests, and farms. I started to wonder about my imminent destination, but decided it best to rid my mind of that thought completely. I focused on the mountains and the woodlands, and the occasional farmhouse.

The miles clicked away, and as they did, I felt I was approaching familiar territory. I'd been here before, after all—and I'm not talking about the location. I tried to shake the feeling off, but there was no way to get rid of it. We had already traveled for nearly an hour on secondary roads, turning every few miles onto even narrower roads and lanes. Eventually, we turned one last time. Dark Hollow Road. Must've been some hellish joke. Each home was worse than the last in one way or another. What was waiting for me this time, at the end of the dark holler?

The Oldsmobile slowed to a crawl. I strained my eyes in an attempt to see what lay ahead. There it was, my next holding cell. An old, ranch-style house. One story, that was a good sign. I had made up my mind on the drive over that if this placement turned out to be another form of hell, then I would run. At least I wouldn't have to jump from a two-story window, breaking a leg in the process.

The first glimpse of my new wardens revealed very little. The pair stood motionless on the front porch, which ran the full width of the house. Their appearance was as plain and unthreatening as the house's. However, their smiles might've been a little too big, and I was surprised their teeth were not filed down to flesh-tearing points. But I knew only too well appearances were deceiving, so I told myself not to get my hopes up.

My caseworker made the introductions. She was officially Miss Kitchin, but I called her Eliza, as we'd been on first-name terms ever since our initial meeting. As for the couple, now reaching out to shake hands with me, they were Little Mary and Bledsoe Ramsey of Nelson County, Virginia. The story was, they'd never had children of their own, so they took in those who had nowhere else to go. *Logical enough,* I told myself, but if history repeated itself, logic would dissipate as soon as my caseworker exited the driveway.

Knowing the Ramseys, Eliza hung around for a little while. Once inside, I found the house to be unusually quiet. It was unlike all the other placements, where there had always been chaos, commotion, or mess, no matter the time of day. Something else that struck me as unusual was that I saw no signs of any other children. I wondered if I would be the only one here with this regular-looking couple. *Unlikely,* I told myself. It was my experience that people took in children for the money, and that was that. Bottom line. And more children made for a bigger monthly check.

The couple invited Eliza to stay for a meal, my first in the new prison. She accepted, so I allowed myself to breathe. After we had finished eating, Little Mary suggested I take a walk and get the lay of the land. She told me she had some catching up to do with her friend, and they would do so while they cleaned up the kitchen together. I figured Little Mary wanted to get the full scoop from Eliza on all the past homes I had survived. Oh, well; fine with me. At least I'd gotten out of doing the dishes.

I'd only been walking for a few minutes when I heard the sound of running water, and it wasn't long before I found myself standing next to a creek. It was neither wide nor deep, but with all manner of rocks scattered about, forming an erratic shoreline, it sounded kind of impressive. I had a flashback of myself as a small child, playing in a similar stream: a little girl, about my age, was running through the water next to me. She tilted her head back and squealed with delight as the cold creek water splashed onto her skin. I felt astonished to have actually had a friend. But there she was, with shoulder-length golden hair, her eyes a sparkling blue, and with a smile that lit up the afternoon. I felt true happiness and a freedom I didn't think possible—

A burning sensation in my eyes brought me back to the here and now. I wiped the warm tears away before they could make the journey down my cheeks. I wondered if it was a true memory. I hoped against hope that it was—that perhaps, at some point in my childhood, I had known such joy.

I headed back to the Ramseys'. I wasn't sure how long I'd been gone; I had never been afforded the luxury of a wristwatch. The doors of an old shed stood open, and I could see Bledsoe leaning over a table. He was deep in his work and didn't notice me as I walked past. For a fleeting moment I allowed myself to be a little curious about his project. I let the thought go almost as quickly as it had come.

Back in the house, I found the two women in the living room, enjoying a cup of coffee. Eliza invited me to join them, so with some reluctance, I did as I was asked. I was well-prepared: Little Mary was going to lay down the rules of the house and tell me what would be expected of me while I was under their roof. But that wasn't the case. She simply told me to make myself comfortable, and assured me that this was now my home, just as it was theirs. Shocked at hearing such kind words, I thought surely my ears would bleed.

Eliza said her goodbyes and asked if I would walk her to the car. She placed her business card in my hand. It had both her work and cell numbers on it; she told me I should never hesitate to call if I needed anything. There was an emphasis on the word *anything*. I shook her outstretched hand and told her goodbye. I even mumbled a barely audible "Thank you." Once she was gone, I stood there staring at the house for a moment, wondering what was next.

The next was more normalcy, a foreign concept to me. Little Mary led me to the bedroom that was to be mine. There stood a dresser, a bedside table with a small lamp on top, and a full-sized bed that didn't sag in the middle. The room even had its own closet, where I would put away my paper bag of belongings. There were no bars on the windows like the ones back in the city. Little Mary told me I was welcome to paint the room whatever color I wanted, and went on to tell me there was a thrift store not too far away, where we could buy a few things to spruce it up. I told her the room was fine the way it was.

Could Little Mary hear the ringing I was hearing so clearly in my ears? If she could, she didn't let on. I swear, I slept so soundly I woke the next morning in the same position I'd started out in.

Over breakfast, Little Mary and Bledsoe told me about the local farmers' market where they sold their goods. I felt elated they'd invited me, though a part of me couldn't help thinking that was because they didn't trust me in the house on my own. Nonetheless, I went into my room and got ready.

There were about a dozen vendors already set up at the

market when we arrived. They sold a variety of wares, such as vegetables, eggs, cheese, candles, and antique furniture. One stall caught my attention. It stood out from the others by a mile, and I was completely drawn in. The proprietor was dressed in a flowing white skirt and a peasant-style shirt, both of which were trimmed with embroidered lilac flowers. She had sandy hair cascading in waves down her back, and the kindest face. Her eyes were bright and enigmatic. On the table in front of her lay a collection of refurbished old frames paned with stained glass. There was one I couldn't help but touch. It was a circular design, and the colors burst outward from the center. The proprietor started toward me, and I pulled my hand away quickly.

"They're beautiful, aren't they?" she said, and I couldn't disagree.

"They most certainly are. If I had the money, I would buy this one." I placed my hand back on the piece. I would never come close to owning it, being dirt-poor and having no family to speak of.

She said, "You're where you belong. I wanted you to know, in case you have doubts."

I looked into her face, directly into her eyes, but didn't reply. They weren't questions. I went back to Little Mary and Bledsoe's table.

After the market had ended, and without being asked, I helped the Ramseys load up their empty boxes; they had sold everything. Mary went over and spoke with the woman who'd been selling the stained-glass pieces, probably making sure I hadn't broken anything.

It was time to go. I took my place next to the door, and Little Mary sat in the middle, next to Bledsoe behind the wheel. The truck appeared to have weathered the years without the rust you usually see on older vehicles. I rolled down my window and took in the breeze as we rode along the country roads. The earthy smells were a treat for my senses: freshly mown fields and wild onions. A little farther along, the sweet scent of lilac wafted through the car, and I tried to breathe in all I could before it was gone. It reminded me of the stained-glass artist and her lilac-trimmed clothing.

Before I knew it, we were pulling into the drive of the little ranch. Bledsoe had us get out right next to the house, and then he pulled the truck into the garage and put the empty boxes away. I went straight to my room and opened the window. I wanted to smell the flowers again, especially the lilacs, and there was a bush just below my window. Little Mary stood at my doorway and gently tapped on the frame. I looked at her in surprise. No one had ever shown me such respect before. Or *any* respect, if I'm being honest.

"May I come in?"

It was on the tip of my tongue to say, "Well, it's your house," jokingly, but I didn't. I'm certain it would've come out all wrong.

"Sure."

"I have something for you."

She held a package wrapped in brown paper, which I recognized from the market, and placed it on my bed. No one had ever bought me a gift before. I was hesitant, unsure of whether or not to move, what to say, or how to act. I felt a smile coming, and did nothing to stop it.

"Don't you want to open it?"

I was trembling with excitement, but noticed the time on the wall clock. "I do, but I want to help you with dinner, first." I hoped she would understand I was feeling overwhelmed by her generosity.

I was excited to finish the meal and the cleanup in order to get to my room. I skipped down the hallway, closed the bedroom door behind me, and sat on the edge of the bed.

Slowly, I unwrapped the present. My heart raced as I pulled the paper away and saw what was inside. It was the small round frame containing the multi-colored glass!

I held it gently and made my way over to the window. The sun was just dipping behind the mountain, so I held up the stained glass, and the orange and red hues from the setting sun shot right through it. It sprayed a rainbow of intense colors across my room and onto the wall behind my bed. I had never in my life seen anything so utterly magnificent.

That night in bed, I felt a strange calmness: a new feeling for me. I was used to being so on edge and het up about everything. I'd never allowed myself to get comfortable until now, I guess.

Before snuggling under the blankets for the night, I set my alarm for just before dawn, so I could go outside to watch the sunrise. It was another good night's sleep.

I'm unsure how long the alarm sounded before I turned it off. I hoped it hadn't disturbed the Ramseys. Quickly, I got dressed, grabbed the stained-glass window, and headed for the little creek, where the sun was making its appearance above the tree-tops. As I held up the glass, it created a rainbow, which appeared to leap across the water. I was mesmerized by the beauty of it all.

"Charlie?" I heard Little Mary's voice coming from the house. Not Charlie Hartless, just *Charlie*. I smiled.

"Coming!" I hollered, hugged the suncatcher close, and ran home. *Home?* That sounded nice.

It was Sunday morning, so we had a light breakfast, then Little Mary asked me to change for church. I didn't own a change of clothes, let alone a Sunday best, so all I could do was stare down at my plate. Bledsoe repeated the request. I continued to look down, this time at nothing in particular.

"If you don't wish to change," Little Mary said, "you'll be fine with what you're wearing. You'll blend in perfectly. But if you do want to check out your other options, you'll find them hanging in your closet." My head shot up like a bat out of hell. Maybe that was not the best thought to have had before going to church, but I was excited to see what was waiting for me. I excused myself from the table and scurried to my room.

An array of dresses, skirts, and shirts were hanging there, in my very own closet! All of them seemed to say, *pick me!* None of the items were new, but they certainly were to me. I chose a peasant top similar to the stained-glass lady's, a white skirt with little green flowers all over it, and slipped on a pair of flip-flops I found at the bottom of the closet.

I was pleasantly surprised by the girl looking back at me in the full-length mirror. It was such a stark change from the dingy gray tee shirts and black jeans I was used to. As for my hair, well, it stayed in a ponytail. I had received no lessons in the grooming department.

The Ramseys were in the living room, sitting side by side on the couch. I rushed in and then paused, suddenly feeling shy. They both agreed the outfit suited me well, but neither made a fuss. I guess they could see I was having trouble articulating how much I appreciated the clothing. I smiled, and they understood very well.

The three of us loaded into the truck and headed off to church. We made a few turns, but it felt as though we were just making a big circle. I looked at Little Mary but decided against asking her about it. A few minutes later, we were pulling into a parking spot. There were no other vehicles, so maybe we were early. The building wasn't really a building at all. It was more like a big picnic shelter. It had a stone floor, and a matching stone fireplace at one end. Two long tables filled the floor area, and in the center were three big support posts. There must have been at least twenty more posts along the sides. I doubted even the heaviest of snows would have pulled the thing down.

I heard voices, so I turned around, expecting to see several cars parked near the truck, but there were none, only people. Had they walked out of the woods or come down the road? I didn't remember passing any houses on the way. I felt myself tensing, and the wall that usually surrounded me was going up rapidly. I didn't trust people. Why should I? They certainly didn't have a very good track record in my life thus far.

I had the urge to run, but my feet felt cemented in place. All I could do was stand there and look at all the people who seemed to be closing in on me. *Shit the bed, Fred,* was the only phrase in my head at that time. It was a good thing I didn't say it out loud.

No one tried to talk to me, shake my hand, or introduce themselves. Each person just walked in casually, and as they passed, they would simply nod a hello in my direction. I decided I was going to keep that wall of mine up, just in case.

Everyone took a spot on the benches, which ran the whole length of the tables. Little Mary motioned for me to take a seat next to her.

Okay, but where's Bledsoe? Just then, I heard him talking. He was welcoming everyone, and then started praying. I was shocked at the thought of him being the pastor, but couldn't quite figure out why. He seemed like an okay guy, and so far, I had no evidence to the contrary.

I couldn't keep my head down or my eyes shut. There was just too much to look at, too much to take in. I discovered different symbols on each of the posts. I only recognized the one for Christianity.

Bledsoe's message hovered around different religions—hundreds of them, in fact. He said there was one thing in common with just about all of them: a higher being. In some way or another, they were all similar. He said it would be odd if, even though we each hold on tight to our own beliefs, in the end, it didn't matter. We all had been worshipping some form of goodness all along. We remained so separate and did all our rituals and routines, thinking our way was the only way. Heaven had indeed been for those who believed and practiced but two things: worship and love the one and only God, and love your neighbor. Not just the one next door but the neighbor across the world. Could it be that simple? It made perfect sense to me.

I felt eyes peering at me, so I looked around at the odd picnic shelter church. Growing up, I had often heard "The building doesn't make up the church." It was the people who gathered within. The congregation: those who looked upon the newcomer. In the crowd, I saw five adult women, besides Little Mary, and five teenage girls, about my age. There were four boys between the ages of ten and sixteen, and twin girls somewhere in between. Being in the foster system for so long, I had become pretty good at guessing children's ages. One element was missing, though: men. It was very noticeable that Bledsoe was the only adult male there.

Everyone started getting up and making their way towards me. I was ready to bolt. Little Mary placed a gentle hand on my arm, as if she knew what I was contemplating. And so the introductions commenced. There was Maeve Keller with a son, Aimesh, and a daughter, Iris. Next was Odette DePriest; her son, Rory, and her daughter, Juniper. Then came Linnea Lawson, with her sons Briar and Coy, and her daughter, Lotus. Aubrey Petit followed with her daughter Posey, and twin girls Harper and Harlow. I bet they were a handful. Last, Coriander Sabin with her daughter Wisteria.

The grown-ups shook my hand and welcomed me. The children giggled and messed about. The five teenage girls, on the other hand, looked me up and down the way teenage girls tend to do when they meet someone new. Especially someone the same age and gender. I don't know if it was a competitive thing, or envy. Either way, it was an archaic act which made me uncomfortable as hell. And I didn't have anything for them to be envious about, in any case. I pictured myself clawing away at their five perfect faces.

The quintet scurried away—undoubtedly, to discuss the new girl. Talk about being a *Flower Child,* each one of them had a name to match.

THE NEXT DAY, I started school. I was more nervous about getting there on time than anything else. Luckily, Little Mary took me for a walk and showed me the path I'd need to take. I found the bridge, following the creek, and was surprised I hadn't noticed it before. It was a bit worse for wear, but kinda pretty, with climbers and creepers winding their way up and over.

I started through the woods until I heard the banter of the teenage girls, not far ahead of me. I composed myself as best I could, and prepared to meet them. I still had the contrasting thought that maybe I should run as far away as I could get.

I was nearing the edge of the woods and could make out a small building.

"Hello, Charlie!" The voice startled me. It was one of the five girls I had met at the church, but I couldn't remember which fucking flower she was.

She must've read my mind. "I'm Lotus. My mother, Ms. Lawson, is the school teacher here."

I relaxed a little, because at least I wasn't going to be alone as

I walked into class.

Of course, when I did, everyone had to stop what they were doing and stare at the new girl. Great. Just great. So much for blending in. I was sick to death of starting new schools and being the strange new girl everybody gawped at. Mind you, I was kinda used to it, though—not fitting in, I mean. And at least it meant I could keep myself to myself, with my nose buried in my journal. I wrote about everything. I had to. It was either that, or sit on my own and stare into space until I disappeared because no one would dare associate with the poor foster child.

"Okay, everybody," Ms. Lawson said, bringing the class to attention. She had bright red curls, and freckles galore. "We have a new student with us, and I thought it'd be great if we all introduced ourselves."

Thankfully, there were only eleven students, so it wouldn't take too long. I thought back to my last school in the city. There were at least forty kids in every class, making a total of twelve hundred.

The teacher went first. She told us how she had gone to the University of Virginia to become a teacher. And she had three children, who were my classmates. Lotus Lawson loved to paint. Coy and Briar didn't have much to say, and played shy.

"We're fourteen," the twin girls, Harper and Harlow, said in unison.

"We like making jewelry—"

"Out of silver."

"*Sterling* silver."

"We especially love making—"

"Rings."

"Yeah. Rings are our—"

"Favorite thing to make."

It was funny how one would start a sentence, but the other would chime in and finish it. They were the first set of twins I had ever met.

Posey, the twins' seventeen-year-old sister, went next.

"I write poetry. In French. My dad was born in Paris." That was all she said. Dads didn't seem to be a topic of choice here. Iris stood up and declared that her hobby was designing and sewing clothes. If she had made what she was wearing, then she really had talent. She'd picked such a pretty fabric. Her younger brother Aimesh had about as much to say, just like the rest of the boys. He took care of the chickens and the rabbits, and did all the gardening. All Rory had to say was, "Yeah, same as me."

Juniper told of how her mom worked long hours as a nurse, so she had her hands full looking after the house and her little brother. Rory grinned and called his sister *tattle-tits*. Juniper blushed, and the rest of the kids laughed. I thought young Briar was going to piss his pants, he cackled so hard.

Ms. Lawson put an end to the nonsense. "All right, children; that's enough. Who's next?"

Wisteria had the whole goth thing going on. Long black hair, pale foundation, acrylic talons—and I do mean talons; they were beyond nails—replete with all manner of symbols. She looked as though she'd just as soon spit on you as look at you. She didn't scare me, but if anyone here was going to cause me grief, it would likely be her. She had advice for me, and it was this: "Get out while you still can."

Ms. Lawson looked distraught. "Wisteria! We are supposed to be making Charlie feel welcome, not scaring her away! Charlie, why don't you tell us a little about yourself?"

I could feel their eyes burning a hole through my already worn-out clothes. I kept it simple by telling them I had just been placed with the Ramseys, and had been living in Lynchburg. I told them I had one hobby, which was writing. "Nothing as fancy as French, though." I looked at Posey when I said that, and she smiled at me.

I leaped back into the safe zone that was my desk. Ms. Lawson thanked the class— shooting Wisteria a look— and assured me I would be a welcome addition to the community.

At noon, she told us we could go outside to have our lunch. My stomach was empty, and I hadn't given the first thought to packing any snacks. Little Mary had given me a backpack as I'd left that morning, though, so I looked inside, and found a lunchbox: not a paper sack but a real, insulated lunchbox! My first.

The goodies inside included a sandwich, an apple, and a bottle of homemade grape juice. All were still fresh, thanks to the cold pack Little Mary had included. I had just sat down at one of the empty picnic tables when four of the seventeen-year-old girls got up from where they were, and came over to sit with me. Wisteria was off on her own a little way away, sitting under the shade of a big tree.

The twins sat at a separate table. They were going on and on about a new wire-wrap ring they were designing. The four boys had already inhaled their food and were now playing tag. Posey told me she was glad we both shared a love of writing, and Iris offered to give me some sewing lessons if I wanted. "Not that there's anything wrong with what you're wearing," she said, "you look just swell."

Lotus said she would like to show me her paintings sometime. Juniper said she had no time for hobbies, what with all the housework and cooking she had to do. I told her that with all her experience, I bet she was an excellent cook. My statement seemed to puff her up nicely, and the other girls smiled in appreciation at what I'd done for their friend. Before I knew it, I had gobbled up my delicious lunch, and Ms. Lawson was calling us back inside.

For a class of only twelve, there were four grades of students, but Ms. Lawson seemed to have the routine down pat, and she made sure no child went without attention. I was amazed by how smoothly it flowed, and how quickly time passed.

The first day of school was over, and we all gathered our things and headed out the door. Lotus, Briar, and Coy belonged to the teacher, so I knew they would walk together. But to my surprise, all the students headed in the same direction. They all told me goodbye, except for Wisteria, of course.

I wanted so badly to follow them, just to see where they lived, but decided against it. They had been nice to me for the most part, and I didn't want to complicate things. I headed in the opposite direction, through the woods, across the bridge, and to the Ramseys'.

Both Little Mary and Bledsoe were in the backyard. They tried their best to look busy, as though they hadn't been standing there waiting to hear how my day had gone.

"It went well," I told them. "The new school's really different than I'm used to, but in a good way."

"That's great, dear! What did you think of the lunch I packed for you?"

"Oh, it was delicious! Thank you so much!" They both grinned from ear to ear. I could see the relief on their faces.

I helped with the chores—nothing much, just a bit of sweeping and putting away some freshly laundered bed linen—then went straight to my room. I had a lot of writing I wanted to do, and for a change, it wasn't all bad.

I was deep into my journaling when there was a knock at my door. It was Iris and Posey. I was definitely surprised; company was one thing I was unaccustomed to.

Iris handed me a bag she'd brought along. "I made these last year, but I've outgrown them. If they fit, they're yours. If you like them, that is!"

I reached into the bag and pulled out a blouse and a pair of capri pants. The detail she had put into the outfit was unreal.

"Wow… thank you! These are awesome! I'm going to wear these tomorrow if they fit." I really hoped they would.

Posey was holding a journal tightly against her chest, as though it would dissipate like a cloud if it were to fall. I understood exactly how she felt. I suddenly missed those notebooks I'd had to leave behind.

The three of us sat in my room and made small-talk for over an hour. It didn't feel too awkward; we talked about writing and creating and I told them I was glad they had come over. It was close to 6 p.m. when they said their goodbyes. I actually looked forward to going to school the next morning.

The rest of the evening flew by with dinner and chores, and I was back in my room by the time the sun was about to set. I had hung the stained glass in my window, and now the evening sunbeams were streaming through it. I stretched out on my bed and let go of all my thoughts, drawn in by the colors that now danced across my room. By the time the sun was swallowed up by the mountains, I slipped into a fitful sleep, tainted with dreams and memories.

I was a small child again, and my blonde friend was there with me. The atmosphere did not have the same joyfulness about it, this time. The air felt heavy and hot, making breathing a chore. I could feel beads of sweat popping out across my forehead, and my heart was racing. I was scared, but the fear was not for myself. It was for her. I could sense that my friend felt it as well. I wanted to grab her hand and run. Darkness was closing in all around us. No—it was more than that. It was more than just darkness. It was a presence, a looming presence, and it meant to cause us harm. No, it was there to cause her harm. Not me…

It was morning, and Bledsoe was knocking at my door. I shook the bad dream away, just as I had done many times in my life. I then dressed in the outfit Iris had given me. It fit perfectly; I felt almost normal—a normal seventeen-year-old girl in the twelfth grade.

After breakfast, I asked Little Mary if she could do something with my hair.

"I'd love to!" she said, and ushered me to the bathroom,

where she brushed out my thick, wavy brown locks. They had a mind of their own and never stayed put. They stuck out here, there, and everywhere. She put some kind of pomade in the palms of her hands and rubbed it through my hair, taking care of all those stray, flyaway strands. She stood back so I could look in the mirror.

"It's so neat! And glossy! Thank you so much."

I walked with a little extra pep that morning, and it wasn't long before I was exiting the woods near the school. To my surprise, Wisteria was the first person I saw. She just glared at me with those dark eyes of hers as I walked nervously by. As I was just past her, she snipped, "Notice anything different about this place? How the boys here are… different?"

I didn't respond, and kept walking. Besides that, I felt too good to let her taint my mood.

After school had let out for the day, Iris told me that on Tuesdays, everyone pitched in to help pack up for the farmers' market, which was on Wednesdays and Saturdays. So, we all headed to the greenhouse to muck in.

As it turned out, their village was only a five-minute walk through the woods, past the school. I could see the opening just ahead. The village… or did they call it a community? I wasn't sure, but there it was, a semi-circle of homes, five in all. The houses faced the woods. Each home was unique, but those five were especially striking. There was nothing fancy about any of the individual properties, but there was something about them. They looked like happy homes. Happiness—that was something my previous foster placements had lacked. Something I had been wanting, desperately.

The group headed behind the first house to the left. I followed. There, at the back, stood a long greenhouse, filled with tomato plants, peppers, and three or four different kinds of squash. Maeve was filling bushel baskets with green beans. The others just automatically chipped in until all the work was done, so I joined in. After helping with the picking, we dead-headed some of the other plants, cutting away any brown leaves and dried-up blooms with secateurs, so they would come back fuller and even more beautiful the next spring. We brushed up the soil we had spilled, and threw it back onto the garden.

I heard Bledsoe and Little Mary's truck pull up before I saw it. Harper and Harlow announced that the dinner truck had arrived. Sure enough, my new foster parents had brought dinner for everyone. There was an outdoor spigot where we got cleaned up before we sat down to eat.

Odette and Coriander arrived home from their jobs, and Linnea and Aubrey came over from one of the houses. There were picnic tables set up under a huge Weeping Willow tree. Everyone grabbed a spot, and after Bledsoe had said the blessing, we all enjoyed the feast. As I looked around at each person, I sensed they were all at peace. Well, all except for Wisteria. She'd complained the entire time she'd worked in the greenhouse. I knew I'd had a chip on my shoulder for years, but that was with good reason. What was Wisteria's excuse? What was her story?

THAT NIGHT, I fought sleep for as long as I could. I feared the nightmares that might come, and I was right.

I saw a tall, thin man, dressed in white linen. He was dark-haired, disheveled, and had several days' growth of jet-black stubble on his sun-weathered face. There was panic in the man's usually calm demeanor. How I knew anything about his typical demeanor was beyond me, but somehow, I did, and it scared me.

Others entered the scene; we were in his private quarters. They chanted loudly, and worked themselves into a frenzy. The tall, thin man was their leader. The other men forced the women to strip, and then dragged them to the altar, where the man stood. He told them that this was what he had been commanded to do, and said he must obey, just as they would have to. The men were ordered to go to the back of the room and bow down. One by one, the man took a turn with each of the women, tossing them aside afterwards to crawl back to their man. After it was over, he looked straight ahead, and his eyes were daggers piercing through my soul. My blood ran cold in an instant—

I blinked, and it was morning.

THE DAYS BECAME routine: school, chores, and getting to know the others. Nights became something to be dreaded, as the nightmares didn't let up.

The weeks slipped by.

It was now October, and we were well into our preparation for the fall festival, which I assumed was going to be held at the local farmers' market. That assumption would prove to be wrong. I had been told it was a big crowd draw, and the community counted on the pumpkin sales, as well as all the crafts and other things that had been made throughout the year. It would take all of us to run the stands for the three days of the festival. I decided this was the ideal opportunity for me to show the community I could pull my own weight and be a helpful addition.

Eliza came for a home study to see how I was adjusting to my new life. I was taken aback at first, because I thought she had come to take me away. Unsurprising, really, considering I'd been taken away more times than I cared to remember. But it was actually good to see her. She had arranged for Ms. Lawson to come over as well, so she could get an idea of how I was doing at the new school. I was delighted to hear Ms. Lawson tell her I was a dream pupil, and that I was advanced beyond my years!

Eliza spoke to me on my own after that. It must have been part of her job to check things from my perspective, too. "No complaints," I said. "I've had fun so far, and I'm glad to be there." It wasn't a lie. I did have plenty of questions yet to be answered, but I didn't tell her that.

Eliza seemed pleased with the visit. She stayed long enough to chat a while longer once Bledsoe came in from the pumpkin patch, and then she was on her way back to the city.

One by one, I got to know ten of the other eleven children here. I had all but given up on breaking Wisteria's ice-cold shell. I just couldn't figure her out. I knew I was something of a pessimist, but I had nothing on her!

I wanted to know more about the adults, but I would have to handle that a little more delicately. All five women in the community appeared to be in their mid-thirties. That didn't include Little Mary; I reckoned she and Bledsoe were in their fifties. Only Odette DePriest and Coriander Sabin traveled elsewhere for their jobs. The others stayed in the community to do their work.

As you already know, Ms. Linnea Lawson was my teacher. She was nice enough, but I was careful not to cross the line; our student-teacher relationship was as formal as you might expect; we were no friendlier than we had to be. I have always been able to tell which people you can get information from, and how deep you can pry. It's something you need to be good at when you're in the foster care system; sometimes, you have to rely on the things other kids tell you about the adults.

Ms. Lawson took her teaching position seriously. She was preparing us for the future. *Our* future. You know, I think I am going to call her *Linnea* from now on, for writing purposes. I will save *Ms. Lawson* for the classroom.

Lotus, Coy, and Briar didn't really talk about their mom much. I could tell they loved her, but they never spoke of her, or their father. Maeve Keller, on the other hand, was open for business, conversation being the business in question. If you worked side by side with Maeve, she would talk your ears off. So that's what I did for several days when I wasn't in school or doing chores. She told me plenty about the women, herself included.

"Well," she said, "we women, we are all from surrounding communities, all still within Nelson County. I hail from Montebello. Lived on a horse farm, don't ya know. Coriander comes from Roseland. Aubrey is from Afton. Odette used to live in Nellysford—it's really good for wine tours, cider, if you're into that sort of thing—and Linnea… let me see… that's right, she was a Lovingston gal before she came here."

I told you she could talk.

Coriander was the oldest of the five, apparently, at thirty-eight. Strange thing was, there was a year between each, so the gaps were even, like staircase steps. Aubrey was thirty-seven, Maeve thirty-six, Odette thirty-five, and Linnea, thirty-four. I wouldn't have guessed it; they all looked about the same age. I guess they were, when you think about it, as there was only a four-year difference from oldest to youngest. That's nothing when you're an adult, is it? I think age gaps seem gigantic when you're a kid, but as you get older, nobody seems to notice, let alone care. They'd all started having children at a young age, too.

"Hmm. When she had Lotus, Linnea would have been… what, seventeen? Yes, that seems about right… seventeen."

Oh, and another strange thing: their firstborns were all girls, and all in the same year. What kind of mad fucking odds was that?

I enjoyed talking with Maeve every day. She would let the answers to my questions flow freely, with nothing to hide. She was as down-to-earth as it was possible to be. I sensed a bit of sadness when she talked about growing up on the farm, though. I supposed she missed keeping horses, and I could certainly picture her working with them. Good thing Iris enjoyed making clothes; I don't think fashion was a high priority for Maeve. The two of them were like chalk and cheese. Aimesh was so much like his mom, though. I could tell by the way she talked about him.

"That boy'd be outside twenty-four-seven if he could, and

knee-deep in turkey shit."

I couldn't help but ask, "Turkey shit?"

"We order it in. Comes by the truckload from a farm down the road."

I couldn't figure out if that meant he was a hard worker, or that he just had a thing for getting mucky. Some boys are like that, right? Anyway, she went on to tell me that the Ramseys hadn't taken on anyone new, until I'd come along. Five women and their eleven children were a *butt-load* to take on. I can't imagine what Little Mary and Bledsoe had been thinking for wanting to help. They must've been saints; they received no financial aid because the women and children weren't in the system. That left me with one ginormous question. Why had the Ramseys taken me on, then? It just seemed strange, since they certainly had enough to handle already, what with their little community 'n' all.

Maeve went on to tell me about Aubrey Petit.

"Aubrey'd always dreamed of going to Paris. So, after high school graduation, that's what she did. She studied art there for a year, and enjoyed every minute of it. She met and fell madly in love with Pierre Petit. He was a free-spirited street artist, and swept her off her feet. They returned to Virginia and settled down, got themselves married. It wasn't long before Posey was born, then three years later, the twins came along. Thing is, though, the fatherhood life seemed too much for Pierre to grasp, and they ended up divorcing. Pierre went back to Paris, and, well, that's the last anyone heard of him."

"They must miss him," I said.

"Harper and Harlow were still in diapers, so I don't think

they even remember him. Posey, on the other hand, oh, she sure does. I believe her poetry was often about him. She learned French early on and has kept up with it ever since."

"That's right—her French poetry. I remember her telling me."

"Aubrey believes Posey writes in that language so as not to offend her."

Aubrey, a small-framed woman with brown hair, had beautiful hazel eyes that seemed to change color to match whatever she was wearing.

Like Linnea and Coriander, Odette had attended the University of Virginia. She'd received her bachelor's degree in nursing.

"Odette specialized in care for women and children who have experienced abuse. She provided nursing care, and advocated for them as well. She has always been tough on Juniper, but I think Odette was trying to make her realize the world can be tough. Rory could be a handful, and that didn't make things any easier." Odette sure looked like a nurse. She kept her light brown hair cropped short, and always conducted herself well—very professional.

Maeve told me she'd intentionally saved Coriander for last, for several reasons. "Coriander enrolled in the university's law program but didn't finish. She dropped out after a year, and took a job with a legal firm, focusing on women's rights. Maybe because of the horrors she'd experienced in the cult."

"The cu—?"

Maeve cut me off. "I do believe Coriander would happily spend the rest of her life fighting for what was taken from her long ago." She didn't elaborate on that.

Coriander's daughter, Wisteria, had her own issues; they were deep-rooted issues, at that. I'd sensed as much. Maeve didn't say much about Wisteria. I guess she felt it would be wrong for her to do so. She did tell me she thought Wisteria could use a true friend; one that would not judge.

As for Coriander's appearance, she looked like a force to be reckoned with. She was a tall, slender woman, with dirty blonde hair and blue eyes. Eyes I imagined had once held a powerful spark, but which had long since been dulled by… well, there's the thing. By what, I did not know. Her features were sharp and chiseled. Maybe it was just due to the seriousness of her presence. Or maybe there was an air about her from being around those rich lawyers far too often. I'd seen just enough of the legal system to know I wanted no part of it, or the fancy-pants lawyers that ruled it.

2

The dreams continued to escalate in their intensity and graphic nature; I slept less and less as the nights went by. If Little Mary noticed, she kept quiet about it. My grades didn't suffer, so I don't think Linnea noticed a change in me at school. Or she did, and she kept quiet, too.

The fall festival was that coming weekend, and we were hoping for beautiful weather. I was a little anxious about being around so many people at once. I'd grown accustomed to life in the small community well enough, but I wasn't sure if any outsiders would be joining us.

I noticed Posey had been hitting her journal harder than usual; I had to admit, I was curious about her French poems. She did tell me she would read some to me "One of these days," but as *these days* never seemed to come around, I wondered if there was something worrying her. I know I'd written nonstop whenever I was on edge. I was surprised my hand wasn't worn out after the past ten years.

It was Thursday; school would be letting out early so we could load everything up for the morning. Set-up for the fall festival was at 5 a.m. The festival was to last three days, and I found out we would be taking up six spaces. I also found out the festival was going to take place at Massie's Mill.

I had no idea of just how much stuff we were taking to the festival. Oh, and did I mention that Little Mary, Juniper and I would be running a food stand? The menu consisted of barbeque chicken, campfire beans, and lemonade. *Crapola!* Not because of the food, just that I don't know much about cooking. I hoped all I'd have to do was serve it up.

Bledsoe would hook up a wagon to the truck for all the veggies, then all the fruits, then the crafts, and finally, the pumpkins. He would make three trips before returning for the tractor and the wagon for the hay rides. Coriander would drive Bledsoe's truck back, but not before hooking up the twenty-three-foot Vagabond camper. It looked like a big, happy submarine. Bright yellow, it was. Dated back to something like 1946, they said. The other vehicles would haul more crafts, clothing, jewelry, and food stand supplies.

IT WAS CLOSE to 5 a.m. when we were finally ready to unload and set up. Exhaustion would've been easy to accept if it hadn't been for the anxiety. And it was only getting worse as the other vendors poured in.

Our six spaces were all in a row, thank goodness. The food stand was first next to the other refreshments vendors. The aromas would make a full-grown tapeworm crawl out of your momma's mouthful to get some of that grub.

Linnea helped Aubrey to run her space, packed full of her stained-glass creations, Posey's primitive signs, Iris' designer-quality clothing, aprons, and really expensive dolls. With Coriander's help, Harper and Harlow had their own spot selling one-of-a-kind, handmade jewelry. Maeve's stand was packed with produce from her greenhouses, along with four varieties of apples and apple cider. Aimesh and Briar were right at home pitching in.

Two of the biggest draws were the pumpkin stand and the hay rides. Bledsoe took care of the hay rides, with Coy helping folk on and off the wagon. In between, Coy worked with Odette and Rory, selling pumpkins. Lotus and Wisteria were next to us, where Lotus did portraits or funny caricatures. Wisteria, the queen of the graveyard corpses, was on face painting. I imagined there was going to be plenty of horny young men lined up to have the Elvira lookalike lean over in front of them and doodle on them while they all but drooled down her cleavage.

And that's probably what had brought Jacob over initially, but when our eyes met, we both knew there was something happening between us. He purchased some food, and we talked for a while. We liked each other instantly. He asked if we were staying on the grounds. He smiled when I said we were, and my insides did little flips. No, it was more than that. There were butterflies in my stomach, and *they* were doing little flips.

Jacob pointed to the other side of the field, where the picnic tables were, and asked if I'd meet him there that night at eight. After he left, he was all I thought about, and as exhausted as I was, the anticipation of seeing him again kept me going.

Once everything got running and we were in full swing, it was mind-blowing. There had to have been a thousand folks who'd made their way through the festival, and that was just the first day. Who the hell knew a fall festival in Massie's Mill, Virginia, would've been such a hit?

Bledsoe took Coy and Aimesh back to the community to get more pumpkins, apples, and vegetables. Coriander took Aubrey and the twins to get the remaining crafts and jewelry. No one would have guessed that so much would sell on the first day. Those who went home to the community would return the next day, which left twelve of us behind to stay the night in the Vagabond. I had never camped out before, either in a camper or a tent. That would've been too much like a holiday.

Just a little before eight, I slipped away and headed to the picnic area. Jacob was waiting on me. He greeted me with a hug. It was sweet and innocent. And so were our kisses.

I told him about the family commune I lived in. He told me

about an incident from ten years back, somewhere not too far from here. There had been a cult, and some of the people had committed suicide. It had been in local and major newspapers.

"The cult leader's name was Aibo, or something like that."

The story left me feeling lightheaded. I needed to get back before they noticed I was gone. He kissed me once more and asked if he could see me again. I told him I could sneak away, and we could meet at the bridge near school on Wednesday.

"You sure it's safe there?"

"I believe so."

I left, but on the way, I could've sworn somebody was watching me. I could feel eyes staring at me. Into me. I hurried along and was relieved when I got back safely. The feeling of being watched remained with me for a while.

The girls were all gathered around the campfire—everyone except Wisteria, who I figured was probably inside the camper, reading a book or something. The women must've already gone inside and called it a night. That means they would have taken up all the beds. Only fair, I suppose. They were our elders.

I plopped myself down next to the others, and I received lots of smiles despite their exhaustion.

"Want some S'mores?" Lotus asked.

"I don't know. I've never had one," I replied.

She listed the ingredients and described how they were made. She demonstrated making one, and then I made my own. It tasted absolutely amazing.

Wisteria finally joined us. "Where'd you run off to?"

"Took a walk under the stars. Did some meditating," I lied;

telling them about Jacob would have been a terrible idea.

Wisteria scoffed. "And what? We don't do enough of that meditating shit already?"

I didn't respond. No one did, and I had to break the silence before my anxiety exploded. "Have any of you heard of a man named Aibo?"

Suddenly, I could feel five pairs of eyes on me. I had never been glared at with so much anger; I could feel it rising like the heat from the fire. Posey, Iris, Lotus and Juniper stood up in sequence like ducklings in a row, and headed to the camper.

"Why would you bring up his fucking name?" Wisteria asked.

"I don't know." I was caught off guard. "I just recently heard his name in passing, so I thought I'd ask. Why does everyone act like I spoke the name of the evilest thing in the world?"

"Probably because you just did. I swear, Charlie Hartless, your name fits you to a tee. How can you, of all people, have no fucking recollection of what happened? I call bullshit!"

"I'm not heartless! How in the hell am I supposed to know what I can and cannot ask when there's a secret behind every corner? I didn't know my question would cause the others to hightail it into the camper."

Wisteria got up and dumped a bucket of water on the burning embers, and stormed inside. I stayed there and watched the white campfire smoke race to the moonlit sky as if it, too, wanted to get as far away from me as possible. I ached for Jacob, and his shoulder to cry on, but that wasn't going to happen until Wednesday night. I needed to find out what Wisteria had meant by the things she said to me.

The cool October air slapped my cheeks, and the sting made me realize my face was damp with tears. I wiped them away on my sweatshirt before eventually rising and entering the now not-so-happy yellow submarine.

I found my place on the floor, and no one spoke a word for the rest of the night.

I was standing outside in the dead of winter, and the icy air was heavy as it bit into my lungs. I pictured my heartbeat slowing as the build-up of frost thickened my blood. I looked at my hands, and saw my fingertips had turned a pale blue color. Time slowed like a slug moving across rocky terrain.

I saw an opening in the woods, which looked like a gaping, nefarious mouth. The trees were stripped of their leaves. Tiny needles prickled against my naked flesh. I looked down and watched as crystals of snow clung to the hairs on my arms. When I looked back at the trees, they were no longer bare; the snow had collected on every branch, giving the appearance of a ghostly burial sheath, draped over skeletal limbs. The ground was quickly covered by several inches. The moon peeked from behind the night clouds, revealing the tiny, sparkling, glass-like shards in the snow. A winter-land of death and dying.

My body floated above the ground, my toes occasionally dipping into the fresh snowfall. I felt only fear. Afraid I would be pulled into whatever waited below.

Then, bells. I was drawn toward the sound. They were tinging a familiar holiday song, something from my childhood. They led me to the church with no walls, which was filled with people in long white gowns. They were all staring ahead, at something I could not see. I floated down the aisle like an unwilling bride. When I reached the end, there was no husband-to-be. In the corner, I saw something hunched over. Waiting. I tried to make out a face, but it didn't appear to be behind a mask. A small whisper told me to run. I tried to abide, but was halted when I turned and faced the congregation. They looked upon me with hunger in their dead but flaming eyes. I bolted, free of their stare, and made my way back to the forest, the white carpet now stained and warm under my feet. My skin was no longer cold. I cried out for help, knowing as I did, no one would hear my screams.

I woke to find myself alone in the camper. I rushed to get ready and go outside. I found the others were already prepping for another busy day. I tried my best to make right what had happened the night before, but they weren't having any part of it. Not yet.

It wasn't until lunchtime that the tension began to ease. Still, I couldn't have been happier when day number two started winding down. I noticed someone making a beeline straight to my food stand, and I was ready when he got there. He was tall, well over six feet, with very kind eyes, which seemed to look right through me, all the way to the other side. Wherever or whatever that was.

As I prepared his order, he told me a little about himself. He was just passing through Massie's Mill on his way to Richmond for a conference. Turns out he was a warden in one of Virginia's toughest prisons. He never offered his name, so I followed his lead. Sometimes, introductions aren't necessary. The simple act of kindness from a stranger was enough.

He smiled. It wasn't like me to converse so easily with a

stranger, even if I was manning the station. But this person was different. He felt safe.

Once his dinner was all packed, and I had secured a lid on his drink, I slid the box close to him. As he handed me the money, his hand brushed against mine and he looked down at me as though he wanted to say something. I waited to hear what it was, but all that came out was a polite *Thank you*, and he was gone.

I know the encounter seemed ordinary, but believe me, it was far from it. I knew without reservation I would remember this person for the remainder of my life, no matter how long that may be. You see, I *heard* him tell me something else. It happened as he walked away, and I heard it—*felt* it, deep within my core. He said, *"Charlie, you are looking for answers that will inevitably hurt people. Guard your findings carefully until you know the time is right. Don't worry, you will know when it's okay to let go of your discoveries."*

However, when I looked up, he wasn't there. I carefully scanned the thinning crowd for him. He was at least a head taller than most, so I was fully expecting to catch a glimpse. I didn't spot him, but I did see movement in the parking lot. I watched as a very old car was driving through the exit. The windows were down, and I could see the driver looking my way. The car was at least a football field away, but I knew it was him. He stretched his long arm out of the driver's window and waved goodbye. I waved back. That was when I felt a tingle in my palm. It was where his fingers had brushed against my skin when he'd handed me the money. Just as quickly as the sensation had arrived, it was gone. This man had somehow gotten inside my head and given me a message. I knew I had just met someone with a unique gift, but I also knew I had to keep it to myself.

The festival closed, and most of the girls had started talking to me again. Not Wisteria, though, and I wasn't surprised. When we were alone after supper, I gathered my thoughts and asked her, "What is it that I should be remembering?"

She glared at me coldly, then said, "All in good time, Charlie Hartless. All in good time."

She walked off, and I didn't feel the need to follow her.

When we were back at the community and everything had been put away, it was close to midnight. The boys had started a good fire in the pit, and everyone gathered around and found a seat. Bledsoe started with a prayer, and then he thanked each one of us individually. Little Mary said the earnings for the past three days amounted to more than sixteen thousand dollars. It had been their most successful festival to date.

I didn't hang around afterward. I excused myself from the gathering and went back to my room in the house. I left the door open, and eavesdropped, just in case the others had something to say about me. Maybe I was being a bit paranoid, but after not fitting in at all in the other foster homes, it seemed the natural thing for me to do. I didn't hear my name come up in conversation. Several moments passed before I heard a knock on my door frame. "May I come in?"

I nodded yes, and dried my eyes, not wanting Little Mary to see that I was crying, but it was too late.

"Charlie? What's wrong?"

I opened up. I asked her about the man Aibo and why I had been treated like garbage when I had mentioned his name.

Little Mary released a long sigh. "I will tell you, but you must brace yourself."

"Brace myself?"

"You must be prepared. What I am about to tell you won't be easy for you to hear. And it's definitely hard for me to tell, but it's time."

She started to tell her side of the story, just like Jacob had done before her. Versions. That's all people had, their versions of what they believed to be the truth.

Little Mary said, "Aibo had been a leader in a commune, sort of like this one. Except Bledsoe was and is a good man. Aibo was the opposite of goodness. When it suited him, Aibo could be charismatic and charming. He accumulated a following of hand-selected people. They all had something in common. They wanted to belong—to reach a higher purpose. To feel something greater than their current circumstances allowed. Aibo preyed on the vulnerable, the shy, the homeless and the rich, who were dissatisfied with the government, and guaranteed them a better way of life. And the most important thing of all, he promised hope to the hopeless.

"There were rumors of rape and torture. The control he held over his flock was intoxicating. But he required more. Always more. Like a heroin addict, chasing their first high. His golden rule was: There could be no resistance. Ever.

"On the day the authorities were going to move in and make an arrest, Aibo had somehow caught wind of it. He convinced some of his followers to take their own lives by way of a lethal drink. Reportedly, the remains of a two-hundred-pound drum of sodium cyanide were found. The white chunks, about the size of charcoal briquettes, were scattered near the drum. And the smell of burnt almonds lingered in the air."

I saw the look in Little Mary's eyes. It was one of remembrance. I said, "You know so much about it. It's as though you were there. Were you? There, that is."

Little Mary seemed at a loss for words. Finally, she answered, "There was lots of publicity surrounding the tragedy. It was in the local newspapers, as well as the evening news worldwide. They showed clips of the bodies. Their skin had turned a cherry red from the cyanide-laced juice they drank.

"That's when Bledsoe and I stepped in. We had our home and the acreage behind it, so we set up a temporary shelter for the survivors. Those women and children found a safe refuge with us. We all worked together, and built homes for each family. Charlie, everyone here is a survivor."

The shock must have registered on my face. Little Mary put a reassuring hand on my shoulder and said, "Wait there a moment. I'll be right back." She left the room and returned less than thirty seconds later with an envelope in her hand. "I'm not sure if this is the right thing to do, but maybe you should look at this."

I opened the worn envelope, and a photograph slid out. It was a black-and-white shot of a man looking straight into the camera. His eyes looked familiar. I didn't know how to respond, so I asked, "Is this him?"

Little Mary nodded *yes*. I tried to hand her the picture, but my fingers refused to release their grip. I saw something in the man's face, and it stirred an echo of feelings. His face made me feel all kinds of sick, and I didn't want to throw up.

"What's wrong, Charlie?"

"This man… I've seen him in my dreams."

IT WAS WEDNESDAY. As a form of gratitude, Bledsoe used some of the money they had earned, and gifted it to the girls for their help at the festival. We all wanted to go to Lynchburg for a nice lunch and a fun afternoon's shopping. I was so excited to be included. Strangely, even Wisteria joined us, even though we still weren't talking. I decided I'd keep a safe distance. Who knows, maybe this would be what we all needed to break the ice. Stranger things had happened.

Since none of us had a driver's license yet, Bledsoe dropped us off at the mall just as it was opening. He handed each of us an envelope with money inside. "I'll pick you up right here, at three this afternoon. Sound good?"

It did sound good. It sounded *very* good! Virtually a whole day's shopping—I'd never had my own money before, let alone the chance to spend any. We were all giddy, even Wisteria, when we said goodbye to Bledsoe and stepped inside the mall.

Wisteria wanted the salon to be our first stop, and we obliged. A beautician took her to a back booth for a cut-and-blow while we stayed in the waiting area. We each took a seat on the comfiest couches I'd ever seen in my life. Padded like you wouldn't believe, and in such beautiful bright pinks and yellows, too. They reminded me of some of the flowers in the greenhouse.

Iris, Lotus and Posey decided to get their nails done while we were waiting, and I was pleased that they asked me to help them select their colors. As the nail technicians were finishing off with a top-coat of polish, out walked Wisteria from behind a curtain at the back of the shop. Our chins nearly struck the floor! We couldn't help but stare at this beautiful blonde, with her hair in fresh, bouncing waves. She looked as though she had just stepped off the cover of a magazine.

"Like what you see?" she asked.

The girls said the same thing at the same time: "You gotta be fucking kidding me!"

"Wisteria, is that really you?" I said.

She smiled bashfully, which wasn't like her.

Once we were out of the salon, Wisteria told the others she needed a minute, and pulled me to one side, so it was just me and her. I felt my heart racing, remembering underneath that new blonde hair was a girl who apparently hated me. I wondered what she was about to say, and without missing a beat, she said, "For far too long, I have done everything to avoid looking or even feeling like myself. I've been living in fear, hiding behind a dark curtain. I want to come out from hiding. I'm ready to be me again. Can you forgive me for treating you so coldly?"

I was taken aback—this, coming from the Ice Queen herself! Nonetheless, I felt tears start to form, and I quickly sniffed them away.

"I never meant to upset anyone when I brought up Aibo at the festival. The evening we returned, Little Mary told me a little about what happened, and I'm so sorry for all of you. I cannot believe that happened. Of course I forgive you."

For a moment, I thought she was going to hug me, but instead, she just nodded and said, "Now that that's out of the way…are you hungry?"

"Starving," I said.

SOMEONE SHOULD'VE SNAPPED a picture of Bledsoe's face when he picked us up and saw Wisteria's hair. "Holy shit!" He couldn't help it; it just kinda came out, but we all started to laugh. It felt good. Not only to laugh, but also to feel like I had a family. Again, I forced back the tears. I knew this was where I belonged.

"Glad to have you back, Wisteria," he said, correcting his last statement.

"It's good to be back."

When we arrived home and knocked on the door, Little Mary nearly fainted! She couldn't believe it, and was over the moon to see that Wisteria and I were getting along. Wisteria was the talk of the household, and Little Mary couldn't wait until the others saw her; there was to be a special church service that evening, with a supper to give thanks to the community.

Everyone unloaded their bags and admired their purchases. I kept mine to myself since all I had bought was new underwear: a couple sets of panties and bras. I wanted new underclothing— not used, from a thrift store. Do they even call it *used* anymore? I've heard them say *pre-loved* more often than not. That's definitely not something that should apply to underwear!

Wisteria put on a striking new outfit, in the palest blue. It was a shock to see her in anything but black. She was still trying to get used to being her true self. I thought she looked beautiful, like a butterfly that had hatched from its cocoon.

Even though no one wanted our day together to end, everyone seemed anxious to get home with their new purchases and get ready for the service. It was due to start in less than an hour. I felt anxious myself, knowing that just a few hours after that, I'd be meeting up with Jacob in secret, at the bridge. I couldn't wait to pick up where we'd left off.

"Is it okay that I stay here until the service?" Wisteria asked Little Mary. "I really want to surprise everyone."

"And I believe you will, in a good way," she replied, smiling.

All the girls left, leaving Wisteria and me to get ready in my bedroom. It felt weird—brilliantly weird—knowing the Ice Queen had melted away and I had acquired a new friend.

Wisteria stared at herself in the mirror. Her thick blonde hair cascaded down her shoulders in big curls. The soft sweater dress hugged her curves and the baby blue fabric highlighted her sparkling blue eyes. The tan belt and the matching knee-high suede boots completed the look. I held not even an ounce of envy; I took in her beauty with appreciation. I was happy being more of a down-to-earth, wears-no-make-up girl, a bit scrappy but kinda cute.

Wisteria seemed satisfied and sat on my bed to wait for me to get ready. I chose one of the thrift store's multi-colored sweaters and a long, rust-colored skirt that complemented it, and regarded my reflection. I thought that would do fine. Only I knew I wasn't getting ready for just the service, but also a date.

"Nervous?" Wisteria asked. It must've shown on my face, but I still felt uncomfortable telling her about Jacob, so I turned the tables on her instead.

"I'm just nervous for you. This is your big night. Aren't you nervous?"

She nodded. "A little, but I'm more excited than anything. I'm ready to finally move forward."

"I'm really happy for you." We smiled at one another.

The church started filling up with the other children, the moms, the Ramseys, and finally, we saw Coriander going in. Once she was seated, we filed in one by one, Wisteria at the end. There were audible gasps, oohs and aahs. Coriander stood and turned to face her daughter. They fell into one another's arms in the warmest, most loving hug I had ever witnessed. Wisteria took the seat next to her mom; from what I'd overheard, this was the first time in many years she'd done so.

Church began, and the message was about the importance of family, whether that be by blood or even adoption, and how it compared to the importance of the unity of the church family. It was very moving. I noticed the moms reaching out to their children and putting their arms around them or giving them a loving smile. My stomach started to knot and twist like a pretzel. Little Mary must have noticed me squirming in my seat: she placed her hand over mine and gave it a gentle squeeze.

Then came that part of the service when Bledsoe asked if anyone would like to share their joys or concerns. As I started to get up from my seat, I saw out of the corner of my eye that Iris was also standing, then Posey, Juniper, Lotus, and Wisteria. Well, I didn't quite know what to do: we hadn't discussed this. So, all six of us walked forward.

Lotus spoke first. "I just wanted to say that it was a joy to spend the day with these girls."

"That's what I came here to say!" said Iris.

Wisteria cleared her throat and spoke softly. "I want to apologize for the worry I've caused. For a long time, I wanted to block everything out, but someone special helped me see that I didn't have to hide away, and I am thankful. I'm turning over a new leaf, which starts with a new me. Here I am!" She took a twirl.

Juniper and Posey reached out, took one another's hands, and announced they were in love. It was truly a joy for them to be able to share something so intimate with the community.

The actual reaction was vastly different than I'd anticipated: Aubrey and Odette looked so pleased, and ran over to hug their daughters. They couldn't have been happier.

That left the last person to speak, which was me. I looked nervously at all the eager faces, as the congregation waited to hear what I had to say. I tried to collect my thoughts, gather my words, and put them in order.

"What I have to say is both a joy and a concern. I, too, enjoyed this afternoon. These five girls, all my age, are so very special. I am blessed not only to know them and call them friends, but also to have this entire community welcome me and make me feel like I have a home, for the first time I can truly remember."

Again, the reaction wasn't what I'd expected.

We headed to our seats, holding hands as we went. Bledsoe prayed, but before the church was dismissed, he added, "We'll now head back to the community, where we will share a blessed meal. But before we eat, we adults have a confession to make—one of both grief and triumph. I must stress that what we have to say shouldn't be uttered within these walls, so with that, you are all free to go."

There was a strange sort of hush that took over everyone, even the young boys. Once we were outside, at the church shelter, the sun had started to set and I noticed the adults had remained behind. I turned and joined my friends, who were on their way back to the community. The girls headed toward the picnic tables around the fire pit, while the boys gathered wood. We watched quietly as they got a roaring fire going. We all sat and stared into the flickering flames, waiting, wondering what would come next. I questioned myself at that point: had I said the wrong thing? Wisteria sat close to me while we waited, and held my hand. *Best friends forever,* I thought. Posey chose that moment to recite one of her poems for us, but this one was in English.

Do I Love You…

The day you left me is hard to recall.

It was many years ago when I was but a child.

Time has passed and I am no longer so small.

Now I run free through the woods like something gone wild.

I regret to say that the day of reuniting may never come.

You filled yourself with gallons of rum.

I'll fly away.

But ere you may sink in the darkest sea.

Just one last meeting is my only plea.

As the adults approached, we heard the crunching of leaves underfoot.

The group arrived with a look of heaviness, as if something was weighing on their hearts, and they gathered in front of us. Coriander cleared her throat. "I shall start."

Silence befell the whole group.

"In the year 1995, a very charismatic man named Aibo started something that he described as the perfect community. He had a way of drawing in even the most intelligent of people and taking hold of them. Within a year, he had about twenty followers. These followers were sent out to the surrounding communities to recruit a particular type of person. Their mission was to find and persuade six young women that following this man would be the true path to happiness. They chose a woman from each of the six surrounding communities and proceeded with the grooming process. And it worked. They followed." She paused for a moment and regarded the congregation. All eyes were on her.

"They were treated like princesses in the beginning. That, however, did not last long, before the process began. Tearing the women down. They were made to feel *less-than*. All their autonomy was stripped away. Men were chosen for them. Posey already had a fiancé, and this threatened Aibo because he was demanding complete control. But he didn't want to lose her, so he allowed the marriage to take place, as much as it pained him. The men were made to believe that they were above the women, and that they needed to make them subservient, catering to their every whim. So the men were brainwashed—gaslighted, too.

Aibo was getting them all primed for his own sick and twisted desires. He paired the couples and performed wedding ceremonies. He had his chosen ones, though, who he kept close at all times.

"Unspeakable things happened at this place, which some of us now recognize to be a cult, a prison. Women were beaten, daily. Often twice, three times a day, and Aibo did not need an excuse. Men were beaten too, if they didn't keep their women under control. People worked like dogs and were treated worse and worse with every passing day until they believed they could do no better. Aibo routinely forced himself on the women, hoping to create a perfect generation of his own children." Coriander's eyes were watery.

"I became pregnant first, and gave birth to a daughter. Aibo told everyone that since I was first, and my name was that of the plant—Coriander—all the firstborn daughters were also to be given horticultural names. That's how it came to be for Wisteria, Lotus, Iris, Posey, and Juniper. There was one more, and that was you, Charlie."

What? I couldn't believe I'd just heard my name.

"It pains me to tell you that Charlie Hartless is not your real name. It is Charity Hardwick."

This time, Coriander paused, to allow me to absorb her words. These were the answers I'd been searching for all those years. It started to explain some of my nightmares, and why I would see the monster, Aibo, in them. It seemed I had been a part of this terrible cult all along. I was a survivor, just like the rest of them.

"This abuse continued for seven more years, and it escalated. Charlie, you were one of his chosen few, and for that reason, he seldom let you away from his home. The others hardly saw you, another reason why some of these girls don't remember you. Your parents' names were Oak and Sunshine. They were nice, beautiful people, and remained close to one another. Sunshine and I had become best friends over the years, and we knew something had to be done before he started hurting the children as well. I gained Aibo's confidence and trust. Enough trust to be allowed to go out of the community, especially to the farmers' market, as our crops were not doing well, and we needed food. That was when I first met Little Mary and Bledsoe. Eventually, Little Mary got it out of me: I told her where I lived, and about the man named Aibo.

"She agreed to help us to escape, but before that could happen, Aibo hurt my daughter and several others. Wisteria never spoke of it, but I could sense the change in her, I could sense the sadness. We had to move quickly. Sunshine and I gathered the information Little Mary needed, and she turned the evidence over to the police. Yet, somehow, Aibo found out. Someone must have tipped him off the police were coming, so he put into action a suicide pact. He gave the tainted juice to the men first, because he knew they were the strongest, physically. Then it was to be the children, in his private quarters.

"On that day, Charlie, it was you and Wisteria. The two of you had become inseparable. Sunshine risked her own life to save you both. She was able to get Wisteria out and into Odette's arms. But you clung to your mom, crying and refusing to leave her. It was as if you knew you were about to lose both of your parents, and you would not let go of her.

"Having come to know the true Aibo, she knew he had no plans to kill himself. He would find some way to sneak off and leave the rest to die. So, Sunshine watched as he prepared the juice. That's when it happened: she saw him leave the cyanide out of his cup. Your mom switched the cups, and allowed him to give you what he thought would be the drink that would kill you. Then he turned to your mom and forced a cup of the liquid down her throat. It was too late for your mom, but she had saved your life, and Wisteria's, too."

Do you ever have that feeling where something is just too much to take in? Where something is so unbelievable, and yet believable, all at once? I couldn't believe what I was hearing, but I could. Almost. All the pieces seemed to be falling into place. I didn't bother holding back my tears. Tears for myself, for those who died, and for Aibo. Why for him?

Coriander continued, "When I arrived at dusk, the police were everywhere. Flashing blue lights lit up the compound. Sunshine lived long enough to tell me she had gotten Wisteria to safety, and that she had kept you from drinking the poison. She had made the ultimate sacrifice. I promised her I would take care of you, and I meant it. But you were nowhere to be found. We were told that one of the policemen had discovered you still clinging to your mom and dad. He quickly grabbed you, and rushed you to the hospital, thinking you, too, had been poisoned. His name was Charlie, and we were told by the other officers on the scene that Charlie had called Aibo 'One heartless sonofabitch.' He'd also said that what had taken place was a truly heartless act. He vowed to get you away from there, and that's exactly what he did. When we searched for this Charlie, he was nowhere to be found. It took all of us—Eliza, the Ramseys, Odette and me—ten years to find you." There was a steady stream of tears rolling down Coriander's cheeks.

"Charlie, I would have taken you in and raised you in a heartbeat, had I known where you were. I am sorry I failed you for so long. But now, I can finally say, welcome home."

I was speechless, even though I desperately wanted to acknowledge what Coriander had just told me. My palms were wet, but my throat was parched. I opened my mouth, but nothing came out. I was lost. I looked to Wisteria for answers, but she was no longer sitting beside me. I couldn't find her. She had probably wandered off to avoid revisiting any of the story. The past.

Instead of speaking, I fell to my knees and wept. I soon felt the presence of all the other children surrounding me. They placed their hands on me, telling me everything would be okay. I had come completely undone by what I believed to be the truth I'd been searching for. I opened my eyes and saw the concerned expressions on everyone's faces. The adults consoled Coriander; she found comfort in their arms.

"This has been a terrible blow to everyone here, and it will take time for us to work through it," Bledsoe said. "But we will get beyond these tragedies, and that'll only strengthen our community."

With tears welling in Posey's eyes, she asked, "Did my dad really return to Paris, or did Aibo kill him? I remember Mom calling what happened 'The Unspeakable,' which was the perfect name, since I could never speak of that day again."

Aubrey went to her daughter, and assured her that as far as she knew, he was very much alive, despite her attempts to contact him resulting in no response.

"I wish I could see him." Posey was shaking now.

Aubrey pulled her close and held her tight. "Me too, honey."

There was another murmuring amongst the children before Rory finally said, "I think we need to know if any of us are the sons or daughters of Aibo. Because I feel like something is wrong with me. I've never truly felt like I fit in here, which makes me wonder if it's me."

During the short time I'd been in the community, I had often wondered what it was that had caused Rory to be somewhat distant. To be different than the others. And now I knew he had been worrying himself sick, thinking he might be Aibo's son.

Odette dropped her face into her hands and bawled. The other four moms didn't fare much better, as the same question came from every child. They wanted to know the truth. I didn't have a mom here to ask, but I, too, was curious to know. "Has there been any blood work done to find out?" I asked as my voice threatened to fail me.

"No testing has been done, so no one knows for sure," Bledsoe replied. "Your moms have discussed it with Little Mary and me on more than one occasion. The decision has been the same every time: what difference would it make? Other than Jacques Petit, all your dads have passed away. That includes Aibo, if he, by chance, did father any of you. All twelve of you are the most caring people I have ever known, regardless of your parentage. Each of you have adjusted very well to life here, considering what you have been through, and you are blessed with talents. This is meant for you, too, Charlie; you are as much a part of this community as anybody. Would knowing that Aibo had fathered any of you make you all of a sudden a different person than you were yesterday? Please think hard about what it is you are asking."

Maybe what he was saying was true. I wasn't so sure. Would knowing make a difference? We are who we make ourselves, and we shouldn't let the past bind us. Isn't that something people say? Little Mary had told me in my room every one of us was a survivor, me included.

Little Mary stepped forward. "I, too, have something to state." I could tell she was anxious from the shakiness of her voice. "It's something I feel must come out in the open. I've intentionally kept something from this community, because I thought it would do more harm than good, were it to come out. But now, I have no other choice. Coriander has already mentioned that we met at the farmers' market and has spoken of how we became friends. That is true, but I encouraged that meeting. I had been hearing gossip about a supposed cult somewhere in the area, and had this gut-wrenching feeling that I needed to investigate. I wanted to find out everything I possibly could. Coriander had been coming to the market for a few weeks, and she always kept to herself. I felt as though she was not allowed to converse with the other vendors, or anyone else. Finally, I was able to get close enough to earn her trust. Eventually, she broke down and told me of the atrocities that had taken place at the hands of the one you knew as Aibo.

"This was heart-breaking to hear, for this Aibo had been a part of my life years before. You see, he was not Aibo when I knew him; he was Adam, my brother. I came… we *both* came from a very loving family. Our parents were wonderful, caring people. My mom's parents came to live with us too, when their health started to fail. Mom and Dad would have had it no other way. I was so fortunate to have had such caring parents.

"Mom became pregnant and gave birth to Adam when I was five. It had been a difficult pregnancy; she was already almost forty when she had me. So, by the time Adam was born, Mom was forty-five. She was sick for the entire pregnancy, with everything from morning sickness to reflux to gestational diabetes, and she was on bed rest for most of the last trimester. When she went into labor, she knew something was wrong. Dad was gone with our only vehicle, and we did not have a phone. My grandmother had delivered many a baby in her time, but she was in no shape to handle what was happening.

"The baby was coming out, except the cord was wrapped around his little neck. Grandma couldn't get it loose. She called me over to help, but it was so tight. The contractions were coming faster and harder. Mom did her best not to push, knowing that if she did, the baby would be strangled. It felt like hours were clicking by, but in all actuality, it had only been minutes. My dad walked in to find us in the midst of the nightmare. He was able to slip something between the cord and the baby's neck, just enough to allow me to get my little hands in there to slip the cord over his head.

"Adam was born, although the damage had already been done. The baby boy had gone without oxygen for more than five minutes. As he grew, I noticed that Adam was not like other children. He developed at a different rate, and would get this far-away look in his eyes, as though he wasn't really there. I was still quite young myself, but I was wise enough to notice his behavioral problems, and to know Adam had lost something precious: the ability to feel remorse. It was as if the lack of oxygen had smothered the part of the brain that was responsible for kindness and empathy, and left behind the desire to control and hurt. Mom and Dad must have known, too, but they acted like everything was fine. They could go on with that farce for only so long.

"Everything changed once Adam was seven years old, and in school. They could ignore the facts no longer. He bullied the other children; even then, he was trying to control people. Not just the other children, but teachers, too. My parents were forced to take him out of public school, and my mom tried homeschooling him. It was torture: that's the only way I can describe it. The stress level at home was through the roof, and he thrived on it. He lived for the chaos. Within a year, both of our grandparents had passed, supposedly from natural causes. I still question that."

I think I'd have questioned it, too. Life with Adam sounded like a living nightmare, even before the transformation into Aibo. I still couldn't shake the feeling that a series of stories was being woven as more information was doled out in small and large doses to me. Some things were just hard to swallow. Did anyone ever really know the whole truth? Doubtful.

Little Mary continued, "By the time I was fourteen and Adam was nine, he had all but ruined our parents' marriage. He controlled Mom, as though he was the master puppeteer, and he intimidated Dad.

"Instead of calling me Mary Beth as everyone else did, he called me Mary Death. For years, he'd call out, 'Mary Death, I am coming for you in your dreams.'

"I tried my best to stay strong for my mom, to be around as much as I could. Lord knows, she needed someone with her, because Dad was afraid of his own son, so he stayed away for longer periods of time. On his last trip home, Adam had just turned thirteen, but he was as big as a grown man. There was a heated exchange between the two of them. The next thing I knew, there was a crashing sound. I found my dad at the bottom of the stairs with his eyes open and his neck broken. He had died instantly. When I looked up, Adam was standing at the top of the stairs with a look of triumph on his face.

"It was ruled an accident, but I knew better. So did Mom. She feared for our lives. She cut the proverbial puppet strings and came up with a plan. She enrolled Adam back into public school, hoping he would act out. If that happened, she knew the authorities would have to be called in. The plan worked; within a mere three weeks, he had been in several fights and threatened more than one of the teachers. He was taken before a judge, and my mom signed the paperwork for him to be sent away to a special school for troubled teens. He threatened us there and then, swearing that he would get revenge.

"Things were peaceful for a while, but then the disturbing letters started to arrive. Mom persuaded a friend of hers to type up an official-looking letter and send it to Adam. It said something along the lines of 'We regret to inform you, but both your mother and sister have been killed in a car crash.' We left our home behind, and everything that was in it, and started a new life. We knew the bank would step in and sell off the property. My mom was able to live her last years in peace, and for that, I am thankful.

"I found my soulmate in Bledsoe, and lived for decades without knowing what had become of Adam. That was, until I met Coriander. When she told me about Aibo, I knew it had to be him. I also knew I needed to do all I could to protect those innocent women and children from any more harm at the hands of my brother.

"I am telling you this so you will know it was not some genetic defect that caused him to be the monster he was. It had been the traumatic birth and the lack of oxygen. Of course, that is not to say that all children born that way will end up with such a dangerous personality. But I know you are all worried he may have fathered some of you, and perhaps you may also have his darkness within. But trust me: I know you don't. When I look into the eyes of each one of you, all I see is kindness. Of course, it's up to you whether you are tested, but you all deserved to know the whole story before you decide. I pray you can forgive me, if my keeping this secret was wrong. Bledsoe and I only wanted to provide a safe home for you all, and give you the opportunity to become the people you were meant to be."

Bledsoe put his arm around his wife's shoulder, and the poor woman nearly collapsed in his arms. It had been one hell of a secret to carry around, and it was finally out. I had to hand it to Little Mary. She was a lot stronger than I would have ever given her credit for. I can't say I would have been willing to get involved with a cult, much less one run by a twisted, sicko brother. A person who wanted nothing more than vengeance. I couldn't imagine the strength she must have needed, after all that, to take in five women and eleven children without knowing how much control Aibo might have still held over them, with no idea if any of them would slit your throat while you slept. I would have to say that Little Mary and Bledsoe were the two bravest people I had ever met. But even after hearing all of it, I still wasn't able to trust. Not completely.

I walked up to them and said, "Forgiveness? Really? As far as I can tell, neither of you did anything wrong. The opposite is true, if anything! You both deserve a medal for what you have done. I know I am the newbie, but thank you for taking me in and showing me what a real family could be. I thank everyone here, because in these few short months, I have known more love and kindness than I can ever remember." Wheels of doubt continued to spin in my mind.

Big tears rolled down Little Mary and Bledsoe's faces. They swooped me up into their arms and reassured me they were tears of joy. I knew that, but I didn't want to spoil the moment for them.

As hard as it was, the discussion was over, and Bledsoe gathered everyone's attention.

"Now, I know that perhaps we might not have the biggest appetite after the bombshell we just unloaded on you, but the food is ready, and we should all try to get something in our system. It'll do your body good. So, if everyone can gather around the table, we will bow our heads to pray and, from this day forward, vow never to forget who we are. I believe it is time we shed our cocoons and blossom into the beautiful butterflies we were always meant to be."

That last part was a little over the top.

As we gathered, I wondered if I should stop and find Wisteria. She was probably at home, lying on her bed, dealing with all this emotion alone, which she'd already been doing for far too long. I decided to give her some space. Maybe she'd join us in a while.

Dinner was a giant turkey with all the trimmings, and I had to admit, the smell had me agreeing with Bledsoe that it would be good to get something in my stomach.

Juniper turned to her brother. "Rory, I'm sorry if I added to your stress by making you feel like you didn't belong. We may have picked on each other, but I thought it was sibling rivalry. Because even though you can be a pain in my ass, I do love you. I love you to bits."

"I love you too," he admitted, which must've been hard to say, considering how he felt. "I just want to drop the subject now. I wish I hadn't said anything. I feel so stupid."

"Please, don't. I understand completely. And if you ever want to talk about it, I'm here to listen. Okay?"

Rory didn't respond. Instead, he reached for a bread roll from one of the baskets.

After Bledsoe had delivered the prayer, everyone ate and began chatting as usual. The healing process was already beginning. While eating my meal, I started to get a weird sensation in my belly, which wasn't from the food. Without trying to cause too much of a scene, I asked Posey what time it was.

"It's almost eight."

Dear Lord. It was a good thing I'd checked. I would've been devastated if I had stood Jacob up, but in my defense, what had transpired wasn't an ordinary event. Still, I liked him, and wanted to get to know him better, to feel him holding me tight. I needed to get going. Without missing a beat, I excused myself from the table and said I was going back to the house to use the bathroom, knowing I'd be sure to return before this whole affair was over. Nobody seemed to be in a rush to go home, not after what had happened. I headed to the bridge, and was almost there when movement caught my attention. I saw two people alongside the path. The male stood facing me while the female's back was to me. She was kneeling before him. I saw the man's jeans down around his ankles, heard him moan in pleasure, and realized what it was I was witnessing. Embarrassed, I was about to turn away when I recognized Jacob's face. He couldn't see me, as his eyes were closed from utter pleasure. It also took me a moment to recognize the woman down on her knees. I wasn't used to seeing her with blonde hair yet.

I shouted, "What are you doing?"

Jacob opened his eyes, and I saw the look of shock within them. Shock that he had just been caught cheating.

Wisteria released Jacob's erect cock from her mouth. She

turned in my direction, delivering a smile so wicked it shook me to my core.

"What does it look like? I'm doing something you'd be too shy to do. And this handsome stud appears to be enjoying every second."

"Jacob came out here to see me!" I heard myself saying in disbelief.

"I know," Wisteria said. She still had a firm grip on Jacob's penis, and was stroking it as she spoke. She owned him, and she knew it. His cock remained hard. "I overheard you two love birds the other night when you snuck away at the festival. I was hiding in the shadows. Several times, I thought you might've heard me, and for a second, you looked my way, so I backed off and let you get ahead of me until you arrived with the others."

I couldn't believe what I was hearing. What reason did she have to betray me like this? We'd just become best friends, or that's what I believed. A short while ago, she had been holding my hand. The hairs on my neck tingled. Another sure sign I should be taking the doubts more seriously. Nothing was as it seemed here in this community. Commune. *Cult?*

"Just to let you know, I never wanted this to happen," Jacob said. "I honestly came here to see you, and I was really anxious, but Wisteria showed up and told me she had a message from you. She said you didn't want to see me anymore—and believe me, that hurt, because I really like you, Charlie."

"Charity!" Wisteria corrected.

"What?" he said, confused.

"Never mind," she said.

"And then things got hot and heavy between us. She practically threw herself on top of me, and before I knew it, she had my pants down."

"Such a man-child you are," Wisteria said, in a baby-like voice. "It looks to me like you were enjoying it." She gripped him. "Proof's in the stiffness."

"Wisteria, why would you do this? Why would you say that?"

"How does it feel?"

"Betrayed is how I feel."

"Good. I'm glad, because that's exactly how I felt a week before you were carried away from all of us. That night when you and I snuck into the big house where he lived."

"Who?"

"Aibo! Who else? We watched as he was doing whatever the hell he wanted to those women. And they let him. Didn't even try to resist. But that was his rule, wasn't it, Charity? We were trying to be so quiet, but somehow, he saw us hiding behind the curtains. He dragged us to the altar, then he turned on me. You just stood there, doing nothing to help, allowing him to beat me!"

I felt sick. "I'm sorry, Wisteria, I don't remember any of that."

"Bullshit! You're full of bullshit! There's no way in hell you could've blocked everything out."

"I really just want to…" Jacob tried to intervene, but Wisteria stopped him.

"What? NO! I'm not finished with you, yet."

"This is all a misunderstanding," he began, but Wisteria turned, and her mouth found him again. I watched in disgust.

She suddenly clamped her jaws around him and bit down with everything she had. Jacob screamed in horror as Wisteria's head thrashed wildly like a rabid dog, determined to kill. She relaxed her mouth, and a shower of blood spewed from Jacob's badly wounded penis. Wisteria smiled with her blood-soaked teeth as Jacob looked down. His face went gray, and he passed out. I ran over to him, and pressed on the wound with my bare hands.

Wisteria's laughter was maniacal as she stared at us. Her face and neck were drenched. She spat out a mouthful of blood like it was soured milk.

Jacob came to, and saw me standing over him. There was so much blood oozing from the wound, my hands weren't enough to stop it. He cried out in pain, and pushed me away. He reached down and felt the jagged tear on the side of his penis. He lost all control.

Wisteria rambled on, not in the least bit distracted by Jacob's screaming. He was squirming, and turning paler by the second. I was afraid he was going to bleed out in front of my eyes.

"Some nerve you have coming here, as though nothing had ever happened. Winning everyone over with your fake innocence. I see through your act, even though you have everyone else fooled."

Wisteria reached behind her, bringing out a long carving knife from behind her back. My blood ran cold. I thought she was going to kill me.

"Remember when I told you that I hid behind an evil which lurked here, and it wanted to come out of hiding? It still holds true, but I won't be around for what follows." Without a second of hesitation, she ran the razor-sharp blade across her neck. Blood spurted from her throat with each heartbeat.

One final smile as our eyes locked for the last time.

Wisteria dropped to the ground, in a pool of her own blood.

"No!" I screamed, and ran to Wisteria. I held her. She looked into my eyes as the tortured life she had lived faded as the light left her eyes. She was gone.

I heard voices behind me and footsteps approaching. It was the others coming to see what all the ruckus was about. I felt Bledsoe reach down, pull me away, and I fell into Little Mary's arms. The others quickly gathered the children in an attempt to prevent them seeing Jacob sprawled out on the path.

Odette, such a skilled nurse, assessed him. She removed her blouse and applied firm pressure.

"Linnea! Run to the school and dial 911! Hurry!"

I told them Wisteria had bit his penis so hard I thought she was going to bite it completely off.

Soon, we were bathed in blue and red lights. It took my mind back to that night ten years earlier when a man named Charles had carried me away to safety. Everything had come full circle. I sobbed hysterically. The flashbacks, the reality of what had just happened, hit me all at once. For a moment, I recalled Wisteria and a man named Aibo together while I stood there and watched. *No.* Let's call it what it was. I had stood there and done nothing as the man had brutalized her. I felt terrible. Why hadn't I tried to stop it? I was a child, that's why. What the hell could I have done? Wasn't there a rule? *No resistance…*

The flashbacks came more often, and in greater detail. I wasn't sure which were actual memories. Someone was holding me back, one of the men. He had such a grip on my arms, I could feel his fingernails digging into my flesh. I rubbed my arms as though I could still feel the pain. Why hadn't that man saved Wisteria? So many thoughts were bumping together in my mind. I felt light-headed and off-balance. I begged for my thoughts to stop as Little Mary held me close.

IT TOOK A while for the community to accept the terrible events of that night, and the news Coriander and Little Mary had told us. We were healing. After two surgeries, Jacob made a full recovery. The entire ordeal weighed heavily on Bledsoe and Little Mary. No one stepped up and asked for a blood test, either. Maybe they decided to accept who they were, not the demons of their past. They were survivors, and nothing could change that.

I had several long meetings with my caseworker, Eliza, about the traumatic events I had witnessed that night. She helped me to work through all the emotions.

One Sunday afternoon, I was sitting on my bed, my eyes welling with tears, staring at the beautiful suncatcher. There came a familiar knock upon the door frame. I turned and saw Little Mary standing there.

"May I come in?" I still couldn't believe the respect she had for me—that she still had the common courtesy to ask.

I nodded, and she came in to sit on the edge of the bed with me. Again, I noticed she was holding something. Another photograph.

Little Mary sat on the bed beside me and handed it over. I stared down at two little girls of around seven, holding hands and smiling. That picture contained nothing but pure love and happiness. I looked up and confessed, "This is the little blonde girl from my dreams, and that's me."

"It is."

"Who is she?"

"Who else? Wisteria. You two were inseparable, whenever that monster let you out of his sight."

"I wish she was here with me right now. I wish we had a second chance."

"Me too," Little Mary said, adding, "It's not your fault. None of it is your fault. She was a troubled child. We tried everything to help her get past what happened, but she couldn't let go. Some people you just can't reach, but not for lack of trying."

I stared at the picture. Letting go of my past and moving forward wasn't something that came easy for me.

"May I keep this picture?" I asked.

"Of course. I thought you might want to."

"I'm going to get a frame for it."

"Hold on." She got up. "I might have one in my room."

Before she reached the door, I called out to her, and she turned around.

"Thank you for everything you've done. I don't know how I can ever repay you and Bledsoe for taking me in."

"We're family, and we love you."

Life went on, and it was good for everyone on the compound. A wonderful group of people, who made up a unique family. My family. For the first time in my life, I was truly happy.

After completing high school, I was accepted into the University of Lynchburg. Returning to the city brought back some of the pain from my past, but it was definitely a step in the right direction. I found myself wandering down memory lane less frequently.

Months turned into years. And before I knew it, I was graduating Magna Cum Laude with a Public Health Major, and a Human Services Minor. My goal in life was to reduce domestic violence and advocate for children's welfare in the foster care system.

It was during my senior year in college when I met and fell in love with Willem DeLong. He was a man with similar values as my own. We wanted to make the world a better place for children.

My first job was a dream come true. I became the first person who had been in foster care to be appointed Director of Social Services. I trained counselors and families to help children, not only to survive past traumas, but provide them with the necessary skills to thrive.

Willem started his career as a social worker about the same time. We were passionate about our jobs to serve the community.

On the one-year anniversary of our first date, Willem proposed, and I accepted. Little Mary, Bledsoe, and my entire family unit were thrilled by the news. They insisted the wedding be held at the outdoor church with Bledsoe officiating. Willem and I had hoped that would be the case.

Two months later, we were married. It was a beautiful ceremony, followed by a joyful reception. I was happy to be surrounded by my loved ones; so was Willem. He had immediately become part of the family. He, too, had been through the foster care system. Luckily, his situation was quite different than my own. His foster parents had treated him with the love and respect all children deserved. Willem had been placed with Mr. and Mrs. DeLong at the young age of three. They were there celebrating with us.

Willem and I devoted our first year to one another, and our careers. The natural progression of life seemed to call for the next step. We became foster parents to a teenage boy who had been through so much, we feared he would never otherwise have been placed with the right family. Willem's parents were so proud of their son, and our decision. Our whole family was thrilled when they found out, especially Little Mary and Bledsoe.

It was a difficult adjustment period, to put it mildly. Months of counseling and classes were needed to get Liam to the point of being able to trust us. But eventually, he did, And we bonded as a family unit. Willem and I knew the day would come when we would move forward with the adoption process. Liam grew to love us, as well as all four of his chosen grandparents and our extended family from the compound.

Nearing our third anniversary, I became very ill, and Willem rushed me to the hospital. Liam insisted on coming along, because he was so worried. We couldn't say no, he had come so far. He needed to feel included, and that made us happy. The nurse had Liam remain in a small, nearby waiting room.

I was suffering from severe dehydration, and worried about Willem and Liam catching whatever virus I had that had caused so much vomiting. The doctor ordered a panel of tests after asking lots of questions. One question in particular took us by total surprise.

"Is there any chance you could be pregnant?"

In unison, we said, "No, we use protection."

As soon as we'd answered, I started counting the days since my last period. I was late. Very late. Life had become so busy, I hadn't been giving it much thought. I'd simply written it off as irregular cycles, which was normal for me.

The doctor returned to the exam room with some news. "Congratulations! The two of you are going to be parents."

Once again, we answered together, "We are parents."

I added, "We have a foster son."

She said, "Wonderful! Your family is growing."

The pregnancy hadn't been planned, but we were happy, and so was Liam. I looked forward to sharing the news with our family. After receiving intravenous fluids to replenish hydration, and medication to help alleviate the nausea, I was released.

We were so excited, we decided to do a recorded video chat with the DeLongs, Little Mary, and Bledsoe. I wanted to have the video as a keepsake for years to come. The rest of the family, we would tell in person over the upcoming weekend.

Willem made the calls and had everything set to go live. I couldn't wait to see their faces when they found out they were going to be grandparents.

I started, "I hope we didn't worry anyone with this rush to

have a video chat, but we have something to share."

That was Liam's cue. He held up a sign which read, *I'm going to be a big brother!*

There were congratulations all around. And questions. They weren't sure if that meant we were taking in another foster child, or what.

Willem said, "Charity has been feeling ill, so we made a quick trip to the emergency room. We assumed it was a virus. We weren't actively trying to get pregnant. Life had other plans for us. We are having a baby!"

There was laughter, and tears of joy. After things had calmed down, we said our goodbyes. It was well past midnight, and Liam had school in the morning. And Willem and I had work. Liam headed to his room, and we were off to ours.

I couldn't sleep. Around 2 a.m., I woke Willem. "Did you notice anything off with anyone's reaction?"

Half asleep, he replied, "I saw the look of surprise. And happiness."

I wanted to talk more, but he drifted right back to sleep.

Something wasn't sitting right with me, so I got up and watched the video. I rewatched it three more times, before it dawned on me. The expression on Little Mary's face, and the look in her eyes, wasn't down to surprise or happiness. It was the look of fear.

After Liam had caught the school bus, I played the video for Willem. He refused to see what I was seeing, assuring me Little Mary was concerned for my well-being and nothing more, because I was like a daughter to them. I accepted his reasoning.

The pregnancy progressed with no more nausea or any other complications. At forty weeks, labor began, and my water broke on the way to the hospital. Contractions started coming closer and more intense. Willem called the family. His parents, along with Little Mary and Bledsoe, stayed in the waiting room with Liam.

Something wasn't right. I could feel it.

After twenty minutes of pushing, the midwife delivered the baby and started calling out orders to the team of nurses.

"What's wrong?" I asked, a little dizzy and still out of breath.

Willem sensed my concerns, and the urgency in the doctor's voice.

He pleaded, "Tell us what's going on. Is our baby okay? Is Charity in danger?"

"Everything's fine. The cord was wrapped around the baby's neck, but he's going to be just fine. Nothing to worry about. We're just taking him to be weighed and checked out and we'll have him back with you, all cleaned up, before you know it."

"H-him?" I asked.

"Oh, yes. Congratulations! It's a boy!"

A boy! And I'd heard it with my own ears: He was going to be fine.

One of the nurses placed our baby boy into my waiting arms. I felt a connection like no other. He was perfect. His tiny hands and feet. His beautiful face. The smell of him.

I breathed in the scent of love, and my heart was full. Willem and I had created something wonderful. A precious life. After everything we had all been through, it came down to this very moment. I placed my finger in the palm of my son's hand, and he instinctively closed his tiny fingers around mine. I noticed the red marks around his neck, where the umbilical cord had been tightly wrapped moments ago.

Everything is *fine*.

ERRICK NUNNALLY

Errick Nunnally was born and raised in Boston, Massachusetts. He served one tour in the Marine Corps before deciding art school would be a safer—and more natural—pursuit. He is permanently distracted by art, comics, science fiction, history, and horror. Trained as a graphic designer, he has earned a black belt in Krav Maga/Muay Thai kickboxing after dark, and first prize in one hamburger contest. Errick's writing includes: the novels: *Blood for the Sun, All the Dead Men*, and *Lightning Wears a Red Cape*; a comic strip collection, *Lost in Transition*; and a short novel *The Queen of Saturn and the Prince in Exile*, available from upstart publisher Clash Books. The following are some magazines and anthologies that he has appeared in: *Galaxy's Edge*; *Fiyah Literary Magazine*; *Lamplight*; and *Nightlight, a Black Horror Podcast*. Eventually, Errick came to his senses and moved to Rhode Island with his two lovely children and one beautiful wife.
Visit **erricknunnally.us** to see more of his work.

AGENT JOSEPHINE BAKER AGAINST THE ISLAND OF HORRORS

Josephine spared a glance at the rolled-up rug in the corner and went back to attending her makeup. Operations tended to leave her in an unfortunate state of disarray. She had one last performance this evening and the dead Nazi in the carpet would keep, until men from the Bureau Central de Renseignements et d'Action collected him for disposal.

A gentle knock sounded at the door and Max called out, "Six minutes, Mademoiselle Baker. I also have a message for you here."

"C'mon in, Maxie, don't be shy." She turned in her chair and grinned, putting on her best coquettish pose—only one of the skills she'd learned the hard way on St. Louis' street corners.

Max was of average height for a man and always sharply

dressed. His ruddy blond hair, parted and combed in waves, framed his clean-shaven, oval face well. "Don't waste those charms on me, Miss Baker, save it for the audience."

Josephine chuckled, knowing full well that Max had no interest in women, but she always enjoyed her friend and assistant's time and attention. And his opinion. "How do I look?"

Max took a moment, honestly assessing her, and said, "Fantastique. Is that the package?" He hooked a thumb in the direction of the rug in the corner.

"Probably still warm."

It wasn't her first kill, and it wouldn't be the last. It had never crossed her mind that she should consider herself a murderer, however, as every man she had killed had meant her—or her loved ones—grievous harm, or even death. She included France as a loved one, so it was hardly a stretch of the imagination to kill Nazis for her.

Max grimaced. "They will be here soon, I hope. In other news, I have this communiqué urgente for you." He held out a folded sheet of paper. "It was mixed in with the fan mail. No return address, bien sûr."

Josephine took the paper and opened it up. Blank: a.k.a. *urgent*. She rummaged in her bag for her special perfume bottle and squirted a fine mist of the chemical onto the page. It smelled of lavender and lemon, a nice touch. Then she held the paper up to the candlelight. As the substance warmed, typed words formed on the page.

She read the lines twice and said, "The Service has relayed an urgent request for assistance regarding a series of gruesome murders across Europe."

"Oh?"

"Oui." Josephine leaned back in her chair and gazed into middle space. "The victims were all SIS and OSS operatives or associates."

"Brits and... Americans."

Josephine nearly spat at the thought of aiding her birth country. She had no interest in being a part of any American endeavor without civil rights concessions. Negroes were still fighting and dying for a behemoth of a country that doggedly maintained racial hierarchy. Still, as much as America had to answer for, it was the Nazis who were at the world like a cursed virus. America had shamefully provided additional inspiration for the bastards in the form of Jim Crow laws and Native American genocides. Turning away the German liner *St. Louis* while it was overflowing with Jewish refugees, allowing an active Nazi political party into the United States... All tendencies that emboldened Hitler's regime and which would be amplified worldwide by a Nazi victory. The bastards were already loud enough.

It wouldn't happen as long as Josephine had a say in the matter, and she had plenty to offer on the subject. The enemy made the choice for her. War had always been a messy business, and Nazis occupying her beloved France were begging to be culled.

Josephine memorized the information and set the paper alight. She dropped the smoldering remains in the ash can and grabbed a pencil and paper. "Make haste, Maxie, arrange a little tour to these locations. Monaco first, then we'll hit the next few spots in Italy. If there's no available venue—"

"—Travel arrangements for a recuperative respite."

"I may have had a touch of pneumonia. Very debilitating." She handed Max the paper and winked. "I've got to have a look at some reports. According to the message, they can be found at dead-drop Gordon."

"I'll have them ready for you after your performance."

"Thank you, Max." Josephine grinned, adjusted her banana skirt, checked herself in the mirror, and made haste to the stage.

JOSEPHINE ENTERED THE empty flat in Monaco, her eyes and gun peeled for anything but the spider's web that settled across her face.

"Ugh." She wiped her gloved hand across her face and spit. "I hate it when that happens."

Max entered behind her, snapped a handkerchief from his coat, and handed it to her.

"Merci. *Blech*. Considering the number of webs in this room, it seems there's not going to be much to see here."

"According to the timeline, Rome and Naples were more recent... events."

Josephine made a sound of agreement and scanned the empty rooms. It appeared that family or, more likely, the landlord, had emptied the place out. No evidence of the grotesque murder described in the file. The door had been found open, however, and the man dead. No question of how the killer had entered, at least.

"Anything, Max?"

Max stuck his head out of the bathroom and said, "Non."

"Probably going to take some time to rent this place, considering what happened here. Who'd want it after that?"

"I wouldn't," Max said, and shivered.

"This scene's too far gone. We're not going to find anything here." She ran one finger along the wall's chair rail, noting the amount of dust.

"Rome, then?"

"Rome." Josephine nodded and turned on her heel. "Plenty of time to get ready for the stage there. I have missed The Olympus Club. Make sure Armand Costellis knows we're coming. That slick little operator always has an ear to a wall or an eye to a keyhole. You sent them the playlist?"

"Oui, Mademoiselle Baker. They'll be ready."

"Excellent."

Josephine sat backstage and put the finishing touches on her makeup, while Max sat on a stool in the corner. She checked her outfit in the mirror: a cap pinned jauntily to one side of her head, wreathed in white feathers; a flowing silver dress, laced with sparkling gems, with a plunging neckline and split from hip to toe. Her evening gloves matched her dress. She smiled at herself and cocked one hip.

"Fabulous," Max said.

Josephine winked.

Olympus, despite its name, was an intimate club with a small stage that was more of a dais. When performing, the audience was mere steps away, the rest of the space filled by the band. She could hear the announcer, Giuliano Fametti, warming up the crowd in Italian. She was glad Giuliano was still the MC at this place. He always did such a fantastic job with his introductions and he set the tone sartorially with his white-jacket tuxedos.

She stood ready, waiting for her cue.

"We have a very special surprise for you tonight, my friends! We were very honored to have her on her very first tour and again the following year. We have not seen her for nearly two years but now… she's back!" Giuliano raised and dropped his hand. The band hit an intense, single note. "Welcome to the stage!" Another intense crash of sound, every instrument blasting as one. "Josephine Baker!" The band hit the opening notes of the first song on her playlist.

She strode on stage, arms raised. The audience roared, so few people making so much noise. Their heat boiled over Josephine. She absorbed the energy and returned it, singing with joy. Costellis was in the front row, watching her with an eager glint in his eye. She winked and waggled her fingers at him. He beamed.

These were the moments she craved, times that reminded her of the happiest parts of her past. Singing, dancing, surviving on her terms. In these moments, she couldn't even remember the bad times, the traumas.

The only other feeling that came close was snatching the life from a fascist.

As the last words of her song left her throat, she danced, letting the band run out the tune, and thought, *Vive la France!*

After the set, Josephine undid her outfit and pulled on more practical clothing. Max waited by the door of the dressing room, a blank envelope in his hand.

"Another note from an admirer?"

"Indeed." He handed her the envelope.

The contents appeared to be a grocery list of mostly meats and one vegetable: broccoli rabe.

Josephine reapplied her lipstick with professional flair. "Max?"

"Oui, Mademoiselle?"

"There's a drop at the corner of Bacelli and Riari. Collect what's there, would you?"

"Certainly, Miss Baker. I'll have it ready for you after your dinner?"

"That'll do."

Max hooked a thumb at the closed door. "There are people waiting for you."

"Let them know I'll sign autographs, but I can't stay long. Where's Costellis?"

Max grinned and said, "He begged me to convince you to meet him at L'Agnello della Vita for dinner. Shall I confirm?"

"You shall."

When Max opened the door, there was a small, disappointed cry among the group. "I apologize for not being Mademoiselle Baker, she'll be out in a moment but can't stay long." The last few words were for Costellis, keeping to himself at the back and failing to look nonchalant. The men nodded in unspoken agreement and Costellis scurried off.

Josephine emerged from her dressing room refreshed and

wearing a more practical outfit for the evening. The small crowd cheered and chattered in Italian, with the occasional phrase in English so she could understand. Her smile was genuine as she signed a few autographs before Max helped her escape. Costellis waited.

Max accompanied Josephine on the short walk to L'Agnello. She turned up her collar and further tipped her hat to remain as anonymous as possible. At the restaurant, Max turned her loose at the host's station and continued on to the dead drop.

The slim man at the station, sorting something in the logbook in front of him, barely glanced at her as he said, "Buonasera signorina. Prenotazione?" Then he met her eyes. "Dio mio. You're Josephine Baker." His demeanor softened, his composure lost for a moment.

"I am indeed, my good man; a pleasure to meet you." She curtsied and an easy smile graced her lips.

"And you, signorina." He bowed his head ever so slightly and straightened. Without a hint of irony, his professional face slid back on and he said, "Do you have a reservation?"

Josephine chuckled and said, "I'm meeting a friend. Armand Cost—"

"Ah, Miss Baker, Miss Baker!" Costellis hustled up to the station and confronted the host. They engaged in a heated exchange of Italian, both gestured with frustration.

The confrontation ended as quickly as it had started and the host said, "Apologies, Signorina Baker; please, allow me to take your coat." He snapped his fingers at someone off to the side of the establishment.

Josephine doffed her coat, hat, and gloves. The host took the clothing and immediately handed them to someone else while Costellis escorted her to their table. A few heads turned, but Josephine kept her eye on their destination. The overwhelming smell of food made her realize how hungry she was, despite the late hour.

Costellis pulled out her chair, disguising his true nature, and waited for her to take a seat before he sat himself. "I took the liberty of ordering a bottle for the table. I hope you don't mind?" Costellis's English was impeccable. Near as she could tell, so were his German and French.

"Not at all, but if I don't get some food into me soon…"

"Of course, of course! Bolognese, if I remember correctly?"

Josephine grinned and waved at her companion. "You do remember correctly, Armand!"

The waiter appeared, right on cue. Costellis ordered in Italian.

"How have you been, Josephine?"

"As busy as ever, Armand, and now that I'm in Rome, dying for gossip."

"Oh, you know I keep my lips sealed. My line of work relies on discretion, of course."

"Of course! Now, tell me of the heroes and villains in your life."

A grin creased Costellis's round face and he leaned back in his chair. "You first, my dear. How is France?"

"Occupied," she said, a cloud falling across her demeanor. She sighed and continued, "It's a depressing state, Armand. This war puts a wet blanket over everything. Get invited to a party, throw a party, it doesn't matter, the Nazis are everywhere."

"Oh, they're not so bad."

Josephine choked back her instincts and held on to a harsh reply. "Really? Stiff, very little fun, always severe—"

Costellis leaned forward. "Until you get a few drinks in them."

"Too many wolves in pretty clothes."

Costellis's eyes glinted. "You are a beautiful woman, Josephine. Can you blame them?"

After two glasses of wine, the food arrived and Josephine was glad for it. Not only was she hungry, she was trying to understand why Costellis was so hesitant to chat.

"That smells fantastic! I'm so very hungry."

Costellis gestured at the plates by way of invitation and they ate in silence for a few minutes.

Josephine paused after a few delicious mouthfuls and said, "I suppose the Germans do bring a certain order to things."

"And a fashionable flair." Costellis watched her eyes as he spoke and chewed around his words.

"Indeed. How are they here?"

Costellis waved his free hand. "Background to our dear leader's men. Still, an… interesting bunch." He raised his thick eyebrows, making his eyes bright and round for a moment.

"That sounds like villains to me. Capes and masks, sharp teeth and pointed ears?"

They both laughed at that, a tense chuckle.

"I think I'd prefer that. Some of these men are… chilling. I met some of them recently, at an embassy party. One of them, a doctor, Beer-something, never smiled, but it was his associates that made me feel like ghosts were passing through me."

"Oh, my goodness."

"Yes, a giant, and a man with a broken face and glasses with one dark lens."

"Who were they?"

"No idea, they never spoke. The doctor never smiled and not a word from his associates. They just… stared."

"Don't tell me they wore all black, too."

Costellis laughed. "Naturally! The one black glove was especially strange."

Josephine leaned forward, openly interested, and baring enough cleavage to sell it. "Are they still here?" She asked the question in a breathy thrill.

Costellis's eyes froze on her décolletage before wandering back to her eager face. "Ahem. No, the doctor remarked they were traveling eastward, no idea where." He chewed for a moment, seeming to regret having shared what little information he'd given her.

"Well, that is chilling. Did they want something from you?"

Costellis blanched and cleared his throat. "Well, I… That is, they…"

Josephine attended to her dinner again, for one bite, listening to Costellis struggle with the question. She considered how the fascists had rattled an old operator like him. "What of the music in Rome, Armand? Tell me, who's rising on the scene?"

Costellis came back to life, relaxing into a subject he clearly felt more comfortable discussing with her. He wasn't exactly a friend, an associate at best. He was a criminal, in fact, and slimy enough that only a woman like Josephine could keep him at arm's length, but this war… these people, they destroyed everything they came in contact with, warping or destroying entire countries, erasing cultures. Curse them and their hellish desires.

The rest of their evening went lightly, she kept the subject on anything but whatever Costellis might be tangled up with. They finished the bottle of wine and Max arrived to escort her back to the hotel.

ROME. A BEAUTIFUL city with filthy corners. Classical architecture thousands of years old and a brand new fascist movement marring everything in sight. Josephine walked on Max's arm to the next location. She wore hat and sunglasses, had her collar turned up, and gloves—her uniform for operations, as much to hide in as functional. The frustration of the night before pinged around her mind. She fully expected to gain more insight from Costellis than she had.

Two Carabinieri chased a small gang of Roma children across their path. Josephine both hoped the children had picked the pocket of a Nazi and that they'd done nothing wrong. Scores of the Carabinieri had defected to join Italy's resistance, but there were still too many who willingly chose to obey fascism's directives. She imagined slipping a dagger into each of their livers and wished for the ability to know which men were willing to enthusiastically oppress others and which were simply trying to survive a vicious warping of Italian culture.

They walked on, leaving the situation to play out.

The apartment in Rome was still furnished and bearing the belongings of the victim. Rather than break in as they'd done in Monaco, they needed a different strategy since the landlord lived next door. Max brokered a bribe in the form of a month's rent and it loosened the owner's morals enough to grant them access.

As they stood waiting while the landlord opened the door, Josephine asked, "What did you hear that night, mio amico?"

The property owner, a sweaty man with a balding head and thick mustache, was slick with sweat and conversant in broken English. He shrugged, turning the lock, and said, "A scream. I come, look, call polizia."

He pushed the door open, bid them to enter and followed them in.

Josephine considered herself fortunate to be wearing gloves when she closed the door and pressed the man against the jamb, a knife to his moist throat.

"Mio amico," she said, "this war has brought us all trying times, yes?"

"Josephine," Max said, and regretted the utterance. She ignored him.

The landlord, shocked into compliance, nodded. He raised both hands, the keys dangling from one finger.

Josephine continued. "The man who lived here died horribly. No one wants such a death, do they?"

The landlord nodded again, a nervous nod, more of a twitch, clearly he was painfully aware of the knife at his throat.

Max watched, tense and uncomfortable. He knew it was a bad idea to interrupt Josephine when she was working. Still, he wanted her to be successful.

"You found the body. What did you hear that night that compelled you to investigate?"

He answered in a burst of stuttering English. "S-Same as I tell polizia. I h-hear scream. Loud, scary. And came. With key, I o-open door."

Josephine nodded slowly, letting the man watch himself in the reflective lenses of her sunglasses. "You heard a scream. Nothing else?"

"No! Nothing else."

Josephine took a deep breath and Max, knowing his friend, tensed even further.

"Lies are what brought us war, mio amico, lies will not save us." She pressed the knife harder against his throat, drawing a bead of blood.

"Please! No, please! I... I heard a... a... noise. Like... *click, click, click*. Nothing more! Maybe imagine! I tell polizia and they say I pazzo—crazy."

"I see. Did you smell anything, feel something else?"

"Smell, feel?" The man cast his eyes to Max, who offered nothing in return but his stillness.

The man tried to sink into the door, to pass through solid matter as Josephine pressed again with her knife. "I don't like to repeat myself, friend."

Max clenched his hands, willing himself to be still, to wait. Assuring himself that Josephine knew what she was doing.

"I… I smell…" The man struggled to remember, blinking rapidly, no doubt trying to think of what would appease the woman with a knife to his throat.

Max stepped forward and said softly, "Just relax and tell her what you remember."

Josephine tilted her head and pinched her lips, a tiny sign of pique.

"Like seed, much seed—please, no more!"

She held the man for a moment longer, unmoving. She pulled away, abrupt and dismissive. The man breathed a sigh of relief with his entire body.

Josephine crossed her arms, the dagger in the hand she held thoughtfully to her chin. They all stood, an absurd collection of sculptures frozen in the moment: Max on the edge of his seat, Josephine seemingly lost in thought, and the landlord with his hands up and waiting.

"What of today?" Josephine asked, "What do you remember about today, mio amico?"

The man sputtered, unsure how to answer. Josephine placed the knife against his belly and pursed her lips.

"Nothing, signora, I remember nothing."

"Good." She pulled the knife away and sheathed it.

Max slipped a handkerchief from his pocket and placed it against the small wound on the man's neck. "Very good, very good, mon ami, let's get you back to your apartment."

"Sì, sì," he muttered, "grazie."

Josephine meandered further into the apartment and said to herself, "Clicking. Seed." Then she began inspecting the floor, walls, and ceiling for clues. The only thing she found was one hair on the door trim below the transom window.

Under her spyglass, the hair had a coarse texture to it, like additional hairs running counter to the length, something she'd never seen on a hair before.

THE INFORMANT IN Naples had disappeared more recently, so they hurried to the scene. Max handled the bags and arranged the hotel for them. Afterward, they walked arm-in-arm to the rooms in question. The location was closer to the docks than civilized people were comfortable with. This did not give Josephine or Max pause, both of them having grown up in inauspicious conditions. It did mean, however, that they were more likely to encounter someone on the streets who presented themselves as everyone's problem. Today was such a day.

The usual set of types that polite society considered uncivilized milled about. Some hawking second-hand items, others putting themselves on the chopping block, the streets quickly became a minefield. Max might occasionally be mistaken for a dandy by some men, but others would recognize what he was with a preternatural gaze. A small group of men near a hotel that likely offered rooms by the hour as well as the day watched them stroll past. One of them, wearing leather and dark looks, peeled off. He wore his black hair combed back and held in place with a prodigious amount of pomade. He ignored Josephine, targeting Max.

"Non mentire, ragazzo, vuoi di più," he said.

Josephine ignored him and Max said, "No, grazie."

"Ah, I speak English, yes? You are French, no? The kind of man who appreciates quality." Ruggedly handsome, the fellow patted his chest with both hands before sweeping one hand through his hair.

"Not interested," Max said, quickening his pace.

The man skipped in front of them. "Don't hide, baby, be yourself. You think you don't want me, are you better than us fags?" He swept an arm to indicate the group he'd left.

Josephine had been deep in thought, only paying attention to obstacles. Now one had presented itself. She slipped herself from Max's crooked arm.

Max hesitated, wanting to de-escalate the situation, but also wanting to see this man who had tried to humiliate him cowed. He feared what Josephine might do and, at the same time, he yearned for what she might do. "Please move aside, sir, I'm not interested."

The prostitute swept a contemptuous hand at Josephine. "You think these people will accept you because of this slip of a thing on your arm?"

Max clenched and attempted to intervene, but Josephine was too fast and snapped a kick into the man's groin. He doubled over with a grunt and she seized his ear in a blur of movement, twisting it and him to the ground. He grabbed her hand—the one clasping his ear—with both of his, attempting to pry her loose. In response, Josephine calmly placed her free hand's thumb in his eye and pressed hard enough to make him believe in the possibility that he might lose some of his sight today.

Max cried, "Mademoiselle Baker, *s'il te plaît!*"

The small crowd of men took halting steps in their direction. Josephine sized up the situation and said to the man she was currently torturing, "Are we done here?"

Through his pained, strangled cries, he responded, "Abbiamo finito! We're done, we're done!"

She let him go and weaved one arm through Max's again, encouraging him to walk.

Curses and other angry sounds pricked at their backs.

Max sighed and said, "Mademoiselle Baker, you can't—"

"Max." She said his name like a period at the end of a sentence. "No one gets to harass you like that. Not when I'm around." She patted his arm. "Don't worry, I'll let you brawl in the streets some other day."

Max chuckled and they continued their journey.

The room in Naples proved more fruitful. Where Monaco had yielded next to nothing in terms of evidence, here there were strange marks on the walls and the ceiling, a loose screw sticking out of the wall vent, and a few coarse hairs caught on the corner of the metal. Hairs like the one she had found in Rome.

The vent nagged at her. Too small for the average man, but perfect, perhaps, for a contortionist or simply a very small person. Maybe. The collected hair, again, looked coarser than any she'd seen before. Under a magnifying glass, she could make out the spines lining the surface of the hairs, and they had a tacky quality to them. *Strange.*

The Allied agent in Bari seemed the next logical stop. *And fast*, Josephine thought, *we're getting closer to… something.*

"Max, book us train tickets in a private box to Bari."

"Oui, Miss Baker. Is our final stop close or shall I book a car?"

Josephine tapped each of her fingertips with her thumb, considering what the future might hold. "Call ahead, arrange a car. We may need to get around quickly."

Max nodded and left the room to make the arrangements. The train ride across the peninsula would give her time to think. So far, the affair felt like a race to the death. The investigation had given her the sense of grasping at air, the outline of something she'd never seen before. If she could just get ahead of this invisible assassin, there could be a chance to stop them, or, at least, uncover their identity and their methods. Despite her own murderous skill set, this phantom killer gave her chills.

JOSEPHINE LINKED ARMS with Max and they entered the train station. She wore a gray half-hat with a veil that partially obscured her face. Wearing her coat collar up, and the addition of understated gloves, helped further conceal the fact of her celebrity—and her skin color. At times, either would produce unwanted effects.

The scent of machine oil permeated the station in Naples. Along with the grime of the city tracked in by countless feet, it was worth wondering if the smell would get into their clothes. The only places without movement in the space were the darkened corners where unsavory men waited. Pickpockets, pimps, and punks. Josephine recognized the type; she'd spent many years growing up among them in America. All around them, ornate iron work and carved marble captured no eyes with their beauty. Not even the intricate skylights caused a neck to bend as everyone was focused on their destinations.

Couples and families hurried about, creating a complex pattern in the crowd as people threaded through each other. Remarkably, there were no collisions and the crowd helped to obscure Josephine's identity while she and Max made their way to the platform and their conductor.

They were escorted to their seats in a private box with little fanfare. In situations like this, Josephine made it a point to place herself just behind Max's shoulder, hiding in plain sight, but outside their escort's view.

Closing the cabin's door, they took their seats, and Max stowed the small bag that Josephine used to carry her tools of the trade. They both removed their hats at the same time and Max smoothed his blond hair. Handsome as ever; Josephine appreciated that he provided the perfect cover at times like this.

"What do you think of all this, Maxie?"

Max crinkled his forehead and said, "The war, your usual part, or this particular mystery we're pursuing?"

"Present course. You haven't had much to say, along the way."

Max's face shifted to puppy-dog hurt and he leaned forward. "Oh, Miss Baker, I'm sorry, I don't—"

"Easy, Max, you're as helpful as ever. And you're no dummy. I'm finding this vexing, so far. It's too unusual. These murderous alboche bastards are everywhere, but this is new."

He took a deep breath, leaned back, and said, "It bothers me too. C'est très étrange, dérangeant. The murders. We have seen the horrors of war, but this feels… different."

She nodded and looked out the window, staying back in her seat, out of sight. There was a knock at the door and the conductor said, "Biglietti, per favore. Tickets, please."

Max rose to his feet and stood in front of the door as it slid open. Josephine caught a glimpse of the conductor's eye and saw his reaction.

Shit. Not today, Lord.

Max closed the door and froze, seeing Josephine's face. "What is it?"

"He saw me, Max, and I don't think his lips are gonna stay sealed."

"Oh, mon Dieu. What can I do?"

"Nothing, I'm afraid. Probably easier to play the part and give the people what they want for a few minutes. I didn't really expect to travel in total anonymity anyway, and I'll need to use the toilettes at some point." She sighed and set out again to pore over the additional reports Max had retrieved.

The files described a heinous, double-puncture wound; swollen, cracked flesh; and the use of an unknown toxin. Speculation included a couple of volatile chemicals and perhaps a two-pronged injection device. It was not beyond the imagination or capabilities of the Axis to have developed such a thing. The file contained possible suspects for the developments of such a weapon. Only one had been seen in Italy.

Dr. Gottfried Biermann, an SS scientist known to the Allies, had been spotted in the country several months earlier. His morbid experiments in biologic hybridization had made him infamous within the Reich before he had disappeared from public view. Cobbling together animals and humans had no place in a civilized society.

Josephine pulled a photo from the folder. "Max, where's the magnifying glass?"

He handed her the glass and she peered more closely at the photo of Biermann. He sat at a Brindisi cafe with four other men. Two of the associates were notable in appearance, the others were typically unremarkable fascists.

"Look at this, Max." She handed the photo over. "What do you see?"

Max struggled with the magnifying glass to see. "Mon dieu, this photo was taken from quite a ways off."

"Hard to get close to men like that. It's what makes my parties so special. They come to me."

Max chuckled. "Which one is Biermann?"

"He's the balding ghoul."

"These two are chilling. The big one, he's a beautiful sculpture, but his eyes are dead. And this one's face looks… broken. His fashion choices are a bit odd, as well."

Josephine took the photo back. "I'm guessing he's a veteran of the Great War. A missing eye would explain the smoked lens in his glasses, and no one with two good hands wears one black glove. No idea about the pretty ape."

Max chewed his lip in thought. "Hm. Makes sense Biermann

and associates would be here. Hitler has been cozy with Mussolini for some time now."

"That he has." Josephine tapped the photo. "According to the assignment, Biermann is a person of interest." She smiled and added an aside, "A target of opportunity."

Max shook his head, amused. "Your enthusiasm for killing Nazis is showing."

"I should hope so." Josephine gazed out the window, a light grin playing at her lips.

AN HOUR LATER, a gentle knock sounded at the door again, and Max answered. The conductor stood in the narrow doorway, hat in hand, with a deep, hopeful look in his eyes. He nodded and spoke in slow, accented English.

"Signorina Baker, very sorry to bother, the engineer has asked if you willing to visit the crew? Just for little bit? He loves you work! Sees you show every time you come to Italia!"

Max stepped farther into the doorway and said, "Please, let Miss Baker have her priv—"

"It's all right, Max. I am happy to meet with them for a few minutes."

He nodded and took his seat. The conductor waited, an expectant look on his face. Josephine smiled, pulled on her hat and gloves, and stood. "Just the crew, yes?"

"Yes, very private. This way, please, Signorina. He will be so happy!" The conductor bowed and motioned.

Josephine left the room and waited for the conductor to lead the way.

Max didn't like it, but he knew she could take care of herself.

"WHAT'S YOUR NAME, young man?"

"Carlos, Signorina, very good to meet you."

She smiled. "And you, Carlos."

They crossed into the next car and through another set of private cabins. Josephine could see a few men waiting in the vestibule ahead.

The conductor slid the door open and presented her to the small group. All of them were in uniform, but the tallest—a man with an impossibly thin mustache, long nose, and very dark hair—wore a different jacket. The other two were clean-shaven with handsome faces, one had brown hair, the other blond.

The tall man made a joyful sound and tilted his head, arms spread. "Signorina Baker! Ciao, bella! Grazie, grazie, grazie for meeting with us! I adore your shows! My name is Antonio." He took her hand and kissed the back of it.

"Oh, my goodness, you must be the engineer of this fine train! I am very fortunate to have patrons such as your good self." She plucked his shoulder and smiled, moving in the ways that made men feel grander than they were, lessons learned before a girl's age reached double digits. These were the selfsame charms that had magnetized her first husband, when she was thirteen years old. Charms she had learned to turn on and off as needed, rather than perform at the whims of society's unequal demands. Her murderous skills had come through hard-earned times, as well.

The engineer introduced her to the other two men: his assistant, Luis, and another conductor, Lorenzo. They both greeted her enthusiastically, though she noticed the latter's face hardened as soon as she'd broken eye contact. Experience told her to be wary of that man. She always listened to her instincts and set to ensuring she remembered his blond hair and facial features. Better to see them coming than be surprised.

"Signora Baker, would you be willing to sign something for me?"

"I'd be delighted, Antonio."

The tall man produced a pad of paper, clearly something he used in his day-to-day work. With the notebook in her hands, he flipped through the pages.

"I know there's a blank page in here somewhere. Ah, here we go! Now, a pen." He made a dramatic show of patting his pockets while his men traded knowing looks. "Penna!" With a flourish, he handed the pen to her.

Josephine signed the blank page and handed the notebook back. She capped the pen, met Antonio's eyes, and smiled as she opened his jacket and returned the pen to the inner pocket from which it had been drawn. "There, you won't forget it now, will you?"

"Oh, ha-ha, I will not, Signora Baker! No, no, no!" Antonio's smile showed nearly every tooth in his mouth.

His enthusiasm delighted Josephine, but she knew better than to extend this meeting any further, so she guided the light conversation to goodbye.

"I'm so sorry to cut things short, boys, but I've been trying to take it easy since a bout of pneumonia last month."

Antonio put on a face of mild horror. "Oh, I am very sorry, signora! I have read that you struggle with that horrible illness."

"It is vexing." She cleared her throat. "Will I see you in the audience the next time I visit Italy, Antonio?"

"Sì, sì, sì!"

Josephine cupped Antonio's long face while the two conductors thanked her for visiting. Carlos led her from the vestibule and she watched Lorenzo from the corner of her eye. He seemed anxious and malicious, at the same time.

"AND HOW WERE your les plus grands admirateurs? Star-struck, adoring, drooling for your culottes?"

Josephine chuckled and said, "Just fans, mostly."

"'Mostly'?"

"One of them felt off to me. Lorenzo, his name is. He was nice enough in conversation, but it felt like he was trying to put a hole in my head when I wasn't looking directly at him."

"And you have enough holes in your pretty head already, eh?"

"I do." She nodded. "This affair has me on edge and I don't want any surprises."

"Understood. Well, tell me what this man looks like and I'll keep my eye out, too."

She described Lorenzo to Max as she rummaged through her

gear, putting a few items here and there. The rest of the ride to the next stop passed without incident.

JOSEPHINE GAZED OUT the window at nothing in particular. Eager to move forward, she was ready to exit the train, but their destination was an hour away. As she scanned the crowd on the platform, a familiar blond caught her attention.

Lorenzo threaded the crowd to scurry into the station's ticket booth. He traded a few words with the attendant there and picked up the phone. The attendant exited the booth and Lorenzo made his call. Josephine watched his lips. She was sure he'd said her name.

Max noticed her intensity and said, "Miss Baker?"

She held out a palm towards him and focused on Lorenzo. Her lip-reading skills were far from perfect, but it helped at parties and other events to be able to see bits of what people were saying.

Max peeked out the window. "Ah, Lorenzo," he muttered.

"Grab a pencil and paper, Max." Her lip-reading experience fell almost entirely within English. Still, she caught snippets of words and committed them to memory. She dictated what she could make out.

Lorenzo hung up the phone and left the booth. The attendant, clearly annoyed, traded a few words with him. Both men gestured dismissively. Lorenzo hurried back on board as the train began moving again.

Josephine sat back and Max pulled out a tourists' book of Italian phrases. Traveling through these fascist territories was difficult even under the best circumstances. Her celebrity opened doors, and she dutifully reported what she could from the inside. As the war burned on around them, the monsters running these nations became ever more paranoid and the fist tightened. It was rubbing off on her.

"Max, do you think anyone suspects?"

"What's that, Miss Baker?" He held a finger on the page where he was scanning.

"That I happen to have been in the room on the occasions that information made its way to the Allies."

Max swallowed, a look of concern creasing his brow. He shrugged and said, "C'est possible. I don't believe, however, that any of them have the imagination to consider your, uh, other activities."

She went back to her thoughts as Max continued to scan the small book. "Here it is: 'Baker, train, I am sure, look for yourself,' and 'I can see.' What do you think all of that means?"

"That Lorenzo is an ambitious toady under the thrall of Il Duce."

"Un problème?"

"Only if his britches get too tight."

Max's face screwed up in confusion. Once in a while, Josephine would drop an American euphemism into the conversation. When she was deep in thought like this, it wasn't worth prying, so he let it go. If it was a problem, he was confident she'd know how to handle it.

THE TRAIN PULLED into the station at Bari, and Max readied himself to go and fetch the car. Josephine pulled up her collar, donned a pair of round sunglasses and pulled down her hat. It was time to be as anonymous as possible. On the platform, she waited with the bags, standing in the shade with her back to a windowless wall.

"Help with your bags, Miss Baker?" Lorenzo's painted-on smile had all the charm of a cigar-store Indian.

Josephine didn't smile. She met his eyes and said, "No, thank you, Lorenzo."

His face danced between emotions for a moment as he unbuttoned his coat to show that he had a gun tucked into his belt. He patted the weapon and said, "Are you sure I can't change your mind?"

She said, "And if I scream?"

"Then I'll kill you here and you'll never know why. Camicie Nere will understand."

Josephine weighed her options, truly curious as to what had led Lorenzo to this moment. "What do you want, Lorenzo?"

"Let's go," he said, "in there, you socialist cagna." He jingled his keys and indicated a storage space for luggage at the depot.

Josephine took a moment to consider what 'cagna' meant. The inflection of the word passing over the lips of a man was unmistakable. She took a slow, calm walk in the indicated direction. After all, he did have a gun at hand.

"'Credere, Obbedire, Combattere.' Is that right, baby Black-shirt? You'll be a big man now, I suppose."

Lorenzo opened the door and pushed Josphine into the room, muttering something in Italian.

His size ensured his push made her stumble forward. She regained her balance and turned, removing her sunglasses now that they were indoors.

Lorenzo rewarded her with a poorly thrown punch to the jaw. It snapped her head but didn't move her feet. She nodded and tucked her glasses into her breast pocket and considered what else to say that might antagonize him or make him think or, perhaps, compel him to give up this foolish course of action. Nothing came to mind.

She scanned the room. Suitcases, trunks, and other baggage surrounded them. Her thoughts narrowed to the task at hand. Rather than tense, she loosened, understanding where her balance and strength were centered and what it meant to move in ways difficult to anticipate.

Lorenzo squared up on her and said, "You Americans, so cocksure of yourselves. Allies with communists, overrun with socialists."

Josephine rolled her eyes and slipped her fingers around the knife up her sleeve while holding Lorenzo's gaze. "Why me, Lorenzo? Why are you doing this?"

"Because I can read! I saw the reports. Put it together and you are the common fact, you were always in the room. No one believes me, but they'll soon see."

"No one believes you because you're a fool."

"I am not a fool!" Lorenzo spat the words. "And with you gone, the truth will shine."

"You are a fool for falling into that Blackshirt bullshit, for believing Mussolini's lies."

Lorenzo reached for his pistol with the slow, menacing, and altogether overconfident pace of a man lost in other men's lies. "An American negress socialist like you will never understand what Credere, Obbedire, Combattere truly mea—"

Josephine stepped forward, and in one motion placed her dagger to his throat, and wrapped her right hand around the pistol grip protruding from his pants. The click of the safety rang ominous to his ears.

"Believe me: this isn't for punching a lady; it's for Travail, Famille, Patrie," she said, and pulled the trigger.

The muffled shot sent a pain through Lorenzo's body, the likes of which he had never known. It forced him to double over, impaling his neck on her blade. The blade slipped easily out of his throat as she stepped aside to avoid the crumpling corpse and the gout of blood.

Josephine ground her teeth and said to Lorenzo's remains, "And I'll never be American, bête."

She realized that Lorenzo's death might help prove him right. Better that he disappear for good, leaving nothing but questions. Casting about the room, she found a trunk the right size and emptied its contents. Then she pushed the body into it, using his clothing to tie off the bleeding wound and mop the bulk of his blood from the floor. The clothes joined Lorenzo in the trunk. Her gloves, she turned inside out and shoved into her pocket.

When Max returned, Josephine was waiting where he'd left her, and the train chugged away.

"Désolé pour le retard, very sorry it took so long. I hope your wait was uneventful." He began loading baggage onto a cart.

"Well, the train crew were calling for Lorenzo earlier. It appears he abandoned his job, nobody knows where he is at the moment."

Max stopped loading the baggage and peered at Josephine. Then he noticed the unfamiliar trunk. "Oh, Miss Baker, non!"

"Oh, Maxie, oui. Let's get out of here."

Max took a beat before he said, "Right away, Mademoiselle. This way to the car."

THE HOTEL WAS clean, unassuming, and quiet. Exactly what they needed.

Josephine peeled off her hat and coat, pleased to shed her "disguise" and be herself again. "Nice job on the accommodations, Max."

"Merci, Mademoiselle Baker." Max bowed his head and clicked his heels playfully. He set to organizing their luggage.

"Max?"

"Oui?"

"Je suis désolé pour le coffre, mon amour. That may have been rash."

"You were cornered, mon cher."

Josephine chewed her lower lip and cast her eyes around the

room, not wanting to meet Max's gaze. "Still. I'm sorry."

A long moment held in the room, a thickening of the air. Max released the pressure. "I'll go take care of that trunk now."

Josephine nodded. "I need to shower."

Max left the room and Josephine stripped on the way into the bathroom. She spun the hot water tap and waited for the temperature to rise. She stood, watching herself in the mirror, naked for no one to see, vulnerable in a way she never was on stage or on an operation.

The passing years had taught her the necessity of hiding bruises and scars, caring for old wounds so that they did not nag. She touched a hand to the light bruise Lorenzo had gifted her. Like every bit of violence men had doled out for her, the pain beneath her skin was sharper and more pronounced. She stood like that, hand to jaw, struggling to tamp down the churning in her gut, a feeling of the past catching up to her. No matter how far she'd run from St. Louis—from America—in quiet, uncertain moments, she could hear the rampaging footsteps of her home country's rage. An entire neighborhood on fire, just across the Mississippi. Screaming, running, leaving everything behind.

The mirror fogged over, obscuring her face, breaking the spell, and Josephine stepped into the shower to cleanse.

Her feelings and clotted blood swirled down the drain. After she'd dried and robed, she found a sweating Max just outside the bathroom, collecting her discarded clothing. She'd left a trail to the bathroom.

"These will need to be laundered, after such a day."

"I'm afraid there are more days like this ahead of us." She

sprawled on the chaise longue and sighed.

"Something I fear as well, mon cher. These Nazis are taking war to very strange and dark places, indeed."

Josephine nodded. Intelligence told of explorations in the occult, pharmaceutical attempts to create supermen, and, of course the death camps. "This locked room murder shit. I swear, Max, I thought that sort of thing was mostly fiction. And the method of killing, itself? Why go to all the trouble of manufacturing a double-pronged injection device to do the job? Too clever by half."

"Poison is a very well established method of murder."

"It is," she acknowledged, "but those injection sites… Too large for medical needles. Putting something in a drink or food, I understand, but…"

"Morbid ingenuity. They are known for such things." Max said his last few words through a blast of exhausted air.

"Max, you're as tired as I am and sweating like a priest in a whorehouse. Take a break, a bath, something. I'll order room service."

Max stood, thinking it over, and grinned. "Oui, Mademoiselle Baker."

THEY WAITED UNTIL early evening the next day before making their way to the Allied contact in Bari. Night crept across the buildings and a light fog rolled in from the harbor as the last rays of light drowned in the west. It was quiet, but neither of them knew Bari well enough to judge whether or not the conditions were unusual. The low-lying fog swirled in the car's plodding headwind, revealing the occasional curl of vapor in the headlamps. Josephine enjoyed these quiet moments, charged with purpose. Another rock to turn over, another target to uncover. Step by step, marching into the future at whatever cost brought peace or something like it.

Max parked the car a half block from the meetup location not far from the docks, in what some would have considered the seediest section of the port town.

"The usual bit, Maxie, follow and watch my back, keep an eye on the street."

"You got it, Miss Baker."

Josephine stepped out of the car and adjusted the Colts holstered at her hips. She wore a wool pantsuit, dyed a vengeful black. Her figure cut a sharp, unassuming silhouette, concealing the daggers in her boots and a few other lethal tricks here and there: brass knuckles sewn into her gloves, the retractable garrote wound beneath a watch at her wrist. A three-quarter, black trench coat covered the entire affair. The addition of a form-fitting cowl and scarf further obscured her features. She kept a quick and confident pace. The contact awaited on the second story of an old building made of sagging stones.

Ascending brick stairs, she caught a glimpse of her assistant at his post, half in and out of shadow. Max made a show of checking his watch every few minutes—to an observer, he was just a guy waiting for someone. He was a good boy, and Josephine would keep an eye on him for as long as she could manage.

Shame on society for demonizing who loves whom. Especially in the face of this horrific conflict. Every hand was needed to beat back the Nazi scourge.

Halfway through the foyer, she heard a scream, an exclamation of unhinged terror. She charged up the steps to the second floor, hearing the unmistakable thump of a body hitting the floor. She unholstered one of her pistols and pressed an ear to the door. Scrabbling, like needles on a typewriter, floated to her ear.

It took two kicks to force the door open. She dove inside, drawing her second pistol, and ended in a crouch off the main sightline to the door. The poorly appointed rooms weren't difficult to take in, it was essentially one space with a kitchenette packed into the corner. A pot of water whistled on the tiny stove. Remembering the previous scene, she made it a point to look up, tracking her sightline with the Colts. Nothing. Just the body on the floor.

Josephine stepped over the contorted agent and turned off the stove. His mouth and eyes were frozen open, his body swollen, and two injection points bulged between his neck and shoulder. She peered closer: it looked like a massive pinch. Muddy yellow ichor slowly flowed from the wound.

A rough click drew her attention. She spun and caught a glimpse of a shadow at the transom window over the door. She surged into the hallway, leading with her pistols. Something far down the hall sounded like a cat plucking at a carpet. She ran toward the sound and heard Max shouting from below.

"Miss Baker! Here, this man!"

An unknown male voice shouted in German, "Zurück! Jetzt!"

Josephine bounded down the stairs two at a time, risking

ankles and knees to ensure the safety of her friend. As she exited the foyer to leap down the stoop, she caught a glimpse of Max taking a punch to the jaw and falling to the ground.

"Max! Are you okay?"

He held his jaw and pointed. "That man, I recognized him! An associate of Biermann's, the one with the broken face!"

Josephine gave chase before the man disappeared into the shadows, the hard soles of his shoes echoing on the cobblestones. The lateness of the hour worked for both of them: cover for him and no witnesses for her. She hadn't decided yet if this man needed to be captured or killed. And why shout "Return now?" If it had been for the benefit of an accomplice, she hadn't seen them.

Three flashes from the shadowy form's pistol gave her the answer she needed. She ducked into an alcove. The wild shots careened down the street, hitting nothing near her. Small caliber, by the sound of it. As the fugitive rounded a corner ahead, Josephine cut behind the building. Vaulting one fence and another, it put her on a straight line to cross her quarry's path. She tackled the man. He easily outweighed her by fifty pounds, but momentum did the job. He sprawled and she rolled to her feet, clubbing him on the back of the neck twice with her pistol butt.

The man issued a pair of painful grunts. She holstered her guns and grabbed his collar before growling in German, "Why are you here, boche, who sent you?"

She saw too late that he was still holding the pistol; this was not a good time to attempt an interrogation. He muscled her off him while rolling to the side, and fired. The bullet zinged past her head. Her own pistol skittered from her hand where she rolled hard. She kicked his arm, stopping his turning motion, before striking him in the liver. He hissed in pain, dropping the gun, but surged to his feet and chopped at her with his left hand as if it were a club. She ducked and stumbled backward a step, unwilling to gun him down. His weapon made small cracks, hers would boom. People would notice the difference and report it, so she holstered the pistol, willing to deal with the situation as quietly as possible.

She could see that it was his left side that had taken damage. He wore a prosthetic across his face, giving it the look of cracked porcelain. The left lens of his glasses was smoked black.

He grabbed his gloved hand with his left and pulled to reveal a long dagger instead of a flesh and blood appendage. He threw the gloved sheath at her and followed with the arm-dagger.

Josephine dodged the flying hand and slipped to her right, into the man's blind spot. He slashed with his dagger, as she expected.

She'd had enough of this encounter. Josephine ducked under the backhanded attempt to cut her and tripped him with a kick to the soft part behind his knee. For the second time, he dropped to the cobblestones, but this time was harder. Both of his pained cries satisfied Josephine, she hoped he'd broken his coccyx. With a knife for one hand and a damaged knee, he labored to get back on his feet.

Josephine scrambled onto his back, and wound her garrote around his throat. Two quick tugs in opposite directions severed both windpipe and arteries. He sagged to the cobblestones, aghast at his own death.

Josephine picked up her gun and took a moment to catch her

breath before she scooped up his pistol. A Walther, of course. "Nazi pig," she spat.

She cast a quick glance around and saw a few lights coming on in the surrounding buildings. Wasting no more time, she dragged the dead man into an alley and checked his person, finding the usual items such as a wallet and keys, a small knife, a handful of coins. The sheaf of papers in his breast pocket proved the most interesting: it bore a series of marks like Morse code, with corresponding letters and German words.

Josephine spared one more glance for the dead man. The rats could have him. She tossed his loosed hand into a garbage can and started her walk back to Max. Her stride was casual, unconcerned, and confident—the shifting of a shadow caught her attention. She was being followed.

TOO SMALL FOR a man, as large as a dog. It moved in spurts, keeping pace with her. She whirled, drawing her pistol, and sighted down the barrel. It froze, performed a series of moves too fast to follow in the dark, and shot down the street towards the harbor. It passed through pools of light and Josephine could barely believe her eyes. It was the largest spider she'd ever seen, and too fast for her to follow on foot.

Headlights lit the street, and she crouched. Max pulled the car alongside her. "Get in!"

Josephine had barely slammed the door when Max simultaneously mashed the accelerator and asked in a harrowed voice,

"What the Hell was that going down the street?"

"Well, Maxie, it looked like a spider to me. Step on it!"

"It's too big! And why should we follow it?"

"If the Nazis have recruited a spider, we need to confirm it or kill it. Maybe both."

Max ground his teeth and kept the vehicle steady. "What's down here?"

"The harbor."

He hoped spiders that size couldn't swim.

They rode in silence for a few minutes, before the lights of the harbor became visible. Max eased off the gas and cut the lights. He paid attention to the street and Josephine scanned the docks as they cruised along. *There*. She saw it making a beeline for a cruiser sitting low in the water. A few men at the gangplank darted out of the way as the spider hurried up the steps. Two of the men followed as the thing scrambled into a crate and they closed the gate on its cage.

"Incroyable. What now?" Max asked.

Josephine watched the men at the crate. They were dressed in a similar manner with white tunics, black jackets and caps. Both were thin, their wrists showing beneath the jackets. One had an Adam's apple large enough to be mistaken for a nose. The other's eyebrows looked like two caterpillars had taken residence on his forehead. All the men were scanning the docks in the direction the spider had come from. One of the crewmen, sporting a thick, gray beard and paunch, marched over from the gangplank to join them. They began to complain in German, loud enough to be heard from a distance.

One of the rangy ones said, "Where is this son of a bitch?"

Midstride, Beardpaunch answered, "Why is this son of a bitch?"

They chuckled with a grim edge that Josephine could hear.

"What duty is this, eh? How does ferrying this horror and its handler help our country?" Adam's apple thumped the crate and it thumped back. All of them took a step back.

"Ours is not to question, boys," Eyebrows said.

Beardpaunch clapped both men on the shoulders and said, "We do the job, we get paid, let the SS take care of the rest. We'll win this time, Der Führer has 'em on the run, I can feel it in my gut."

"That's all you can feel in there?"

When their laughter died down, Beardpaunch looked out at the harbor and said, "Seriously, where is this son of a bitch? We have to launch soon."

Max said, "Josephine?"

"I need to get on that ship. Open the trunk."

Max hopped out and joined her, doing as she said. "You can't be serious."

Her only answer was to look into his eyes for a fraction of a second. She pulled out a small gear bag and stuffed a few items into it. "Eyes on me, Maxie. Follow, no matter what. If I get caught, do not try to spring me. Notify the BCRA."

"They don't trust me, Miss Baker, I'm not an official operative. Most of them don't even consider me to be a man. This is the kind of information you need to deliver."

"*Max.*"

He sighed, grabbed a pair of binoculars, and got back behind the steering wheel while Josephine pulled her cowl tight and made her way to the ship. She made sure to circle around and come at the boat from an angle. Its hull was painted in a camouflage pattern that would make it difficult to see on the horizon, especially at night. The men continued to scan the gloom, no doubt watching for the spider's handler. She had no idea how long they'd wait. It was imperative she get aboard.

Going straight up the gangplank was a no go. As capable as she was of scaling an anchor chain, the damn things were too greasy for a solid grip. Especially considering she'd have to swim in filthy harbor water in order to scale it with wet hands. Gangplank it was, then.

Josephine crawled along the dockline, staying in the ship's shadow. A window slammed open above decks and she heard a new voice.

"Where the fuck is Manfred?"

Beardpaunch answered, a bitter and disgusted tone in his voice, "No idea, Captain."

He ain't gonna make it back at all, boys, she thought, *just hang in there a bit longer*. At the base of the gangplank, she eased underneath and began an upside down crawl toward the ship. At the hull, she found a bare handhold along the rim separating the deck from belowdecks. She shimmied toward the aft and hauled herself up by the scupper and over the gunwale. From there, she snuck around the portside, opposite where the men were conferring.

"Has that… thing… boarded?"

All three answered at once, "Yes, sir."

"Crated?"

"Yes, sir."

"Any sign of Manfred?"

"No, sir!"

"God damn that goatfucking prick! Secure that fucking horror and cast off lines! We're going. I'll be damned if we have to explain to these SS bastards why we were late on the return."

Caterpillar brows said, "But, Captain, Manfred is the one who secures the—"

"Secure that crate and see to your duties, or be docked! Start the engines!"

The men set about their duties, muttering obscenities about what they had to do and what they believed would come of it.

Even Nazis were capable of revulsion when it came to spiders, Josephine concluded. It was time to take stock of the ship's crew. There were the three on deck, of course. She eased a hatch open and went below, where the horrific smell of sheep assaulted her nose.

A disheveled and portly man sat near a small enclosure, dozing. A few raps on the hatch above the enclosure roused him. He went about the task of selecting a sheep. Another series of raps on the hatch made him look up and shout with disgust, "Festhalten!" Then he wrapped his arms around a bleating sheep and hauled it up and out, under his arm.

Josephine followed, matching his steps, as the sheep, held backwards, watched her. The animal's emotionless stare gave her chills. At the top of the ladder, she used the bulk of the man to obscure her turn in the opposite direction to find the bridge. She slipped out through a porthole and scaled the side to peek into the bridge. Two men stood, one holding binoculars and wearing a captain's cap.

The captain looked disgusted. He swore under his breath and yelled, "Lines secure?"

"We're away, Captain," came the answer.

"Take us out," said the captain.

The pilot gave the vessel some throttle and spun the wheel.

Shit. Josephine hoped Max would follow. In the background, above decks, she heard the cries of the terrified sheep as it was fed to the spider.

To Hell with doubt, she *knew* Max would follow. *How* he would do it was the question.

MAX WATCHED THE men untie the boat, wrapping lines to hooks. A puff of smoke issued from the stacks. "Oh, la vache…" He fidgeted, knowing it was going to be a long night and wondering how he could follow.

"A boat, obviously, Max, toi imbécile." But he didn't have a boat. *Yet*.

He keyed the engine to life and eased the car into a space off the wharf proper. He opened the trunk and pulled out his coat, watch cap, and gloves. His eyes barely left the German boat as he moved.

The vessel's engines roared and it began pulling from the

dock as men tossed unbound mooring lines aboard and hurried to follow and retract the gangplank. Max pulled on the coat and cap, shoved the gloves into the pockets, and ran toward the docks. As the ship chugged slowly out of the small marina, desperation bubbled in his chest, fueling his frantic search.

A boat, any boat, even a simple one, that's all he needed. Each one he passed was too large. He'd never handled a boat before and wanted something smaller, like a car.

There.

As the dock lengthened, smaller boats were moored farther from land.

He sprinted down the planks and hopped into the first motorboat. It was secured to the dock with multiple lines and partially covered with canvas knotted to rails on both sides. That wouldn't do. Max scrambled out and ran again. He hopped into a small, uncovered motorboat and searched for an ignition.

No keys. Were they back on land, with an attendant? Locked away? He cursed himself for not having checked before running down this far.

He looked out into the harbor. The ship—with Josephine—chugged toward open waters.

"If I were keys, where would…?" Max rifled underneath the control panel and moved around to the seat cushions in the rear. Beneath one, he found a storage compartment. Inside: keys.

"Dieu merci."

The vessel wasn't much more than a smudge in the night, its few lights snapping off. Max inserted the key and hesitated. This was a diesel engine. Lines needed to be primed and the starter motor engaged. He fumbled about, searching his memory for his uncle's tedious lessons. He'd been only twelve the last time Oncle Phillipe had run through the process for him.

"Dieu, aide-moi," Max mumbled to himself as his frantic fingers flipped and turned what he hoped were the proper valves and switches. The engine fired up when he turned the ignition, and Max sighed with relief. Then he unmoored the lines and gave the boat enough throttle to navigate out of the port.

JOSEPHINE'S VESSEL WASN'T more than a vague shadow in the distance. He angled the boat at the shape and prayed for guidance. Not that any god who allowed *homosexuels* to be persecuted could be trusted, but it was all Max knew. So he pressed on.

Josephine squatted behind the sheep pen and relieved herself. The stench of the animals would cover anything she could produce with her own body. The man tending the animals dozed again, snoring, with his arms crossed over his belly and his cap pulled over his eyes. He'd be easy to kill—they all would—in Josephine's estimation. But killing Nazis and their collaborators was a secondary mission tonight. The mystery of this monstrous spider needed to be unraveled first. By her estimate, the journey couldn't be more than a day, based on what she'd seen of the ship's stores. She satiated her hunger with a liberated can of wurst and began poring over Manfred's notes again, hoping to make sense of them and use them against whoever waited at the end of this ocean journey. She was once again reminded of

Morse code. A series of dashes and dots, some notes in German on the backs of pages, lists of words and numbers. She flipped back and forth through the papers and noted numbers next to lines of code marks. It wasn't a sophisticated cypher: the words corresponded with marks and vice versa. Some numbers, some letters, rudimentary stuff. It was a simple language, not worthy of coded messages to avoid the Allied forces, and easy to master. To what end, though?

MAX HADN'T UNCLENCHED his teeth since beginning this journey. The sight of the spider and Miss Baker's stoic determination to see this through were the only things keeping his hands steady on the wheel. He maintained as much distance behind the vessel as he could manage. The damn thing was difficult to see at night, but the breaking dawn made the task somewhat easier, casting a hazy silhouette on the horizon. He fought his nerves and eased back on the throttle a bit more. There was no telling what might happen if he were spotted.

It appeared they were making their way to a small island somewhere in the Ionian Sea. Or, at least, he hoped it was the Ionian. They'd left the heel of Italy behind more than a few hours ago.

As the angle of their path continued to nose toward a jagged series of peaks on the horizon, Max was reminded of a crocodile's toothy smile. Watching the menacing landscape get closer and larger only heightened his dread.

The ship steamed forward, navigating a narrow pass into a

natural harbor and disappearing into a massive cave on the side of what Max recognized as a volcanic isle. He navigated his smaller craft to the side of the isle, out of sight, and dropped anchor.

"Oh, mon cher ami, où nous as-tu amenés?"

THE BOAT JERKED, startling Josephine awake. The sounds of shouting and lines being tied floated in the air. The keeper of the sheep mumbled to himself and cleaned the pen with mechanical motions. He began the tedious project of hauling the remaining two animals up the ladder, one by one. Josephine remained still long after he had finished, listening for any sounds of movement above and around her. Satisfied, she slipped out from behind the pen and eased her way along the bulkheads until she was on the deck in the open air.

A massive cavern stretched above her and a long dock lined the inside from the cave's mouth. A few men roamed about, performing tasks they seemed unenthused for. The crate holding the spider was gone. She peeked farther over the rail and felt a sharp pang of terror. A U-boat, long and black, was moored far into the cave. She determined that there were two missions at hand: disrupt any naval operations, then find and neutralize the source of the spider attacks. In order to accomplish this, she needed to be quiet. No gunshots, no explosions, no killing. Not yet, anyway. Then there was Maxie. Had he managed to follow? If he did, she'd find him somewhere offshore. She hoped.

MAX SCANNED THE island with his binoculars. There was no activity other than the occasional bird on the sharp rocks. There were few plants on the island, not much to speak of other than the cavern he had seen the ship loading into.

He lowered the binoculars, cracked his knuckles, and moaned to himself. "Affamé." *A Frenchman should not go this long without proper rations.*

When he raised the binoculars again, there was Miss Baker, waving her arms over her head.

"Bien sûr! She's fine. What now, my problem girl?"

Josephine held her hands chest-high, lowered them, and bobbed with palms down.

"Ah, *wait*. Oui."

Josephine pointed at herself several times, then her eyes, and spread her arms wide.

"*Keep the lookout*, okay."

Max raised his thumbs up to her until she acknowledged the gesture. Then she made her way back down the pockmarked hillside and disappeared again.

"Well, then…" Max sighed with relief before the fear of what was sure to come flooded back in. He peered over the side to see if any spiders were swimming his way.

JOSEPHINE MADE HER way back down with care. The many handholds that brought her up the hillside would tear her to ribbons going down if she were not careful. Her agenda was to start with the U-boat and take her time on the dock, working through one craft at a time. Despite appearances, the sub would be the easiest to rig, it was full of explosives. The fuel within the rest would serve fine for the smaller crafts. Getting on the U-boat, however…

One guard stood on the dock. Though "guard" wasn't quite the right word. The man was taking a break, smoking a ciga-rette. *Why would they need a guard on such a secluded island?* Look-outs and other equipment above might only draw attention. A barren rock in the Ionian Sea? Not so much. That kind of arrogance, Josephine could work with. The real problem would be getting on the boat without killing anyone.

The tall crewman stubbed out his cigarette and hustled back to his duties on the submersible. Josephine watched from among stacks of crates along the walls. There didn't seem to be anyone else on the docks. There'd been little activity ever since the boat she'd stowed away on had emptied.

Josephine waited to see if he'd close the hatch behind him. In the meantime, she skimmed the crates for their contents: supplies for living on a barren island, nothing useful to her in the moment. It was useful for giving her an estimate of how many Nazi vermin infested the island, however. A little less than half the stores were hay and silage. Feed for the sheep. Perhaps Biermann preferred mutton, or the spider did. Proba-bly both. Regardless, there were approximately thirty people running the installation. No doubt it had taken more manpower to build, which meant the Nazi regime had paid some serious attention to this place. She wondered if they knew about the spiders, or if Biermann were operating as an ally of the Reich. Was this another facet of Hitler's mad plans? What some considered tactical brilliance she saw as unhinged power plays, a child's understanding of war planning: effective only for destruction.

Josephine crept up to the side of the sub and ascended the ladder to peer down into the hatch. Moving as quickly as possible without making a sound, she leaned in to make sure the area was clear, and descended the ladder head-first. At the bottom, a tuck and roll brought her to a ready crouch. She shifted her weight and the tall man she'd seen smoking on the dock appeared from the forward hatch. He froze, opening his mouth and turning his head to shout.

Josephine surged forward, striking him in his exposed throat. He gagged, unable to utter a sound. He interrupted her next move by throwing his bulk at her. They stumbled backward, caroming off metal. His weight, applied recklessly, was too much for her. Taking the risk of being crushed or concussed by his bullish ways, she drove her thumbs up into his eyes.

The man roared, clawing and grabbing at her. She slid under his grasp, and thrust upward on his jaw. The man's head slammed into the low ceiling.

She followed by kicking him in the crotch, taking his head in the crook of her arm, and dropping her entire weight to the deck. A crack, muffled by the soft flesh of his neck, signaled an end to their engagement.

So much for not killing anyone.

It was a death she would not mourn; however, it would slow her down some.

Josephine collected some rope and a massive wrench before hauling the man out by the neck, lowering him into the water on the outward-facing side of the sub. He sank under the water, tied to the wrench. Then she set to work rigging the U-boat's engine and collecting some of the munitions to rig the other crafts.

A few men had come and gone while she was doing the painstaking work. No alarm was raised, she hadn't been seen, nor had her victim been discovered.

In her travels back and forth, she saw access to what looked like ventilation for the facility. It would be a tight fit, but the shaft was wide enough for a small person to slip through, and that was curious. Why build them this size?

She flexed her shoulders and massaged her aching muscles, noting the bruises the past twenty-four hours had left. Then she got back to work. No Nazi would leave this island alive.

Once inside, she listened carefully, and followed the sounds of activity. Snippets of German floated on the air, along with the hum of machinery. She passed a small mess hall, bathroom facilities for men and women, a machine shop, and an armory. As interested as she was in the armory, it'd be a devil of a time sneaking into a locked, reinforced room. She wanted to see the heart of the operation.

As Josephine moved along, deeper into the system, the acrid scent of sulfur tickled her nose. The ventilation followed the passageways, branching and turning at right angles. As she crawled, she familiarized herself with the basic layout of the place. They'd carved a simple grid into the rock of the island. Why? And what did the spider have to do with it?

The nexus of the vents ended at the apparent nerve center of the operation. A large vent went straight up to open air and a series of fans ground lazily, circulating the fresh air through the system. A massive generator powered the entire facility. It nestled over a glowing pit, humming and churning out power. A series of panels with lights, knobs, dials, and buttons lined one half of the cavern. Men and women in lab coats operated and monitored the machinery.

The other side of the space was dominated by a gigantic vault door with cables feeding into it and hydraulics along one edge. The snarl of cables and lines was too complex for Josephine to determine their origin, or where they terminated. The most interesting aspect of the space was the man giving orders as if his mouth was on fire.

Dr. Biermann ran the facility with the proverbial iron fist. He moved from station to station, giving orders in an even, stern voice, with the occasional query to those carrying clipboards or reviewing printouts.

What an unremarkably boring and typical fascist, Josephine thought. *Almost too worthy of assassination.* Her fingers itched for his throat.

Getting at him would be too difficult. Her skin color alone was already a high barrier. She counted five guards on rotation, meandering about the room and along the scaffolding over the vault. None of them appeared to be on high alert. It would be simpler to blend in if all these subordinates wore matching masks, like in the funnies. And she was deadly curious about the vault. What could be behind the heavily reinforced structure, why would they build such a thing? The Nazis were meticulous record-keepers. If she could find a file room or a clerk's office, she might also find some answers. Her prodigious memory didn't produce any such office, so she backed into the ventilation system to continue her survey of the facility.

Unexplored branches stretched ahead as she shimmied backward then forward, farther into the system. Her sense of direction told her she was on the other side of the vault. Somewhat remote, it could be a space where the mundane act of record-keeping was practiced. From the narrow vent, she could see little of a darkened space. Just the type of environment that could hold hundreds of file cabinets. Much easier—although less satisfying—to flip through files than massacre hundreds of Nazis in her quest for answers.

Josephine pried off the vent and peered in. Dark, motionless. She twisted around and lowered herself into the room. Her feet slid against the wall until she dropped to the floor. She'd have to find a cabinet or a crate to get herself back up into the vents.

There had not been a sound after her entrance. Then a tapping caught her attention. A pattern. After a pause, the sound repeated. In the gloom, she could see something moving in time with the beat. She reached to her holster, feeling the familiar steel of her Colt's grip. Using her left hand, she pulled a flashlight from her pocket. She aimed both at the form, which was low to the ground, and snapped the light on.

More gigantic spiders than she could count stood silent in the room. The one doing the tapping was bigger than the others, roughly the size of a motorcycle; to the rest of the knee-high creatures, it tapped the ground with a foreleg. An electric strike of fear took her heart, faced as she was with overwhelming odds. This was her end, but she'd go out fighting. Her finger tightened on the trigger and the massive spider continued to tap. Something familiar tickled her memory.

Manfred's notes. The tapping matched the code. She lowered her weapon and concentrated. The word "HELP" was repeated at a mechanical pace.

"Oh!" Josephine exclaimed. A reaction rippled through the spiders and they froze. She swallowed her surprise and angled her flashlight upward to illuminate them all. Then she bent and tapped the ground using the code. "WHY?"

"YOU. KILL. MNFRD."

She responded. "YES. ENEMY."

"YOU. FRIEND. HELP. EGGS."

The vault, Josephine thought. Biermann had somehow captured this creature's spawn. The *how* of it didn't matter. If she could free them, then she'd have allies against these bastards. She tapped a new message out. "YES. ME. HELP."

The spiders rippled again, seemingly excited by the prospect. The large one started tapping again. "KILL. BRMN. KILL. ALL."

"YES," Josephine tapped back. "KILL. THEM. ALL." They needed a plan and the only one she could think of was audacious and would put her in tremendous peril. It was perfect.

JOSEPHINE WATCHED FROM above. There was no reasonable way for her to access the chamber from below, but she could see a series of spaces where the artificial walls didn't quite meet the cavern's ceiling. The scaffolding around the chamber was limited. And patrolled by one guard. As earlier, security was lackadaisical on the small island. Assistants would occasionally access the catwalks to check various gauges and adjust valves. The network of pipes and wires, she surmised, monitored and maintained the stability of the volcanic pocket where Queen's eggs were kept.

Queen. Yes, perhaps that's what I'll call her, she thought.

Pipes, wires, and some vents. She eyed the tangle of metal and determined her route. The lone guard, bored and slumping, strolled off of one catwalk and disappeared back inside the facility. According to her count, she had about two minutes before the guard reappeared. Easing the screen off the vent, she crept out and reached up. There was a handhold, so she checked her gloves and slid out. A pull-up allowed her to see a narrow ledge above, which she slipped onto. Keeping an eye out for any assistants wandering the catwalks, she slid along the ledge to a series of pipes leading to her goal.

Below her, a technician walked along the catwalk, his hard heels pinging off the metal. She froze and tracked his progress. The man's eyes were focused on a clipboard, not looking up at all. He took some notes on gauges along the wall and went back the way he had come from.

Josephine reached up, testing the security of the pipes above her head. She slid her legs out and dangled over the space, feeling some heat through the pipes. Hand over hand, she moved along the pipe and the wall. Another lab-coated collaborator appeared. A woman, her hair pulled tight into a bun high on the back of her head. Josephine held her position, unmoving, not willing to blink or breathe. The woman below her glanced left and right before pulling out a small box that rattled from a pocket within her coat.

Josephine could feel heat building up in her palms. Fatigue was the least of her problems—the pipes she traversed were hot, and only getting hotter. The woman checked again to be sure she was alone and swallowed the pills. Josephine was sure her eyes cut across her dangling form, but stillness made for amazing camouflage, under the right conditions. None of that would help her hands, however; they were burning now. She wanted to let go and drop to the catwalk for relief. She silently pleaded for the Nazi drug addict to move along. The woman took several deep, calming breaths before continuing.

Moving hand over hand—faster than she was comfortable with—Josephine traversed the space and swung her feet up to the slim ledge on the other side. The guard sauntered onto the catwalk as she rolled onto her back. She removed her gloves and waggled her hands, allowing them to cool while the guard walked slowly around the space and back through the doorway. When she checked her palms, she saw no damage and moved on to her next task. The gap between wall and ceiling was just over her head. She bent up and peered through the opening.

The cavern sprawled below in an eerie red glow. Craggy walls cast sharp shadows around clutches of milky white globes. The heat from veins of slow-moving magma caressed her face. It was clear how Beirmann had enslaved the intelligent spiders. Proof enough for Josephine. The Nazi scourge had managed to victimize yet another race and it was time for them to pay. Next, she confirmed the deadly arrangement of explosives and sophisticated vents that held the volcano in stasis.

Satisfied, she steeled herself for the return trip and made it across without having to stop once.

AFTER CONFIRMING FOR herself that the spider's eggs were indeed within the vault—no easy feat—Josephine and Queen plotted the chaos that would free them—also, no easy feat. The vault was certainly wired to explode.

It took several rounds of repetition to communicate ideas in the crude language Biermann had developed to communicate with the arachnids. The type of orders he would give them had little to do with thoughtful consideration and more to do with locating a target and killing them. Josephine couldn't hold the decision to cooperate against them. She was without children, but determined to have many someday, and she'd already determined that she'd bathe the entire world in blood to protect them.

There were two goals for her human hands: one, acquire the

device Biermann kept on his person that would trigger charges within the vault and, two, open the vault for the spiders to get in. The only thought she could come up with after establishing this plan was bitterly sarcastic.

The spiders set about their tasks and Josephine readied herself for the oncoming impossibilities.

THE LARGEST SPIDER entered the control room. She was allowed some freedom to receive Biermann's orders while the rest of her brood remained imprisoned away from the vault. Not much of a prison, for sure, if Josephine could accidentally break in. Which meant they could purposely break out. The threat to the eggs was the only thing holding them at bay.

This had been the hardest part to convey, that they needed a distraction to put Biermann off his footing, to have him focus on one strange problem after another. The spiders seemed mostly preoccupied with ambushing the Nazis. A strategy that would only ensure more deaths for Queen's people than Biermann's. Queen—Josephine had resolved to think of her as such—would need to trust her not to condemn her babies to oblivion. It had been difficult, but she'd managed to convey that as much as they all wanted Biermann to die, the children were not a sacrifice to that end. And neither was she.

Queen approached Biermann alone. Scientists and soldiers alike made way for the giant spider. Revulsion and fear splashed across their faces as the eight-legged mother made her way to the doctor. For his part, Biermann fished a boxy device from his pocket with a covered switch that he flipped open, and held a thumb over the button. She froze several feet from him and began tapping.

"GIVE. EGGS."

Biermann sneered and held himself in a rigid, backwards-leaning position so that he could peer down his nose at her. "Nein. Käfig!" He gestured to a cage near the vault.

One of the techs carrying a sheaf of papers appeared at the doctor's elbow. A small man who shuffled and remained bent along his spine, subservient. "Doktor Biermann—"

Biermann snatched the pages and snapped at him, his German clipped and brutal.

The man flinched in answer and backed away, his hands raised.

"HAD. DEAL. DONE. DEAL." Queen walked over to the vault door and indicated a button and lever assembly. "FREE," she tapped.

"Nein, verdammt, käfig!" Biermann stamped out, "NOW."

Queen seemed to struggle in place. Josephine hoped she wouldn't overplay the moment with Biermann. She needed to resist, but only as much as necessary, to make Biermann think he was her superior. Queen tapped all eight of her legs in a cascade of sound and skittered into the cage.

From her perch, Josephine watched—was that sweat on Biermann's brow? She observed as a guard locked the cage with nervous jerks of his hands. Queen slammed the bars and the man tumbled backward onto his ass.

Josephine smiled to herself. *Damn, that girl is strong.*

Biermann scoffed, closed the device, and went back to whatever horror he considered his work.

Content that she had all the information she needed, Josephine lowered herself into the hallway just outside the nerve center where Biermann lurked, and removed her hood and scarf.

JOSEPHINE PUSHED THE doors to the center open in a burst and sang the first words of *J'ai Deux Amours*, her most famous song—and her favorite. An ode to France, her second love. She danced along, headed for the center of the room in a series of stuttering steps and gyrations.

On dit qu'au-delà des mers
They say that beyond the seas
Là-bas sous le ciel clair
There under the clear sky
Il existe une cité
There is a city
Au séjour enchanté
At the enchanted stay

The monsters in the room stared in disbelief. Who among them didn't know her face? Hadn't heard her songs or seen her movies? How many of them didn't fetishize her brown skin or desire her in the most carnal way?

Stunned, Biermann stared, his mouth slowly opening and closing. One of the guards asked another, "Ist das Josephine Baker?"

She sashayed up to Biermann and circled him like a cat, writhing her body in ways she knew he rarely saw.

Et sous les grands arbres noirs

And under the big black trees

Chaque soir

Every evening

Vers elle s'en va tout mon espoir

Towards her goes all my hope

J'ai deux amours

I have two loves

Mon pays et Paris

My country and Paris…

In a blur of motion, Josephine drew one of her Colts from beneath her coat and smacked Biermann across his jaw while snatching the device from his coat pocket and slipping it into hers. His glasses flew to the floor and blood gushed over his fingers as he dropped to his knees, palming his wounded face.

It took two shots to crack the lock on the cage. The firing of the gun snapped the soldiers from their gaping stance and they hurried to bring rifles to their shoulders. But… the spider was loose.

Queen burst from the cage, the door slamming as loudly as Josephine's gunshots. Her eight-legged motion unnerved the uniformed men. The others—women and men in lab coats—screamed and ran for the doors, causing further disruption. They did not wish to fire through their own people.

Josephine had no such compunction. She emptied one pistol, killing two soldiers and one of the technicians before running toward the vault. Queen surged past her, going in the other direction at incredible speed.

Automatic fire strafed the floor near her. She dove and twisted to land on her back, sliding across the floor and firing up where the shots had come from. A soldier cried out as the thick .45 bullets made him dance and tumble off the catwalk and down to the floor. She rolled behind a bank of equipment to reload her pistols. Across the large room, she saw Queen reach Biermann. The Nazi bastard scrambled backward on all fours, too slow to escape. He slapped the floor, banging out, "NO" before the spider surged over him and pierced his neck with her fangs. Blood spurted onto the floor and Biermann's legs shot out straight, vibrating at an unnatural speed. She struck twice more before he stopped moving.

Live by the spider, die by the spider, Josephine thought, uncaring. Then she made a mental note never to cross Queen. That meant completing the most important job of getting that vault open. She banged hard on the panel in front of her. "NOW."

Josephine rose to a crouch and another soldier stepped in her path, rifle raised. She pushed the barrel of his weapon to the side and fired three quick shots into his belly, pushing him backward as two more Nazis fired at her.

Bullets grazed her hip and shoulder. She fired back, clenching her teeth against the impact of bullets on her Boche shield.

Above her, the two soldiers screamed and flailed, firing wildly as spiders poured from the vent, ran along the wall, and enveloped the men. As all three of the Nazis collapsed, a final wild shot grazed Josephine's scalp and sent her world spinning. Warmth spread down the side of her face and she swam through cotton to keep moving. Her limbs felt leaden, barely responsive. She struggled to keep her focus on the mechanism that ran the vault door. She leaned against the frame, inched along its warm metal. The other side was still hot, hanging over magma.

How far away was the latch? How long before she could reach it? The sounds of chaos in the room rushed into her ears and she felt a quantum of stability.

There—the gears and levers, the button. She pulled one lever after another, releasing hydraulic pressure, drawing back locking bars, and mashed the button.

The vault began to grind open as bullets pinged around her. Several soldiers fired from cover at the doorway. Barely able to aim, she shot back, drawing their full attention. Spiders began dropping on them from above. Their screams made the dangerous maneuver worthwhile.

Queen ran past her, making a rasping noise Josephine hadn't yet heard from them. Several of the smaller ones followed her into the vault. Josephine peered in, leaning hard against the steel framing, feeling the warmth of the room add another smothering layer to her unsteady body. An explosion sounded far away. Then another. The booby traps she'd set at the port were working. They were killing themselves.

The bastards had tried to escape this, to avoid the hard lesson their own actions brought upon them. For France, they burned; for the Jews, the Roma, the *homosexuels*, and everyone the Nazis had determined defective or unclean. They were destroyed by their own hands. Josephine felt remarkably pleased with the results.

Within the vault, the spiders gathered up kin the size of puppies on Queen's directions.

Oh! The eggs must've hatched! How cute the little ones look, like eight-legged puffs of dandelion. She sagged to the floor.

Queen walked into Josephine's line of sight. She looked at the great creature and tapped the ground with a weak fist. "GO."

The giant spider gathered Josephine up and set her straddling upon her back. The animal smelled like a field of sunflowers and seeds. The hairs on her back, though stiff, were not coarse at all.

Air whipped over Josephine's face as she rode the spider through the corridors. They ran swift and even, eight legs thrumming around her. Like a wave of vengeance, Josephine and the spider army made their way out of the facility, cutting down any who found themselves in their path. She held her head high as a smile slowly peeled across her face. Feeling safe and invincible at once, for the first time in her life, she closed her eyes and enjoyed the ride.

Is this how white men feel? She cackled aloud and held on as tightly as she could manage. At the first taste of ocean air, the spider stopped, and lowered Josephine to the ground. She looked around. They'd come out at a different point, well away from the burning docks.

"THANK. YOU," the spider tapped out.

Josephine said, "You're welcome, and thank you, Queen." Then she remembered she needed to tap out the message, but Queen placed one of her clawed paws gently on Josephine's hand.

The great spider bowed, straightened, and made the rasping noises again. She picked her way to an outcropping and the horde followed. They all disappeared down a long crevice where the island folded on itself.

The cool ocean air felt good, revitalizing. The setting sun left a gorgeous streak of orange and red across the blue ocean, mixing to purple at the edges. The silhouette of a small boat made its way toward her position.

"Maxie," she said, a grin spreading across her lips. Behind her, she heard panicked voices. It seemed that there were survivors and they were coming closer. She made her way down the hill to greet her loyal friend.

"Josephine! Mon Dieu, I saw the explosions at the dock and—I knew, I just knew that you would make an exit elsewhere so I circled the island and, oh, here you are. I didn't expect to see you with the spiders, though." He shivered.

"They were lovely, Max; you should have seen them cut through the Nazis." Josephine tossed one leg over the bow and rolled onto the boat, lolling on her back and elbows before triggering Biermann's device. The explosion could be felt in the ocean; a gentle wave pushed the boat back. Warm air and more of the island's personnel rushed out of the exits. The ground shook, and overhead, the hilltop cracked open, revealing the hot blood of the earth's core. The survivors yelled to them, begging for help.

"Time to go, Max!" She smiled and waved at the terrified Boche on the hillside, blowing kisses as Max maneuvered the boat into deeper waters and pointed its nose back toward Italy. A couple of guards stood perplexed for a moment before shouldering their rifles and firing. Bullets thwacked into the water around them.

Max ducked behind the wheel and said, "They're shooting at us!"

Josephine laughed and watched as the last of the island's oppressors stumbled and choked to death in the deadly, volcanic gases. "What a gorgeous sunset, eh, Max?"

"Oui, Mademoiselle Baker, très beau."

CHAPTER ONE: NAUTICA

Nautica fell in love with a Man who wasn't a man. But of course, she didn't know that at first.

She was young when she first saw Him. A tall Man, standing in a meadow of wildflowers outside her village, His hair the color of rich earth, the wind caressing it as though He were holy.

She had stopped still, her chubby hands full of wildflowers. They were all colors, beautiful and strange, red and blue and yellow. Nautica loved this meadow, this place, where flowers of all kinds grew, and where the trees whispered to her at night. But now, trembling in front of this stranger, she felt for the first time that she was an interloper, that she didn't belong in this place of magic. She looked down at her sturdy shoes and grimy knees, and frowned.

The Man didn't move, but suddenly appeared much, much closer to her. Nautica blinked.

"I'm sorry," she said. She didn't speak often because she rarely had much to say, and her voice sounded creaky and awkward. "I didn't know anyone would be here."

The Man didn't respond. His strange stillness reminded her of a deer raising its head and sniffing the air. She was certain she smelled like Dirty Little Girl and clumsy human things, like earthenware pots and outdoor fires.

Nautica clutched her flowers tighter.

Help, cried one. *Not so tight.*

You're hurting us, another whispered.

"Oh, I'm so sorry," Nautica answered, opening her hands and letting the flowers fall. They sighed gently as they landed with their brethren, strewn about like tiny pieces of colorful fabric.

We love you, a white gardenia said prettily, and kissed Nautica's foot. Nautica smiled and glanced up. The Man was gone. She peered around the glen, but everything was as it usually was: The sun dappled the ground, birds called out to each other, and squirrels chittered angrily while the flowers twined their leaves together and hummed.

Still, Nautica backed away, unwilling to turn her back to the grove, unwilling to feel vulnerable. Despite its apparent normalcy, there was a strange current that ran through the very earth itself. It made Nautica's feet buzz and traveled up her body and to her fingertips. Her blood ran just a bit faster, her heart pounded slightly harder.

She slowly stepped away, farther and farther, until she felt safe enough to turn and flee. She ran home, stumbling through the undergrowth, her braids trailing behind her, and she didn't stop until she had reached the tiny little town of Paradise. Nautica ran through the dirt streets and burst through her front door.

MAMA WASN'T HOME. She seldom was. She was either full of drink or lifting her skirts for the neighbors or had gone on an adventure without her small daughter. It really didn't matter anymore, the wheres or even the whys. It mattered only that Mama was gone, and Nautica was alone again, and now she was trembling in her small, simple house after seeing something strange in the woods.

She curled up on her pallet under a tattered blanket, her body feeling cold despite the exertion. She counted her breaths to calm down. One. Two. Three for Mama. Four for Nautica.

The Man in the grove. Why was He so different? Why had He unsettled her so?

Five for the flowers. Six for her blanket. Seven breaths to fill her lungs with calm, cool air.

The way He moved, or *didn't*, was what had caught her attention. That quietness—the way He had seemed several yards closer to her even though He hadn't changed position and she hadn't heard His steps in the grass.

I hope I don't see Him again, she thought, even as her fingers curled as if she were holding imaginary wildflowers. *He's unnatural and strange and I need to stay away from Him forever. I shan't ever go to the meadow again.*

She let her eyes flutter closed for just a second, recalling the way His hair had blown in the wind; it was the only thing that had moved. She wondered if it would be as soft as fox fur.

I hope He's there next time, she admitted to herself. *It's so seldom that something interesting happens in Paradise.*

AS SHE GREW, Nautica would catch glimpses of Him now and again: in the grove, hidden in the trees, occasionally at the edge of town. One morning, she woke up, shivering in her cold house, and thought she could see His stillness and eyeshine in the darkness. When she blinked, He was gone.

Nautica's mother was found face-down in the dirt, her body broken and bruised as though it had been trampled by a herd of wild horses and then tossed out with the other trash. Yet, things got better after that.

For a while.

"It's time you marry," her neighbor, Mrs. Mott, said to Nautica. Nautica was outside, trying to fill the holes in the house, stuffing them with straw and mud and everything else she could think of. The chill of the night was becoming almost too cold to bear.

"I'm not that interested in marriage," she said, just as her hair escaped its braid and stuck to the mud she was working with. Of course it did. She would have to chastise it later, perhaps by giving it a rather stern trim.

"Nonsense," Mrs. Mott answered. "Every woman is interested in marriage."

"I'm not."

The mud was cold, and her hands felt frozen, but Nautica diligently continued her work. Scoop, mix, patch.

"Who is going to take care of you?"

Scoop, mix, patch. Nautica blew the hair out of her eyes.

"I don't need anyone to take care of me. I'm quite content on my own."

Make her go away, her hair whispered into her ears. *We don't like her.*

Quiet, Nautica commanded it.

"Don't be silly, my dear. A single woman like yourself should have a spouse."

The mud winked at Nautica, threw up its arms, and slid out of the crack. It oozed down the side of the house, grinning naughtily. The wind immediately howled through the hole and into the house.

"I don't need a husband," Nautica said through gritted teeth. She glared at the mud, which snickered. She thickened it with more dirt and hay.

Scoop.

We can kill her, her hair suggested. *We can wrap around her throat so strongly that her breath catches, and she is quiet, and the world will be beautiful again.*

A tendril snaked toward the neighbor. Nautica pushed it down with a filthy hand.

"Why, look at yourself." Mrs. Mott clucked her tongue. "Such a mess with dirt and twigs in your hair. Why, if you were married—"

The mud scoffed and burrowed deeper into Nautica's hair, where it rolled around and made a delightful mess.

"—then you would be prompted to care for yourself properly."

"I care for myself just fine, Mrs. Mott," Nautica said. Her hair growled playfully and pulled itself toward the neighbor. Nautica beat it back.

"Now, my Brand, he's of age. He's a fine, strong man who could do things like this for you. Why, he'd have these unsightly holes patched up in a jiffy."

"It's too bad he isn't home to help me do it now," Nautica said. She felt the tight smile on her face, but was afraid to do anything else, lest she bare her teeth in less acceptable ways.

Mrs. Mott looked aghast.

"He wouldn't help without reason, dear one! That would be taking advantage of his good heart. But if you were *married*, that's another thing entirely. If you were to marry my son and be my daughter-in-law…"

Then I should surely die.

We can make that happen, too, her hair said in a brittle voice. It pulled tight against her throat, a noose made of itself, and squeezed, squeezed, squeezed.

"No," Nautica breathed.

"No?" Mrs. Mott asked sharply. "Simply no? Are you too good for marriage altogether? Or are you too good for my son?"

The mud oozed over Nautica's shoes and into her thick, cotton socks, lapping her ankles with an icy tongue.

Die, die, die, sang her hair, each note dissident, and it yanked hard across her neck. Nautica gasped with what little breath she had left, and scrabbled at it with frozen fingers.

"Because listen to me, you useless piece of refuse, you are not good enough for my son! For anybody." Mrs. Mott's voice was biting, her words clipped off in her anger. Nautica reached for her with one hand, the other firmly entwined in her hair. The woman smacked her hand away. "I was being gracious, offering you the chance to have a normal life with a normal family. Inviting you to be in mine. You and your sad strumpet of a mother were nothing but a weight on this town. What do you have to offer? A girl who is soft in the head and talks to animals and wildflowers like they speak back. You're insane."

She kicked Nautica, then kicked her again. Nautica's eyes bulged, unable as she was to even wheeze anymore, and Mrs. Mott finally looked at her. Her eyes rounded in horror.

"What is this? You're having a fit?"

No. I've worked too hard to live. I can't die like this.

Stop it, Nautica mouthed. She had no breath, no voice. The mud ran up her body, coating her legs and sliding under her dress obscenely.

Mrs. Mott took a step back.

"Unnatural," she mumbled.

Stop it, Nautica silently repeated, and tears filled her eyes. They ran down her face and mixed themselves into the mud that slid up her neck, invading her open mouth and shoving itself down her throat. Nautica tried to claw it out, but it was too firm, too thick.

I'm patching this hole so the wind doesn't get through. The mud's mocking voice was dark and old, primitive and strange. It wasn't the giggling child that it had masqueraded as earlier. It was as old as the world itself.

It's futile to fight me, it said, and swallowed Nautica's mouth in a deathly kiss.

Enough, her hair said breezily. *I'm tired of this game.*

It yanked upward with all its might. Nautica struggled, but she was moving slowly, her body feeble. Her feet lifted from the ground, her toes dragging against the earth, and she was pulled higher, higher, higher into the sky, kicking until she could kick no longer, fighting until there was nothing left. She hung suspended in the air, dark with mud, shiny with tears and blood where her fingers had torn at her hair and her face and her body. She rotated slightly, her fingers stretching toward Mrs. Mott, who stood far below her, mouth agape.

Mrs. Mott's lips moved, saying something, but Nautica's eyes closed, and the stony sunlight and myriad of voices blended together like the sound of the stream, and finally the horror stopped.

CHAPTER TWO

Nautica's head hurt. It pulsed each time her heart beat, sending fresh pain through her. She wiggled her fingers and toes in the way that she always did when she woke up in the morning.

"She's awake," a voice bellowed, and Nautica groaned. She reached to cover her head with her hands, but couldn't move. She opened her eyes.

Rope. Her hands were bound in front of her with rope.

"What is this?" she tried to ask, but as her throat was swollen, her voice torn, she made little more than a squeak.

"Quiet, witch," the voice spat. Nautica blinked, her eyes getting used to the hazy darkness. Sunlight filtered through weathered wooden slats. She peeked outside and saw her little house. She studied the silhouette of her captor and knew exactly whose barn she was in.

"Brand Mott? Is that you?" she asked hoarsely. "Why am I bound?"

He sneered at her, his ugly face contorted even more than usual.

"My mother told me what you did. You will be sentenced and punished for your crimes," he said.

"What crimes? What is this? You have no right to keep me here. I haven't done anything wrong."

He came closer, looming over her. Nautica scrambled to her knees. She wasn't sure she had the strength to stand quite yet, but she couldn't simply lie helplessly on the ground in front of him.

"Your kind is full of tricks and deceit," Brand said. His eyes were usually dull, dark holes, but now they were soulless. Nautica searched for some sort of kindness or compassion there, any type of light at all, but they were icy pits. She shivered from more than the damp cold.

"My kind?" she asked, trying to sound calm. "Brand, you've known me since we were children. I am your neighbor. I am the same kind as you."

He reared back, and Nautica cringed. She looked desperately around for help, but they were alone, and there was no aid to be found.

I'm always alone. After all this time, nothing has changed.

Her hair caressed her cheek gently. It kissed her ear.

"You are a harlot, like your mother! You enticed me with your body and tried to enchant my mind. And after we are married, then what? Would I sire wicked children and taint my family line? You were so close to your goal. We were in marriage talks."

Nautica dropped her head, her shoulders shaking. From tears? From a nearly hysterical laughter brought on by the utter bizarreness of the situation? She covered her face with her bound hands and tried to catch her breath.

"Save them. Your tears won't move me," Brand said bitterly.

"No, I suspect they won't." Nautica touched her unsteady hands to her lips. "Brand, I am sorry if you ever thought I was leading you on. I don't want to get married, you see, to anyone," she said, as his face twisted in anger once again. "To anyone,

Brand. What is my experience with men?" She looked up at him, turning her face toward his darkness, and felt her heart drop at his coldness. "What is my experience with family? My mother brought home strangers, and one of them killed her. This is my example. I'm sure marriage is a wondrous thing, and I know people crave it, but to me, it has always been a horror. Men are violent and frightening, and I have always done my best to stay away from them. Because…" She looked pointedly down at her wet, muddy dress, at her bound hands, then once again searched for humanity in his face. "Do you see?"

He's not going to fall for it, whispered her hair. *Oh! Turn away!*

"What?" she said aloud, but the pain came then, hard and bright like the sun. Her head rocked back, and she was in a cosmic universe. Stars fell behind her eyes, a whole shower of them, and the chiming sound they made was the most beautiful thing of her entire life.

Brand hit her again, and her cheek opened to show him her everything. His hands were strong from working in the dirt, from coaxing life from seeds and strangling weeds and wielding heavy tools. The fragile skin and bones of a mere woman had no power to resist him.

"Even now you try to entice," he said, and kicked her once in the ribs for good measure. Nautica gasped and curled in on herself, still bathed in light from the cascading stars behind her eyes. She gagged into the ground, breathing in mud and everything filthy that was mixed into it. It was cold against the unholy heat of a thousand suns that exploded behind her eye and her cheekbone.

"You're going to die," Brand promised, and Nautica heard a door slam. Writhing, she coughed, and tried to stem her tears. They did nothing, anyway. God didn't respond to tears any more than Brand did. She cowered and wiped the mud from her eyes.

He's coming, and there's more of them, a rat warned from the corner, and Nautica scrambled to her feet. She staggered back, pressing herself against the wall. Brand burst in through the door with a small group of men and grabbed her by the hair.

"Go," he said, and pushed her roughly outside. She balked, but he balled his fist and punched her in the back. She nearly fell, but his grip on her hair righted her. She looked around wildly as they marched her along the streets, stopping in front of her house. Nautica's eyes caught and landed on each face. There was the mayor of the town, his mustache trembling with what looked like rage. There was the midwife who had delivered her, shrieking words so vile that Nautica could hardly process them. There was the blacksmith, the pastor, and the little boy who ran around and let the animals out of their pens when he was bored.

The girls she had gone to school with.

The boys who had tried to kiss her behind the trees.

There was every person who had professed to love her at one time or another, but she could barely recognize them, their faces were so distorted with hate. They were bearing torches, and she shied away from the fire.

"I don't understand," she said, but her voice was shouted down by the crowd. She didn't need to understand. She just needed to pay.

Mrs. Mott joined the crowd, pushing through from the back. Her eyes blazed, and she cuffed Nautica across her already puffy mouth.

"Witchcraft," Mrs. Mott intoned. "I saw it myself, right here. This woman sang the devil's praises, cursing and snarling at me. Then she howled and rose into the sky, riding the airflow like a force of evil."

"I did *not*," Nautica answered, but Mrs. Mott wouldn't be stopped.

"Who knows what she's been doing in that house alone? What wickedness she has conjured? We all know there has been a blight on our crops, on our animals. Lands that were long fertile are fallow."

"I couldn't possibly—" Nautica began.

"The tailor's dog was found turned inside out. The moon is carnivorous and chitters at night."

"This is madness," Nautica cried, but she looked, and she saw, and her quiet heart sank and broke in two with a quite literal snap. She felt a small piece of it give way, and there was only room for despair.

"You're really going to do this," she said softly. The crowd screamed and cried and roiled, but a few villagers had the decency to look ashamed.

"I never did anything to you, but you're going to do this." Nautica slumped, the weight of realization far too heavy on her slim shoulders, but then she straightened. She smoothed the features on her bloody, swollen face, her back straight and proud. Her filthy, tattered dress looked regal, the mud a badge of honor from the earth. Her hair flew around her face like a halo, although it hissed and spit at the mob. Nautica's eyes were quiet. They were a meadow, a grove, a magical sanctuary full of wild-flowers. She was a mountainside in a tornado, a steady, rocky shore withstanding a hurricane. The ground held its breath.

"Inside, then," Mrs. Mott said. Her voice sounded rough. "Give her that much dignity."

Brand pushed Nautica past his mother and into the house. Here was Nautica's neat little pallet. Here was her single dish. Here was a wooden spoon worn shiny by years of careful use. Nautica craned her neck to see Mrs. Mott, but the other woman had turned away resolutely.

"Lift your arms," Brand said, and tied her wrists to an over-head beam. She had to stretch uncomfortably, standing on her toes. Her arms would be throbbing in a few minutes, but she was afraid this was the least of her worries. The other men wandered through the house, looking for something to loot. She had a nicely knitted pair of socks that was quickly pocketed, but that was the only thing of value. Such a hovel. Such humiliation. Nautica blinked quickly. Shame was such a funny thing.

While the men hooted impatiently and held their torches, Brand's mouth turned down.

"I could have saved you from all this," he said hoarsely. "You wouldn't have had to stay here."

Nautica's lips twisted. "You mean in poverty? You proclaim you wanted to save me, yet you're the one lashing me to my home." She stared at him through her good eye, for the other had swollen shut. "Is this how you save someone, Brand Mott?

To me, this looks like an execution."

He winced before pulling his lips back from his teeth. Nautica watched him change, pinpointed the exact second his anger overtook any compassion he might have had.

"The thought of you tainting my bloodline is disgusting," he said, and spit at her feet. "Men! Burn the place down."

Nautica wanted to shout. She wanted to heroically tear herself down from the beam and beat every last man to a pulp. If she could, she would have turned their flames back on them and forced them to run for the creek to put themselves out.

Don't look, her hair said, and slid itself over her eyes. *Shhh. It's much gentler this way.*

Nautica wept. She heard raucous laughter and the strange, airy sound the flames made as they roasted her pallet, as they tasted the walls of her home and found them delicious. The men stampeded outside, and she was left with the merry cracking of her life being torn and devoured by the fiery teeth.

More, the fire groaned. Its voice started small, but became deeper, darker. Louder and full of greed. *More, more, more.*

Her tears seeped into her blindfold, made of her own hair. The wetness evaporated off her cheeks nearly instantly. Her skin singed, burned, and she tried to pull herself away from the heat, her feet pedaling uselessly in the air as she tried to find purchase.

It's all right, her hair comforted her. It began to stink, curling in the heat when the flames got too close. *We'll be with you, after all. We…oh. It's Him.*

Nautica thought she heard the shattering of glass as the small window blew out, but her world was a gibbering, nearly mindless place of noise and heat and light flickering behind her closed eyes. She fought harder, trying to pull herself up, as if keeping her feet off the ground would somehow save her.

Look at Him, her hair said dreamily, and floated away.

Nautica was scattered, frantic. She opened her eyes and there was nothing, nothing, simply an inferno that gnawed at everything, and which in seconds would be gnawing at her, too. The heat forced her to sweat, which was licked away immediately in the dry air. As her skin reddened and blistered, she opened her mouth to scream.

And then she saw Him, the Man, standing outside her window, poised as if ready to run, His eyes reflecting raging fire.

So still. So calm. Soon He would bound away and save Himself, but right now, they held one another's gaze. He was nothing like Brand, who was filled with darkness and dead, rotted things. The Man's eyes held worlds. The cosmos: full of life and everything that ever was, and had been, and would be. His hair blew back from His face, twirling in the fiery wind, shining with falling embers, and it was like looking at the face of a god.

Oh, He's so beautiful.

A spiraling ember landed on His cheek and went out. Nautica saw a tiny red spot where it had touched.

Run, she thought at Him, and He started, blinked. He tilted His head, His eyes bright, wide moons.

Run, she thought again. She was coughing in the smoke now, breathing it in, her already tender vocal cords swelling and charring. *You will die if you stay here. Go.*

His face was so ethereal, so serene. Nautica tried to hold that calmness inside her mind, to face her death with as much dignity as she could, but the flames were running across the wooden beam, now. They licked the rope before devouring it. Nautica's hands and wrists were touched by flame. They burned.

As she tipped her head back, a dark, guttural scream wrenched from her mouth, and she heard all of her agony in it—the burning, the biting, the abandonment. She shrieked, and years of pain poured out. With it, she felt each cuff across the face from every man her mother had ever brought home, felt every time a girl had turned away from her at school. The physical pain of carrying water and fixing house beams without anyone to help her. The disgust that twisted in her gut when Brand leered at her, or stood even taller so as to loom over her. She cried and howled, and her hair followed suit while the fire laughed and laughed and laughed.

Stop, said a voice in her head. It was exquisitely beautiful, soft and sad. *No more.*

Taken aback, the fire paused. Nautica's hair rubbed the soot out of her eyes. The air cleared briefly, the smoke frozen in place, and Nautica managed to catch a short breath.

She couldn't see Him through the haze and the flame, but Nautica knew the Man was still at the window; His eyes were beacons that she could feel rather than see. Her body ceased writhing and unconsciously pointed itself toward Him.

Come, He said to her, and everything started up again. The fire took great big bites from the rope, feasting on it and on her fingers.

The rope snapped.

CHAPTER THREE

The rope snapped. That's really all that needed to be said, wasn't it? Three words, encompassing a miracle.

The rope snapped.

The fire shrieked.

Nautica fell.

Her body hit the ground hard, and what little breath she had was knocked from her. But in her head reverberated the word *Come,* and she nodded. Yes, she would come. If He said to do it, she would take heed.

Over the ground she crawled, still coughing, and dragged herself to her feet using the windowsill. Struggling, sucking in great breaths of smoke, but refusing to give up. She pushed and pulled, cutting herself on the shards of glass stuck in the windowsill, her hair singeing and crying for help, but she struggled on.

No, you don't, the fire hissed, and it grabbed her skirts with immense force. Nautica tried to pull away, but the fire bent down and chewed at her hem. Her heavy skirts went up in flames.

She beat at it with bloody hands, but it burned oh-so-cheerily, oh-so-brightly. Never had anything blazed as beautifully as this lovely skirt with a frantic woman trapped inside.

Come, the voice said again, and it was made of sunlight and gold. It sounded so familiar, and Nautica thought of barley fields and wildflowers and the first time she had ever seen Him standing in the grove, when she was still a child.

She went still. The flames laughed and tore at her clothes and hair with great teeth. Unmoved, Nautica calmly unbuttoned her skirts and stepped out. Her petticoats were plain and covered in mud, but she wore them as if they were of the finest silks. Her hair was ablaze, her head a torch, but she crawled out of the window, as she had many a time as a child. Her bare feet hit the muddy ground. There stood the Man.

Even through the smoke, He smelled of grass. His stillness overwhelmed her, and she thought, *This is how I die. There isn't enough oxygen to my brain, so I am seeing an angel where a simple man stands. But this peace feels ever so much better than the terror, and I am so tired. If I fall here, I will close my eyes gladly.*

The Man reached out a hand, His fingers long and slim, His nails black and shiny like hooves. From root to tip, He ran His hand over her hair, and the flames were snuffed out. He reached out His other hand and took both of hers in His. He didn't break their eye contact, but simply brought her hands to His lips. His kisses soothed, felt cooling, and even though she couldn't look away from the starshine in His pupils, she knew her skin was knitting together.

She didn't ask how. She didn't care. All she knew was that the unbearable pain was ceasing, her bubbling skin smoothing. He reached out that calm hand and touched her face. Her crushed cheek swelled, the calcium joining again. Her eyelid shrank and she could open her eye. Tentatively, she touched her tongue to her split lip, and it was now whole. For the first time, the Man's eyes left hers, as He followed the movement of her tongue. His gaze soon flicked back up.

Run, He said, echoing the words she had thought to Him. The fire cavorted, tearing down the rafters, and Nautica was certain the men still capered on the other side, as well. She clasped the Man's hand, and they ran the back way to the forest.

She was fast, but, oh, He was faster. Nautica's legs were sore and stiff, and her bare feet quickly sustained cuts from the rocks underfoot and the deep roots in the ground. The Man ran in front of her, leading her along, sure-footed while she stumbled.

"You… should go," she panted. "Escape. I will… follow."

She released His hand, and, strangely, the mere act cut her heart. She watched His fingers begin to slip away as she fell behind.

No. His voice in her mind was commanding. He spoke with a resonating authority, as if He wouldn't even entertain the fact that she wouldn't obey. *Do not let go.*

But I can't keep up, she thought. He grasped her hand tighter, His grip warm and sure.

Then I will carry you.

There was a flash of space, a piece of quiet carved out of the hecticness of their race. The woods went silent—no waving grasses, no whispers of trees, no chirring of insects. Just a silence that felt great and whole and powerful…

…and Nautica was running alongside a hind, a deer so big and sleek that He towered over her. His muscles bunched and flexed as He bounded without a sound. She had a grip on His antlers, which were regal and adorned Him like a crown.

She gasped, and the stag turned to her, the entire forest reflected in His calm eyes.

Hold on, He said, and tossed His powerful head. She tightened her grip on His horns, biting her lip as He dragged her across

His back. She struggled to straddle Him, nearly slipping off as He flew beneath her. She held tighter to the cluster of antlers and situated herself. She laid down low and wrapped her arms around His neck.

The stag smelled earthy and fresh, and His fur was surprisingly soft. She remembered the first time she had seen Him, wondering if His hair was as soft as a fox.

"Yes, it is," she murmured into His clean fur, and buried her face in it. He was soft and strong and warm, and smelled like ponds and hope. Had she ever been so content in her life, even after all that had happened? Was this moment simply one she wanted to remember forever?

Yes. Yes, it was.

CHAPTER FOUR

Nautica didn't fall asleep while on the stag's back, but still she dreamed. He bounded through the fields and the forest, across streams and ravines, and Nautica saw the very land itself come to greet Him. The earth pushed up under His hooves to give more purchase; the trees bent out of His way. She saw balls of light following them, zipping alongside, keeping pace. They seemed quite interested in this clumsy human clinging to His back.

Nautica's wounds had certainly healed some, but not completely. Her head hurt and her face itched where new skin struggled to grow. What about her house? Where would she go now? How would she survive? Her head lolled against the strong body, and she concentrated only on holding on. That was all she needed to think about now. That was all that mattered.

It was dark, and the moon stood fat and greedy in the sky. She licked her lips as she gazed at Nautica, who pressed her face more firmly into the soft fur. She couldn't stand to see the moon's teeth, the way she snicked her incisors and chased away the stars who ventured too close. The forest itself was full of stars. They spiraled lazily from the sky and mingled with the fireflies. It was so otherworldly that Nautica had to turn away again.

The hind slowed, and then stopped. Nautica slowly sat up and watched Him test the air.

"Is it safe?" she asked.

He tossed His head, and she carefully slid to the ground, her hand lingering on His back.

"Thank you," she said rather awkwardly, "for helping me. I don't think I would have survived."

And you want to live? He asked. He flicked an ear and bent to taste a mouthful of grass. His antlers gave off their own light. Luminescence. It was so lovely.

"I suppose I do," she said, and stroked the stag's neck. He straightened and turned to look at her. Nautica ran her hand over His ears, and gently down his muzzle. She saw each fine hair, each whisker under His chin. His eyes held planets, the Milky Way, everything.

"What are you?" she asked. "Do you have a name?"

He dipped His head down to the grass again, munching languidly.

I have no need for such things.

"What should I call you?"

Why is there a need for you to call me anything?

Nautica flinched slightly. Ah, yes. She was getting ahead of herself. All these years, when she had seen Him, she had wondered. What was His name? Where did He live? *What was His family like? —If, indeed, He had a family.* Did He walk across the stars? Did He drink moonlight?

Now she saw Him, proud and somewhat arrogant, but it was an arrogance earned by simply existing. Beautiful and strong, sure and glowing like a celestial being Himself. How presumptuous of her to assume she would be allowed to speak His name.

"I'm sorry," Nautica said, and made an awkward curtsy. This made her feel even worse. What does one say to some Otherkind after He has saved you from death? One is merely grateful, she decided, and that was enough.

"Thank you," she said again, and smiled. She saw herself reflected in His peculiar eyes. "I'd better get going now." On realizing she was still stroking His muzzle, she dropped her hand and turned.

That strange weight, that pause in time. A star, mating with a firefly, hovered in front of her, suspended mid-act. Puffs of dandelion fluff, disturbed by her feet, floated in the air, unmoving. Then the atmospheric weight lifted, and the world moved at full speed again.

Where are you going?

Warm fingers enveloped her hand. She turned around to see Him standing there, tall and tranquil, silent, and very nearly divine. His eyes lit from the inside, with that same luminescence as His antlers.

Nautica's mouth was dry.

"I… I don't know."

Where will you sleep?

"I don't know," she repeated.

What will you eat?

Her head dropped. A tear fell from her eye, and a yellow daisy opened its mouth to catch it.

You can't go back to your village.

"No," she replied. "They'll kill me."

He entwined His fingers with hers.

There's not another human village for miles.

Nautica looked at her feet, at her torn, dirty, burnt dress, her hair singing sad songs as it soothed itself. She closed her eyes as He wiped a second tear from her cheek. He pulled back His thumb, examining the soot. He touched His thumb with His tongue.

"Have you ever seen tears before?" she asked Him. She could hardly breathe; her chest felt so tight, and her heart was beating like the danger drums.

I do not cry, He answered. *I do not understand it.*

"It means… well, many things, I suppose," she said. "Happiness or sadness or despair. We cry when there's too much emotion in our bodies and we must let it out."

What too-much are you feeling?

She shrugged. "I'm not sure," she said uselessly. "So many. Gratitude. Fear. Sorrow. Awe. Too much to understand."

The breeze was a naughty thing, chilling her as it crawled

through the scraps of her dress. She shivered.

You need to nest. Be warm.

Warmth radiated from their clasped hands. She took His hand in both of hers and held it to her cold cheek.

"Yes. Where do I nest? Where do I stay?" Maybe there was somewhere close by, a hollow tree or something she could use as a shelter. A fire was out of the question, and the mere thought of it made her stomach twist. But if He sent her in the right direction, surely she could find something. She was resourceful. She didn't give up.

With me, He answered.

Nautica blinked. "What was that?"

Nest with me. Stay with me.

The intensity in His eyes pinned her. She saw herself within them, yes, but not merely her reflection. She saw them walking together in the forest. She had flowers in her hair. He was a Man, He was a hind, He was a god. And she was under His arm, by His side, in His heaven on earth.

"For… just a little while?" she asked. Her lips trembled and her voice was shaking.

He smiled, then, for the first time, and His teeth were white and strangely sharp and human and inhuman at the same time. It was so lovely that she reached out and touched His mouth.

Stay with me always, He said, and it was the simplest, most heartfelt proposal in the entire world. He leaned forward and kissed her, and she thought, *I wonder where He learned to do this,* and *He tastes like fresh water from the stream,* and *This is where I was always meant to be, my whole life, and somehow, He knew it.*

CHAPTER FIVE

They had a daughter called Fawn. Perhaps it was too on the nose, or perhaps it was a hidden joke, or perhaps it was the most perfect name in the world for a tiny scrap of a thing with fragile, human skin and luminescent hair.

Nautica explained the uniquely human habit of naming things, how it was used to identify and classify, and to address, of course, but also how names were personal and Had Meaning, and how calling something by its name gave you, the caller, a power as well as the called.

"There are tales of controlling demons if you know their names," she said. The hind lay quietly in the meadow with His head in her lap. Whether a Man or a hind, Nautica stroked His head. "They're considered that important."

I shall have a name, He said. *You shall be the only one to use it.*

Her heart fluttered. "Yes? What would you like me to call you?"

He had star showers in His eyes.

She tried again. "What pleases you? What would you like to hear me say whenever I call you?"

The shower of stars changed into flowers that bloomed, faded, and rose again. Centuries passed in a matter of minutes as He thought. She saw the entire cycle of existence.

Mine, He answered finally. His voice was proud. *Whenever you refer to me, call me Mine. You're the only one who can.*

She blushed, and He smiled, and when she said His name, although He was a stag, He nearly purred.

"MAMA," FAWN SAID aloud. "Is there just us?"

She had deer-colored hair and celestial-colored eyes, and her voice sounded like the wind blowing through the wildflowers. She was perfect.

"No, there are many more creatures in the forest. And humans even farther on."

"Did you ever meet any?"

"Yes."

Nautica hummed and swept the tiny house she and Mine had built from wood and stone, while Fawn organized the carrots and potatoes they had pulled from the garden.

"Tell me about them?"

"About humans?" Nautica kept her face placid, her voice friendly, but her muscles clenched in fear, as if preparing to run.

"What are they like?" her daughter asked.

Evil and cruel and horrendous, Nautica thought. *They'll burn your home and take your life away without caring.*

"Did that happen to you?" Fawn questioned.

Nautica quickly cleared her throat. Her bitter feelings swept her up, and she had briefly forgotten how well Fawn could hear the Soul, even without Nautica projecting it.

"I'm sorry, love," she said to her daughter. "I was careless. Let me tell you something else about where I am from."

She described houses ("A bit grander than this," she admitted, "but with none of the love") and different types of clothing. Tables and dancing, and what music was. ("It's difficult to explain, but there are more instruments than just our voices and drumming on trees. Imagine something with strings, and metal, and tubes you can blow in. It would change your life.") She described sitting in a room with other children and listening to the elder tell stories.

"Other children?" Fawn asked. "There's more than just me?"

"Many more, dear one."

"Why don't we ever see them?"

Nautica smiled. "They live rather far away. But maybe one day."

Maybe one day, because the wind whispered of something coming. Maybe one day, because something slithered through the grass. Maybe one day, because—

—*Your town of Paradise will be destroyed,* Mine told her. He pranced beside her, nuzzling her hair with His snout.

"Why is this?" Nautica asked. The earth shifted and Mine transformed so He could hold her unsteady hands.

It is better to see, He said. *It is a two-day walk.*

"I'll get Fawn ready."

The girl was dressed in soft, sturdy skins. Nautica placed some vegetables and apples in a sack and slung it over her shoulder.

Up or down? Mine asked His daughter.

Up, she responded. Time paused and her father dipped low, bowing so His little one could hold His antlers and clamber onto His back.

"What's Paradise?" Fawn asked her mother, and Nautica paused briefly.

"Paradise is here. *This* is paradise. But it's also the name of the town I come from."

She talked until the little girl fell asleep. Nautica walked with her hand buried in her husband's fur.

What do I need to know? she asked Him, trying to keep herself resolute. *What threatens Paradise?*

Everything, Mine answered, and Nautica felt the weight of the words. He snuffed and the grasses bent before him. *The earth itself is rising up, since I stole the town's most precious thing.*

"What was that?" she asked, shivering even though the night was warm. "What was this precious thing?"

His eyes were crescent moons.

You. I stole you.

MINE WAS FULL of secrets, and so, apparently, was Nautica's family.

Your affinity for the earth, He Sent. *Have you not wondered?*

"Wondered what?" Nautica asked. She gently patted Fawn's sleeping body, safe and secure upon her father's back. Her daughter's locks discreetly glowed.

Few can hear flowers, Mine said. He tossed his majestic head. *Few can hear Me.*

"My heart breaks for anyone who cannot hear You, my love."

He nuzzled her hair, and even after this time, her cheeks flushed.

I care only about you and our little one.

"Certainly, others matter," Nautica said, generously.

They do not.

She reveled in this, this feeling of being special, of being His alone. Her fears of her childhood town settled. She felt safe and capable with Mine by her side. With Him, she could do anything.

"If nobody else matters, why are we heading back to Paradise? What is so important?"

Mine was silent. Eons came and went. Baby birds were hatched, grew, and fell from the sky to their deaths. Rivers carved canyons out of red rock.

Long ago, He said, *your women were given power.*

"Power?" she breathed.

An ability.

Nautica shuddered. It felt so ominous, like a dark responsibility.

"What ability?" she asked. "Communicating with the elements?"

More, He answered. She sensed He was choosing His words carefully so she could best understand. His hesitation alarmed her.

"Is it important?" she asked. "Is it something I must learn to do?"

Let Me show you.

Mine stopped and pressed His forehead against hers.

Calm, He said.

Birds sang in the forest. Nautica breathed in the scent of moss and stone while her husband's warmth grounded her.

Look, He commanded, and she gazed into His peculiar eyes.

She saw Paradise from a long time ago when the houses were small and new. The land ran unchecked. Plants frolicked and rose to bump against a woman's outstretched hand.

That must be an ancestor, she thought, and her heart glowed.

The woman lived a simple life in seconds. Washing, hanging clothes to dry, laughing with friends, drying her eyes. Then she was snatched by a group of men and dragged away, kicking fiercely.

"No," Nautica whispered. Mine pressed closer to her.

Look, He said again.

The land decayed. Flowers bared their teeth and the wind grew claws. It beat against the homes, pulling them apart plank by plank. Rocks fell from the sky, and water gleefully held itself back from parched mouths.

"What is it doing?" Nautica asked. "Why is the land acting like this?"

She is not there to stop it.

"That's our ability? To pacify the elements?"

Yes.

"I can do it, too? Unknowingly?"

Yes.

Startled, Nautica stepped back.

"Mine, why didn't anybody tell me?"

The hind began walking again, His footsteps sure in the undergrowth.

It is secret.

She trailed behind.

"The townspeople don't know?"

No.

"Did… did my mother know?"

He dipped His head, shrugging gracefully.

Nautica frowned.

"It's a secret so clandestine that even we don't know?"

Mine's ears swiveled, catching sounds His wife couldn't hear.

Some struggled, He said nonchalantly, then paused for a mouthful of grass.

"How do you know this?"

I watched many of your line.

Nautica felt a sharp pang in her heart, a ridiculous jealousy directed toward the women who had lived before her. Her family, her blood, and yet she seethed at the mere thought of them catching Mine's eye, of the relationships He must have had before she had come along. He had lived lifetimes, and perhaps had chosen a new wife every few rounds or so.

My love.

"Yes?" she asked miserably. She was so silly, so ludicrous. Of course she wanted Him to be happy, to never be lonely, to have someone by His side. But, oh, how she wished it could always be her!

My love, He Sent again, and this time it was with *feeling.* She felt His adoration, His protectiveness, His awe when He had seen her in the meadow that first time. *She has light,* He had thought to himself, and watched this human girl-child wobble around on youthful legs. Mine, before he was called Mine, had watched her grow, and sing songs of the Old Ways, and chatter with the milkweed and rebuke the small stream when it was too boisterous. Instead of a girl-child, she had become a doe, with soft, intelligent eyes and a grace that left the grasses dancing around her ankles. Bucks from her village wanted to mate with her, give her a litter, and the stag had thought, *This feeling. Why?*

This feeling caught in His throat like thistles, this thought He could not understand. It made Him want to trumpet and slash His hooves at the other human bucks, made Him want to lower His head and tangle their antlers together, only these humans didn't have any antlers, any defenses. They were weak and soft as fawns. He was forced to linger on the edges of the town, or occasionally slip inside the borders to rest outside her door and listen to the faint sound of her breathing.

If you are hurt, He thought, but what more could He add? If she were harmed, cut down by teeth or claws or man's metal swords, what was He, in His Otherkind majesty, supposed to do about it? She belonged to the human world, not His, no matter how much He wanted her.

And He did want her.

Then she was beaten, and tied, and her home set aflame. The stag crept to the window to see her struggling, to see her hair blowing about her face, her skirts catching, this being of light and wonder and beauty bewitching in the firelight—

—and she met His eyes.

His breathing slowed even as His heart sped up. Her eyes were cascades of starlight.

He held out a hand, not knowing if she could see it through the inferno.

Come, He had said. The world stopped as He held His breath.

His fingers shook, looking so desperate and grasping as He reached towards her.

Never had He, god of the wood, been so helpless.

Never had He, an ancient being horrifically in love, felt so foolish.

Come.

She came and placed her hand in His. He grasped on to her, pulled her toward Him, and they ran.

I'm never letting you go, He thought, careful not to let her overhear. *You're mine. Mine, mine, mine.*

"Oh," Nautica said now, and covered her mouth. "Oh, I didn't know that's how you felt."

His gaze held stars, held supernovas, held black holes full of mysteries and delights.

Wife, He thought tenderly, and let His heart crash through her mind, completely unbridled. *Darling. My secret witch.*

You are the only thing I have ever wanted.

THE MEADOW WAS just as she remembered it. It was vibrant and lovely, and yet...

"It's sinister," she whispered.

Yes.

"There's something wrong with it."

Yes.

Mine, in human form, held hands with Nautica and Fawn.

"This is where I first saw your father," Nautica said. "He was the most beautiful thing I had ever seen."

"He's alright," Fawn said, and sped away, twirling and dancing with new flowers, who twirled and danced back. A buttercup reared and struck her ankle. It put its face to the wound and drank deeply.

"Daddy!" Fawn cried. She stumbled backward and fell. "What's wrong with it?"

"It's feral, darling," Nautica said, pulling Fawn to her feet. "Is there more?" she asked Mine. She couldn't look at Him but stared toward the village. "Does it get worse?"

His silence was heavy. It held the weight of pregnant thunderclouds, of tension before the breaking of a storm.

"I see," she said. "Let's go."

AT DUSK, THEY reached the village. They stayed at the edge of the forest, watching the townsfolk as they trotted to and fro, doing their chores.

"Look at all those homes!" Fawn squealed. "There are so many."

"There are enough," Nautica answered distractedly. Her heart hurt. It squeezed in a way that made it hard to breathe. Mine kissed her temple.

We don't have to go closer, He said. *You can sense it from here.*

And she did. A rot, a viciousness. Something with teeth ran through the town, under the ground. It poisoned the brook. It fell from the sky like fire. It rose from the grass like a coiled snake.

"Mama," Fawn breathed, and Nautica hushed her.

A man strode to the edge of the town. He held something in his hands.

Nautica shied back, but Fawn leaned forward.

Down, Mine told her, and the little girl crouched to the ground.

The man glanced around surreptitiously and then took bites of whatever he was holding. Bread, maybe. Nautica couldn't tell. But when he had finished, and raised his head, Nautica gasped. She recognized that craggy face, that devious look. She whimpered deep in her throat, and instinctively covered her mouth.

Mama, are you scared?

No, darling. Just startled. Shh.

Yes, she was scared. She was terrified. Fear leaked out of her pores, and she wore panic like a perfume. If Brand had any awareness whatsoever, he would be able to smell her, to track her like a hunter following a blood trail.

Calm, Mine told her, and she remembered Him saying that so long ago, when her house and her dress and her hair were on fire, when this man before them had tied her to the wooden beam, when everything had burned down around her and she was starting to burn, too...

He did that to you? Fawn asked, and she growled low in her throat. Her tiny body tensed up, ready to run after this man, ready to defend her mother from things that had happened long before she was born.

Why does she have to be so astute? Nautica thought, and she was going to say something to placate her daughter, to warn her of the importance of being still, as still as her handsome father, when a woman with yellow hair and a little boy walked up to Brand.

"Here you are," the woman said. "We should go inside before it gets dark."

"I'm hungry, Papa," the boy said. He had Brand's untamed thatch of hair, but somehow it managed to look charming. "Can't we find something to eat?"

"Not tonight, son," Brand said, and Nautica nearly gagged in revulsion at his familiar voice. She would recognize it in her sleep, in the dark, through flames and horror and hellfire. "There's no food left. Maybe we'll find something in the morning."

But he just ate something himself! Fawn said furiously. *We just saw him!*

Shh, Nautica warned. *He can't know we're here.*

Or he'll hurt you again. Will he hurt me, Mama?

I won't let him, Mine said, and His voice was pondwater-cold and burning-house-beam hot at the same time. Nautica turned to Him quickly. His eyes were wild, His nostrils flaring, the edges of His form blurring as His body flickered.

Mine, she said desperately. Was the evil of the village affecting him? She put her hands on either side of His face. *Mine! I need you here with me.*

Brand's son began to cry.

"I'm hungry, Papa. You said we'd find food today, but it's

been days and days. My stomach hurts."

His mother swept him up in her arms, her golden hair cascading over his small body.

"I'm sure if we look hard enough tomorrow, we'll find something. Tonight, let's have a little water and it will help fill your tummy, hmm?"

Brand cursed and turned on his heel.

"You two are wastes," he said. "If I had married my Nautica, I wouldn't have to deal with this."

Nautica froze. Her family was silent beside her.

"Well, you didn't," Lem's wife bit out. "You brought me to town, and *I* am your wife. *This* is your son. I can't compete with a dead woman. I won't even try anymore."

"I tried to save her," Brand said. The dirt stirred at his feet in an unusual way. It crawled up his leg like a vine. "I tried, but—"

"You failed, Brand," his wife shouted. Her hair blew in a sudden wind that wasn't there before; a wind who laughed and moaned and licked the side of her face with invisible tongues.

Nautica drew back in horror. *What is going on?*

Mine's eyes were still full of madness, His human face transforming into a muzzle and back again. *It's feeding. You need to hold it back.*

But how can I? Nautica asked. *And what's happening to you, my love?*

The woman with golden hair dropped her son to the ground. He squirmed away while she launched herself at Brand, beating him with her delicate fists.

"I hate you!" She screamed so loudly that her voice tore. "I wish you had never brought me here. I wish I'd never had seed with you. You selfish, useless, poor-excuse of a man!"

Brand pulled back, and the punch to her face made an ugly sound. She fell to the ground. Nautica put her hand to her cheek as she remembered her own experience with him.

Brand hit her again, and her cheek opened to show him her everything.

Before he'd dragged her outside by her hair. Before he'd tied her up. Before he'd set her home on fire.

Brand kicked his wife twice, hard, with his rugged farm boots. Then he knelt beside her to hit her again. His son screamed and crawled toward his mother, and Brand slapped him across the face as casually as if he were swatting away a pest. The boy crumpled into the dirt.

She didn't even hear Fawn leave. Nautica simply blinked and there was her daughter, a tangle of brown skins and brown hair, her feet hitting the ground with the cadence of hoofbeats.

Fawn, Mine cried, but He was on His side, breathing hard, His limbs becoming legs and arms, and then deer legs again. His eyes were set far too wide for a human and a deer, transforming back and forth so quickly it made Nautica's head spin.

"I'll get her, my love," she said, and she was racing after her child, flowers springing from the earth and blooming behind each footfall.

"Fawn!" she yelled, and she realized she had never screamed her daughter's name before, that things were peaceful at home and their names, oh-so-precious, were always said with love. But the second she had come back to Paradise, the weight of her humanity had fallen heavy upon her.

She ran faster, kicking her feet as though she could fly, as if she, too, were a doe in the forest. Light, light, fast, fast, wary of the danger of man.

FAWN REACHED THE weeping boy and threw her arms around him. He was covered in dirt and had blood running from his nose.

It's okay. Don't cry, she said, but it was as if the boy couldn't hear her at all.

Boy? She asked again. The boy's ugly father turned away from his sobbing wife to face Fawn. "Boy?" she said aloud.

"You little brat," Brand hissed, and raised his hand. Fawn held the boy tightly and squeezed her eyes shut. "You have the nerve to—"

He didn't finish. The blow didn't fall. Fawn cautiously opened her eyes to see a mountain in front of her, the force of a gale, the steadfastness of a boulder.

Mama, Fawn said, and Nautica's voice was full of love and fury as she answered:

Take the boy and run.

Mama, I don't want to.

Run, Fawn, her mother barked, and Fawn was on her feet, dragging the boy upright. She pulled him behind a nearby house where they both crouched down. Fawn peeked around the corner to watch.

The man stared up at her mother. The expression on his face

would have been funny if his eyes weren't so scary.

"This can't be," he said. He scrambled to his feet, and Nautica jumped back.

"No closer," she warned.

He took a step forward, reaching for her, and Nautica shouted.

"I said no closer, Brand!"

The man, this Brand, stopped moving, but his hand still hung in the air as if he would caress Nautica's face.

"You came back from the dead," he breathed. "You were dead, but you stand before me."

"Check on your wife, Brand. I know exactly how you choose to use your fists."

"Nautica, I would never—"

"Step back, Brand, or I will…"

Nautica tapered off, the words ceasing like a falling rain. Fawn strained to hear them.

Brand smiled, and Fawn recognized it.

Predator, she thought, and growled low in her throat. If she'd had a knife, she would have gripped it. But Daddy had her knife in His pack. Fawn searched for Him at the tree line, but He couldn't be seen.

"Or you'll do what, Nautica?" Brand stepped forward, One step, two. He was nearly close enough to touch Fawn's mother with his big, hitting hands.

"I'm warning you," Nautica said, and gathered herself as if she were about to spring. Fawn watched the wind wrap around her mother's body, blowing through her clothes and spiraling her hair into the sky. It spoke the strangest of things, about revenge and bloodthirst and the need to be satiated.

It has been so long, the wind whined, and roots and vines slithered from the ground.

Yes, so long, they agreed. A thorny tendril rubbed its face against Brand's leather boots while another twined in the broken bride's golden hair.

You had been holding us back, a bramble said. It lashed across Nautica's leg. Fawn saw a thin stripe of blood appear and run down into her mother's shoes. *All this time, for so many generations. But then you left…*

Yes, you left, the wind sang, and the lust in its voice was obscene. *You left, and we were free. First, we were afraid, but then we gathered strength. And we grew, and watched this village very closely, and saw these people, and what they really are—*

What they really are, a bluebell said, and bared its teeth.

—and what they are is sad, is cruel, isn't worth saving. So, if you would just let us—

Just let us, cooed a butterfly, its proboscis coated in blood.

Things would be ever so much better, a frog croaked, its voice strangely human, and it hopped over to burrow inside Brand's wife's mouth. She barely managed to cough and pull it away.

"All this time?" Nautica asked. She trembled, her body ready to flee, ready to fight. She flicked her eyes and met Fawn's gaze.

Find your father, Nautica told her. *You're not safe here. Take the boy and run to your father.*

The wind grew brisk as the clouds darkened. Thunder rumbled and Fawn felt it in her chest, but she could not move. She blinked moisture out of her eyes. Was she crying? No, it was only mist from the rain that was beginning.

"All this time, I've been holding you back, somehow? The very living things of Paradise? You want to attack the people of the village?" Nautica's voice sounded awed.

Brand laughed.

"You're crazy. Crazier than ever. Who are you even talking to?"

The wind roared, shrieking and howling at Brand. He turned his face against it.

All this time, Nautica thought. *When I told the plants to behave and the wind to quiet down. When I let my hair sing and cautioned it against wrapping around twigs and tree limbs and other people, I was telling the land to—*

Calm, Mine said. His voice was weak, but fueled with anger. She saw Him out of the corner of her eye, staggering toward them. He was limping heavily, His strong legs seemingly too thin and fragile to carry Him, His antlers a glorious crown on His head. *You have Otherkind blood flowing through you, from way back. That is why you can communicate with the very land itself. That's why you can communicate with me.*

"Look at the size of that buck," Brand murmured, and reached for his knife.

Fawn, come to me, Mine said. *The evil of this town is affecting me greatly. We must go.*

But I can't leave the boy, Fawn told him. *He's hurt. His daddy will kill him.*

It isn't up to us to interfere, Mine said. Struggling to breathe, He dipped His majestic nose to the ground.

Let us, chimed the rain, and it hit as hard as arrows, it hit as brutally as sharp rocks. It drove itself into their eyes and bubbled down their mouths and noses.

Mama, Fawn cried, and the rain struck the dirt, mixing into a thick, menacing mud. It wrapped its arms around Fawn's ankles, and sucked her down.

Mama! she screamed. The mud wailed, the malice emboldened by the rain, and it pulled Fawn deeper and deeper into the earth. Worms attached themselves to her body and began to feast. Her calves, her knees, and her thin thighs disappeared under the ground.

Brand's son struggled to pull her out, but the rain turned to snow in an instant, obscuring his vision and making his fingers too cold to move. The freezing wind buffeted him, knocking him hard into the stone house. He collapsed onto the ground, unmoving.

Daddy!

Let us rage, whispered the wind, the rain, the earth, the sky. *Let us destroy and devour. It is time.*

"Stay away from my daughter," Nautica shouted, and the elements shrieked back. They bit and snapped, tripped and struck out. She had cuts on her face and welts on her body. But still she commanded them, *No,* they couldn't take her child and *no,* they couldn't consume this town. There was still beauty here in the humanity. *Somewhere,* she thought desperately. *There must be.*

Mine struggled to His daughter. The snow became ice, and He closed His eyes against it. It tried to chip and slash at His eyes, turning the moons to bloody suns, but He limped closer. The stone from the building tore itself away with a great yell and rumbled toward Him, hitting Him hard on the flank as He sidestepped away.

Come, He called to his daughter. *Come,* He said, the first thing He had ever said to her mother. She had heard the story of that fiery night, told plainly and without emotion, except that her mother's eyes hid secrets and tears inside. "Your father's voice," she had said, and her own voice bloomed. "It was everything. *Come,* He said."

Come, He demanded now, as Brand left his broken wife moaning at his feet. Nautica held her hands out defensively, trying to keep the evil of Paradise at bay.

We crawl through the streets. We live in the refuse. We poison the wells and the water. And it's time, it's time, and you cannot hold us back, the evil said, and sank its fangs into everything that moved. Nautica turned her back to Brand and focused on Mine and the children.

Calm, she thought, and held her hands out. *Come to me, birds of the field. Come to me, zephyrs. Calm your anger and sate yourself with me.*

The great churning of the earth paused. The soil tested the air. Nautica nodded, her smile beatific, but her eyes darted toward her family.

Yes, come, she said, and pulled the top of her dress down to expose her neck. *Taste just a little. A little will be enough.*

The earth reared toward her, a tidal wave of soil and decayed vegetables. The wind sprang forward with its mouths open, teeth sharp and ready. Nautica gasped as the evil tasted and tasted and tasted. It supped. It gulped. Her legs shook, but still she stood, and would stand, until her husband and child were safe.

Mine bent low, and Fawn grabbed His luminescent antlers, her hair glowing softly in response. Mine pulled Himself backwards, step by painful step, pulling Fawn from the hole.

Daddy, the boy, she said, and her father, whose blood ran from His eyes and seeped into His muzzle, nodded. He knelt low, and Fawn used all her strength to help push the boy onto her father's back.

Hold on, she told him, and then remembered that he didn't speak with Soul. "Hold on," she said out loud. The boy threw his arms around the stag's neck, his small face contorted with pain, and Fawn *hated* his father, *hated* the man that had shown her what humans could be. The very first human she had ever seen besides her mother, and it had to be this monster?

Child, her father said, and Fawn clambered onto His back. He was shuddering under them, but He lifted His head to the air, triumphant and strong, and she felt His body coil.

He sprang, He sprang, King of the Growing Things, Lord of All Nature, and as He leapt into the air, Fawn's heart leapt with Him. *Let's leave this terrible place,* she thought, and she clung to the boy in front of her, her legs clamped around her father's lean body, and she turned to her mother with a grin.

Mama, we're going home, she said, but her mother was struggling to breathe, struggling to stand. She was drowning in the rain that pooled around her nose and mouth, scrabbling at the icy wind that froze her hair and made it chime. Roots and bugs and mud and refuse crawled over her body, making holes to drink here, tearing at flesh there.

My love, her father bugled, and it was a sound Fawn had never heard before. He was in pain, and desperate, and she felt His body shudder as His very Soul rent, and she felt His despair. Despair: that's a human emotion, not one worthy of the God of the Woods, and for a brief second Fawn saw with a knowledge beyond her years how her father's love for her mother had corrupted Him.

You're a god no longer, she thought, and was full of sorrow. This is how you kill a god. You make Him love, and love makes Him both powerful and weak at the same time.

Fawn felt Him waver. Should He take the children farther away, or run directly to His wife? Fawn studied her mother's face, the way the muscles moved under her skin. Through her suffering, Nautica caught her lover's gaze. Her eyes were fierce and full of fire. They reflected the holy shine of the hind's antlers, the fawngirl's hair.

Mine's anguished face hardened. He snorted and pawed the ground. Then he turned and bounded away.

Faster, faster. Fawn held on tightly as her father took her far away. Her mother became smaller in the background.

Traitorous tears, fat and hot, ran down Fawn's face. They dropped onto the boy's wild thatch of hair, so like his father's. The boy turned and roughly grabbed her hand.

"I'm sorry," he said, and his human eyes were dull and flat like stones. They didn't glow at all. "I'm sorry about your mom."

They reached the safety of the trees. Her father stamped

loudly.

Hurry, He said, and His voice was cold. His gentleness was gone, His ears flattened along His neck. Fawn slid to the ground and helped the boy down.

Stay, Mine commanded, and once again He was racing toward the village, toward His wife, toward the only thing that could propel Him toward this area of evil and hate. As He drew closer, His fur came off in patches. His skin began to peel, exposing veins and muscle, and the air squealed in horrid delight. His lips pulled back from His curiously sharp teeth.

Fawn watched Him, feeling so afraid, feeling so proud, and she quietly crept closer. She bounced on the balls of her feet, the nervous energy almost too much for her to handle.

Mama! Mama, hang on, she called. A flock of birds erupted from the trees beside her. *We are safe, and Daddy is coming.*

Her mother was kneeling in the mud, but she raised her head at Fawn's call and staggered to her feet. Now that her child was safe, she no longer needed to distract the evil. She could tamp it down.

Enough, Nautica cried, and although her voice was weak, her spirit was strong. She needed to get back to Fawn. She needed to return to Mine. She needed to mother that little boy until his golden-haired mom was well enough to take him back.

She didn't have time for this.

Stop, she commanded the wind. Her will battled with it, her nostrils flaring. *No more!*

Enough, she told the mud, the rain, the snow, the sky. *Calm yourselves. You have supped on my blood. That is enough for now.*

"What is this madness?" Brand said. He cursed. His eyes were wild pinwheels. "You command the very earth itself?"

The water slid from her face. Nautica took a great gasp and the air was good.

"It is enough to save you," she said, and wildflowers fell from the sky like stars. Petals landed on Brand's hair, and he shrunk back.

Mama!

Nautica heard Fawn's voice and turned. She saw her husband racing toward her, the way His fur hung in weeping patches, the way His skin pulled away and showed her bone and gristle.

"My love, no," she said, and reached out for Him.

FAWN SAW EVERYTHING as if it were happening in slow motion. Her father bounded toward the village, racing to save His beloved. Nautica, her hair saturated with petals and rain, reached for Him, her mouth forming a soft "o."

The man, this Brand, darted from behind her. He screamed something about witches, and how she should have burned the first time. He pulled his shiny dagger from its sheath.

Oh, how it glittered in the misty light!

Oh, how swift and how surely it slid across her mother's throat!

Oh, how lovely her mother looked as she fell, sinking to the ground in the man's arms. Brand yelled and cried, burying his face into Nautica's hair as the wind ruffled, spun around them, and eventually became still.

My darlings, Fawn heard. The words were Sent with such love. *My darlings.*

Mine trumpeted, a sound so loud and fierce that Fawn quivered. She hugged the boy next to her, who smelled so very human and not like Otherkind at all, and she couldn't look away.

Her father, mad with grief. Her father, Lord of All That Lives, but not the Lord of Anything That Dies, sprinted to her mother and the killer who held her.

Love! My love, He shouted, but His wife did not move. Brand sat there, cradling a dead wife that was not his, his foot touching the woman who was. Brand, the epicenter of all this killing, this ugliness, who knew how to do nothing except hurt with his big, thick hands and his mind full of hate.

The hind's hooves came crashing down on Brand's face, his skull, his arms, his killing hands. Mine shouted words that didn't make sense in the human language, and some that didn't make sense in Otherkind. His grief was a torrent, an ocean, and as He stamped and bones broke beneath Him, He hardly noticed.

Daddy, Fawn cried, but her father was beyond her. He had become a thing of horrors, a god of justice, and then a god of vengeance. Brand's ruined face was little more than bone chips and red paste pounded into the ground, and the earth feasted upon it happily.

I curse you, I curse you, Mine repeated, and the elements yipped and capered. Nautica was gone; there was nothing to hold them back. They opened their jaws and swallowed, swallowed, swallowed great pieces of the livid lord, sucking the marrow from His bones and sharpening their teeth on His antlers. They brought Him down as he thrashed and fought, swimming into His nose and mouth. Vines infested His bloodstream and spread out in His lungs, where they bloomed malignantly. Lightning arced down from the heavens, which opened in their joyous sorrow, and illuminated the darkening sky. Fawn watched as her father struggled, then slowed, and eventually came to an end, laying His head in His dead wife's lap.

The world ceased.

The stars in His eyes

flickered

and went out.

CHAPTER SIX: FAWN

Fawn had never known such terror, had never recalled such horror. She watched her mother bleed out, watched her father lose Himself in his vengeance, saw Him devoured whole. The earth shook and the houses began to crumble. Night fell, and so did the stars as they zipped down to take pleasured bites from the tasty morsels screaming in the village.

Fawn squatted down and covered her hands with her ears.

It isn't happening. It isn't happening.

"Girl," the boy said, shaking her elbow.

It isn't happening. This isn't real.

"Girl," the boy shouted, and his voice was thick with tears. Fawn looked up, and saw her own gibbering fear reflected back at her.

He too, had witnessed the madness, the trauma, of watching his father beat his mother nearly to death, and of seeing his father obliterated.

Fawn's teeth were chattering in cold and shock.

"I'm sorry my dad killed your dad," she said.

He nodded back. "I'm sorry my dad killed your mom. Really sorry. But we have to g-go. I think… I think…"

He couldn't finish his words and Fawn understood. The village was a howling mass of yips and screams, some human, some not.

"Your mother?" she asked.

He shook his head, his eyes large.

Coward, she wanted to say, but that wasn't the right word. *Cautious.* The likelihood of his mother surviving wasn't good. Fawn's superior eyesight, even in the dark, told her that something leggy crawled through the open hole in his mother's cheek. She wasn't moving. It was time to go.

She slung her little pack over her shoulder,

—*Mustn't think of Father carrying it on His sleek back*—grabbed the boy's hand, and started to run.

They ran, back the way she had come, away from this cesspool of humans and hate and wild things that tore and bit and swallowed. She ran, her usually lithe feet clumsy, and she tripped over roots and tore her clothes. She stumbled and fell over stones that seemed to come out of nowhere to trip her, and she couldn't see, she couldn't *see,* and she finally realized it was because her tears had blinded her.

"Stop, please," gasped the boy, and he was breathing so hard that he was wheezing. His lungs sounded sick and unhealthy, and Fawn wondered if they were black inside, stuffed full with soot and dirt like everything else in that town.

"I can't run anymore," he said, and collapsed in the field, in the meadow where Fawn's parents had met, and when she realized this, she fell beside him.

"I'm just a little boy," he said, by way of explanation, and when the children crumpled together like puppies searching for warmth or care, they sobbed so openly and without shame that the animals of the grove, and the grasses and flowers themselves crept close to watch over them.

So tragic, said a sprig of lavender, ruffling its flowers. *Their tears are so delicious, and yet I feel almost sorrow watering myself with them.*

They really are so very small, the nighttime sky said, bowing low over them. *Too small to survive on their own. Whatever shall they do?*

We'll think about it tomorrow, said a strange flower with glistening petals. As it snuggled up to the weeping children, it gave off a faint light that matched Fawn's hair.

Yes, tomorrow, said the grove. *We'll sort it all out in the morning.*

THE MORNING CAME and nothing was sorted. A dirty, sweaty Fawn looked at a swollen-faced boy.

"What is your name, boy?" she asked him.

"Lem," he answered. "What is yours?"

"Fawn."

He nodded once and his stomach rumbled.

"Oh, are you hungry?" she asked. "I have some food in this

bag."

She rifled through and found some carrots and potatoes. The boy took two carrots and ate hungrily. She watched him.

"When did you eat last?"

"It's been days, Lem said. "There's no food in the village."

"I saw your dad eating something right before you and your mother found him."

The boy's face fell, and Fawn felt her cheeks flush. What was this feeling? This strange flutter of sadness for hurting someone? She hadn't experienced it with her parents. They just *were*.

She thought of the human words her mother had taught her to say in such times if she were ever to meet another person.

"I'm sorry," she said.

Lem shook his head and chewed noisily.

"It doesn't surprise me. It sounds like him."

"I don't think you like him much," she said.

"He didn't like me at all, so perhaps that is fair."

Fawn studied her damaged skin, ripped from their flight through the woods. She heard the music of a brook.

"You need to wash your wounds," her mother had taught her. "You can't simply lick them like your father does."

Fawn's vision blurred again, and her face was wet. She busied herself at the stream, splashing water everywhere to hide her tears.

Lem joined her. He avoided looking at her face.

"Are you a witch?" he asked.

Fawn snarled.

"Why would you say that?"

"Your mother was a witch. She cursed us and that's why

everything happened in Paradise. Are you one, too?"

"What do you mean, everything happened in Paradise?"

He talked of stories his mother had told, that after the Witch of Paradise was burned, the land had soured. Evil things crept around at night, seeping through the cracks in the doors and poisoning the trees.

"Branches would catch us," he said. "Trees would snap and crush us. I had a sister, once. That's how she fell."

"Mama wouldn't curse anyone, even though she said everyone treated her terribly."

Lem looked embarrassed.

"I'm sorry. I wouldn't have."

Fawn frowned. Lem took her hand. They stood there knee-deep in the brook, in the dappled sunlight, and Lem's cold, damp hand didn't feel at all like her mother's touch. Fawn pulled away.

"I won't treat you that way," he promised. "Never. I'll help you build a house."

"A house?" Fawn asked, smoothing down the hides of her dress nervously.

"Yes, a house. In the village. With a gate, so nobody can come in if you don't want them to. We can even paint it."

Fawn turned and climbed onto the bank.

"I don't want to live in the village. Are you mad? Why would I ever go back?"

He blinked at her.

"Where else would you go?"

She stopped abruptly.

"To my house. To my home. In the forest."

"Where? How do you get there?"

"I don't know," she admitted.

"Who will take care of you?" Lem pushed. "You're still too small to be on your own."

Fawn's lip trembled.

The summer breeze is a terrible nanny. Butterflies are beautiful but they can't bring in the water. Flowers are cheery but they can't help you fix a roof or scavenge for food or cure the meat.

"Then come with me," he said. "I don't have any parents, either. Surely, we'll find someone who has lost their children and will care for us until we can live by ourselves."

Fawn hesitated.

"It's the only way," Lem said. He held out his hand.

He was a little boy, and she a young girl. They stood in the grove where her mother had come across Mine in His perfect stillness. Lem moved with every breath; he jittered and shook, the veins thrumming with his heartbeat. He didn't command the Otherkind like her father, or the elements like her mother. His eyes didn't contain scenes of the forest or the mysteries of the universe. They were flat and dull, and the pupils widened and constricted as he looked at Fawn's face, but she saw herself reflected in them. Beneath the brokenness of his imperfect, human eyes, she saw kindness.

He continued to hold out his hand.

"Come," he said. Something in the words shook her, an echo in time. She reached toward him with trembling fingers, and the gesture felt vaguely familiar.

"Come," he said again, and Fawn took his hand.

CHAPTER SEVEN

Fawn and Lem lived with an old woman who needed children with strong backs to help her till and harvest and thatch the roof. They slaughtered animals for food and gathered firewood. When the land screeched and slithered and yelped in starvation, Fawn would tell it to hold its tongue. She soon discovered that nobody else could hear it. The leaves, the grass, the squawk of birds—they couldn't be understood by anyone in Paradise.

"What a silly girl," the old woman said. "Her head is always in the clouds."

"She has no idea I saved her life twice today," Fawn told Lem. He was older now, about fourteen, and tall enough that his head scraped the doorway. He was starting to look more like his father. "The earth nearly devoured her both times."

"She's lucky to have you," he said, and meant it. He grew, and Fawn grew, and the old woman grew and grew greater in years until she died.

"I'm leaving this place," Fawn told Lem. "The din of the village is too much for me. Men touch me and women stare at me, and the flowers grow wrong here. Their heads are always upside down. I need room to breathe."

"I told you I'd help you build a house," Lem reminded her, and he did. They built Fawn's new home shadowing the glen where her parents had met. The grass was fresh, and they built the house next to a green hill. The house was one small room with a clean stone floor and cheery windows. A tree with strong branches grew proudly next to the door.

I will cause pain and destruction to your granddaughters, the tree informed her.

Then you're no different than anyone else here, she answered.

Her home was cozy and afforded her the escape she needed. Sometimes Lem stayed with her, but mostly he stayed in the old woman's house in the village.

He grew taller, and stronger, and his body began to bend with time.

"Why don't you love me?" he asked Fawn.

"I'm very fond of you," she said. "Look, I bore your daughter. That is its own form of love."

"Yet you keep me at bay," Lem said, and he wept those big, dopey tears that had no purpose nor luminesce at all.

If you love him, he will die, the wise tree warned her. *It is part of the trade. Your line has the power to wrestle back the elements in town, but in exchange for love.*

You know what happened to my father? Fawn asked. *My mother loved Him very much.*

Yes, the tree replied. *Her love was a poison that brought Him down in the end.*

Fawn bared her teeth.

It isn't a fair trade. Saving these horrible people at the cost of true love? I don't want this gift.

The tree batted its branches lazily.

Who said it's a gift? it answered.

LEM FOUND ANOTHER woman in the village who could truly love him. His father hadn't murdered her mother, and that really is a very important basis for everlasting love. He would visit Fawn every now and then with something to trade—feed for her chickens if she would prepare medicine for his sick son, for instance, or simply to visit their daughter. He would listen to Anise chatter about what the tree at the front door had told her, or what the silly flowers were gossiping about. Lem's eyes would predictably drift to Fawn, who simply smiled. Her mind was unchanged, and because of the lack of romantic love, Lem lived a good life before dying of a normal, natural, not-at-all-curse-driven illness.

"It hurts to crave what you cannot have," he told Fawn the last time he saw her. She had come to visit him at his home with a packet of healing herbs, and greeted his wife and son warmly.

"My friend," she said, and held his hand between her own. She nodded toward his family in the other room. "You have wasted so much time. What you truly sought was here all the time."

He tried to lift his hand to her cheek, but she stepped back.

"Goodbye, Lem," she said, and left the house.

She raised Anise to be strong and capable and knowledgeable in the way of curses and healing spells and keeping the secret of their family line. She admonished her to seek companionship if she wanted, but never to fall in love. One day, Fawn looked at her child and thought, *She will do wonderfully*. She remembered her mother's laughter and riding around on her father's proud back, His antlers shining like spiderwebs in the moonlight. She lay down and let herself die.

Anise grew straight and tall. She fell in love with a man who had a soft smile and wide, brown eyes as beautifully lashed and as gentle as those of a cow. They made love in the flowered glen and Anise had never been so happy.

Naturally, that could not last.

CHAPTER EIGHT: ANISE

More than anything in the world, Anise wanted to travel. She was tired of Paradise, where the ground constantly grumbled and threw fits under her feet. She was weary of the small-minded people who looked at her so queerly and turned from her when she ventured into town.

"Hello, stepmother," she called cheerily to her dead father's wife. The woman took her son by the hand and walked briskly away, her golden hair shining. Anise watched after them with a feeling that wasn't quite love, not quite hate, but which was far from neutral indifference.

Perhaps it was loneliness.

Perhaps it wasn't.

Anise stepped out of the store with a paper bag of groceries and waited patiently as an old truck rumbled by. She was about to start the lengthy walk home when she saw a man.

A man she didn't know. A man she didn't even recognize.

This could be interesting, she thought.

She marched straight to this man and pushed her hair behind her ears.

"You look lost," she said to him. She eyed the military duffle bag slung over his shoulder. "Freshly back from the war?"

He nodded. He smiled, and a small dimple appeared near his mouth.

Even more interesting.

"There are a few places to stay in Paradise," she mused. "Unless you're looking for someone in particular? Tell me who, and I can point you the right way."

This man could definitely make a woman happy.

The man blushed and looked at his feet.

"Are you embarrassed to be lost?" Anise asked.

The man shook his head.

"Do you speak?" she needled playfully.

He nodded again, and Anise laughed. She linked her arm through his.

"Oh, you are darling! Tell me who you're looking for and I'll escort you. It will be dark soon."

The man looked at her arm looped through his. He rested his calloused hand atop hers.

"You're the woman I want to make happy," he said. "That's why I was a bit shy. I'm pleased to hear you say it."

Anise froze. "What?" she said aloud.

C-can you hear me? she Sent. *Who are you looking for?*

You, he answered. His face was very serious, but his eyes were warm. *I've been looking for you.*

ANISE STEPPED BACK abruptly and dropped her groceries. She covered her mouth with her hands.

You spoke to me through Soul, she said. *Nobody has ever been able to do that except my mother.*

I can't do it all the time, he admitted. *It wears me out.*

"How?" she asked, speaking audibly. "How can you do this?"

He bent down and picked up her spilled bag. He set the flour neatly inside. Oranges. A red lipstick and a book. He straightened and held her groceries carefully.

"I've always been a bit sensitive," he said simply, and shrugged. "I catch the wind every now and then. The moon loves to curse at me. Just a little, here and there. But you, I heard about you. At least, your village, and the secret witches who live there." He held his arm out like a gentleman. "Miss. If I could perhaps escort *you* home?"

It was a long walk, but they chattered. Anise inquired about what was in his duffle bag, and he told her it was full of nothing and everything in the world at the same time. He clucked at her chickens and greeted the tree by her front door. He waited politely until she invited him inside. He studied the tiny house with the gentlest eyes Anise had ever seen.

"What is your name?" she asked.

"Anthony. Anthony Patton Anders."

"My name is Anise."

"I know," he said, and showed that darling dimple again.

Dinner was simple and extravagant and comfortable but thrilling at the same time. Anise wanted to know everything.

"What was it like, traveling the world? I've never been out of this wretched town. I bet you have the best stories."

"I do have stories, but perhaps they aren't the best," Anthony admitted. "I traveled, but only to foxholes and to face the horrors of war. I can tell you what gunfire sounds like, and how it smells when something explodes close to your head. Children are ragged and broken and can never play with anyone ever again. I can tell you that rations keep you alive, but they don't bring near the joy that this glorious soup and fresh-baked bread does. But I want to know more about you."

Anise's mouth turned up.

"Nobody's ever asked me about myself before," she said, and the plant on her windowsill shivered and suddenly burst into bloom. The other plants and flowers around the house followed suit. It was a visual cacophony of joy.

"You were really searching for me?" she asked timidly. Oh, it was so unlike her to be timid! Yet her heart was doing something strange, as though it were filling up with something warmer than blood and more nourishing than water.

Anthony reached across the table and took her warm hand.

"I think I've been searching for you all my life," he answered honestly. His brown eyes were so kind, and she thought for a second that they were full of starlight, but it was just the reflection of an errant firefly that had made its way into the house.

"I want nothing more than to leave this place," she told him, gripping his fingers hard, her eyes glowing with faint luminescence. "I want to leave Paradise. The nature outside town is so lovely, but it's horrid within. I'm supposed to be responsible and stay here to help the people, but I don't want to. For once,

I want to do something—"

Simply for yourself, he said, and Anise was surprised that her eyes were full of tears. They fell down her face, leaving a trail of bioluminescent shine, and Anthony wiped them away.

"I don't know why I'm crying," she told him. "I'm not sad at all. There are just so many emotions."

"Show me your favorite things here, and then we shall leave," he promised her. "We'll go wherever you like. I'm good with my hands. I'm good with animals. I can find a job anywhere."

"Let me take you to my very favorite place in the whole world," she said, and pulled him to his feet. They stepped out into the moonlight. Anthony was right: the moon was cursing him, his family, and the horse he rode in on.

"What does she have against you?" Anise asked.

Moonlight dotted his hair as the moon grabbed great handfuls of it. "Hmm? Oh, is she after me again? I don't know why, but she's quite the vulgar mistress," he said.

Anise led him to the meadow.

CHAPTER NINE

The meadow was full of stars. It was a glen of wonder. The moon ceased her abuse and started snapping, catching errant stars in her mouth. She bit down and left shards of the universe in her teeth.

"This place," Anthony breathed. He held his hands out, palms down, as if he were to touch the grass. But he didn't touch the grass, or the flowers, or the trees, or anything. It was too precious. It was too sacred.

"Silly," Anise said, and she plucked a dahlia and tucked it behind Anthony's ear. It leaned over and whispered the most delectable of things. Anthony touched its petals softly.

"It feels…" he said, and couldn't finish. Feels like magic. Feels like joy. Feels like the furthest thing from war he had ever experienced.

It does, she said, and then she was kissing him, the first romantic kiss of her life, not counting that one time with the mayor's son when she was a child. Anthony's lips were full and warm, and most importantly, they were kissing her back. They didn't drive her away because she was different. They didn't treat her poorly because they didn't understand her rancor and bitterness.

Anthony tried to pause the kiss, but Anise bit his lip in chastisement and pressed herself closer. She was hungry and lonely and angry and hopeful and had so many feelings to pour into this man if he would only let her.

That's why I'm here, he said, because his mouth was too full of the taste of Anise. *I want to give you everything you want.*

What she wanted was closeness. What she wanted was love. She wanted to throw a stone through the windows of her house and call up the river to drown the Paradise in a paranormal flood. She wanted to pick up her skirts and flee somewhere far, far away.

Take me from here, she said, and she was pulling at his clothes and fumbling with his buttons.

I will, I will, he promised, and when they sank into the grasses, the moon had the decency to turn away.

A WOMAN IN love is a dangerous thing. A woman of this line, even more so.

Anise and Anthony stayed in the town for six days. Six days of him whittling by the fireplace. Six days of his wonder when she bent the fire left and right, laughing at the expression he wore. She packed everything she needed in one small suitcase that she had purchased in town.

"Finally leaving?" the store owner asked her. "Took you long enough."

"I hope you burn in Hell," she said merrily, and skipped away.

"Where to?" Anthony asked. "I have a bus ticket to Cincinnati. After that, we can go anywhere."

"Then let's go anywhere," she answered lightly. "Let's pick a place with a beautiful name. Or somewhere you always wanted to be."

Are you coming back? the water from the stream burbled.

"Never," she swore.

The night has eyes. They shone in the dark.

Will we sup on bones and sinew while you are gone?

"See if I care," she responded. She had one good hat, and put it aside for the next day's journey.

All the little children! the Night Eyes exulted. *So tender and so sweet. It has been so long since I devoured a child.*

"Devouring children?" Anthony said. He looked at Anise. "What exactly happens if you leave?"

"I'm not sure." She shrugged, but her face darkened. "Nobody has left for generations."

"One of your ancestors did. Maybe a great, great grandfather, or so. That's how I know of your line. The secret witches of Paradise who use magic in today's world. I had always hoped it was true, and here you are. You're like a dream. But are you putting children in danger?"

"I-I'm not sure," Anise stuttered. "I know that if I don't pay attention, the ground rears up and attacks the townspeople. But they are unbelievably cruel," she assured him when his brown eyes lost their sweetness. "Just terrible, angry people who hunt each other all the time. Perhaps it would be a blessing to let them disappear. Removing a blight from the world."

Anthony's eyes went dark, and Anise was afraid of him for the first time. He clenched his large hands, and she vaguely wondered what they had done in the war. They were strong and powerful and the bones under them suddenly seemed foreign and threatening.

"I need to take a walk," he said in a measured voice, and stepped outside. Anise heard the moon snicker.

Anise wasn't heartless, and this heart pierced her.

Perhaps the evil of this land is affecting me, too.

She grabbed her shawl and a lantern. She spirited down the dark, dirt road toward the village.

What are you doing? The fireflies asked.

She didn't answer.

Anise was tired and out of breath by the time she reached the village. She stepped quickly down the streets until she came to a plain stone house.

She knocked and waited impatiently until the door opened.

"What do you want?" her dead father's wife asked coldly.

Anise steeled herself. The woman was unpleasant, but this was important.

"Take your son out of the village," Anise said.

The woman leaned forward, her yellow hair spilling over her shoulder. "What was that?"

"Take your son out of the village. It isn't safe. I think there is going to be a disaster of some sort. Soon. Maybe even in the next few days."

The woman snorted. "Who told you that?" she mocked. "The wind? The fluffy little forest animals?"

"I'm being serious," Anise said.

"I don't believe you," the woman told her, tossing her golden hair back. "You and your entire line are full of madness! Just sitting there on the edge of the woods being strange."

She started to shut the door, but Anise blocked it with her foot.

"Listen," she said, and her voice was a hiss that rivaled the snakes of the field. "I do not like you, but your son is of my blood. He is my half-brother." The woman flinched, and Anise's eyes blazed. "Yes, we share the same father, as shameful as that may be for you. And the boy has done nothing wrong. So, when I tell you that he's in danger, you had better believe I mean what I say. Take him from here and keep him safe."

She removed her foot, and the door slammed in her face. She gripped her dress with white fingers.

There. She had done what she could. Tomorrow, she and her love would leave this place, and all would be well.

She just had to make it through one last night.

ANTHONY DIDN'T COME back until morning, and Anise had not been able to sleep all night. She plucked at her bags and whispered to her plants and told her chickens that she loved them. The tree next to her door assured her not to worry.

"But what if he leaves me?" she said.

You've been alone before, the tree answered.

This didn't make her feel any better.

The sun came over the horizon and so did Anthony. She wanted to fling herself into his arms, but she was afraid. Always, this fear. She was too worried to hide it behind snappy words and grand gestures. She leaned in the doorway, with bags under her eyes and trepidation radiating from her like old sunshine.

Anthony swept her up in his arms.

"I'm sorry," he said. "I get like this from time to time, and it is better for me to leave. I don't want to hurt the ones I love."

He loves me, she thought, and her potted plants swooned.

Anise hugged him back, not even embarrassed at her relieved desperation, and soon she swept her little house, touched its eaves gently, and shut the door behind them.

They walked to town in silence and boarded the bus without a word. Rainwater pressed itself to the bus windows and studied Anise before falling to the ground and turning to mud.

She's really leaving, it told the others. *We're finally free.*

Anise felt happy, and relieved, and then pensive, and eventually ill. The farther they got out of town, the more the pressure increased in her head. Her eyes still shone after an hour's drive. By two hours, she had lost her smile. Three found pain pooling behind her eyes. At four, her stomach twisted and felt like it was turning itself inside out.

"Stop the bus," she gasped weakly, and at five hours away from Paradise, she was on her hands and knees, retching toads and worms and mushrooms into the grass of Podunk, Ohio.

Anthony crouched beside her, rubbing her back.

"It's okay, my love," he said as crickets spewed from her mouth and scattered. "You'll be all right."

I think I'm dying, she sputtered, and gagged as a snake with gray and white scales oozed from her mouth. Her throat convulsed and the snake hissed. Its forked tongue flicked and Anise's eyes were round saucers, the luminescence running down her cheeks and wetting the wretched, wriggling creature. Anthony reached forward and tugged the snake, ignoring it as the creature struck his hand. The snake was two feet long. Three feet. Four, five, six. Anise heaved wracking sobs, her hair falling out of its neat curls and sticking to her face. The snake slipped out, its tail hitting the ground with a slap, and slithered away.

Darling, she cried, and her body was shuddering, her skin covered in welts and bites from the creatures and sticks she had vomited up. Her Victory Red lipstick was smeared.

"I'll take you home," Anthony said, and held her until the next bus came. The ride home was silent except for the raspy breaths from her damaged throat.

I'm torn apart from the inside out, she gasped. *What is this?*

"Maybe you can't leave," Anthony said. He caressed her hair, pushing it back from her sweaty brow. "I've heard the women in your line can't leave Paradise, but who would have thought it was true?"

I can't go back there. It's a prison, she sobbed, and her tears really were a thing of bitter beauty, glittering down her face with their otherworldly light. She cried for hours, until she was a limp, sodden mess leaning on Anthony's shoulder. Paradise was a dark, abandoned place when they returned home.

You're back, growled the night air. Its teeth were sharp.

You're back, spat something black and lanky that slithered down a tree.

"You're back," Lem's wife said. She had a suitcase in one hand and her son in the other. She was about to board the last bus out of town.

"You can stay if you'd like," Anthony told her. He gathered Anise under his arm and shouldered most of her weight. "Anise has returned."

"Pity," said Lem's wife, but she regarded Anthony and Anise with new eyes.

"Are you getting on?" the bus driver asked impatiently. "I have miles to go."

Lem's wife hesitated.

"I think not," she said, and the bus pulled away, its wheels spinning gaily.

The golden-haired woman and her child returned home. So

did Anthony and Anise.

Such a pity, a sinister vine said, and lashed at Anise's face. She tripped over a root that had surreptitiously raised itself.

Hold yourselves back, Anthony commanded them. *You don't have the authority to defy her.*

The wind spit in his face. It leered at Anise and lapped the sorrow from her cheeks.

Welcome home to your grim destiny, the tree said, and stood silent guard as they stepped into the clean, freshly swept house.

CHAPTER TEN: CLARKE

Anise loved Anthony so wholly that it became unholy.

My love, please take me in your arms.

My darling, don't be gone too long today.

Lover, tell me a story. Make it grand.

They married in the little stone church in Paradise. Anthony wore his military uniform, looking sharp and sleek in his regalia. Anise wore a simple white dress with a crown of flowers, and her bouquet whispered its congratulations as she walked down the aisle.

The town came out, love, Anthony thought. *Perhaps there isn't as much animosity as you think?*

Anise tossed her hair back.

Of course they came. There's so little to do in town, who would miss this?

Anthony laughed, and it was like the ringing of bells. For perhaps the first time, the church felt hallowed.

After their vows and their kiss that was more than a kiss, he held her close while they danced.

"I will always love you," he whispered, and Anise snuggled close. Outside, the moon rolled her eyes.

Love is strong, but so are curses. Over the years as Anise held her groom, he transformed in her arms. The curse ran from her mouth to his, from her tongue down his throat and deep inside. His gentleness began to tatter like the skin of a lordly stag peeling from His bones.

"Where have you been?" Anise demanded, cradling her round stomach. "Were you at the pub again?"

"Stop harassing me," he slurred. "I need a bit of space."

"Why do you keep leaving?" she asked later, holding their now-toddler's tiny hand. "I only want to be with you and little Clarke!"

Anthony's features hardened, his former military haircut now unkempt and down to his chin.

"Why don't you leave me be? Why must you keep me all to yourself? Man isn't meant to live in such isolation."

The first time he laid his hands on her, striking her across the face so hard her entire world spun, he fell to his knees before she did.

"Oh, my love, my life," he whispered, and wiped the blood from her mouth before burying his face in his hands. Little Clarke didn't know who to run to first, her mother or her father. "What have I done? What have I done? I hear whispering in my head all the time. In the day, when I'm trying to work. At night, when I long to sleep. It tells me that you loathe me, you despise me, and when I argue saying it isn't true, it turns to convincing me that I loathe *you,* despise *you,* and sometimes I fear it is right!"

He stayed away that night, and for two nights thereafter. Where? Where was her Anthony? Was he in the town, in the forest, in the arms of another woman, or another man? She didn't know, she didn't know, and the not knowing was eating her up inside.

"Not now, Clarke," she said, when the little girl cried for food. Anise sat by the window, her face rumpled, and the lipstick worn from her mouth.

Clarke scurried through the door and out into the garden, where a fresh potato unearthed itself for her.

Your daddy is a devil now, it told her as she ate, and as she devoured its delicious flesh, Clarke nodded.

"DADDY?" CLARKE ASKED. Her mother lay motionless in the bed, her hand sprawled across the sheets like something beautiful. Her nails were broken, and blood glistened at her fingertips.

"Daddy?"

Daddy was a demon. He had the face he presented to the world, and then he had his Real Face, his New Face. She could see the devilish bones of his Real Face undulating under the human mask he wore. It rippled under his skin and sometimes peered out from his pupils. Clarke could read the story behind his brown eyes, and she didn't like it one bit.

"Daddy, Mama isn't moving."

Daddy wasn't moving either. His breath was laced with alcohol and his shirt was bloody. He looked like a fresh kill from the forest. He looked like a man who had come home from the war, but the war had found a home in him instead.

Clarke stood between them, her beautiful, red-laced Mama on the bed and her dashing father, so handsome in his brutality, so regal in his sins.

You're all alone now, the potted plant told her, rubbing its bud against her hand. *All alone in the big, wide world. Whatever are you going to do?*

Mama wore a necklace of rubies. They ran down her throat like ribbons, drenching her in crimson silk, and it was the most beautiful and most horrific thing Clarke had ever seen.

I'm free, Anise's blood sang as it danced along the edge of Daddy's knife. *I'm free of Paradise, free of the world.* But its voice was growing weak, and by the time Clarke took the shining knife in her tiny hands, her mother's blood had slowed.

It stopped.

Clarke held her mother's hand. It was chilled like porcelain, and just as pale.

Daddy, Clarke Sent, and for just a second, her father briefly stirred. *I saw everything. I saw it all. The way you looked at Mama; the way she looked at you. And it isn't your fault, I know that. Mama wasn't supposed to love you. She said it was all her fault. She told me not to love anyone, either.*

Tears come naturally to a small child. They come even quicker to a little girl who is without a mother and will soon be without a father. The moon told her so.

I always knew this would happen, the moon said, disgust fat and heavy in her voice. *I have known it since the beginning.*

Clarke kissed her mother's cold, cold hand and put it against her warm cheek.

"What am I going to do now?" she said aloud, and kicked her small feet back and forth, back and forth, like a child would. For that's exactly what she was: a little child, in a big world, and the weight of it crushed her brittle shoulders.

CHAPTER ELEVEN

Her daddy opened his eyes. For a second, they were the old eyes that she loved, clear and brown, soft and gentle. She had seen a dog with such gentle eyes once, and asked to take it home, but then its owner had come running and herded it back. Clarke had cried and cried that night, but both her mother and father had comforted her.

"Daddy," she said now, and Anthony turned to look at her. His little girl, his darling little angel! Oh, her luminous eyes! Oh, her dandelion-fluff hair!

He reached for her, and she threw her crimsoned arms around him. The knife glittered in the moonlight, and her pink nightgown with the ruffled hem was stained with blood.

Blood.

on the battlefield

Blood, on his child.

Blood

in the crevices, between his fingers, between his lips, between the pieces of his frayed soul.

Clarke pulled back, her cheek rosy and red from where she had rubbed it against her father's stubble.

"Daddy, Mama needs help." She pointed with the knife. "Her blood isn't singing to me anymore."

She looked at her father's face, saw the way it twisted up. She thought for a second that he would start crying from his strange New Face eyes, but they were rolling around in a scary way.

"Your mother," Anthony said. He pushed Clarke away and stood up. He crossed to the bed and peered at his wife.

You promised to love me forever, her blood said weakly. It trickled from the wound at Anise's alabaster throat. *Turns out forever isn't that long.*

The blood sighed and was still.

The house felt very empty. It held its breath.

Clarke felt the shift, felt the change. The energy in the house bucked, bent in on itself. She watched her father's face go blank, frightening, like an old doll without any personality at all. She felt the very moment her beloved Daddy stepped back, hiding his soul away somewhere safe, and the thing that owned the New Face filled his shell.

New Daddy flashed his eyes at her.

"What did you do?" he asked. His voice was dark, measured in a way that Clarke hadn't heard before, and she saw horrors in his eyes. Bombs and barbed wire and children covered in shrapnel. Rifling through the pockets of dead men and gnawing at their bones because it was so cold, the earth was frozen so hard, and he was so very hungry, hungry, hungry.

Clarke took a step back.

Her father stepped closer.

"I-I didn't do anything," she stuttered. Her voice, like her hands and her body, was small, so humiliatingly small! She wanted to be a giant. She wanted, no, she needed to be a bird with strong wings so she could fly high up in the sky and escape here, because she saw the crossbones in her New Daddy's eyes.

"You've slain your mother," New Daddy said. His face changed expression even while it seemed not to move. "My wife. My love."

"You did it, Daddy."

She heard a growl, a bark of pure madness, the sound of a hundred wolves howling and yelping at once, and New Daddy dropped to all fours. His bones lengthened. *Bones aren't supposed to bend that way,* Clarke thought.

"You killed her," New Daddy keened, and his face elongated into a snout. But only for a moment. Clarke blinked and saw her father standing upright, his face normal and kind again. Then the flash was gone, and he was a feral animal, glaring with devilish eyes through his sweaty hair.

Run, said the moon, and Clarke took another step back toward the door. She reached behind her and fumbled for the handle.

Run! the moon screeched, and Clarke whirled, pelting through the door, racing into the night with the knife still in her hand.

Her father screamed, and it was worse than anything she had

ever heard. Worse than the taunting of the village girls, worse than the burbling her mother's blood made as it clotted. Her father was gone, and New Daddy was in his place, and New Daddy was going to kill her.

She ran, feet flashing in the moonlight, her hair and ribbons streaming behind her. New Daddy ran from the house on his hands and feet, licking his chops with a tongue that was far too long to be real.

The wise tree by the door lifted its roots, tripping New Daddy, the Man-Who-Once-Was-Anthony, the Man-Who-Would-Never-Be-Anthony-Again. It yanked back its branches and let them fly, lacerating New Daddy's morphing face.

Run, shrieked the vines and thorny things. They threw themselves in New Daddy's path, winding and weaving themselves into a barricade that barely slowed the man-beast down.

The earth rose, creating hills and holes and crevices for New Daddy to fall into. The brook forced itself down his throat. Bees stung his face and birds pecked at his eyes.

He slowed, he slowed, but he would not be stopped. He fought thorn and briar like Sleeping Beauty's prince. He conquered earth and sky. The wind shrieked and stung his watering eyes, but he pressed on.

There was a war, you see, still going on inside his soul. The enemy had taken the thing most precious and was skittering away through the grass like a shadow. Anthony pursued, his eyesight sharpened and focused on the girl's red, red hands.

It's the blood of my love, he managed to think, but then the thoughts were swept away, crowded out with feeling and emotion and hate and hunger. The villain fled, and he followed behind, his nose to the air to catch her scent.

With no more air in her lungs, Clarke was forced to use Soul.

Daddy, Clarke Sent.

She screamed her father's name, but there was nobody to respond. Her father wasn't there, had ceased to be, no longer existed. There was only the monster who loped along on all fours, now staggering to his feet and running like a man, who seemed to swish through the grass like something made of demon and shadow.

Help, help, she called, and it was the voice of a very tiny girl, a pretty little thing with a few loose curls in her hair and a nose that turned up a bit too much. Children shouldn't have to flee the darkness, shouldn't be considered enemies of war. She kept her grip on the knife, ready to slash if he caught up with her—*of course he'd catch her, it's unavoidable, there's no way she could escape*—

but the thought of tearing his skin made her ill. The thought of his devilish blood burning along the blade with her mother's made her already twisted stomach turn even more.

Would his blood sing to me? she thought, and faltered.

No, whispered the moon, who wasn't used to being silent. She bent low to see more clearly.

Don't give up, urged the flowers, the grasses, the wind, the sky. *You're so close.*

Clarke recovered her footing and tried to speed up, but this misstep was all it took. She was nearly to the meadow, the glen that had always called to her, and it was here that her New Daddy caught her, and she fell.

CHAPTER TWELVE

ew Daddy grabbed Clarke by her hair, yanking her head back so hard her feet simply ran out from under her. She hit the ground with a sound that made the moon herself wince. It was the sound of bones breaking, of stars colliding, of universes wreaking havoc.

Clarke wanted to cry out but had no breath. She wanted to scream his name deep in her Soul, but her thoughts were too fragmented. She couldn't remember his name, didn't know what to call him, and so she simply wept.

She wept and held her knife like a precious, deadly doll. It was all she had left of her mother. Maybe it would protect her.

All this time she had heard pounding feet and trampled grass. She heard her own heavy breathing and Father-Not-Father's bestial cries. Now the meadow was oddly silent, strangely calm, and even her breath made no sound.

Clarke saw the stars above her. Fireflies lazed here and there, glowing without concern. She saw the flowers bending, their mouths moving as they called out to her desperately, but there was only silence.

How beautiful. How otherworldly.

If she was going to die, this was the way she wanted to go. Peacefully, in a beautiful place, with what remained of her mother close to her.

Please let me go like this, she prayed to whatever it was she prayed to, and she saw her murmured words ascend to the skies with the fireflies. The stars took her desires, spun them into fabric, and dressed themselves in their new finery.

How extraordinary.

How utterly lovely.

Her New Daddy's face came into her view, dark and sinister, his brows pulled down and his mouth pushed too high up in a toothy grin that wrapped all the way around his face. The warmth and coziness of the earlier moment evaporated, replaced with those black, soulless, wretched, wretched eyes.

Sound returned, crashing into her like an ocean wave, and it was full of roars and curses and screaming. She wanted to cover her ears with her hands to block it out, but her fingertips twitched uselessly, her body still unable to move.

Her father spoke to her without moving his lips. It wasn't Soul; it was something else, something darker that came from within, like a well spewing out black water. He pressed images into her mind.

Fire. Teeth. Running through the forest, chasing a little girl, only the little girl was dressed in ragged skins and wore the mask of her mother upon her face. He had to slay this creature, this corrupt fae of the forest, because she had stolen his wife.

His wife.

Clarke was bombarded with scenes of Anise, of her cocky smile, of her grabbing Anthony's arm with sure, strong fingers. She laughed, throwing her head back and showing her throat.

that throat, wears a smile of a different kind, now, the shadow voice sneered,

and it was pale and vulnerable and the lines of it made something in his young-man's heart lurch. Clarke saw her parents doing something with their bodies she didn't understand, but the image was saturated with love around the corners. She saw her mother on her hands and knees in the dirt, throwing up something long and creepy, her mascara running down her face, bathing it with that ethereal inner light. A wedding, her mother smirking at the crowd, her mother weeping quietly on the floor with her hands around her stomach, a baby covered in blood and mucus and kisses, her mother pushing Clarke behind her as Anthony raged after another night out drinking.

No, her father said, and the voice almost sounded like him again. *No.*

Her Daddy's memories pushed into Clarke's mind, so violently that she tried to crawl away.

Her mother's battered face, one eye swollen shut and the other looking at him balefully. It glowed with her eerie tears. Anthony studying his own hand, still balled into a fist, covered in blood and shimmering light. Anthony staggering into the town, into the houses of random, willing participants, and they did that body thing again except this time it didn't feel lovely and warm, but hateful and angry and coarse. Clarke gagged.

"No, I don't want you to see," her father said, and covered her eyes, but it didn't stop the onslaught. Rutting, that was the word. Violence as he left the town for a day or two to stalk, to frighten, to hold the knife to the faces of helpless women in front of their children as he took, and took, and took.

Call us, whispered the leaves on the ground. They fluttered, pushing against Clarke with all their might. She choked on the images of desecration, scrabbling against the earth feebly.

Use us, a yellow daisy said, drifting by on the wind. It tore itself apart—

she loves me, she loves me not

and a petal slipped between Clarke's teeth. She bit down reflexively and tasted the universe.

Green, growing things. Starlight. And love, so much love. She couldn't love a man like her mama had, because look where it had gotten her. But she could love the universe. Love the flowers and the wetness and the creatures in the soil. Love them like they loved her. And it was a love, no, it was a *love,* and this *love* was powerful and eternal.

She traded love for *love,* and that wasn't such a bad trade at all.

Her father sobbed, scratching at his eyes, leaving bloody furrows in his skin. Clarke turned her face to the sky and shouted, *I am the last of my line! I need your help!*

She took the knife in her hand and stabbed it deep into the earth. The soil licked her mother's blood from the blade and moaned.

Yes, the universe said.

That was all. Simply *yes.*

The earth roared. It opened its maw and bellowed. Rocks and bones, fossils and things long dead scrambled to the surface. They fell on Anthony, ripping at his skin and dragging him down.

Help! Clarke shouted again.

The fireflies gathered, a ball of iridescent, glimmering light. It came to her as one, lifting her gently to her feet, setting her upright. They settled in her hair and her clothing, licked her scratches and nestled into her ears. They landed on her cheeks, and for the first time, her tears held their own glowing light just like her mother's.

Help! she called, and the zephyr hardened, sharpened, became a thing of fury and fangs. It was a freezing gale, slicing at her father with silvered claws, biting at the soft parts of his body with needled teeth. He yelled something, but his voice was carried away in it. It blew his hair over his eyes and down his throat, choking him as he cried. It mixed with the rain and became a hurricane, tossing him to and fro. Creatures of the deep emerged from the water, attacking with poisoned barbs and tentacles.

Turn away, child, the moon said, but Clarke couldn't. She was stuck fast, caught in the awe of the elements' power, heaving with guilt at what she had summoned, what she had done, how she had condemned her father for murdering her mother, but she was doing the same thing.

Human life means little, the moon said, and then she floated somewhere else in the sky. Her interest in this particular entertainment was done.

The power. The enormity. Clarke's hair blew back, her child's eyes wide, her pupils reflected horror and carnage and misery. It was her own war. This was her own battlefield.

Daddy, she thought, and the sheer guilty weight of the thought pushed down and settled like a blanket on the glen.

Oh, said the hurricane, and its cyclical winds slowed in shame.

Mm, said the earth, and it noticed the shell-shocked expression on Clarke's face, the way her eyes and soul seemed to have gone someplace else. It withdrew its teeth from Anthony's throat.

The vines and thorns pulled away, leaving his ravaged skin. It was torn and full of holes. Muscle shone through in some places; others revealed bone.

It's not his fault, Clarke thought. A firefly floated over and illuminated her father's handsome face.

It's not your fault, Daddy, she told him, and he looked up with gentle, brown eyes so full of sorrow that Clarke rubbed her eyes with the balls of her fists and wept.

Her father reached for her, looked at his bloodied hand, and let it drop to his side.

He bowed his head low, his hair a dark tangle in front of his face. Clarke had never seen anything so utterly forlorn and broken before.

I'm sorry, he told her, and the words held weight.

"C-can you come back home?" she said, her breath hitching. "Can you still be my daddy?"

Her father raised his head, and for a second the wolfish features flashed underneath his normal face.

"I can't," he said, and there were traces of the New Voice, the dark thing that nibbled the edges of his words, but he mostly sounded like himself. "There's something… else… inside me now, and I'm afraid…"

I can't keep you safe, Clarke heard.

I'll put you in danger.

I'll rip your pretty little head off your body and drink your blood. Tear your limbs off and put you back together wrong, nice and clean, so we can play and play and play and—

Clarke shuddered, and her father nodded.

"I'm just afraid," he finished.

The breeze pushed into Clarke's hand like a warm puppy.

"Who will take care of me?" Clarke asked her father. "I'm awfully small."

Her father looked off into the distance.

"Somebody in the village. Tell them what I did. Tell them I attacked you and ran away. Somebody will take pity."

"But I hate everyone in Paradise."

"You cannot leave," he told her. "Maybe for a visit, but your intentions must always be to return." He met her eyes. "Paradise is your home, little one. You will live here, and you will die here."

Clarke wanted to say more. She wanted to run to him, to sit on his knee, to wrap her arms around him and demand that he love her forever. Her daddy must have heard her think it, because his smile was bitter.

Turns out forever isn't that long, he said.

He turned away and staggered painfully through the meadow. Her heart cried out, but she managed to stifle it.

Something shimmered in the distance. There was a pressure in the air, a sudden weight, and a grand stag stepped out of the forest. He was ghostly, translucent, and muscle and skin hung from His body like a torn flag. He wore a majestic crown of softly glowing antlers. His bare skull grinned at her father, but He radiated a calmness that made Clarke briefly close her eyes.

Her father looked at the stag for a long time, and then gingerly put his ruined arm over the creature's back. He leaned against Him heavily. They took careful steps together.

The hind spoke, and His voice was as tranquil as still water. *Come*, He said. *Anthony, come.*

CHAPTER THIRTEEN: ITALIA

Clarke lived in the little one-roomed house on the outskirts of Paradise.

I will be the death of you one day, promised the tree by her door. It basked in the sun.

Clarke tossed her long wheat-colored braid over her shoulder. "Sure, why not?" she said. "We all have to die sometime."

She kissed the tiny bundle in her arms.

My sweet baby, she whispered. *My darling one. My sweet little girl.*

MICHAEL BURKE

Michael Burke is a lifelong fan of fantasy, science fiction, and horror, propelled into these realms at a tender age when he discovered his father's cache of pulp novels. A passion for comic books soon followed. In 2000, Michael co-founded the Eisner-award-winning comic and collectible store, Comicazi, in Somerville, MA.

When not sorting the comic stacks at work, Michael can be found at home, releasing the hobgoblins of his mind into story form. He has had several short stories published both online and in print, including *The Horror Zine*, *Monster Fight at the O.K. Corrall*, and the '80s-themed anthology, *Totally Tubular Terrors*. He also has a weird western novella, *Last Sunset of a Dying Age*, in Crystal Lake's Dark Tide series, and a small sword and sorcery collection, *Fragments of a Greater Darkness*, from Tule Fog Press.

Michael is a member of the New England Horror Writers' Association and lives outside of Boston, MA in a house with more books than he can possibly read, which doesn't stop him from acquiring more. He continues writing every chance he gets. He lives with his beautiful and patient wife. His inner 11-year-old thinks middle age isn't all that bad.

Vengeful Spirits

Smoke curled in the sky, a charcoal ribbon fading to light gray as it drifted ever higher, eventually dissipating into the blue vault. Sunlight glinted off hundreds of panes of glass like a celestial necklace beneath the impermanence of the hazy stain, which briefly marred the view above. The Victorian elegance of the massive Arcade Building drew many eyes from the bustling streets below.

A sour odor permeated the air in the narrow alley, where the tall man in the drab blue sack suit wrinkled his nose. All manner of pungent smells lingered in the alleyways of large metropolises. He withdrew his gaze from the magnificent building, glimpsed above the confines of the alley, and continued ahead.

The tall man knew the odor to be fermenting alcohol; he

walked confidently down the passageway, his leather Oxfords clacking smartly on the dimpled asphalt, as he considered the current state of things. A foraging dog looked up at him as he passed. The man clucked to himself and patted his valise absent-mindedly. Perhaps there was something in his Book to mask the scent that so assaulted his nostrils. He sniffed as the scent only intensified the farther down the alley he trod. Yes, he would make that research a priority when he reached his destination.

It might also be wise to contact one of his associates once settled. Indeed, the manufacture and the sale of spirits were presently illegal, but as he well knew in his current custodianship, this focal point in humankind's history was a necessary one.

America, Finland, the Russian Empire—and others—had banned alcohol consumption. The views of those who walked the corridors of power had put a stranglehold on the people. Yet, many rebellious souls contended against the current regime. Here in Cleveland, as in many hidey-holes across the United States, elaborate operations were in place, engaged in combatting the present constraints.

It was a good fight to be waged, despite what would follow. The man knew this—what would soon come. For he was privy to the guidelines of society's progress as well as its promise of greatness—and its potential for self-destruction.

The Books told him and his brethren all. He was proud to share in such knowledge and to be counted among such a prestigious institution as the Unknown. And to be the bearer of his singular responsibility.

The man pushed down his *esprit de corps*, as he termed it, and concentrated instead on contacting one of his associates. They could have been anywhere in the world. All he knew for certain was that no Unknown were currently in Cleveland, for none of the Nine were to occupy the same space at the same time. The danger was too great.

He stopped at the end of the alley, wrinkling his nose once again. His hand darted in his pocket and came back with a key. Shadows bunched in corners this far down the passageway, but patches of sunlight still gleamed amid the scattered debris. The man could still glimpse the marvelous architecture of the Arcade from his position. He nodded in appreciation of the structure, then cast his wary eyes around the dirty alleyway. *Empty.*

He inserted the key into the well-oiled lock, entered swiftly, and closed the door. He failed to observe the pair of narrowed weasel-eyes that tracked his path. The click of the lock on the other side lasted for a second in the sour air.

SAM NEARLY TOPPLED a pile of dirty cardboard boxes, ducking out of sight when the stranger turned to scan his surroundings. That would have ruined things. But he had managed to compose himself and remain silently hidden.

The well-dressed man often made his way down here. What business did someone as well-to-do as this guy have at the end of an alley? It made Sam wonder. The back doorway of the building he'd entered was only a block away from Mr. Dalitz's setup. *Too close.*

It was usually pretty quiet around here. Too quiet, in fact, especially for Sam, who was becoming a little tired of the place and craving more excitement. Sam, a squirrely little chap, had first noticed the tall man a couple weeks ago. He had thought nothing of him, but he seemed to have set up shop. And he wasn't part of Mr. Dalitz's organization, as far as he knew.

The guy had to be a fed. Sam would find out. And he'd take care of matters. Then Mr. Dalitz would have no choice but to integrate Sam into the Mayfield Road Gang.

The eager, nervous little man scurried to the doorway. He fumbled in his worn, corduroy hip-level Coatee jacket for several seconds, eventually pulling from a flap pocket a small lock-picking kit. Sam quickly inspected the contents and selected a tooled steel pick.

After nearly two minutes, Sam abandoned his first selection and tried a different pick. Perspiration beaded on his upper lip. "Shit! Too long." He was a much better lockpicker than this! Mr. Dalitz would never have him if he performed this poorly. Determined, Sam renewed his efforts, and after another twenty seconds, he quietly sprung the lock. Taking one last scan of the alley to check nobody was watching, he ducked through and pulled the door shut quietly behind him.

He stood there for a moment, letting his eyes adjust. Sam was getting the sense he was standing in a wide corridor. Hulking figures loomed on either side of the room, running the length of the chamber. As his vision adapted to the low light, he could see that the figures were statues. Mostly of people. Some were holding everyday items, but others were accompanied by things he did not recognize but which seemed to be some form of tool. As he peered closer, he saw the stone figures represented a number of ethnicities: Chinese, African, Mexican. Some of the clothing looked weird, old-timey and outdated. He didn't know much about art, but he could appreciate the fine details of the clothing and items the figures were holding. And every one of the statues was near lifelike. Sure, he had seen statues before, but he could not recall ever seeing such detail, especially when it came to the faces.

Until now, he hadn't had cause to venture inside, but now, here he was, in the dark, his mind racing with a multitude of questions. Why would this fed have so many statues of so many different people? What was this building? Sam didn't really have any answers. He only knew he needed to get more information, and the only way to do that was to go deeper into this place.

He shuddered as he passed between the statues. Though he knew they couldn't see, Sam still felt the pressure of an unseen gaze. The things gave him the creeps.

CANDLES FLICKERED IN the overstuffed library, casting writhing shadows across the shelves so that the lettering seemed to crawl across the spines of the books. Sulphur hung heavily in the enclosed space.

Truth to tell, there was electricity in the building and lamps aplenty throughout the room, but the tall man preferred the candlelight—especially here, in the library, and whenever he wished to contact one of his fellows. It somehow made him feel more attuned to his secret brothers and sisters and the responsibility they all shared. As for him, he was merely the latest caretaker of this knowledge in a long lineage. He did not regret having taken up this mantle and sacrificing all for it: family, romance, wealth. There was no way to put a value on the riches he safeguarded. His family were his fellows in this monumental task, although he had limited contact with them. Despite that fact, his heart was full.

The man removed a massive tome from his nearby valise and clutched the black-bound book to his chest, folding his lanky legs beneath him to sit cross-legged on the floor, the creak of settling timbers and the sizzle of burning wicks the only sounds. The room itself seemed to be holding its breath. The man did not move but sat there on the floor as though he were in a trance.

Sam watched from the shadows. The fine hairs on his arms and neck stood on end. It was like static electricity in the air before one of the thunderstorms that rolled in off Lake Erie: everything was still.

If he was going to find out anything for Mr. Dalitz, now was his chance, while this mook was in a trance or whatever. Nervously, Sam stole from behind the bookcase where he was hiding and crept forward on silent rodent feet, drawing his leather-weighted sap from inside his Coatee.

The man didn't seem to notice him.

A great, black-bound book lay in the man's lap; he had both palms flat on the cover and was resting his chin on his chest.

Sam chanced a look around, hoping this guy's trance was a

deep one. More books were piled on the tables around the room, but none of them were as impressive as the one he was holding. Crumbling papers jutted from metal tubes. These things—and the strange vessels and rods also atop a table—made Sam doubt this guy was a fed. Where were the guns? What about a radio setup to contact his FBI buddies? Perhaps he was some kind of loon, but either way, rat or nut job, Sam figured the safest thing to do was to take him out. Besides, this place gave him the heebie-jeebies.

Sam raised the black sap and hesitated. The air had changed somehow, as if a storm had finally arrived. He thought he could hear a voice far away, echoing in his head.

The mark didn't move.

Sam had to get out of this strange place: he was spooked, and he didn't know why. Shaking, he brought his blunt instrument down across the back of the guy's head, hitting him again as he fell forward.

Having little use for books himself, Sam couldn't really explain why he'd decided to take the big, black-bound volume from beneath the man lying still on the floor. His only interest was in becoming a made man in the Mayfield Road Gang. But take it he did. *Maybe Mr. Dalitz will know what to make of it.*

Sam slipped out as quickly and as silently as he could.

In the wake of his departure, the candle flames fluttered like angry serpents, the shimmering orange light casting a glow on the blood pooling around the body on the floor.

THE ROAR OF the engine rumbled through the darkness. Night birds took flight as the big, shadowy speedboat, *Nectar of the Gods*, lanced over the placid waters of Lake Erie toward the shore.

Mary Santos waited amid the reeds at the run-down dock. The place had been shut down and neglected, due to Cleveland's growing economic concentration on machine tools and industrial equipment. Which made it the perfect locale for her to conduct her illicit activities.

She pushed her shoulder-length dark hair from her face and narrowed her keen brown eyes. The waters of the bow wave before the fast-approaching craft flattened so it appeared as if the boat was riding on the water instead of cutting through it. As the child of a fisherman who came from a long line of those who worked the waters, as well as being a student of boats, she certainly appreciated the hull configuration of the *Nectar*, its vee-bottomed hard chined characteristic. Any edge that could be gained in this line of work was crucial; it was always best to stay one step ahead.

The timbre of the engine changed, and the boat slowed, coasting to a halt beside the rotted wooden berth standing sentinel against the tide. Mary shook her head free of her musings. "Richard. Incoming. Get the boys ready."

"Yes, boss," came the deep-throated reply from a large shadow farther back.

Trusting her man to handle matters, Mary stepped from out of the reeds onto the narrow stretch of sandy beach.

"Where's Moe?" came a gruff voice from the deck of the

powerboat.

Mary ignored the curt question, instead climbing expertly aboard the deck of the *Nectar*. She cast her gaze about the deck. After a moment, she said, "Is it all here?"

"Listen, doll," the heavy-set, cruel-eyed captain said, "I don't answer to dames. Especially ones that try to pass themselves off like men. What's with the pants? And who the hell are you?"

Mary sighed. This wasn't the first time she had had to deal with this. But she certainly knew how to handle it. "I'm Mary. And I oversee all operations here on the lake. You must be new. You can take what I have to say as Mr. Dalitz's word."

The captain's expression hardened.

"Now," Mary continued, undeterred by the stocky man's demeanor, "The *Nectar* is an eighty-foot boat. I'm expecting you have quite the cargo to unload to my men ashore. Let's get this done quickly before the cops show up."

Mild shock showed on some of the crew's faces. "We, uh, had some hassles on the Canadian side. We're a little short."

Mary stepped up to the captain. She was a couple of inches taller but gave up much in the way of weight. She didn't care for the smirk on this *desgraçado's* face. He needed to be taught a lesson.

"I expect to pay for the agreed shipment. It's your job to deal with any hassles on the other side."

"I'll make good on the next run," the captain said.

Mary glowered. "I think you're looking to skim a little and make something extra on the side. Maybe with one of Mr. Dalitz's competitors?"

She noticed the man's Adam's apple become pronounced.

"I saw how the *Nectar* was riding as she came in. You're not short. You have a full hold."

The captain backed up a step, suddenly nervous. Mary stepped closer, holding his gaze and maintaining the same distance.

One of the crew moved to intervene. "We don't take orders from mouthy bitches."

Mary launched a rabbit punch directly into the captain's face. She felt the crunch of his pug nose beneath her knuckles and he collapsed in a heap, wiping away the blood and tears with the back of his hand. Mary towered over him. "You don't want to piss me off, or Mr. Dalitz will be the least of your worries."

The crew stood aghast, then gradually began offloading their cargo to Richard, who directed the crates into a pair of trucks. The captain clambered to his feet, embarrassment and anger warring in his eyes.

Mary deboarded the *Nectar of the Gods* as Richard oversaw the unloading operation.

"I'll wear goddamned pants if I want."

A COPPERY TANG tainted the air, causing a metallic taste in the back of the throat. The young woman knew what that meant, what she was bound to face when entering the room.

With the dust motes dancing in the sun rays stabbing forth from the window, the whole room resembled a grainy old photograph. She carefully inspected the outer rooms, making sure no one else was present, checking that nothing looked out of place. True, she had not been here before, but all the Unknown had certain items and tools pertaining to their singular responsibilities only their brethren could discern if the matter warranted it. Besides, she wished to stave off confirming the inevitable.

Seven was gone.

His mental communication had been prematurely halted. It was possible things weren't as dire as she feared, but the Unknown could ill afford not to investigate. She was closest, and it had still taken her a day to get here. The woman made a mental note to speak to either Eight or Three about improving their methods of transportation. One of them would surely have an answer.

Enough delay.

She steeled herself before entering the library. It was gloomy. The candles Seven had so abundantly collected lay fallow. She groped along the wall and found a brass plate; as she flicked a porcelain switch, a nearby lamp sprung to life. The stench of putrefaction was already evident but seemed to grow stronger with the advent of the light, as if it were finally illuminating the fate that waited for all.

Number Four shook her head, dispelling the thought, only to behold a grimmer reality. Her brother lay in a widespread pool of blackish blood, the back of his skull caved in. She catalogued the scene while she wrestled with the horror of it all, her mind racing with the chemical equations of decomposition and exactly how long ago Seven had perished.

Then, she noticed. *The Book is missing!* The Books were never far from their keepers. If Seven's was missing, then it must have been stolen.

Four systematically searched the library, pawing through the voluminous books stacked on tables and shelved on racks for the black-bound tome. A similar volume to the one she carried in her bag. She felt her stomach fall away. That waiting fate, which she had earlier dismissed, now loomed ever closer.

"I'M HERE TO see Mr. Dalitz."

Sam flinched when the big mug silently and efficiently patted him down. The other guy simply stared hard at him. These guys knew him. Why were they giving him the business? Yeah, he'd never been to Moe's office before, but he'd had dealings with him these past nine months. Well… not actually face-to-face, but Mr. Dalitz knew his name. He'd certainly know his name when Sam revealed his news, that's for sure.

"What's with the book?"

"It's for Mr. Dalitz."

The burly guard tilted his head. It seemed to Sam the guy was considering his claim.

"I'm going to need to take a look at it."

"Come on," Sam whined. "You guys know me. I'm bringing Mr. Dalitz a gift. There's good stuff in here."

"That book is big enough to hide a small piece in a fake page or something," the guard said. His companion twitched his hand to his chest.

"Hey, g-guys, it's n-nothing like that," Sam stammered. "I just keep an eye on things around the Arcade for Mr. Dalitz. This is something I think he might be interested in."

"We know who you are, stoolie." The guard sneered. The other man lowered his hand.

Sam begrudgingly handed the book to the big man. He watched as the guard skimmed through the pages with meaty fingers, seeking the supposed weapon he had accused Sam of hiding. At one point, he upended the book and shook it, hoping to dislodge something.

Sam winced. He didn't read much, but he found this guy's treatment of the book offensive. He watched the guy scrunch his face in bewilderment as he scanned the words on random pages.

His inspection done, he nodded at his companion. "Follow me, rat."

Sam fell in step behind the guard as he was led through a heavy wooden door into a small outer office. File cabinets lined one wall; a framed picture of what looked to be the Boston city skyline was on the opposing wall. Sam thought Mr. Dalitz was from the East Coast but he wasn't positive. He glanced at the picture again. All he knew was that it certainly wasn't Cleveland.

An unoccupied desk with a phone sat in front of another door. The guard picked up the phone and muttered something Sam couldn't hear, then replaced the receiver. When he did, the door behind the desk swung open with a low, electric buzz.

The burly guard put a paw on Sam's shoulder and propelled him through the doorway.

"Thanks, George," a nasally voice said.

That's *this big mook's name? He doesn't seem like a George,* Sam thought even as he regarded the well-dressed man sitting behind yet another desk at the end of the room.

"The guy said this is for you, Mr. Dalitz." George stepped forward and laid the black-bound book on the edge of Moe's desk. It was an odd book, like no other book he had seen in his life. The black leather seemed to absorb all light, a yawning square of darkness.

"That'll be all, George."

A furrow wrinkled George's brow. "Are you sure, sir?"

"I'll be fine." Moe smiled.

George nodded and exited the office.

"Have a seat, Mr. Norton." Moe indicated a straight-backed leather chair in front of his desk.

Sam said, "You know who I am?"

"I make it a point to know everyone who works for me. Now, please, take a seat."

Sam hurried to the proffered chair and sat down. He took a moment to luxuriate in the plushness of the leather. *I can't believe I'm in a meeting with Moe Dalitz. I knew good things would come to me if I kept my nose to the ground.*

Moe steepled his fingers beneath his chin and gazed hard at Sam. "Now what do you have to tell me about this book, here?"

"Well, Mr. Dalitz," Sam began. He took a deep breath, still amazed at where he was. "As you probably know, I keep an eye out for any suspicious activity in the Downtown Flats Warehouse District. You know, cops, feds, anyone snooping around your gang operations."

Moe blinked once.

"Well, I know you have a speakeasy in The Arcade. And a gin still in one of the nearby warehouses. I figured that was a likely spot for any heat to come down on you, so I've been watching." Sam was nervous, but as he continued, and Mr. Dalitz quietly listened, he felt emboldened to finish his story.

"So, I noticed this tall, well-dressed guy hanging around a lot. Guy had to be over six feet, lean, white guy. Always in a suit. Hung around mostly in the next alley over from your warehouse. Every day. Sometimes several times in one day. In and out through some locked door. Struck me as weird, right?" He looked for affirmation to his question, but Moe simply waited for Sam to continue.

"So, I followed this guy down the alley and watched him go in his place. I made him for a fed, and he had some setup in that building near your place, so I picked the lock and slipped in. I knew you'd need solid info on what this guy was about before I came to you.

"All's this guy had was some big library in there. No radio, nothing that tipped me off to him being a fed or being any danger to you and your gang, Mr. Dalitz. When I came up behind him, he was sitting with this book in his lap in some kind of trance. I clubbed him over the head and took the book. I figured it must be important and I wanted you to have it. You'd probably know what to do with it."

Moe leaned back in his chair and uncrossed his fingers. He stared at Sam a moment before speaking.

"I appreciate your interest in my security, Mr. Norton."

"I knew you would, Mr. Dalitz—"

"Don't interrupt me," Moe growled.

Sam shrunk back in his chair.

"What I do not appreciate is undue attention being brought to my doorstep. I work very hard to maintain a balance in this city, and foolish actions such as yours disrupt that delicate balance."

"What?" Sam leaned forward. "But, Mr. Dalitz…"

"You killed that gentleman, Mr. Norton. That area is now a crime scene. The police currently swarm over that alley and the surrounding area."

Sam rose to his feet. "No way! I couldn't have!"

"You most certainly did," Moe said, pulling open a drawer and withdrawing a sinister black Colt M1911 pistol. "Fortunately, the balance I maintain will divert attentions from my warehouse, but this is an unforgivable offense on your part, Mr. Norton. I'm afraid there is no place for you in my 'gang,' as you so distastefully put it."

Smoke and fire belched forth from the barrel of the handgun and Sam's chest sprouted a crimson hole. Scarlet leaked from his heart and he fell back, sliding off the edge of the leather seat. Sam breathed in ragged gasps, and he could not tell if it was the pain of his swiftly ebbing life or the shock of not having realized his dream of becoming a made man in the Mayfield Road Gang. The last thing he heard was the office door being thrown open.

George and his companion stood in the doorway, guns drawn, staring down at the corpse of Sam Norton.

"Everything's fine, boys," Moe said, placing the Colt on his desk. "One of you get a cleaning crew in here and supervise the disposal of Mr. Norton."

"Yessir," George said. He and his partner left the office.

Moe Dalitz regarded the black book on his desk for several minutes before finally reaching for it. He could not deny feeling a strange thrill on opening the cover and seeing what lay within. His mind swirled with possibilities.

"I WISH YOU wouldn't take such chances. These types of guys can be real bastards. Especially to a woman."

"I can handle myself just fine, *meu querido*," Mary said as she shifted the baby on her hip. "Get me the formula for little Felix here," she said, indicating a full bottle on the kitchen counter.

Alfred disentangled himself from baby Sarah on his lap and rose to his feet. He made his way into the kitchen and retrieved the bottle. "Still," he said, and handed it to Mary.

"Still nothing. Guys like that speedboat captain are all talk. Besides, I had my crew with me if things had gone south."

"Yeah, but I don't have to like you going out there and doing this kind of work. You should be—"

"I should be *what*?" snarled Mary, with a sudden heat in her tone. Felix started to wail. "Home? Taking care of the babies because that's a woman's job? The hell with that! Besides, you don't complain about this nice house, the car, and the money that my work brings in. I do this job because I can, and I'm good at it."

"I've heard this before," Alfred said. "It's 1923, hon. This state of things can't last for much longer. Then what? I'm only concerned for the future. Your job is illegal and can be danger-ous. If even the *least* bad thing that happens to you is getting arrested, where does that leave Felix and Sarah?"

Mary looked at the bawling baby in her arms, then to the living room and her wide-eyed daughter; the little girl seemed scared and did not understand why her parents' voices were raised. Mary wasn't sure she had an answer for her husband, but one thing she was sure of was that Moe Dalitz rewarded loyalty and hard work. And she had done good work for the Mayfield Road organization.

The jangle of the telephone cut through the pregnant silence. Mary moved to the candlestick-design contraption and picked up the mouthpiece. "Hello?"

After a few moments of intent listening, she returned the unit to the receiver. She gently placed Felix in his crib and gathered her things. "I have to go."

"Another errand for Moe?"

"Yes." Mary sighed. "I need to check on something. I shouldn't be too long."

"Well, be careful."

Mary pecked her husband on the cheek. "Back before you know it."

THE FOURTH PRECINCT station house occupied a lot on the corner of Wilson and Perkins Streets. The large Norman-style stone building, complete with a towering steeple at one end, was a bustle of activity. Cops came and went, many with cuffed perps in tow. Squad cars peeled out in clouds of burnt rubber and dust while others pulled in, disgorging more officers.

Prohibition's unforeseen drawback was the number of arrests. The existing jail system was insufficient to hold the number of offenders to the law. Thus, the prisons filled up quickly and makeshift holding cells had had to be fashioned swiftly, and cases were rushed to an already strained court system. Perps found guilty of bootlegging alcohol or running illegal speakeasies—hell, even entering or being found in one of the establishments after a raid—were processed into the burgeoning legal system. Then, to relieve the crowded local jails, officials shipped criminals elsewhere, sometimes even out of state, for lack of accommodations. This was an incredible strain on resources at the municipal level.

Organized crime prospered, and things slipped through the cracks. On both sides of the law.

Mary climbed the steps to the station house, making way for the two officers roughly manhandling a handcuffed young man through the double doors. She turned and watched as the cops dragged the stumbling youth to a waiting squad car.

Chuckling softly, she returned her gaze to the entrance. She pushed her way through and took a moment to get her bearings. She had been to the Fourth only once before, and that was nearly seven months ago. She had been running a similar errand for Mr. Dalitz then, too, but this time, she was to meet with someone else.

"You've been in one cop shop, you've been in them all," Mary said to herself. She adjusted the high collar of her black leather jacket and turned left. Judging by the racket coming from around the corner, the admittance desk had to be over there.

"Mrs. Santos?" A hand gripped her arm suddenly.

Mary cursed out loud at herself for being taken off-guard and shook herself free.

"What was that?" asked a squat man in a brown suit. He had a patchy beard and a flattened nose.

Mary swiftly regained her composure. "It was Portuguese. You startled me, that's all. Bates?"

The man nodded. "Detective Jack Bates."

"I understand there was a murder in the Warehouse Flats and that someone was brought in." Mary checked around to see if anyone was listening in, then decided that would have been impossible, given the noise of the place.

"We had a person of interest, found at the scene. Well, outside the scene, in the alley."

"Were they running?"

"No," the cop said. "They looked worried when the blues arrived, but honestly, I find people of that… *persuasion* always look worried around cops."

"I'm not here for your backward insights." Mary's mouth formed a tight line.

"And I'm not here to take lip from some dame, in *my* precinct house."

Mary locked eyes with Bates. "You're here to look out for Mr. Dalitz's interests. I believe you're paid very well for your discretion."

The fireplug squirmed beneath Mary's stony gaze. He tried passing it off to his ill-fitting suit, smoothing his sleeve, and eventually breaking eye contact. "Mr. Dalitz has nothing to worry about. I arrived on scene after the blues and redirected traffic away from his establishment. Any paperwork pertaining to this will also be handled the usual way."

"Good." Mary nodded. "What about the person you brought in? Where are they?"

"She cooperated fully with us, and she'd done nothing other than being in the wrong place at the wrong time, so there was nothing we could hold her on. Said she was some kind of scientist, too, if you can believe that shit. Didn't really make her for the murder, and with the cells here full up, we had to let her go. I told her myself that she was still a person of interest, so she was not to leave town anytime soon."

Mary nodded, digesting the information.

"We good?"

Mary looked up, focusing once more on the unpleasant man before her. "Yeah. I'll let Mr. Dalitz know." She turned and made her way to the exit.

Bates leered at her retreating form, then disappeared into the bustle of the station house.

THE TRIM, FORTYSOMETHING man pulled the silken black hood from his face. He leaned over the desk, enrapt at the pages before him. He gazed intently at each page for several minutes before moving on to the next.

Finally, he looked up. "How did you come by this again, Moe?"

Moe Dalitz tensed his shoulders as he stared across his desk. He was only a little perturbed by the directness and familiarity of the man in his office. Most everyone addressed him with respect and not without a touch of fear, for he was an important man. A powerful man. Wise, too, for all that.

Moe had spent the better part of the night and the morning leafing through the black-bound book. It was fascinating stuff, even if he did understand only a portion of what was written therein. What Moe did understand, however, was that the information—the knowledge—now in his possession would help grow his burgeoning empire. He could even rival Capone. Or surpass him. And what a feat that would be.

But he knew enough to realize that he needed help.

"Well, Eddie, it was brought to me."

"Bishop Kane, if you would, please," Eddie said, his voice as smooth as reptile scales.

Moe rankled at the admonition. *Who the hell does he think he is? He works for me.* Moe breathed in through his nose, calming himself. His leg shook with unrealized adrenaline, though, and he placed his hand upon his knee as casually as he could, as if he were merely shifting position in his chair.

"I assume the bringer of this gift has been… rewarded?" Eddie asked.

Moe raised an eyebrow.

"Of course," Eddie answered, with a flash of his too-white teeth.

Moe leaned forward, placing his elbows on the desk. "What I've gathered from this book is that I can revolutionize bootlegging operations. I can cut way down on operating costs, increasing my margins. But a lot of what I see here reads like mystic hocus pocus. Which is where you come in."

Eddie straightened, finally tearing his eyes from the book. He got up and meandered around the office, tracing his finger along the crown moldings, gathering his thoughts, processing what he had seen. "I don't know the origins of this book, but it would seem to deal a lot with alchemy. At least, according to this initial observation."

"Isn't that the whole turning-metal-to-gold thing?" Moe asked.

"That is the layman's definition of the science, yes." Moe simmered.

"Alchemy was an ancient art, believed by some to be sorcery, magic. It is merely unexplained science, wherein the alchemist changes the physical properties of matter. Although I do confess my ignorance as to the exact catalyst the alchemist would use to transform matter. I might be able to gather more information for you if I could study the book further?"

Moe sat back in his chair, a smile playing across his full lips. "I don't think that's necessary. We can work on it together."

"I only seek to advise you as you wish, Moe. You're a busy man and I would certainly be glad to assist you in this matter without taking up your valuable time."

"I appreciate that, but it is best the book remains with me. I can create a list of questions for you when we next get together to discuss the book."

An impasse of wills had been reached. Both men plastered fake grins on their grim features and held each other's stare.

The phone on Moe's desk rang. The pair stared for another ten seconds until Eddie blinked. Moe picked up the receiver. "Yeah? Show her in. And what'd I tell you about that kind of talk?"

The far door opened as Moe hung up, and George ushered Mary in. His face was flushed. He looked over to Moe and swiftly departed after an indication from his boss.

"Mary, a pleasure." Moe stood up. "George looked a bit flush. Was that only from my reprimand, or did you also have something to contribute to his discomfiture?"

"I don't rightly take to being called a tomato. So, I let him know that tomatoes can be acidic as well as sweet. Sir."

Moe laughed from the belly. "What I could do if I had ten like you!"

Mary smiled. "Am I interrupting, Mr. Dalitz?" Her eyes flicked to the black-robed man standing beside Moe's desk.

"We were just wrapping up. This is Eddie. He's my… astrologer. Eddie, this is Mary Santos."

Eddie stepped forward, his hand slipping forth from a voluminous sleeve like a serpent striking from a hole. "Bishop Kane. Pleased to meet you."

Mary took his hand. It was sweaty and unpleasant. She caught how he stiffened at being addressed by his first name. She hadn't pegged Mr. Dalitz for being into the occult but secret societies were all the rage in places like New York and Hollywood. She had heard that movie stars like Douglas Fairbanks and Clara

Bow were members of cults. Hell, she wouldn't have been surprised if Charlie Chaplin ran one. Why not a Cleveland bootlegger like Mr. Dalitz?

Whatever Bishop Kane purported to be into, Mary suspected that it was more than simple astrology. Whatever. She didn't care for the man. Mr. Dalitz's business with him was none of her own, as long as it didn't impact her livelihood.

She released Eddie's hand.

"I'll be in touch shortly, Moe."

Mr. Dalitz's jaw tightened as he gritted his teeth and cast a lingering look at the heavy, black-bound book on his desk.

Moe swiftly closed the book when he noticed Mary's attention upon it. "Now, what do you have for me?" He forced a genial tone.

"Your guy inside has assured me that he's taken care of the crime scene. No one will disturb your warehouse. And he will take care of the paperwork."

"That's good."

Mary cleared her throat. "There's something else, sir. They arrested a woman on-scene but released her. It looks to be a case of her being unlucky and in the wrong place."

"Okay."

"I'm told she's some kind of scientist."

A momentary flash of concern darkened Moe's features, but it vanished just as swiftly. "She was told not to leave town while the murder investigation is ongoing."

"Okay, okay. Good. Stay on that, would you, Mary? On top of your regular duties, of course."

"Of course, sir."

"That'll be all." Moe stabbed a finger at something on his desk. Immediately, the office door opened to reveal George waiting in the doorway. Mary walked forward, a sneer curling her lip as she approached the big guard. George avoided her glare.

Moe slumped into his chair once the door had closed. A scientist? That seemed too much of a coincidence, especially considering what Eddie had told him. That woman scientist—or whatever she was—had to have been here about the book. He reached for the heavy tome and pored over the pages.

MARY'S MIND TUMBLED with thoughts. She made her way down the busy sidewalk, letting the sun warm her face. The faint hint of a breeze off Lake Erie stopped her from getting too hot.

The sensation put her in mind of a far simpler time, as a girl in Madeira, working the fishing docks with her family. She was expected to be at home washing and cleaning, but she had never abided such preconceptions, even at a young age. Mary could do anything her uncles and the young men of her village could do. And when she had backed up her bravado, her father had relented and let her work alongside the men, albeit begrudgingly.

Although, Mary recalled, the breeze off the sea in those days had carried more impact, as she had been dressed appropriately for the job she was doing, not wearing breeches as she was now, with long socks and a blue men's shirt. She loosened the necktie at her throat and doffed the jacket, swinging it over her shoulder.

Feeling cooler already, she let her mind come back to what she had seen in Moe's office. Something, some power struggle, seemed to be happening between Moe and his… astrologer. Eddie Kane. *Bishop* Kane. Mary snorted. A pair of women looked askance at her as they passed, scrunching their faces in disgust.

"*Cuide de sua vida,*" Mary tossed back at them in her native Portuguese. It was a public street! Who were they to cast judgement upon her? *More people should mind their business.*

The women hurried on, and they vanished swiftly from her thoughts.

If Eddie Kane were a bishop of anything, it was of bullshit. Mary did not buy his title or his act. And she was puzzled by Moe's connection with him. He had shown himself to be a shrewd judge of character and to have a strategic mind. He had hired her, hadn't he? To oversee his operations coming in from Canada? And he had contingencies in place for every conceivable leak in his network that she could see. So, what exactly was Kane's place? Mary didn't know, but she figured she'd find out soon enough if she kept her eyes and ears open. Being aware of her surroundings had served her well thus far. One thing she did know was that Kane had evinced an instinctual dislike in her. Since departing her small island home off the coast of Portugal and using her sister's identity to enter the United States, Mary had learned to trust her instincts. Those instincts had served her well in her dealings with men and the lies behind their smiles. She had traveled across an ocean on her own and had got by for several years.

Mary was a highly valued operative in a successful bootlegging operation, while also being married and having two children. She was always hearing how women could not do this or shouldn't do that. And those restrictions inevitably spilled from the mouths of men.

Then there was that strange book on Moe's desk. Were they arguing over it, or about something in it? She had seen Eddie cast his gaze at it before leaving. A lingering, lustful gaze, almost as if it were a woman. *That's ridiculous! What the hell could be so desirable in a book to elicit such a response?* And she could swear Moe had had the same yearning to go through that book and had just been waiting to usher her out.

Mary stopped in front of a cigar store newsstand. A variety of luridly splashed pulp magazines and staid newspapers rustled like leaves on a tree of stories both fantastic and factual.

Mary wasn't sure why she had stopped there. She wasn't the biggest reader. She did keep up with the news and enjoyed a tall tale or two but had never really stopped at a newsstand to look over the offerings. It must have been that she had that odd book on her mind.

A simple blue cloth hardcover with some yellow gilt caught her eye; Mary picked it up. *The Nine Unknown* by someone named Talbot Mundy. *That must be a pseudonym,* she thought. Flicking through it quickly, she discerned that it was some manner of adventure story. Not her thing, at all.

"That's brand new this week."

She looked up to see a friendly, middle-aged man exit the cigar store. Obviously, the proprietor. "Yeah?"

"Yep. Another crackin' adventure of Jimgrim and his men. Like *Lion of Petra*. That was a good one."

Mary nodded and replaced the book.

"Aren't you getting it?"

"My, uh, husband is a big fan. But I need to check if he already picked it up. If not, it'll be a wonderful birthday present for him."

"Well, you remember where you saw it first," the man said. "Have a good day."

"You, too," Mary replied, and hurried off, a little disturbed by her sudden notion to pick up the book. By the time she had gotten back home, the origins of her motivation were as forgotten as the book's title was mysterious.

HE HAD SPENT the past two hours in his private darkroom and was pleased with the results. The occultist mentally congratulated himself for employing the tiny camera situated within the buttonhole of his robe when meeting with Dalitz. Best now to share what he had learned.

Bishop Kane kneeled on the floor of the small room in his basement. He rocked back and forth, his head cast downward, the hood of his robe obscuring his features. A low moan escaped his lips.

He straightened suddenly and threw back his hood. His forehead was dappled with perspiration and his eyes were wide, as if he were staring into an abyss. Gloom shrouded the chamber, barely held back by the feeble glow of regularly spaced candles. Globs of wax tarred the floor at the base of each one. Sulfur tinged the air, along with a trace of vinegar.

"Is it done?"

Eddie started. His eyes flitted about the darkened room. Although he had expected the question, the scrape of that voice never failed to make his bowels clench.

"Almost. I need to see a few more passages."

"Witless fool! Why summon me if it is not yet done?" The candle flames flickered angrily.

Eddie swallowed, his fear rising in the face of the sudden spectral anger. "I do not wish to rouse his suspicions, so must play the part of humble supplicant. I am steering him to my will. One more meeting, I would think."

"My will, you mean. Do not forget your place."

"Of-of course, Master. I meant n-no offense," Eddie stammered.

The flickering of the candles slowed.

"I thought not. Now be about your task."

A presence seemed to vanish from the chamber, a passing of wind from an unseen breeze. After several minutes, Eddie's knees screamed in objection to his kneeling position, and he rose stiffly to his feet.

As he extinguished the last candle, he could have sworn he heard a voice whisper: "Soon."

JACK BATES STOOD outside the alley mouth working his jaw, the fine hairs of his sparse beard glinting red in the glow of the siren lights. He looked once more down the alleyway, where the darkness loomed like an open throat.

Violent heaving, followed by wet splatters on the pavement behind him, pulled Bates from his musings. He turned to see a young cop hunched over and spilling his dinner all over the street.

"Hey, rookie. You better handle a simple murder scene better than this." Truth to tell, Bates didn't blame the kid. He kind of wanted to puke himself. The mere thought of what was down that alley was enough to make anybody sick.

"S-sorry Detective," the rookie said, wiping his chin. Sick glistened on his dark blue shirt and his eyes were wide and fearful.

"I get it, kid. I've never seen anything like it. Go clean yourself up."

The kid hurried off, thankful to be away. Bates swallowed audibly and proceeded back into the alley with his flashlight.

Two other cops were on the scene. One officer was jotting notes a distance away from the bodies, while the other took photographs and stepped gingerly around them. More dry heaving could be heard just past the range of the intermittent flash bulb light.

"Wood? That you?" Bates yelled. A muffled affirmation came in reply. "Get the hell outta here, Wood. Go out the other side of the alley."

As the footsteps quickly faded, Bates addressed the note-taking cop. "What do we have?"

"Near as I can figure, this dame here was a pro skirt." The cop didn't look up from his notepad but made a slight indication with his foot. "These two guys musta went off the track over the deal. Or she did. I don't know. We're still sorting all the pieces."

"No shit," Bates said. "Somebody here went insanely violent. You like this scene for a fourth person?"

"Don't think so," the cop said, keeping his face buried in his notepad. It was as if he didn't want to look at the savaged corpses at his feet, the jagged holes that had been torn into their flesh. Viscous blood spattered the walls and the ground and pooled all around the victims.

Bates's stomach churned as he surveyed the carnage. People couldn't tear each other apart like that, could they? An animal, maybe? Some crazy monster of a killer? The flash bulb's popping froze horrific pictures of jangled limbs and sticky entrails onto his mind's eye. He was sure not to catch any winks tonight. Maybe not for the next few nights.

Bottles of booze littered the scene alongside a dented flask. The scent of alcohol mingled with the tang of copper in Bates's throat. "What's up with all the booze?"

"Right now," the cop said, finally looking up from his notepad and staring straight into Bates's face, "that's my main reason for discounting another person of interest and thinking these poor saps did this to themselves."

MARY LEANED ON the rail of the pier as a cooling breeze off the Cuyahoga blew through her hair. This was a little outside her scope of operations as assigned to her by Mr. Dalitz. Sometimes, though, she knew a manager had to make difficult decisions; that didn't stop her from feeling as if she was doing something wrong.

Ever since the meeting with Mr. Dalitz, Mary's gut had been telling her something was up. She was out of sorts and second-guessing everything. That wasn't like her. But too many events were adding up; there had to be something big brewing. Rumors of sudden violence, Eddie Kane, the double murder, and the woman scientist who had been picked up outside the scene and was still a person of interest.

Mary liked her work. She was good at it. Regardless of what Alfred said, they were able to enjoy the finer things in life because of what she did. Sarah and Felix didn't want for anything. They had far more than she'd had as a child. And shouldn't a mother provide for her children?

The heavy tread of boots on the wooden planks grew louder. Worry still coiled in Mary's chest over the puzzle forming back in Cleveland, and how it might affect her work, but that concern was dwarfed now by the approaching figure and the guilt that flared in her heart.

The heavy, bearded sailor stopped before Mary, his oval face bearing a wide grin.

"Greetings, *mijn liefste!*"

Mary rolled her eyes. "How many times have I told you not to call me that, Henk? I am married with children." She couldn't entirely hide the smile from her lips, however.

Hendrik Stanley reached a hand to her arm and guffawed. "As you say, I remain optimistic." She did not resist the Dutchman's touch.

"So, Mary, what compels you to have this secret meeting?"

"I need to know if you've seen or heard anything unusual in the past few weeks. Things are happening back in Cleveland, and I suspect it may have something to do with operations."

Hendrik frowned. "This is a lucrative side gig for me. I'd hate to see this particular well dry up. But, to answer your question, there has been more than the usual attention leveled at St. Pierre and Miquelon. As you know, those islands are the warehouse for your… merchandise."

"Hmm. That's not good, I would think. Dealings with the French ownership and the logistics through Canada are currently above my pay grade, but I do like to stay informed in case I need to seize an opportunity. I wonder why there's so much attention there?"

"I know nothing of such things. Only that I've been doing what I do for a time, and I know the traffic such an establishment generates. By my count, it has increased. Is there a higher demand for what you provide?"

"Nothing beyond projected parameters. I couldn't speak to other operations' needs. Even so, if demand is increasing, an increase in traffic makes sense. I don't know. It just doesn't sit right with me somehow."

The echo of nearby footsteps carried on the wind.

"We should wrap this up," Mary said.

"I shall keep my eyes and ears open for you."

"Thank you, *meu bem*." Mary smiled at the big sailor. She shouldn't have been encouraging him with such affectations, but she couldn't help herself. She watched as Hendrik disappeared into the lowering gloom.

IT WAS LATE. Later than Mary's usual home-time. And she was later still for having stopped off at the cigar stand. Thankfully, the hardcover she had perused the other day had still been there, and she had purchased it.

It was plainly a conciliatory offering. She knew it, and Alfred would know it. The guilt welled up in her chest again. She hadn't done anything physical, but she was straying into the gray areas of her heart. It wasn't fair to him. To her family.

But he'd probably think the reason for the gift was work-related. She had to manage some mooks, or a shipment ran late, or some cops wanted a little extra take. These were regular occurrences; nothing out of the ordinary. And she reasoned that it was work-related. It simply hadn't anything to do with *her* job. But she was making it her business. It was simply unfortunate that Hendrick was whom she'd had to meet. She regretted how easily the lies had slipped from her tongue.

Mary stood outside her house, bracing for the inevitable discussion that would certainly devolve into yet another disagreement over her chosen line of work. She pulled the book from its brown paper bag and turned it over in her hand, as she had done that day on the sidewalk.

She still wasn't sure why she had stopped and selected that book. Or why it had seemed to call to her on her drive back from Cuyahoga. She figured there was some reason, and that it would reveal itself at some point.

"I'm surprised that has seen print. Many in the west would scoff at the contents of such a book, but Mundy is well-traveled and has a keen perception of the world."

Mary whirled, and with her free hand, swiftly and smoothly drew the three-inch snub revolver from beneath her coat. It was a .32 Smith and Wesson Safety Hammerless, commonly known as a Lemon Squeezer. She liked it for the internal hammer, which allowed for quick drawings from an internal pocket without snagging. She did not drop the book.

"Who the hell are you, and why are you lurking about my home?" Mary leveled the snub at the figure, who emerged from behind a tree. She narrowed her eyes at the stranger's dark, impassive visage.

"You're the woman they arrested at the murder scene and later released." Mary lowered the gun a little. The stranger did not appear armed, nor intent on any mischief.

"Yes. I was responding to my associate's summons. Alas, I was too late."

"I'm sorry." Mary wasn't sure why she was apologizing, but she sensed this woman was, if not a friend, then at least an ally. "Who are you?"

"That's not as important as what I have to warn you about."

Mary stiffened. She didn't care for the shift in conversation.

"There is a coming disturbance. This point in time is a crucial flashpoint in the history of man."

Mary let out a long breath she hadn't realized she'd been holding and relaxed somewhat. She thought this woman might be from a rival organization looking to move in on Mr. Dalitz's territory. Instead, it turned out she'd apparently escaped from the funny farm.

"I can see by your expression you don't believe me. That is unfortunate."

"I don't have time for this nonsense. Why don't you tell me your name and I can help you find your way back to where you need to go."

"I gave up my name—"

"Everyone has a name," Mary interrupted. "Now, why don't you—"

"The name you currently use is not your true name. Why is it so hard for you to believe, then, that I have none?"

Mary reeled back. "What…?" How could this woman have known that? "Who the hell are you?"

"I stand against the coming threat. That is why I am here. And I believe you can help me."

"Listen, lady, I want no part of whatever shit you're talking about. I have plenty on my plate. Now, why don't you get out of here?" Mary waved the revolver.

"You do indeed have plenty on your plate. You sense it, do you not? Your instincts are screaming at you, but you are not listening."

Mary was breathing loudly through her nose. Waiting. Listening.

"You sense something about the circumstances surrounding my former associate's death. You met someone recently who may play a large role in the threat I am here to stand against; they trigger a distrust, a wariness in you that you cannot explain. You even now return from a meeting which your instincts drove you to arrange as you seek answers."

How the hell could this woman, this stranger, have known all of this? Was Mary being watched? Was she being set up to take a fall?

"Your mind is swirling with questions about me and how I could possibly know these things. I know these things about you because I suspect you are a nexus being. There are several instances in your past that cannot be explained by modern science, such as your time on Thompson Island. Such events are drawn to you as the rod draws the lightning."

Mary gasped. There was no way anyone could have learned about her trials on Thompson Island all those years ago. Could the things this stranger was saying possibly be true? Was there some… *evil* coming?

"Some of the answers, you hold in your very hand. How else would you explain your affinity to such a book?"

"I-I don't know," Mary stammered. She looked at the book she was loosely clutching; she had forgotten it was in her hand. *The Nine Unknown.*

This was all too fantastic.

"My associate's death leaves an unfortunate void that will soon need to be filled. But the incoming threat is a far more pressing issue. Follow your instincts. They will serve you well."

"What about you?"

"I will continue as I have been doing, don't worry. This is not the last you have seen of me."

Terrific.

Then she was gone. Mary cast her gaze about the front yard but there was no trace of the mysterious woman. All that remained were cryptic words, and more questions.

Mary gazed once more at the book. *Some of the answers were in my hand.* Perhaps she had better wait before giving this to Alfred as a gift. She considered getting back in her car to start reading, but she knew she'd be in for a hell of an argument if she was gone for the rest of the night. Best to tackle the fight waiting behind the front door and study up later on the possible battle ahead.

THE GLASS HEIGHTS of the Arcade Building reflected the last rays of the setting sun. Far below, in the gloom of an alley, a door slammed open. The earthy rhythms and fast beats of jazz spilled into the twilight, followed by raucous laughter. Half a dozen smartly dressed people ambled casually, albeit mechanically, from within.

Alarmed cries echoed from within the speakeasy, calls to the group to come back inside and alerts to beware of the police. But the shuffling group paid the cautionary yells no mind. Their eyes were glazed over as if they were drugged, yet they somehow remained mobile. As they neared the alley mouth and entered the main street, passersby gave them a wide berth, sensing something wasn't quite right about these six people with their strange, uniform gait and dead-eyed stare.

Only when a large man in a suit rushed forth from the doorway they had exited did the walkers come to life, as it were. He was apparently a security guard; as he laid hands on the rearmost woman in the strange, shambling procession, it was as if his mere touch flipped a collective switch.

The woman reacted suddenly, savagely. She turned, clawing at the man's eyes. Her companions halted and joined her in beating back the hapless man, who had been seeking to deter them from reaching their destination.

The shuffling pack horribly—yet silently—tore the security man apart. They ripped at him with hooked fingers and crimson-stained teeth, spitting out gobbets of red flesh. All the while, their eyes remained void.

When the man's screaming ceased, the walkers calmly turned away from him. They stood still for a moment, with their blank eyes and blood-spattered finery, and regarded the gathering crowd. Then, the walkers proceeded apace. Several of the observing crowd broke and ran, gibbering in terror at what they had just witnessed. Others simply stared, aghast.

Still more men poured forth from the alleyway that housed the speakeasy, stopping short at the sight of their mauled, broken fellow. They each withdrew pistols and called for the six walkers to stop.

The strange group continued on, neither stopping nor giving any indication they had heard the yells for them to stop.

Smoke and the barrage of handguns filled the busy street.

Screams from the horrified witnesses punctuated the thunder of gunfire, and the stamp of fleeing footsteps was the bassline in this symphony of murder. The six zombie-like patrons jerked spasmodically as hot lead cut their puppet strings and they collapsed soundlessly.

Police sirens sliced through the cold, silent aftermath. The gun smoke wafted upward into the fast-vanishing sunrays reflecting from the top of the Arcade.

MOE DALITZ GINGERLY closed the heavy tome. He rapped his knuckles upon the cover, enjoying the sound of the muffled knock against the black leather. Often, he performed this action after concluding a meeting with Eddie Kane, the Bishop of the New World Order. Whatever that was.

Moe sipped from his tumbler of fine whisky. He knew Kane had aspirations of his own and even harbored designs on the book at his fingertips. The bishop obviously knew more about the book than he was letting on. Moe wouldn't have been in charge of the Mayfield Road organization if he couldn't read people—and excel at manipulating them.

But for every hour he spent poring over the book with Kane, Moe would spend another hour with it by himself. It all seemed to be crazy fantasy, like the yarns in those new pulp magazines some of his men talked about. Yeah, he kept an ear to the ground when it came to what his subordinates were up to. One had to. If not fantasy, it was at least some kind of pseudo-science. But if he let himself disregard that notion, Moe could see—feel— that the words in that book hinted at more. Even if he only half understood the words on the page. He just couldn't shake the feeling that this book was important and could lead to his assuming even more power.

So, if Kane could help him decipher some of the mysteries within, Moe would let him. He would let the ambitious pretender believe he had one over on him. Religion and belief were useful tools and Bishop Kane was still of value to him. Whatever the cult leader was planning to do with the book, Moe was ready for him and wouldn't hesitate to rub Kane out as soon as he showed himself to be a threat to his greater plans.

Moe started when the phone rang. He grabbed it immediately. It was late, but he knew his men wouldn't be calling if it weren't important. Besides, it didn't hurt appearances to let them know that he was available at any hour. It made them wonder if he even slept and how much he really saw. This kept most of the crew in line, knowing that the big boss man could be watching.

Moe replaced the receiver and furrowed his brow. Half a dozen people had been shot and killed, leaving one of his joints in full view of a crowd. This wasn't good. It would be difficult to tie off all the loose ends in something like this.

Moe took a long pull at his glass then curled his lip in frustration. Too many things had been going wrong lately. He'd need to consider putting Kane on this. The cult figure could maybe smooth this over in a way that he couldn't, and which would allow Moe time to further some other plans.

He reached for the phone again but stopped before lifting the receiver. Could Kane have had something to do with these incidents? The thought burrowed in Moe's head, but he couldn't make the connection work. He leaned back and considered his next move.

EDDIE KANE PACED the floor, prowling in his basement like a hungry leopard, waiting for prey to meander into his field of vision. He was heedless of the minor chaos his flowing robe was causing as he moved back and forth. Candle flames fluttered, threatening to fan into a larger conflagration as they licked at nearby scrolls. Strange pottery and artifacts teetered on shelves, some tumbling to the floor with a loud crash. Of late, meetings with Dalitz had vexed him. He cursed the mobster, he cursed his current role, he cursed simply to vent his anger at not yet having achieved his goals.

Honestly, though, deep down, Kane felt as if he might be the prey, and what he awaited, the predator. That cold realization burrowed in his gut, and he sat with that notion for a while, letting the dank sweat of it trickle down his back until he allowed his mind to fully grasp his glorious plan. Fear would not rule him, no. He only had to play the subservient lackey for a little while longer.

With the knowledge in that book, he need not fear anyone. Not Moe Dalitz, not the demon he pretended to serve, not anybody. His vision for a new world was close! Everything was just about in its proper place. His recent experiments had borne ripe fruit. Now he only awaited the proper time to implement his goal, his vision.

If only he could possess the book. But that sly bastard Dalitz was too canny to let it out of his sight. Oh, to be able to plumb the depths of that precious tome at his leisure!

It was a happy circumstance that he suspected the origins of the book in the gangster's possession. There had been whispers of it through the centuries, and its companion volumes, too. Only the slightest of clues hinted at what the books meant or which doors they opened. An ancient Chinese emperor was supposed to have entrusted nine unknown guardians to safeguard the secrets within. He did not know if these guardians were immortal, or if others assumed the mantle when the time was right. He did not even know if the emperor truly existed. History had never been Kane's strong suit, but he did appreciate the lore of the arcane and believed that sometimes, history and magic intertwined.

A sudden cold seeped into the chamber. Eddie could feel it creeping through his limbs despite his heavy cloak. He could see his hot breath in the air.

Heita was here.

Kane kneeled and bowed his head, knowing the demon-spirit tolerated nothing less than complete subservience.

"You have the knowledge you seek?" The hiss issued from the shadowed corner of the room.

"Yes, Master. The tests have gone well."

"Good. Then it is time."

"Yes. I merely wait upon your grace."

"As is your place, human." Laughter like crunching leaves rustled in the air. "You have permission to begin recruiting my subjects and start my reign upon this sphere."

A shimmer flickered in the corner. Silence lingered and the

chill in the air slowly dissipated while Eddie clambered to his feet and approached cautiously. There, crouched in the shadows, was a covered receptacle adorned with strange, hellish runes. Eddie touched it tentatively. It was slick and warm, and sloshed at his gentle touch as if there was something inside, perhaps a fluid. He lifted the vessel, and his stomach churned a little at the thick noise from within the demonic pottery. Kane could guess what was within but did not care to let his mind wander. This was the lever which would realize his ambition. To rule over humanity, over the mindless herd. He would become a new emperor, one to rival the purported Chinese emperor from the mists of legend.

THERE WAS SOMETHING in the air. The breeze was warm with only the slightest bite to it, hinting that autumn was in its final days, and winter would soon drape its cold shroud across the land. The night sky was clear, and stars could be seen over Lake Erie away from the lights of the city. Those celestial points winked like the eyes of a capricious god observing the folly of man.

Mary shivered as the notion skipped through her head. She didn't know where such a thought had come from. That was not typically how she looked at things. It had to be the book. That damn adventure fantasy story. She was letting herself get carried away with the romance of the adventure and the damn conspiracy talk from that strange woman on her front lawn the other night.

Mary cursed her gullibility. "*Mulher tola*. Why am I buying into this stuff?"

She ground her teeth. Letting herself get distracted by this nonsense would only serve to hurt her chances of promotion in the Mayfield Road Gang. She'd worked hard to gain the trust of Mr. Dalitz and command the position she was in. And she didn't want to jeopardize that. She had a family, and she had big plans.

Still… that nameless woman and her stories. As mysterious and distrustful as she seemed, Mary simply couldn't discount what the woman had said. What she knew. Deep down, Mary realized there was some truth in it. Something in the air, indeed.

The rumble of an engine intruded on the night's stillness.

"They're coming in, boss-lady."

"Thanks, Richard. I hear them. Is the truck ready for off-loading?"

"You bet."

Mary nodded at her subordinate and turned back to the black waters of Lake Erie. There were heavy clouds, and it made the night darker. She could just make out the speedboat's shadowy mass on the water. The boat wasn't running any lights, but that wasn't unusual considering what they were hauling.

Still, uneasiness clawed at Mary's guts. She'd overseen dozens of these transfer runs, and, so far, there was nothing out of the ordinary about this one. "Be ready for anything," she said. She watched as Richard almost comically cocked his head, and his face went through a small gamut of expressions from alertness and appeasement to confusion and concern. She inclined her head once at the man and returned her gaze to the fast-approaching boat.

The Nectar of the Gods cut its engine and coasted into shore. The boat clumsily moored at the makeshift dock Mary's men had set up for these drops. No hands were seen on deck.

Richard motioned to two of his men. "Secure the boat."

A stocky figure detached itself from the shadows on deck; it appeared to be the same cruel-eyed captain that Mary had knocked onto his ass weeks ago. She sighed, then stepped forward. "*Que diabos*! You could jeopardize the whole operation coming in as foolishly as that."

She was hot under the collar and wouldn't mind knocking this *filho da puta* on his pins a couple more times. Her native tongue came more readily when her blood was boiling, and this ugly little man had caused that very thing. Her job was hard enough, *por deus*, without some chauvinist making it more so, never mind running the risk of capsizing Mr. Dalitz's entire bootlegging operation.

"You know, I think I will kick this *desgraçado's* ass," Mary muttered. She put one booted foot on the dock. "Hey!"

Nothing. In fact, the captain's silhouette dipped below the bridge out of sight and did not reappear.

What the hell? That was not what Mary had expected. She removed her foot from the dock and looked back to her men. Unvoiced questions were writ on their faces. This did not sit well with her.

Mary reached inside her jacket for the .32 Smith & Wesson. The Lemon Squeezer was a five-shot revolver that she could reload quickly. As she grabbed it, a voice in her head screamed at her. It was like the long, loud whistle blow at a major port of call. Her pulse hammered in her ears. She drew her gun and held it ready.

From out of the shallows on either side of the *Nectar*, shadowy forms erupted from the water. They burst onto the sand in halting, jerky motions, but did not move any less swiftly for it. The figures moved as if they were discovering the workings of their own limbs and bodies.

Mary had seen them before. She had made a point of memorizing their faces. She had always taken note of men who looked askance at her, be it for underestimating her or for more predatory reasons. They were the crew of the Nectar. Mary was unsure if they were even men anymore. They were more slavering beasts in the shapes of men. Spittle flew from their wide mouths, and they gnashed their teeth so hard Mary thought they might crack. They propelled themselves forward as if they were great apes, loping and running on their knuckles across the shifting sand, eyes wild and burning an unnatural red.

It was *that* look, the realization that no human had eyes that color, which prompted Mary to act. She squeezed the trigger, firing two shots into the nearest snarling visage. Warm, wet crimson spattered her face and chest, and for a moment, Mary was blind. She smelled smoke and copper, and the echo of thunder rang in her ears. Richard and her men fired into the advancing horde. She heard screams, both human and inhuman.

Mary shook her head wildly, shaking the blood from her eyes. Tears streaked through her vision as she watched tongues of fire stab through the haze of the night and bodies crumple to the dark ground. She cast about for the captain of the *Nectar*. He did not appear to be one of the horde that had rushed the beach.

She heard a growl to her left and whirled and fired at the looming shape. With a piercing cry, the form fell.

Wet, crunching sounds reached her ears, along with unholy screams she recognized as having emanated from her own men. Staccato gunfire sounded and the horrible noises stopped.

"Boss!"

"Richard!" Mary yelled.

The big man stumbled to her through the impromptu battlefield, avoiding the creatures sprawled across the gore-stained beach.

"You OK?"

"Yeah." Mary reloaded her snubbie. "How many did we lose?"

"Four. Me, Archie and John are all that's left. What the hell were those things? I ain't never seen nothing like that."

Mary tightened her grip on the Lemon Squeezer now that it was fully loaded. "Me neither. It's like they were men but also wild, primitive."

"Not all of them, boss."

"What do you mean?"

Richard led her to a nearby corpse. The figure was basically humanoid, but shiny scales glistened in the dim light. It also appeared to have two small horns sprouting from either side of its head. Its crimson eyes stared sightlessly back at them.

"It's a demon," Richard said.

"I don't believe in demons," Mary snarled. "I've seen some strange shit in my day but I'm not buying into demons." She shuddered as she recalled the horrors she had witnessed on Thompson Island years ago and cursed the mystery woman for dredging up that foul memory. She had nearly forgotten that experience.

What the fuck was going on?

"Why are some of these demons and some not?"

"I don't know. Maybe some of them weren't fully transformed. Where's the captain? You know, that stocky *merda* who gave me lip last time?" Mary started scouring the beach, inspecting the corpses.

Richard trailed behind, hurrying to keep up with her frenzied pace. "I thought I saw something at the cabin when they docked."

Mary halted and Richard stumbled to avoid colliding with her. She sprinted as fast as she could back to the *Nectar*, leaping onto the wooden dock and vaulting the gunwale of the speedboat.

Richard joined her in time to discover that she had the captain cornered in the small stateroom of the boat. The man did not look at all perturbed to be staring down the barrel of a revolver.

"I think something's wrong with him, boss."

Mary nodded, glaring at her intended victim. "What do you know, *merda*?"

The captain stared straight ahead. It was as if he had gazed into infinity and been struck dumb.

Mary backed off a few steps to stand even with Richard. The

captain didn't appear to be searching for an escape, and besides, the only way out was through the two of them. And he didn't look to have been as monstrously transformed as his crew. Were those… *monsters* trailing the *Nectar* through the water? Or were they being smuggled into the city?

"You can't stop what's going to happen."

Mary and Richard started at the sudden voice. It was guttural and choking, and dripped with contempt. It sounded almost unnatural, too, as if speech were forming from a throat not meant to utter words.

"Mrs. Santos," the captain croaked. His mouth didn't quite shape the words properly. His eyes had a strange light in them, as if someone else were peering through them.

Mary leveled her gun at the captain, who was now crouching forward like some squat little toad.

"What you did here was inconsequential. The time is nearly upon us. You can join the movement. I would have use for someone like you." The captain-thing leered at her.

Revulsion brimmed in Mary's throat. She emptied her .32 Smith & Wesson into the heavy, swaying body before her. It slumped down the stateroom wall like a slug, trailing crimson.

"W-what the holy fuck?" Richard stammered.

"We need to get to a phone," Mary said, reloading. She recognized that faraway voice. She had heard it only once, but she had made a habit of marking men and their deceptive smiles.

Bishop Kane.

"EINDELIJK! I'VE BEEN trying to reach you all night!"

Mary held the phone receiver away from her ear, the voice on the other end was so loud and frantic. "What is it, Henk?" The big Dutchman was typically unflappable, but she could not help but be concerned by his tone of voice, especially after what she had witnessed.

"I knew you were scheduled to pick up a shipment tonight. I was hoping you'd stop in at the Erie safehouse before heading back. I have seen something suspicious. A boat has departed for Saint Pierre and Miquelon."

"Where are you?"

"I'm at the port in Sydney, Nova Scotia," Henk replied. "A small party cast off due east without following procedure. That would seem the most likely destination if one were to leave in such a way."

Mary considered Henk's words. Was he right? Lots of undercover, secretive runs were being made back and forth in this line of work. What was it about this one that had him in such a dither?

"What prompted you to call about this, *meu querido*?" Mary hoped that their familiar playful banter would calm him. A lot had happened tonight, and she was still trying to sort it all in her mind.

"There was a man aboard the boat. Definitely in charge. He was wearing a black robe with a hood over his head. It was just out of place. It gave me a bad feeling."

Kane.

"You couldn't be more right," Mary hissed.

"What?"

"Nothing. Sit tight. I'll be in touch." Mary hung up even as she heard Henk begin to sputter on the other end. She turned to Richard. "You have any connections in Sydney or at Saint Pierre and Miquelon?"

"Archie worked at the depot there for a spell," the big man replied.

Mary directed her attention to the freckle-faced man Richard had indicated. Her stare was hard. She waited for him to speak up.

"Uh, I did," Archie said, nervous beneath Mary's stony focus. "I worked guard detail overnight. Most activity was done during daytime hours, but some business happened after that."

"And?"

"And, uh, there's usually a small detail for overnight security. Should be six to eight guys on duty per warehouse."

Small enough to be overcome by an organized force, Mary thought. "Any additional crew nearby to help out or reinforce in case of a raid?"

"Nah," Archie said. "Most of the workforce is quartered on the mainland. Along the Nova Scotia ports. Nothing in America, so as to avoid any legal hassles. 'Bout fifteen miles away, so a pretty quick trip."

Mary's mind raced. *Damn. Kane could already be there. Don't know what he's up to, but if it involves what we just saw, it can't be good.*

"All right," she said. "I've got to call Mr. Malitz. As soon as I'm off the line with him, you call the security detail at the depot and warn them. Richard, get started rousting some of the boys. We gotta be ready for anything."

The men nodded and left the room.

Mary quickly dialed Moe Dalitz's office number. She momentarily questioned the wisdom of disturbing him at this hour, but she had already pressed the last digit. The crime boss picked up after the first ring.

"Mr. Dalitz, this is Mary."

"What's going on?"

Worry snaked through her stomach; Moe did not seem as calm and collected as usual.

"There was a problem with the drop. The crew of the *Nectar* are dead. We had to kill them."

"What? What happened?"

"They… attacked me and the boys. The crew was insane. Crazy, like wild animals. We had no choice but to defend ourselves." She decided not to mention the scaly things also present at the scene. Mr. Dalitz was a practical man, and monster stories would likely not go over well, considering the botched operation.

A long silence stretched across the phone line.

"How many did we lose?" Moe asked eventually.

"Four," Mary said.

Silence.

"Sir," she ventured, "I… think Bishop Kane has something to do with this. Do you know where he is?"

She could almost hear his teeth grinding.

"No."

"I have reason to believe he may make some move against the big depot off the coast."

"What kind of move?"

"I don't know, sir. But I've been informed he was casting off from Sydney less than an hour ago."

"Damn it!" Without another word, Moe disconnected the call.

Porra!

She didn't know what to do next. She wasn't expecting Moe to hang up on her. Obviously, something was going on with him, and her news didn't help. Well, she didn't have time for that. The nagging sensation that something incredibly bad was about to happen only grew steadier in her gut.

Her thoughts kept dancing back to her talk with the woman in front of her house. She and her maddening, mysterious ways, and her vague talk of things greater than this world. But Mary could hardly refute the horned, scaled corpses she had recently seen and dispatched. The things that had killed her own men.

Kane was an oily salesman type with his own agenda, but demons? Did he summon monsters? Was he a villain looking to rule the world? That was just fanciful talk, like in the damn book she couldn't help leafing through.

"Mary." The voice came from nowhere, low and flat.

She whirled, half expecting Richard or Archie, as they were the only other ones at this halfway house. But they always addressed her as *boss* or *boss lady*. She didn't like it, but there was no way she would allow the familiarity of first-name terms. She *was* their boss.

The impassive face of the unknown woman gazed back from the shadowed corner.

"You! How did you get here? Where are my men?"

The Unknown's dark eyes did not waver. "Your men are fine. They are unaware of our presence. We have much to discuss, and little time to do so."

"*We?*" Mary clenched the grip on her revolver.

Two more enigmatic figures melted from the very walls of the small office. Gloom huddled in some corners, but the room was lit. How had she not seen three people there? How had she, Richard, and Archie, for that matter, not been aware of them? It was impossible. Mary raised her gun. The strange things the mysterious woman had told her before seemed just a little more real now.

"*Está bem*, what in the hell is going on? Who are these people?" Mary waved her gun at the man and the woman accompanying the Unknown she had met previously. Somehow, that name, Unknown, seemed fitting.

"These are my associates. They stand with me against the impending threat, the one of which I warned you."

Mary's gaze shifted back and forth between the two strangers. The man was Indian and seemed to bear a great weight, not unlike those wise men… yogis, were they called? The woman was very old, her face a sunken deposit of fissures and cracks; Mary could not discern her ethnicity, only that she was neither American nor European.

"I suppose these two have no names, either, right?"

"All who serve in our order have relinquished the folly of names. They are unnecessary," the Unknown said.

"*Cristo todo-poderoso*, give me something to work with, some reason to trust you!" Mary shouted, her frustration finally getting the best of her. "I just fought scaly monsters, by god. And I don't even believe in monsters."

The first Unknown woman said nothing. She appeared to be weighing her options. Finally, she spoke. "As I said, we truly have no names. If you must have something to call us, you may call me Four. My associates are Six and Eight." Four indicated the man and the old woman, respectively.

Mary sat with that explanation for a few moments. "Fine. I don't like it, but it's something, I suppose. Now, what's going on?"

"Humanity approaches a crossroads," Four stated. "An individual seeks dominion over humankind. He utilizes dark forces, brought into play, in part, by an object of ours. This object was in the keeping of our fellow, Number Seven, but stolen when he was murdered."

Mary recalled Four speaking of an associate when they had first met. Mysterious objects, secret societies, scaled monsters, it was all a little much to swallow, but she wasn't one to deny what her eyes showed her. She had killed monsters. Three mysterious strangers stood before her, spinning a tall tale. Part of Mary wanted to laugh, to leave, but she could not shake the feeling in her gut. What was it that Four had said to her on her front lawn? *Your instincts are screaming at you, but you are not listening.*

"I think I know who's behind all this. His name is Kane," Mary said. "What can I do? He's far from here."

"I anticipated the enemy would be several steps ahead, thus I called on my fellows for assistance. The need for such action outweighs the danger. They will speed you to your destination."

"Wait," Mary said. "Kane is on his way to the North Atlantic, I believe. Hell, he's probably already there. How are your friends going to get me there? And what about you? You've been pestering me about this whole damn thing. Why aren't you seeing this through with me?"

"There are means of travel my fellows and I are privy to that you do not know," Four said, with the same steady tone that so frustrated Mary. "As for myself, I will join you just as soon as I complete an errand, a most important one."

Six and Eight moved forward as one, standing to either side of Four. Mary instinctively retreated in the face of the Unknown. These people scared her, deep down where she dared not look.

"Do not fear," Four said. "Simply close your eyes and you will soon be where you need to be."

"What? If things are as serious as you say, we don't have time for games. We need to hurry."

"We play no games here. You are simply not ready to digest the method of travel which will be employed. It is best if you close your eyes and trust that we can do as we say."

Mary took a deep breath and held it, all the while staring hard at each of the three Unknowns in turn. Each stared back. None so much as blinked.

"All will be explained," Four said. "I promise."

Mary released her breath in a long sigh. Her fingers were sweaty on the grip of her gun.

"Fine." She hesitantly closed her eyes.

THE SOUND OF waves crashed through her ears and the familiar scent of salt spray filled her nostrils. It smelled and sounded like the ocean, but that couldn't be possible. The nearest body of water was Lake Erie, and that was a five-minute drive away.

The air was cooler. Cooler than it had been less than an hour ago at the dock. A gull cried in the distance. Mary knew something had happened. Something was different.

"*Heilige onzin!*"

She recognized that voice. She blinked, focusing on the man before her.

Henk?

"H-how are you here?"

"I've been here since we spoke on the phone! How are you here?" the Dutch sailor said, wonder illuminating his face.

"I-I'm not sure…" Mary stammered. "I was at the doss house, the cabin just off the drop dock on Erie."

"That's over seventeen hundred kilometers away, Mary. That's impossible."

Mary reeled and stretched out a hand for support, finding it on a wooden pylon. She took a few moments to collect herself; she looked up to see the concern etched across Henk's lined, bearded face.

One moment, Mary had been facing that unknown woman, Four, and her companions, Six and Eight—and the next, she had found herself here. In Sydney, Nova Scotia. She couldn't explain to Henk *how* she had got here, but she knew *why*.

Mary straightened, a resolute expression crossing her features. "I know it's impossible, *meu querido*, but here I stand. And there are more impossible things in this world than we can speak of. You and I are of the sea, and on some level, we know this to be fact."

She smoothed her hands down the length of her black leather coat. "Let us deal with the now and leave the impossible behind. We need to get to Saint Pierre and Miquelon and stop the hooded man you saw. His name is Eddie Kane. Is there a boat here that can get us to the depot as fast as possible?"

Henk scrunched up his face. "Aye. *The Cyprian* is a forty-foot power boat. It docked a few hours ago. The captain owes me a favor. Methinks he'll let me take a quick trip to the depot. We should make landfall within the half hour if we leave now."

"You get that ready. We'll need guns. Lots of firepower."

"I can get us a pair of Thompsons before we cast off."

Mary grinned. In her experience, Henk was nothing if not resourceful. "Tommy guns should be perfect. I have a feeling we'll need one more thing, though." She looked around the dock, then turned back to the Dutchman.

"They still do blast fishing in these parts, right?"

Henk nodded.

"Where's the dynamite?"

EDDIE KANE STEPPED over the bullet-riddled corpse of the security guard as if it were not in his way. His leather-soled shoe nearly slipped in the pooling blood, but he paid it no mind. The occultist merely regained his composure and continued to the edge of the catwalk.

Placing his palms on the railing of the second-story mezzanine, he gazed over the length and breadth of the massive warehouse. Large vats lined the far wall. Kane knew they were filled with alcohol, and he would address those soon enough. Or rather, his servant would attend to those containers when the time was right. Instead, he needed to direct his attention to a smaller scale before he could fully enact his plan.

The artificial lighting generated by the abundant gas discharge lamps glinted off the metal rings on Kane's fingers. The self-styled religious leader knew well the power of perception. He realized that these rings were mere costume jewelry, but they appeared exotic and helped further his performance as a learned man. Soon enough, however, Kane would have riches enough to seize as many jewels and as much power as he could desire.

Kane turned with a sudden flourish of his silken black robe. He strode to the stairs at the end of the mezzanine and proceeded downward with a measured pace. The click of his soles echoed loudly, and Eddie smiled, visions of power dancing through his mind, as he stroked the black lacquered box in his hands.

He entered a small office. Before him, his two most trusted

acolytes held three men at gunpoint. Eddie knew these captives to be the remainder of the security detail at the depot.

"There are no more guards?"

"No, Bishop Kane. The morning shift does not sign on for another several hours."

"You're certain? I can ill afford any surprises this near to my goal."

Before any of the acolytes could answer, one of the captive security guards spoke up. "You may have gotten lucky getting in here, pal, but if all you're trying to do is cut out the middle man by seizing this place, let me tell ya, you're fucked."

Kane grinned, his eyes alight like a wolf cornering its prey. "Let me assure you, my plans are more far-reaching than your small mind can fathom."

With that, Kane released the clasp on the box and withdrew a long, translucent vial. A viscous fluid with the appearance of crude oil slopped thickly against the glass interior as the occultist held the container to his eye. "Fetch me a bottle of booze." Kane tossed the order over his shoulder to his disciples, keeping his eyes on the strange liquid.

"Here, Bishop," one of the acolytes said after a few moments.

Kane turned to behold his lackey holding an unmarked bottle of clear fluid.

"It is gin, I believe, sir."

"As long as it is alcohol, it matters not what it is. Pour two glasses."

The acolyte searched through some cabinets and found some tumblers. He poured two fingers' worth of gin into each glass, then waited.

Kane returned his attention to the vial and stared at it. *At last, I am at the threshold. All I need to do is step across, and this world will be mine.*

Presently, he withdrew a fat piece of yellow chalk from within his robe and sketched arcane symbols on the tiled floor in front of him, muttering as he did so. Then, he laid the dusky vial in the center of his markings and straightened. Kane raised his arms above his head and incanted, repeating the mantra over and over for several minutes. The word *Heita* was heard multiple times.

The lighting in the office flickered. The captives, and even the acolytes, shifted nervously. They could all sense something had changed in the room. Ghost clouds of breath misted in the suddenly chill atmosphere.

"Is it time?" The question dripped from the shadows.

"It is… Master." Eddie bit off the last word.

"Begin."

Kane continued his mantra once again, but more stridently and with swifter cadence. His eyes were wide, as if he were a madman.

Suddenly, he stopped, and swayed at the edge of the chalk-drawn sigils. It was as if he were suffused with some strange energy, to which his body was struggling to acclimate.

He soon bent and retrieved the black-filled vial. Uncorking it, Kane watched as inky tendrils of smoke puffed through the narrow glass mouth. The wisps pulsed, as if waiting.

Kane walked over to the two glasses upon the office desk. As he poured a sampling of the ichor into each gin-filled tumbler, the contents of the glass turned translucent. Curls of ebon smoke wafted over the rim of the glass, almost as if the contents had released a breath.

Kane gripped one of the demon-soaked gin glasses near the bottom, careful of the rim, and slowly made his way to one of the captive security guards. The restrained men again found their voices and noisily struggled away from the occultist's advance as best their bonds would allow.

The acolytes waved their guns at the frantic men; the prisoners silenced somewhat, the occasional low moan or grumbled curse escaping their lips. Kane regarded each man in turn, before he finally approached one with the glass.

The intended victim shook his head and craned backwards. One of the acolytes moved behind him and held his head in place while another of Kane's disciples trained a gun on the prisoner. Eddie waited until the man's mouth was forced open, then he upended the glass into it. The man swallowed involuntarily.

Kane turned on his heel and fetched the next glass. He went to the second guard, who retreated even more vehemently, but to no avail. He, too, was forced to ingest the demon-stained gin.

The two men sat stock-still in their chairs. Both were flexed, arms bulging, muscles corded, as if they were jungle cats about to pounce on unsuspecting prey.

"Begin," that bodiless voice sounded once more from the shadows.

Kane nodded to no one, but he knew his affirmation had been seen. He cared not one whit if Heita had seen him obey or not, only that this next step brought him closer to realizing his dreams. "Relax."

The two men slumped in their chairs at the occultist's order but remained alert for the next command.

"Untie them," Kane ordered one of his followers. The disciple hesitated until Kane turned an angry eye upon him. "Do it."

The acolyte untied the two captives warily, but the blank-eyed men did not flinch. The man hurried back to his place, facing the now-freed prisoners.

"Now," Kane said, "hop on one foot."

Both men did as they were told until commanded to stop. Kane continued with a series of increasingly ridiculous orders, which the men enacted without hesitation or complaint.

"Stop."

The two guards ceased. A hiss of air came from above—an almost spectral breeze where there should be none.

"Kill the man in the chair."

The third security guard, still bound to his seat, widened his eyes in fear. When his fellows turned their heads toward him, he began scampering backward in his chair, scraping his feet frantically, his efforts succeeding only in toppling him over onto his side. The two possessed men fell upon their once-companion, savagely biting him, and tearing at him with hooked fingers. The serene look upon their faces as they did these things did not change.

Eddie Kane smiled. His grin widened as the wet, tearing sounds grew louder.

MARY SCANNED THE shore ahead from the prow of *The Cyprian*. False dawn tinged the sky with wisps of pink amid the indigo. All seemed quiet on the land, all except the thrum of the powerboat's engine.

"We made it through the 'Mouth of Hell' with hardly a worry," Hendrik said.

Mary looked back at her companion. She furrowed her brow in question.

"It was the strait we passed through. Normally, the currents are fierce, but we're in luck this morning." The Dutchman smiled ruefully as he slowed their approach to the dock. "There are eight islands here. And many distilleries and warehouses among them. How do you know which one this Kane person is on?"

Mary stared hard ahead. "He's here. I know it." Her thoughts drifted to the book she had purchased for her husband. *The Nine Unknown*. Echoes of her life sounded in her mind, and she knew that sometimes stories—no matter how crazy—could have substance; they could be more than tall tales. She had experienced it; no matter how far she had pushed those experiences down, she knew the truth.

Hendrik guided *The Cyprian* into a mooring along the docks of the large island, Grande Miquelon. Mary had decided this was the ideal place to start after a hurried history lesson of the archipelago from Hendrik. Together, he and Mary swiftly tied off the boat. There were few eyes about at this hour to see their approach, but there were eyes, nonetheless. Fishermen were always up this early. And the business of smuggling knew no off-hours; such were the pros and cons of bootlegging.

Mary hurried to the edge of the dock and cast her eyes to the row of warehouses looming in the pre-dawn gloom. She had never laid eyes upon this hub of operations, from which her current livelihood stemmed. She was impressed. This chain of islands warehoused untold gallons of alcohol waiting to be smuggled into the United States, Canada, and most certainly, other countries. She knew Mr. Dalitz was not the only boss who bootlegged—Al Capone, in nearby Chicago, was reputed to be in the same business—and there were certainly other small fish. The people wanted their vices, after all.

She turned at Hendrik's approaching footsteps. "Which of these buildings does the most business with Mr. Dalitz?"

The Dutchman squinted and pointed to the massive structure at the left end of the row. "There. I have made several pickups and runs for the Mayfield Road Gang out of that place."

"Then that is where we'll find Kane."

"I still do not know how you know this, or what is going on, my dear."

"I'm not sure I know myself. I do know that Kane is a slippery bastard, and I didn't like him when I met him. He's up to something. He has that look."

Hendrik nodded.

"And I have it on good faith he's the threat here. Strange things have been happening stateside," Mary continued. "Reports of people in and around speakeasies found dead, as if killed by an animal. Also, accounts of people going wild and attacking others. And before I called you..." Mary hesitated.

Hendrik waited for her to finish.

"…I was on Lake Erie to pick up a scheduled drop from the *Nectar*. And there were… monsters. Scaly, reptilian things. And the crew were acting as if possessed or hypnotized. They killed four of my men."

Mary set her jaw, collecting herself. Hendrik placed a beefy hand on her shoulder in a gesture of comfort. She patted his hand and pulled away. "Locations, places where booze is available, seem to be the common thread. The only thing that makes sense is that the alcohol was poisoned. Maybe Kane is here seeking to contaminate a larger supply? I don't know why he would do this or what purpose it would serve, but I've got to try to stop him."

"Why you?"

"Because I know." Mary hefted her Thompson SMG Model 1921 automatic rifle. "And because I can."

THE PUNGENT SMELL permeated the entire warehouse. It was sharp and made the nose crinkle. But Eddie Kane paid no attention. The robust odor of fermented alcohol mingled with the close, metallic air of the space. Traces of copper lingered, evidence of the bloodshed in the adjoining office. It was a small sacrifice on his road to rule.

Kane stood in the center of the wide room, dozens of large vats lined up along the walls surrounding him. He took stock of his acolytes—six in all, each guarding a passageway into the concourse in which they stood—and at the sour faces they made at the sharp stench filling the chamber. The occultist smiled.

Soon.

Very soon.

Fat candles, dripping globs of yellow wax, ringed the edges of the room, each one placed before one of the vats. Their flames beckoned like ethereal fingers for Kane to begin. He would not kneel to summon the spirit as he had done before. He saw no need to do so now, on this, the cusp of his ascension to power.

Kane began the familiar chant, speaking the words and passages he had learned. Syllables that had not been spoken in millennia. They slipped from his tongue like the vilest honey. He heard the scuffle of his acolytes' boots across the cement floor and the fearful murmuring of their voices. Kane peered upward. The edges of the air before him fluttered, and a wraithlike silhouette seemed to form, as if drawn by an unseen hand.

SPECTRAL FLICKERING LIGHT lured Mary and Hendrik farther. The pair had encountered zero resistance in the warehouse, which she thought odd. Factories and warehouses on a scale such as this operated around the clock, and at the very least, there should have been a skeleton crew for the graveyard shift. And, considering the business nature of this warehouse—and most facilities on this island—it was *not* a good sign they had seen no one.

Could she have been wrong? Was she letting Four's tales fuel her paranoia and disbelief? Mary wasn't sure. Her head told her one thing, but her gut screamed differently, and she couldn't ignore its cries anymore.

The echo of strange utterances came distantly to their ears and Mary exchanged a look with Henk. She saw uneasiness writ across his features, and those unusual words, distant and unintelligible, also filled her with irrational dread. Henk nodded to a metal stairwell leading upward to a catwalk. It would be best to get an overall view of this place and hopefully get the drop on Kane. Mary shouldered her Thompson and moved up the stairs, careful to make as little noise as possible with her boots upon the grated metal. On a landing halfway up, they halted. The voice grew louder, and they stopped, trying to puzzle out what was being said, but to no avail. To their right, a heavy wooden door was slightly ajar. Mary and Henk passed silently onto a mezzanine level and gazed out upon a bizarre scene.

The ghost light which had beckoned them glowed bright as they moved onto the grated catwalk. Far below was a spacious concourse area filled with large vats, pallet racks and other shelving. Candles shimmered along the floor ringing the chamber. Six armed men, each standing guard before an entryway into the large space, were turned toward the center of the room. The unmistakable figure of Bishop Eddie Kane, swathed in black, stood there, arms spread high and wide. Light rippled strangely along the lines of his obsidian robes.

Suddenly, he ceased.

Above him, yet still below Mary and Hendrik, the very air seemed to ripple. A form coalesced, translucent like a dream becoming flesh. A haggard face appeared slowly, as if it were pushing through a membrane, cloudy and indistinct, before it came into sharp, terrible relief. Its mouth looked sickly, lips sagging, and its teeth were rotted. Its eyes, however, were horribly clear and burning with hate.

As a body formed beneath that hellish face, limbs flowing like murky liquid, pearly fire flickered downward along its throat to where a stomach opened in a ghastly torso. Glimpses of burnt organs could be seen through the pale flames.

The smell of vinegar burned the air.

"I am here," the thing spoke, every word punctuated with a burst of the pale flames at its throat, each syllable an eruption of hate.

"Indeed, Heita," Kane said. "And now that you are, you will implement my vision for this world."

"Beware, lackey." The ghost-form's eyes blazed. "You serve *me* in my quest for vengeance."

Kane laughed. "I now have the means to bind you to my will, spirit. There is much to be learned from the Books of the Unknown." He stroked the black box in his grip.

Ghost fire burned brightly. Heita said nothing. But the wraith's eyes spoke volumes as they burned downward at Kane.

"I care not for your desires upon this world nor your mission of vengeance," Kane said. "Yes, I know your story. You were punished for spoiling wine into vinegar. I also know you have great sway over the properties of alcohol. I wish you to convert the fluid in these vats so as I can command those who drink of it."

"Why should I do this thing?"

Kane lifted the vial from the box and held it before him as a powerful talisman. The inky fluid within thrashed against its glass confines. "This should be all the answer you need."

Heita floated backward.

"You know it, I see." Kane smiled. "And you know this has the power to affect even you."

Heita hissed. Sparks of pale fire sizzled in the air.

"If I do this thing for you, what promise do you make me? I wish vengeance upon he who wronged me. He and his kin."

"Do this for me and they are yours."

Mary's palms were sweaty on the grip of her submachine gun. She couldn't believe what she was watching. But there it was…

…a fiery, floating ghost, seeking vengeance. And even crazier, Kane bartering with this thing for the fate of the world as if he were haggling at a market. The slick occultist was a madman.

She turned to Hendrik. "We have to stop this."

"Aye, *mijn liefste*." The Dutchman nodded slowly.

Mary straightened and racked her Thompson. Then she rained fire on the scene beneath her feet.

THE LOUD, METALLIC ratchet sound bounced off the cavernous space and both Kane and Heita looked up. The thunder of automatic gunfire exploded within the concourse, sounding as if the end of the world was nigh.

Perhaps it was.

Kane covered his head and bolted for cover, hot, stinging bees flying all around him. He watched as four of his acolytes fell in a crimson mist before they could even bring their guns to bear. Through the cacophony of death, the cold laughter of Heita could be heard clearly.

"Fucking phantom," Kane snarled as he dove clumsily out of sight behind a pallet of hardwood kegs. It galled him to hear the blasted ghost laugh while whomever was on the catwalk threatened to disrupt his plans. And he cursed having to cower behind these crates.

The sudden silence was deafening. Kane chanced a peek over the top of the keg in front of him. The stink of pitch lining the cask filled his nostrils, and his eyes watered. Gunsmoke hung heavily in the air, and he could see the cold, ivory silhouette of Heita observing events. Two figures rushed down a gangplank from the catwalk: a man and a woman. They dodged the gunfire his remaining faithful aimed their way.

The man—a large, bearded sailor by his dress—returned fire, providing cover for the woman as she loaded another magazine. Kane peered closer—*Mary Santos!*

More shocking, though, was the black lacquered box he spied in the middle of the floor. Damn him for a fool! He had dropped it while running for cover. He needed that for his plans to come to fruition.

A worried scream yanked Kane's attention back to the events in the concourse. The big sailor was down. Mary dropped one of the last two acolytes, presumably the one who had shot her companion, with a blaze of bullets. Now, she was alone. Alone against himself, his last servant, and Heita.

The spirit didn't seem to recognize that Kane no longer held the means to keep him at bay; it appeared amused by the standoff between Mary and the acolyte trading fire. *I should make a break for the box,* Kane thought, *but it's still too far away.* The Santos woman was closer to it and could drop him if he didn't time it right.

Kane hovered, half hidden behind the pallet of kegs, waiting for his chance.

MARY DARTED FROM behind the stairwell and sprayed bullets at the last of Kane's men. He was around the corner of the corridor entrance, and she didn't quite have the angle on him.

She whipped her head aside as a bullet dinged off the metal railing right next to her.

Head in the game, Mary!

She pulled the trigger, and the Thompson coughed twice before jamming.

"*Porra!*" Mary kicked at the shell casings on the floor. She saw the acolyte tentatively duck his head out, then smile. He stepped more clearly into view, raising his gun.

A scuff of shoe leather behind her alerted Mary that Kane was likely skittering from under his rock. She still had the .32 Lemon Squeezer. Faced with danger on two fronts, Mary let her instincts guide her. Flashes of Felix and Sarah, and Alfred's warm smile danced across her mind's eye, and she prayed she would be able to see her family again. She hurled the Thompson to the right; the autorifle made a racket as it careened over the floor.

The acolyte's gaze instinctively tracked the sliding weapon, and Mary effortlessly drew the snub revolver from inside her coat. She was thankful she had had the foresight to carry the Smith & Wesson for its easy unholstering.

She fired two shots, both direct hits to the chest. Crimson stains spread evenly across the man's torso as he fell, lifeless, his gun clattering to the floor. Trusting in her accuracy and skill, Mary whirled before the acolyte's gun fell, knowing Kane was likely to come up behind her. She fired two more shots.

A *thunk*, followed by the tinkle of breaking glass, then a pained grunt.

Mary steadied herself, keeping her Lemon Squeezer aimed forward. She had one shot left. She needed to assess her situation.

Kane kneeled on the floor before her, no more than twenty feet away. He cradled a bloody hand, paying little attention to the wetness soaking his sleeve. Instead, he gawked in horror at the shattered remnants of the black box on the floor; shards of glass winked in the light and a strange, inky cloud drifted upward, disappearing in the dawning sunrays coming through the high windows.

"You fool!" Kane screamed.

Mary moved closer, wary still. "I've been called worse. It's all over." She eyed the debris.

"You bitch. You have no idea what you've done."

"My idea is to take you to Mr. Dalitz instead of the police." Mary's jawline was tight.

A cold shadow fell across the pair.

Mary retreated a step and looked up to see the fiery ghost had now taken notice of them. She swallowed, feeling a chill on the back of her neck. The *fantasma*, however, did not seem concerned with her.

"You wronged me as I had been wronged in the past." Heita glowered at Kane.

The crippled cult leader, for his part, glared back. "You are a short-sighted fool, Heita. You have done nothing in your unlife but nurse hatred when you could have had so much more with the abilities you command."

The bilious pale fires rippled along Heita's unearthly form for several moments. A terrible smile split his rotted face.

"Perhaps I have been short-sighted. You are correct. I can see no better way to redress myself of this than by adopting your vision."

Surprised realization lit Kane's face as his jaw went slack. "That is *my* plan! You can't!"

"I can. I also considered making you a victim of your own 'plan,' but centuries of nurturing vengeance against one long gone have taught me it is best that I simply end you."

Horror grew on Kane's face.

"And I have you to thank for my newfound perception."

Mary watched in awestruck terror as Kane trembled on the floor. The cult leader tried to climb to his feet but fell back to his knees. His horror-pained features began to slowly melt. First, his eyes popped and bubbled, then dribbled like jelly down his waxy cheeks. His skin sizzled and liquified, flowing from his robes into a steaming, fleshy goo. It happened in an instant, but it felt like an eternity to Mary. The stink of hot vinegar scorched her nostrils, and she swallowed the bile rising in her throat.

"Now, what to do with you…"

MARY QUIVERED IN fear despite herself. Heita gazed down upon her with those shining, hateful eyes. She could see the pseudo-pulsing of his organs through the opalescent flames of his spectral torso.

She had faced several odd and terrible things in her short life, but never had she been at such a disadvantage. No allies. Henk was likely dead. Whatever means she might have had to control this monster, she had already destroyed. She had one shot remaining in her snubbie, and seriously doubted this hellish thing would give her time to reload. Besides, what good were bullets against a ghost?

This was it, then. Mary thought she'd have had a longer run of it than this. And she certainly hadn't expected to go out this way. Visions of her family misted her dark eyes, and she regretted that she would not get to see them one last time.

She would go out defiantly, not whimpering like that bastard, Kane. Mary set her mouth in a hard line and raised her gun to the grisly ghost. "*Vá se foder, fantasma!*"

Heita's laughter pierced her ears like sharp talons plunging into her brain. She grimaced and fired off her last shot. The baleful cackling and the echoes of the gunshot faded into the cavernous space.

Mary blinked, unsure of what had happened, whether she were dead or not. The air seemed to pop like a soap bubble bursting. It was a sensation she had recently felt, and she wondered if any of what had just occurred was real.

She lowered her gun to behold the three mysterious figures she had last seen on Lake Erie; that meeting seemed like a lifetime ago but had taken place only yesterday. The woman, Four, and her cohorts, Six and Eight.

They ringed around Heita and stood firm in defensive postures. Each of them clutched a book, heavy tomes swathed in black leather. Their free hands were splayed forward, as if waiting for something. Mary backed away, sensing this fight was not hers. The Unknown must have traveled here by the same method they'd used to send her to Sydney. It made sense. If they could send others, why not themselves?

As Mary retrieved her useless Thompson—she could no longer reload, but she drew some small comfort from holding it—she fumed over why they had not assisted earlier. Perhaps her friend would still be alive if they had.

Mary had never checked on Henk. There had been no time, under fire as she was. Rage and grief and the urgency of the situation dictated her conclusion. She hurried over to him, all the while aware of the standoff brimming behind her, and slid beside Hendrik's supine form. Blood stained his face, pooling beneath his head. She ran her fingers across him, feeling for a pulse, heedless of her now wet, sticky fingers.

Mary could find no entry wound anywhere on the big sailor's

head where most of the blood was centered. All she could find was a long, wicked gash across his temple; a stray bullet had only grazed him.

"*Bastardo sortudo!*" Mary replaced her empty Thompson with the big sailor's nearby rifle, for what good it may have done.

"You," Heita hissed, slowly revolving to take in each of the Unknown encircling him.

"Yes," Four said in her low, flat tone.

"Ashoka's current lackeys. You will not stop me." Heita flared, glowing white hot. Only his rotted teeth were visible through the unholy flames.

Hendrik stirred at the sudden onset of heat. Mary held up an arm to ward off the surge.

"*Wat maakt het uit?*" the Dutchman swore, squinting in pain. He pulled himself to a sitting position and stared ahead in awe.

"Might just be the end of the world, *meu amigo.*"

The three Unknown maintained their positions, hands spread forward at Heita's attack. The glare subsided, and thick protoplasmic matter splashed away from each of the Unknown like rain from an umbrella. The fluid plopped in creamy yellow pools on the warehouse floor around the three mystics.

Mary could swear she saw each of their books emit a peculiar light during that surreal exchange, but she couldn't be sure. It was so bright.

"This world is not yours, Heita," Four said. "It is time for you to depart."

The three Unknown stepped inward as one, tightening the circle about the angry phantom, and held the books forward. The books did indeed glow, or rather, they seemed to eat the light surrounding them. The Unknown closed the circle further.

Heita thrashed like an animal trapped in a cage. His eyes blazed cold fire.

Mary now clearly saw the light of the three books intensify. A gossamer tether formed between them. A fourth anti-glow emanated from the chest of Four, connecting to the ethereal chain.

The vengeful spirit screamed wordlessly. The pale fires of his twisted, terrible body sputtered and died out. Glimpses of his internal organs, so horrifically visible previously, now turned cloudy. Heita's face flowed into the collapsing mass of his body. Very shortly, a wet splash reached Mary's ears, and she saw a stain upon the warehouse floor.

A hint of vinegar tinged the air.

MARY BREATHED IN the sharp, stinging sea wind. No matter what she did in her life's journey, or how far away she was from home, she would always love that smell. It was part and parcel of who she was. Madeira lived in her heart.

She gazed out over the North Atlantic, digesting the last several hours.

"Mary."

She turned to the speaker. She marveled once again at their location. Moments ago, they had been in a warehouse in the aftermath of some strange, mythic contest for the fate of the world. Now, they were in Sydney, standing in the shipyard. Sailors and fishermen bustled about their tasks, and she thought for certain some of them were about the business of smuggling, although she did not recognize anyone in particular. No one seemed to pay her and her companion any mind.

"You have questions."

"I do. I'm not even sure where to start."

"The beginning."

Mary cocked her head, annoyed.

The faintest trace of a smile played across Four's lips.

"Will that *fantasma*, Heita, return, or is he gone? Who was he?"

"Heita is banished. We converted him to water. We thought it a fitting fate for he who was punished for spoiling wine into vinegar."

"But, vinegar can't spoil, can it?"

"Entropy comes for all," Four replied. "We merely sped up the passage of time. He reverted to simple water."

"How can you do these things?" Mary was trying to wrap her head around this mumbo jumbo. The term sprang so easily to mind, but she should have known better. Especially after what she had just experienced.

"We just can."

Mary sighed. "What about the alcohol in the warehouse? Was it contaminated? Did Kane or the spirit succeed in doing that? My friend and I didn't see anything."

"The fluid in those vats is fine. My associates and I made sure of it. We also rendered inert the explosives you and your friend had planted."

Mary scrunched her face. "And what about Henk?"

"He will not remember this travail."

"You can't toy with his mind," Mary sputtered.

"It is for the best."

"Are you going to make me forget?"

Four did not say anything at first. Instead, she simply gazed at Mary, who seized the opportune gap in questioning. "I will not be made to forget my life. Who are you to exert such decisions?"

"We are the Unknown, shepherds of humanity. It is our burden to decide such things."

"Why the hell would you let things get to such a state that Kane nearly achieved his ends? You could have come with me to stop what happened. You and your friends," Mary shouted, "where the fuck were you?"

"As I told you," Four reminded her, "I had a more pressing errand."

"What could have been more pressing than the possible end of the world?"

"This." Four removed a black-bound book from inside her voluminous cloak. "Your superior had this in his possession. It does not belong to him."

"Did you make him forget?"

"Some things, yes."

Questions lit in Mary's eyes. Four saw them. "Moe Dalitz has a destiny beyond his current station. He will realize that destiny from some of the knowledge he gleaned within these pages."

Mary chewed on this answer. "And what is my destiny?"

"Now we come to the crux of it," Four said. "You are at a crossroads."

"I am?"

"Yes. My companions and I are of the Nine Unknown. Yet, we currently stand at Eight. That is the matter which brought me to Cleveland."

"You… want me to join up?" Mary asked.

Four merely stared at her.

"I have a family and a job, people who depend on me. Besides, you've never told me what you do beyond mystic half-truths. I need more than that."

"What do you want?"

Mary took in a breath, held it, then blew it out. She needed this woman to give her something, some measure of good faith. "What's your name?"

"I have no name."

Mary sighed, and turned to go.

"Ruth."

Mary stopped.

"Ruth Ella Moore. I have some small aptitude for micro-organisms."

Mary extended her hand. "Hello, Ruth."

Four hesitatingly took Mary's hand. "I tell you this fact, so that you may more easily come to your decision. Never again must you refer to me by my relinquished name. I am Four."

Mary nodded.

"The Nine Unknown have existed for millennia, founded by an ancient emperor, Ashoka. We each safeguard a Book that holds secret knowledge which would be dangerous to humanity until they are prepared to learn of it. There must always be Nine." Four held forth the tome.

Mary took it. The Book was smooth and heavy. She gazed at the black leather cover.

"This is Alchemy. You would become Seven."

Mary's fingers brushed the edge of the cover. She was tempted to open it.

"Hold!" Four said. "Before you crack these pages, you must know what you need to give up."

Mary turned her plaintive eyes to Four. She suspected her answer.

"You will no longer be Mary Santos. You will no longer be a mother and wife. You will be Unknown and serve the greater good from the fringes of society, shepherding them as we do."

Mary's fingers fell away from the Book cover.

"I have been in communication with my fellows, and we are in agreement. You are a suitable candidate to join our ranks as Seven. But you must leave your old life behind."

"I'm not sure I can do that."

"Time is short, for we must be Nine before long. If not you, then I must find another."

Mary had always thrived on adventure and seizing life by its horns, but she had never quite embarked on such a road as the one which lay before her.

Alfred, and Felix, and Sarah. The idea of never seeing them again pulled at her. The corners of her eyes watered. She rubbed her belly thoughtfully, torn between desires.

"Can I think about it?"

Four considered for several moments, then eventually nodded her assent. "I will return for your answer. Soon. In the meantime, I must have the Book back."

Mary nodded. She stared into the ebon blackness of the Book's leather cover and imagined where its pages might lead her.

Hesitating, she slowly held out her hand. Gulls wheeled overhead, crying out to the sky and the sea. Mary felt the weight leave her grip as she relinquished the Book of Alchemy. Her eyes took on a faraway cast.

She had a decision to make.

TOM DEADY

Tom Deady's first novel, *Haven*, won the
2016 Bram Stoker Award for Superior
Achievement in a First Novel. He has since
published several novels, novellas, a short
story collection, and the first book in his
middle grade horror series. Most recently, he
compiled *The Rack*, an anthology celebrating
the bygone days of mass market horror
paperbacks. He has a master's degree in
English and Creative Writing and is a member
of both the Horror Writers Association
and the New England Horror Writers
Association. You can find out more about
Tom and his work at **www.tomdeady.com**.

CHAPTER ONE

Roan Devlin closed his eyes as the elevator rattled along the mine shaft. It did no good: he could still hear the grinding of the pulleys and smell the fear of the men huddled around him. Another cave-in, in one of the new shafts. Everybody had made it out alive but that didn't erase the memory. The panicked yelling after the dynamite had gone off. The thundering rumble that had shaken him right to the soul. The cloying dust filling the shaft. The split-second surety that this was it, this was the day he would die in the mines. *Just like Da.*

"Coming, Roan?"

Patrick Laughlin's voice pulled him back to the present.

The elevator was empty. Patrick stood staring, head cocked to one side. "Yeah, sorry, mate." He stepped out of the elevator, relieved to be on solid ground, the weight that had been on his chest all day finally lifting.

"You okay?" Patrick asked as they shuffled behind the other men and headed toward the equipment shed.

"I'll be right as rain after a pint. I need to wash the taste out of my mouth. The taste of this place." They tossed their helmets and tools into the lockers. "Maybe the second pint will clear my head of that shit." He gestured toward the mine shaft.

Patrick nodded. "It's a bloody miracle nobody was killed. Well…"

Roan turned. "What?"

Patrick looked around, then gave his head a quick shake.

Roan understood. Too many big ears around. Some of the other miners were all too willing to run straight to management with any scuttlebutt. They fancied it would get them in the mine bosses' good graces and earn them the easy duties.

When they were out of earshot, on the way to the saloon, Patrick said, "Word is, MacGreggor fucked up the blast."

Roan scoffed. "Wouldn't be the first time."

"Yeah," Patrick agreed. "But it'll likely be the last."

"Jackman fired him?" It would be unusual. Management was having trouble keeping the crews filled. There was talk of a group from Ireland whispering in some of the miners' ears about the dangerous conditions and the low wages. The word 'strike' had been spoken in hushed tones at the saloon. Usually, the bosses would just keep the sloppy workers away from the blasting crew.

"He's been sent to Tunnel 17," Patrick said.

"What's the big deal with 17? Can it be any more dangerous than the rest of that deathtrap?"

Patrick scoffed. "How long you been going down, now?"

"Just five months."

"And you haven't heard the men talking about Tunnel 17?" Patrick sounded bemused.

Roan shrugged. "This and that." Now that he thought about it, Tunnel 17 had only been whispered about, and only briefly at that. "Is it some sort of demotion? A punishment?"

Patrick didn't answer for a long minute. "Just keep your nose clean, and don't get sent down there."

"I don't under—"

Patrick stopped abruptly. "You know," he said, "I don't fancy a pint after all. I'm heading home."

Roan watched him go, confused by the sudden, skittish behavior. He decided he *did* fancy a pint, and continued toward the saloon.

Working the mines was the last thing he had wanted, but since the Panic of 1873, times had been tough. He'd held a good position at Jay Cooke and Company, starting out as a runner but eventually learning some accounting and moving up the ranks. After they'd filed bankruptcy and the New York Stock Exchange closed down for ten days, the economy had crumbled. Banks toppled like dominos, followed by more than fifty railroad companies. Jobs were scarce; *good* jobs were nonexistent. Roan had slunk home to Serenity, Pennsylvania, tail between his legs. The mines put food on the table.

The crack of a whip sounded off to his left. He turned to find a man trying to urge an overloaded mule forward. The man drew back his arm, about to give the poor animal another lash. "Here, now!" Roan called, striding toward the pair.

With a scowl, the man lowered his arm as Roan approached. "Unless you have a talent for getting stubborn mules to move, I haven't time for you." He turned back to the problem at hand and raised the whip.

Roan lunged forward and twisted the weapon from the man's grasp. "There's no talent to it," he said. "You just have to be smarter than the mule."

The man's expression went from confused to angry. He stepped forward but Roan cracked the whip, stopping him in his tracks.

"You've got her overpacked," he said calmly. "Lessen her burden and she'll do her job."

The man glared at Roan, then regarded the mule and the load weighing her down. He sighed and nodded.

Roan handed him the whip, then helped him unpack the mule. He shook hands with the man and headed to get a beer.

The saloon was unusually quiet. Most evenings, the men were happy to throw away some of their hard-earned wages to blow off some steam after their shift, but tonight was different. The accident seemed to have left many of the workers sullen. But there was something else. A wariness Roan hadn't seen before. Conversations seemed tense, eyes shifting suspiciously.

He saw a couple guys who worked on his crew. After getting

a beer, he made his way through the crowd to where they stood. "Evening, mates."

"Evenin'," one muttered. The other just glared.

"Why so glum, boys?" Roan said, trying to break the tension. "We all made it out."

The two men, John Moore and Sean Graves, exchanged a glance.

Roan tried to gauge the reaction of the odd pair. Moore was a hulking giant, as though he had been carved from the very mountain he mined. He wore a long beard that hid most of his features, other than his brooding eyes. Graves was small and frail-looking, always needing help with his duties. He had a scrawny, rat-like face that no beard seemed to want anything to do with. They were thick as thieves, though. Roan suspected that Moore did the lion's share of Graves' work. Or he had some sway with the mine bosses to keep Graves employed.

Moore straightened to his full height, his face hardening. "You see MacGreggor here, enjoying a pint?"

The room went quiet. It was as if they'd been waiting for something, a confrontation. Violence to alleviate stress, allay fear.

"No," Roan said. "But I heard he wasn't injured."

Graves shook his head and muttered something Roan couldn't make out. He was brave enough when Moore was nearby.

"Don't worry about MacGreggor," Moore said. "But don't be so fucking cheery after a cocked-up blast, either."

Roan didn't like the look in Moore's eyes. They were no longer brooding, but cold and steely. His body was rigid, every muscle a coiled spring. Ordinarily, Moore was generally the calmest fellow on the crew. A gentle giant.

Roan was in no mood for a fight, especially one he couldn't win. Hell, the way Moore looked, Roan might end up in the infirmary. Or worse. "I'm sorry, John. I didn't mean any harm. I really thought MacGreggor was all right. *Was* he injured?"

Moore glared at him, eyes narrowed, as if trying to assess his sincerity. Then his face softened. Roan let out a breath, feeling the electricity in the room diminish.

"MacGreggor's been sent to work Tunnel 17," Moore said, his voice barely above a whisper. Graves held his glare a moment longer, sneered, and the pair shuffled away.

Roan took a pull on his beer, but it tasted bad. He put the half-full mug down on the bar and left the saloon. He walked the quiet streets, trying to recall everything he'd heard about Tunnel 17. That's when he realized he hadn't heard much at all. Like he'd told Patrick, it had sounded like a sort of punishment. The shit duty you get when you screw up. Then why were Laughlin, Moore, and that cocksucker Graves so bothered about MacGreggor?

CHAPTER TWO

The next day, the elevator ride down to the shaft was uncomfortably somber. Entering the mine was never a cause for celebration; it was a dangerous place, and you could never be a hundred percent sure you'd be taking the ride up at the end of the shift. Or if you did, that you'd have all your limbs still attached and your eyesight and hearing intact. But that day was eerily quiet and there was an undercurrent of tension that was almost palpable. The same crackle you could feel in the air before a thunderstorm rolled through. The tightness in Roan's chest made his breaths shallow. Still, he kept his mouth shut and his eyes down, not wanting to give the look or say the word that might set someone off.

At the shaft, he waited for Jackman to hand out assignments. He was jumpy, the walls seeming closer, the air cloying. The other miners seemed on edge as well.

Jackman usually kept the same pairings and duties most days, but after an accident he would sometimes mix things up, ordering teams to work together who had never done so before. Like he was trying to keep them off-balance, distracted. Or maybe so the new teams might not feel comfortable talking about the incident.

Roan, to his great dismay, was paired with Graves. It wasn't the words at the saloon that had annoyed him, Graves was just not a good worker. Roan thought him lazy and careless, a some-times-deadly combination in the mines. Graves looked no more pleased with the situation than Roan, nodding brusquely as they prepared to start drilling.

The day wore on, with none of the usual joking and raucous storytelling. A shadow was hanging over the workers after the accident, but there was something else afoot. At lunch break, Roan pulled Laughlin aside and asked him what was going on.

Patrick pulled him deeper into a side tunnel, well out of ear-shot. "People are tired of being treated like animals, risking their lives down here for shite wages," he hissed. Then he looked around, making sure nobody had approached. "There's talk of a strike… and more. And I think I'm going to be taking part—"

Footfalls sounded nearby. Patrick gave him a hard look and scurried away.

Strike? thought Roan, cold dread squirming in his gut. And what had Laughlin meant by "and more?" Roan had heard the rumors before about strikes and unionizing but it had never come to anything. Usually because the mine owners would find out the source of the talk and send some 'associates' to have a talk with the troublemaker. And the troublemaker's family, if necessary.

Roan ate his lunch in solitude, not tasting any of the meal his wife had put together for him. He conjured up a dozen scenarios of doom, all ending with him trapped in the mine. What would he do if the men were to rally for a strike today? His options were limited, and none seemed very safe. He could side with the men and put himself at risk of retaliation from the mine owners. Or he could show up for work the next day and cross the picket line, forever marking himself a traitor.

Another idea struck him. He could try to straddle the line and hope it would be over in a day or two by telling Jackman he was sick and needed to stay home for a few days. It might work… or it might ostracize him from both sides. *Fuck.*

He went back to his station for the afternoon shift, unsure of what tomorrow would bring. He and Graves would finish drilling the blast holes, then they would begin the tedious task of setting the dynamite and preparing the fuses. Roan found himself distracted, trying to size up his fellow miners to determine which side they were likely to fall on.

"The fuck you doing?" Graves bellowed.

Roan looked down. The drill was smoking, the bit close to snapping from overheating. He'd been on water duty, responsible for ladling water over the bit before it became too hot from the friction of boring into the rock. He gave Graves a meek look and reached for the ladle just as the ominous sound of the bit snapping echoed in the shaft.

Pain erupted in Roan's head and he staggered backward, his helmet flying off. The back of his head slammed against the mine wall before he landed on his ass. He grabbed his left ear. Liquid, warm and sticky, poured through his fingers as all sound in the mine seemed to cease. Then the shouting began, almost immediately drowned out by the emergency horn.

Rough hands pulled him to his feet. Jackman barged through the crowd, scowling. "What happened here?" When Roan didn't respond, he fixed his glare on Graves.

"He looked like he was daydreaming," Graves spat. "When I asked him what in the bloody hell he was doing, the bit overheated and snapped."

Jackman pointed at Moore. "Get him up top." He turned to O'Banion, who had been paired with Moore for the day. "You're with Graves."

"Christ, I thought you people knew the mines? First, the colossal fuck-up yesterday, now this?" He shot Roan a look, then turned and pushed through the crowd. "Back to work, everyone. Show's over."

Moore put an arm around Roan's waist and helped him

toward the elevator. "What the fuck, Roan?" he growled. "Do ya have a big head from the saloon last night?"

Roan shook his head, sending a battalion of pain marching through it. "I never finished my first pint," he said. The mine seemed to tilt. "I was just—" He stopped himself. In his daze, he was about to say he was thinking about the strike. "I was thinking about MacGreggor. And Tunnel 17."

"You gotta clear your head of that foolishness," Graves said. "Lest you'll end up there yourself."

The idea chilled Roan. Though he hadn't figured out exactly what the tunnel was, he knew he wanted to stay clear of it. Was this a big enough mistake to warrant Tunnel 17? They'd reached the elevator, but it swam in and out of focus, as though it was moving away, then coming closer.

Moore helped him into the car then shut the cage. He rang the bell for the operator to pull it up.

Roan reached a shaky hand toward the big man. "Moore—"

CHAPTER THREE

Roan regained consciousness as the elevator shuddered to a stop. Moore was staring at him with an expression of mild amusement, laced with a touch of concern.

"Welcome back. Reckon you scrambled your brains a touch. Think you can stay with us until we get you home?"

Roan tried to nod but wasn't sure if his head moved. A deep ache had settled into his neck. "Yeah," he croaked. "What happened?"

"Drill bit snapped." Moore heaved Roan to his feet. "Graves said you bollocksed it up."

Roan remembered Graves yelling at someone, but the rest was fuzzy. "Thanks for helping out."

Moore shrugged his giant shoulders. "All the same to me, mate. I get full wages because of the circumstances." Moore returned the equipment to the manager and started walking with Roan, half carrying him. "Besides," he said, glancing around, "I'm not sure you want to be around later, anyhow."

Roan frowned. "What? Why?"

Moore scoffed. "Get your head out of your ass, Devlin. Jackman and the rest of the bosses are in for a reckoning. There're some folks in town that came to help. Advocates for us miners. There's going to be a meeting of sorts after today's shift. As long as the bosses don't catch wind of it," he added.

Cold fear spread through Roan as he recalled Patrick Laughlin's words. It was finally falling into place. *There's talk of a strike... and more.* "The Molly Maguires," Roan whispered. Moore's grip tightened.

"Don't be saying that name aloud, ya fool," Moore hissed. "It's time we got what we deserve," he added softly.

The Molly Maguires had once been spoken of in mythical terms for their violent, sometimes murderous methods of activism. Lately, there was more and more evidence that they had made their way to the United States. Pennsylvania, to be specific. There was talk that they were already active in nearby mines, wreaking their special form of vigilante justice in the name of the struggling miners.

"MacGreggor, too?" Roan asked.

"Are you daft from hitting your head, or just a fucking idiot?" Moore's voice dripped venom.

"Maybe both," Roan replied. "I'm new to the mines. People are still skittish around me." He laughed. "Maybe they think I'm a spy for the bosses." He felt Moore's eyes on him. Roan stopped, shaking himself from the big man's grip despite the tendrils of pain that reached from his head down his neck. "Tell me what's going on with MacGreggor." He held the giant's gaze.

Moore sighed. "It's not MacGreggor you need to worry about. It's Tunnel 17."

"Spill it, Moore." Roan was losing patience. "What's with all the Tunnel 17 secrecy?"

"There's not much to spill," Moore said. "People get sent to Tunnel 17. They never come back."

"Never?" Roan exclaimed. "The work is so bad that they just quit? Has anyone asked them about it?"

"You're not getting it, mate. It's not that they don't come back to work. They're just…" Moore snapped his giant fingers, louder than a gunshot. "Gone."

"What do you mean?" Roan was waiting for the punchline but quickly realized the big man was serious. "What do the families say?"

Moore shook his head, his long hair swaying back and forth. "Gone. Every time. The bosses always have a story. Left town in a hurry. Had family down south. Got a better job in Boston." He looked back at the mine, scowling. "It's all bullshit."

The headache had taken root, and Roan was struggling to

follow the conversation. "What do you think is down there?"

Moore's gaze was so intense Roan had to turn away.

"I think there's a deep hole filled with bodies."

Roan blinked. It felt as though his eyes had turned to dust. Everything hurt. "You think they're killing miners? And the families, too? Why would they?"

"I'm not sure about the families," he said. "Could be they're sending them away with enough blood money to keep them quiet. As for why?" He held up a ham-sized hand and squeezed it into a fist. "Control. They rule with fear. But that's going to end."

Roan's stomach seemed to be trying to crawl up his esophagus. He didn't know if it was the knock on the head or Moore's story that was causing his nausea. They'd started walking again when the landscape in front of Roan blurred and started to spin. Moore kept him from falling again.

"Forget taking you home," he said. "We're going to see the doc."

Moore half dragged, half carried Roan to Doc Wilson's. They were in luck. Doc was in the office and reasonably sober. He took one look at Roan, let loose an exasperated groan, and motioned toward the table.

Roan looked about the office with trepidation. He never got sick, and this was his first injury so he'd never had cause to visit the doc before. The shabby condition of the room and the equipment made him question the wisdom of being here now. Not to mention the unsteady, half-slurring, bleary-eyed Doc. He sighed, knowing there was no alternative.

Doc cleaned the wound on Roan's ear, chuckling that there was a good chunk of it still down in the mine. Roan didn't find the humor in it. He shone a flashlight directly into Roan's face, and it felt like the sun itself was blazing there.

After a few other tests he said, "You've got a brain commotion. The medical journals are starting to use the word 'concussion' now. This means you have taken a traumatic blow to the head, and you might have a headache and experience some dizziness for a few days. Maybe vomiting. Bright lights, excessive noise, and too much activity will likely make it worse. Take a couple days away from the mines." He pulled a flask from his pocket and drank deeply, signaling they were done.

Moore walked out with Roan. "Lucky break, as it turns out. You'll miss all the excitement."

"What's going to happen, John?" Roan asked. "It sounds dangerous."

"Going down in the mines every day is fucking dangerous," he snapped. Then, quieter, "We're trying to make it *less* dangerous."

"I've heard stories about the mine bosses. And management," Roan said. "And after what you told me about Tunnel 17…"

"It's the only way," Moore said.

THEY REACHED ROAN'S house, and his wife, Sara, came running out. "Oh, my goodness! What happened?" She looked at his ear with an expression of pure horror.

"Just an accident with the drill," Roan said. "I'll be okay. I have to rest for a couple days."

As she hugged her husband, the armies of pain began marching double-time. His stomach squeezed in on itself, then violently ejected its contents. He barely had time to pull away from Sara before it happened.

"That's my cue," Moore said. "He's all yours. If you need anything, you come get me," he said, and headed off.

"John," Roan called after him. He turned back. "Please, tell me how the… meeting goes?" Moore nodded, then he was gone.

"SO, WHAT'S THIS meeting you're all worried about?" Sara asked.

Roan had spent the last twenty minutes explaining what had happened in the mines and assuring his wife that he was going to be okay. He'd thought—hoped—it was the last of it, so he could get some rest. But of course, she'd picked up on his last comment to John Moore. Very little got by Sara.

Roan sighed, ignoring the pulsing pain in his head. Sara deserved to know what was going on. "The miners are fed up. Tired of the low wages, the deathtrap conditions, being held hostage by the town."

"Strike," she breathed, her eyes filling with fear.

"Yes," he replied. "But that's not all."

Her face tensed, the color draining out of it. "Not…" She looked toward the window, afraid to say the name.

Nodding, Roan said it for her. "The Molly Maguires."

"Tell me you're not thinking of throwing in with that lot," she said sternly. But her voice cracked on the last word.

Roan explained that he didn't know what to do, and went over the short list of options. "The accident was a blessing in disguise," he said. "Now I get to see how it plays out without betraying the miners or getting in Dutch with the bosses." Spoken aloud, it sounded so cowardly.

"What about—"

Roan held up a hand to stop her. "My head is about to fall off my shoulders, love. Let me get a couple hours' kip and we'll talk. Maybe John or Patrick—"

"Patrick, too?" Sara shrieked.

"Patrick, too," he sighed. "Sara, please?"

She nodded and scurried away, leaving him to his pain and his bad thoughts.

ROAN SAT UP, clutching his head in his hands as pain shot down his skull into his neck and shoulders.

"Roan?" Sara's voice was soft, tentative.

"Mmmm," he managed, eyes clamped shut.

"You were…" Sara paused. "You were dreaming."

Roan took a deep breath and slowly opened his eyes. Sara came into view, blurry at first. "Was I?" Something plucked at his memory—

"You were moaning, and saying the name Buddy over and

over," Sara said. "Wasn't that—"

"God," Roan said, cutting her off. The dream came back to him all at once. *Not just a dream, a memory.*

Roan had been eleven or twelve when the stray had wandered onto their land. He'd known better than to ask his dad, so he had worked on his mother until she'd relented and said he could keep it, but it would be his responsibility. Roan had readily agreed and had gone to clear out a nice spot for his new dog—Buddy, he'd decided to call him—in the barn.

Things had been okay for a while, his father reluctantly agreeing that Buddy was a good dog. Then Da had broken his leg when a wagon lost a wheel and fell on him. Soon after, he'd taken to drinking, and taken to it with a zeal.

Roan soon realized that the drink turned his father into someone else, and learned to avoid him. Buddy wasn't so lucky. Roan had come home to find the dog cowering in the barn, its fur caked with dried blood. He'd run to his mother in tears, and she'd explained that his father had had a bad day and taken it out on Buddy.

There were a lot of bad days that fall, and Buddy paid the price. Roan had tended to fresh wounds almost daily. Finally, he'd come home from school and found Buddy listless and unable to get up to greet him. The poor thing had lain there, weakly licking Roan's hand.

He later found out Da had beaten the dog with the blunt side of his hatchet, inflicting so much brain damage the dog couldn't move its legs. Da—sober for a change—had explained with tears in his eyes that Buddy would have to be put down.

Roan had gone to the barn with his father. He'd sat with the dog for a long time, talking to him and patting him. When Da cocked the rifle, Roan had touched his arm, then held his hand out for the gun. Buddy was his dog; it was his responsibility. He'd never forgotten the look in Buddy's eyes just before he pulled the trigger. It was as if he'd known.

"Good Christ," Roan said, tears welling all these years later. "Maybe I should be put down."

Sara gasped. He'd told her the story, but he didn't think she understood the depth of his pain. "Go back to sleep," she said, and left him to his memories.

CHAPTER FOUR

A warm wind whispered through the trees. Thomas McCabe took a final drag from his cigarette, dropped it to the ground, and heeled it into the soft dirt. The small gathering of men in the clearing—lit by the soft, bluish light of a half-moon—shuffled nervously around him. McCabe counted fewer than twenty miners. *Not enough.*

"Gentlemen," he boomed, calling the meeting to order. "Thank you all for coming out. You're here because you're tired of toiling in the mines to make the owners rich while you can barely afford to feed your families, giving half your wages back to the owners at the company store." There were a few mutters of assent. "You're here because too many of you, your family, your friends, are subject to deadly working conditions. You're here because you want a better life for yourselves and your families."

"Hear, hear," a voice called from the darkness.

"For too many years," McCabe went on, "miners have been mistreated. Overworked, underpaid, your very lives put at risk, all to line the pockets of the mine owners." More muttering, getting louder. A good sign. "The mine bosses wield an iron fist, punishing workers for minor offenses. Docking wages. The mine mules are treated better than you are!" This was met with raucous response. He had them.

"Gentlemen—" McCabe stopped, his head cocked to one side. One thing he'd learned as a Molly was to stay alert at all times, keenly attuned to his surroundings. The snapping branch he'd heard didn't sound like a deer.

Torches blazed to light just beyond the perimeter of the clearing, and the group of miners went quiet. McCabe took stock. There were at least ten torches: they were surrounded. Unless each torchbearer was alone, and that was unlikely, this wasn't going to end well.

"Stay calm, gentlemen," McCabe said, his voice quiet but steady. "Looks like we've got a few folks too shy to join the meeting." He yelled out, "Show yourselves!" The miners panicked, turning wildly from side to side, as if looking for an escape route.

As the torches moved closer, the circle tightening, McCabe reached under his duster and pulled the shotgun from its custom leather holster. He wondered if any of the miners were armed, because the owner's henchmen sure as hell would be.

"Make yourselves known, cowards!" McCabe called.

The torches were extinguished, pitching the clearing back

into relative darkness.

Then hell broke loose.

The woods erupted in a cacophony of howls and branches breaking as the mob crashed through the underbrush toward them. As McCabe expected, they were greatly outnumbered. The assailants were armed, but McCabe was relieved to see they carried clubs instead of guns. He and the miners would take a beating, but they'd live to fight another day. He returned the shotgun to the holster and jumped into the fray.

He ran to the closest fight, swinging and kicking. He was a big man, tall and wide, with plenty of combat experience. He was powered by the strength of his convictions. The opposition was easy to identify, as they all wore burlap hoods. McCabe went for the knees whenever he could: a vulnerable spot, the easiest way to render an opponent useless. The throat was another weak spot but had deadly consequences.

He dispatched several of the assailants, taking a perverse satisfaction at their cries of pain, then went after the biggest of them, hoping the miners would carry their weight and not try to flee. He wrestled a club away from one of the men and used it viciously, raining blows down until bones cracked and the man's pleas stopped. The yelling and screaming around him seemed to go on forever as McCabe waded deeper into the fracas. He was beginning to think they might get out of this almost unscathed.

McCabe squared off with a hooded man waving a metal rod back and forth like a saber. They parried with their weapons, looking for a weakness in each other. McCabe feinted one way then swung mightily at the man's knee. He sidestepped the blow and caught McCabe on the shoulder with his club, numbing his arm and causing him to lose his grip on the weapon. McCabe moved closer to avoid a second hit, kneeing the other man in the thigh. He grabbed the man's hood, hoping to twist it enough so he couldn't see. Instead, the hood ripped off.

McCabe glared at him. *I know you.* The man's eyes bulged as he scrambled to get his hood back. Unable to do so, he put his fingers in his mouth and uttered a shrill whistle. Then he turned and disappeared into the darkness. The hooded men all followed, leaving McCabe to survey the damage.

SOME OF THE miners had fled; those who were still there had taken their share of lumps. McCabe found John Moore, one of his first and most fervent allies in Serenity.

"How did you fare?" he asked.

Moore turned his battered face to McCabe. His face was swelling already, and blood coated the lower part of his beard.

"Gave as good as I got," Moore said thickly. "So, I guess it's a draw."

The big man's expression betrayed his buoyant spirit. He was in a lot of pain. "Let's take stock," said McCabe, "and get anyone who needs help to Doc."

The clearing had sounded like an infirmary after the attackers had fled, the moans and groans louder than any conversation. Then shouts of anger rose above the din. McCabe ran over, a cold fist closing on his guts.

A small group huddled around a prone figure. One of the men turned to McCabe. "He's dead." The rage written all over his face overruled the fear in his voice. "You said nobody would be hurt."

"I'm sorry," McCabe said weakly. Moore stepped beside him; he was glad for the support. This could get out of hand quickly. "We need to find out how they knew about the meeting."

The miner—McCabe couldn't remember his name—jabbed a finger at his chest. "A man's dead, and all you care about is your fucking meeting?"

"If there's a rat among the miners, we're all in great danger," Moore said. He tried to soften his voice to exude concern, but the words came out cold.

"There is no 'we,' McCabe," the man spat, wheeling on him. "We're out." Murmurs rose from the other men.

McCabe shook his head and shouldered through the miners. The body was face-up, sightless eyes pointed to the heavens. The left half of his skull was caved in. A dark pool of blood was seeping into the dry soil. McCabe knelt and bowed his head. Ignoring the questions and accusations raining down on him, he reached over and closed the man's eyes, then stood, solemnly.

"Someone needs to tell whatever passes for the law around here," he said. He met each miner's gaze until one of them finally said "I'll go to the constable," and slunk away.

"Does this man have a wife? A family?"

Moore touched his arm. "A wife and two children."

"I'll tell the wife," McCabe said. "The rest of you, go home. If you need Doc, tell him you got into a scrape at the saloon. Tell him you fell out of bed. Not a word about what happened here. I don't care if you're in or you're out, but not a word."

Grumbles were the only response as the miners shuffled away.

"I'll go with you to see the widow," Moore said. "It's going to be rough."

"Thanks, John." McCabe heaved a great sigh. "Won't be my first and I'm sure it won't be my last." With a final, mournful glance at the dead man, McCabe headed out of the clearing.

CHAPTER FIVE

Roan is caught by the bosses, conspiring to strike, and sent to Tunnel 17. He's alone in the cave. Even though he can't see anything through the impenetrable darkness, he knows the chamber is vast. Bigger than it should be. Then, he hears noises. Shuffling things and slithering things. It all echoes hauntingly, sometimes seeming distant, then right next to him whispering in his ear. Then, he feels the hot breath on his neck. The smell of death, rot. He realizes he is holding a match and is about to strike it, to reveal what is in the tunnel with him—

"Roan, wake up."

Roan gasped and sat up, pain shooting through his skull as he pulled from the worst dream he'd ever had.

"What is it?" he asked groggily. His heart was trying to escape his chest, and he was bathed in his own fear-sweat.

"John Moore is here," his wife replied, with an edge to her voice he didn't much care for.

Roan dragged himself out of bed, standing still for a moment to see what kind of fresh hell his head was up to. The pain was still there, a dull, throbbing ache that pulsed in time to his heart-beat. He wasn't dizzy or nauseated, at least. Taking it slowly, he made his way out to the main room, where he found John Moore, holding his hat in his hands. His face was cut and bruised, his expression a portrait of pain and sorrow.

"Thanks for coming, John," Roan said. "Can I get you a drink?" The big man shook his head. "Did that happen at the meeting?" Roan gestured vaguely toward his face.

"I'm afraid I've got some bad news," he said softly.

Roan waited, shifting his gaze to Sara. She looked terrified. "Go on," he said. "Let's hear it."

"The meeting was a set-up," Moore said, anger seeping into his voice. "Hell, maybe not. Could be just a rat. Anyway, they knew where we were meeting and they came to break it up."

"They?" Roan asked. "The bosses?"

Moore raised his shoulders and let them slump. "More likely hired cronies. None of us escaped unharmed, including McCabe. But…" Moore took a deep, hitching breath and let it out slowly. "Patrick was killed."

Sara gasped and burst into tears. Roan gaped at Moore, too shocked to even offer his wife comfort. "Patrick is dead?"

Moore nodded and Roan saw his eyes were bright with tears. Finally, Roan went to Sara and hugged her. She buried her face in his chest and sobbed.

"Did they…" Roan wanted to ask if Patrick had been shot. Or lynched. But it would only upset his wife.

Moore seemed to understand. "He took a blow to the head. I don't think they meant to do it, but—"

"But he's just as dead!" Sara shouted, pulling away from Roan and turning on Moore. "And his wife is just as much a widow. The children just as fatherless! You people and your grand ideas. What would a strike do but take food out of our mouths? And now poor Elizabeth has lost her husband!"

Moore looked at the floor. Roan tried to pull Sara back in to hold her, but she shook him off. "You'd better think long and hard about what you do next, Roan." Her voice was a hiss, low and firm and full of power.

"Sara—"

She cut him off with a raised hand, as if she was going to shove him. Then she left the house, closing the door gently behind her.

"I'm sorry, Roan," Moore said meekly. "I should have waited…"

Roan shook his head. "She would have found out. I'm sure it'll be all over town soon, if it isn't already." The stiff pain in his head and neck was spreading, tightening his shoulders and gripping him miserably. "I appreciate you letting me know. What happens next? You know, with the Mollies?"

"I'm not sure," Moore said. "McCabe, that's the man who approached us and held the meeting, is wiring his people. He's asking for reinforcements, but…"

Roan didn't like the word "reinforcements" or the way Moore had trailed off. The town didn't need any more death. It certainly didn't need a war. "But what?" Roan pressed.

"I've got a bad feeling," Moore said. "It's not just that they knew about the meeting. There's something McCabe isn't telling me. And we lost a lot of supporters tonight."

Roan thought it over. "Do you think it has anything to do with Tunnel 17?"

Moore jerked his head up. "Christ, Roan, I hadn't even considered that. But if he doesn't know anything about it, I think it's a good place for him to start. Maybe he could find out what they're doing and use that for leverage. It's sure as hell safer than a strike."

"I think it's sensible," Roan agreed. "Has anyone ever tried to look for themselves?"

Moore's visage darkened, flashing him a warning. "Don't even speak of it."

The pain had been ebbing and flowing in Roan's head and neck. Now it seemed to gather behind his eyes. A great pressure formed there. He rubbed his temples. "Someone has," he said.

Moore heaved another one of his deep sighs. "Aye, someone has." There was a long pause. Roan didn't think he was going to continue. Finally, in a defeated voice, he did. "I've only heard tell of it. I don't know if any of this is true, or just another story the bosses keep alive to scare us, to keep us in line.

"There was a man who went looking on his own. His friend had been sent there, and when the friend's family pulled stakes and left without a word, he took it upon himself to investigate. Snuck back in after the second shift detonated. It was crazy: a fool's errand, to be sure."

Roan reached the point of exasperation, his head throbbing in time with his heartbeat. He felt as if his eyeballs were being squeezed out of his skull. "For God's sake, man. What happened?"

"He came back barmy," Moore said. "He was babbling about something in the mine. A devil or a demon or some such madness. They locked him up in Dismount."

"Dismount?"

"An asylum, just northwest of Pittsburgh. He was quite mad, whatever he saw."

"What do you think happened to him down there?" Roan asked. "What did he really see?"

"I couldn't say. The stories start with his own—some sort of demon, to some monster, a creature that's almost human but…" Moore shook his head again, regarding Roan earnestly. "I still think he probably saw a big hole filled with dead miners. Isn't that enough to make a man daft?" He sighed. "Just leave it alone, Roan. Will you do that?"

Roan closed his eyes. "I need to rest. Thanks for keeping me apprised. Will you be going down tomorrow?"

"Unless they tell me otherwise," Moore said, and made a sound that might have been a laugh. "What choice do I have?"

CHAPTER SIX

McCabe slammed his glass on the bar and motioned to the bartender for another. He was taking a risk just being there after what had happened in the clearing, but he was too angry to care. Part of him hoped one of the bosses would show up—No, not one of the bosses. *Him.*

McCabe nodded at the bartender as he refilled his glass.

"Looks like you had a rough night," the bartender said.

"I've had better. Quiet in here tonight."

The bartender shrugged. "It'll pick up when the night shift lets out."

"The mine pay for this place?" McCabe asked. In a lot of mining towns, most of the businesses were subsidized by the mines.

The bartender's face hardened. "I don't take a penny from them," he said gruffly.

"I'll drink to that," McCabe said, and downed his drink. The bartender lifted the bottle, but McCabe shook his head. If he got drunk and one of the bosses did show up, things might get out of hand. "How'd you end up running a saloon in a mining town?"

The bartender reached across the bar. "Name's Cal Townsend."

McCabe shook his hand. "Thomas McCabe."

"Had a good job in Philly. Saved some money. Ran into a little trouble and had to leave... unexpectedly." Townsend smiled wanly. "Heard Walker Brothers was planning on digging here and managed to get a property claim before they took it all. They tried to buy me out, of course, but I turned them down."

"And they just gave up?" McCabe had heard how the mine owners liked to control every profitable business in their towns and would go to any lengths—legal or otherwise—to get them.

Townsend's smile thinned. "Took some persuading, but they eventually acquiesced."

McCabe appraised the man. He was tall and lean but had a hard look about him, as if he could take care of himself. But he spoke like he was well educated. A strange combination for a barkeep in a shithole Pennsylvania mining town. "Doesn't sound like it was an amicable business deal."

Townsend laughed. "You could say that. They tried to strong-arm me, but I've still got some very… *influential* friends back in Philly."

"They leave you alone now?"

"They still mess with me but it's nothing I can't handle. They send ruffians in to stir up a fight, break some tables and chairs in the row. They sink a bit more cowardly, trying to interfere with deliveries, things like that."

McCabe shook his head. The damn mine owners were some of the richest men in the state, yet they couldn't let a business owner get his share of the profits. Which was exactly why McCabe was there. "I think maybe we should have a talk sometime. Somewhere a little less public."

Townsend raised his eyebrows, then glanced around. "So, it's true?"

McCabe winked. "I just think we should talk—"

The doors flew open, and a group of men poured into the bar.

"Time to go to work," Townsend said. "But maybe I'll see you around."

McCabe nodded, then turned to watch the new patrons. The night shift must have let out, though he hadn't heard the detonation that usually signaled the shift's end.

"Four beers," a burly man called to the bartender, pulling up a stool next to McCabe.

"Evenin'," McCabe said.

The man nodded but said nothing. Three others had taken station along the bar.

"Didn't hear a detonation," McCabe said amiably.

The miner watched him suspiciously. "Boss called it off," he said.

McCabe noticed the men were fairly subdued. None of the usual after-shift rowdiness exhibited by men happy to have survived another day in the mines. "Trouble?"

The man glared. Then the bartender brought the drinks and said, "Robert May, this is my friend, Thomas McCabe."

"Pleasure," McCabe said.

The man looked him up and down, a hint of recognition in his eyes. "Good to meetcha." He took a long pull on his beer, draining half the mug. "One of the boys—damn rookie named Bingham—dumped a cart of slag. Broke one of the boss's legs. Called off the blast and sent the poor slob to Tunnel 17."

MCCABE TOOK A final drag on his cigar and stomped it out under his boot heel. He didn't like this part of the job but he knew it was important, so he did it with the same stoic efficiency that he used for everything. The dusty soil softened his footfalls as he approached the small shack that looked like every other rundown shack on the road.

He paused outside, ear to the door, but heard nothing. He knocked softly, then heard someone muttering before shuffling steps approached.

"Who's—"

McCabe slammed a shoulder against the flimsy door, sending Graves backward. He slipped inside and closed it behind him. He was on Graves before the wiry little man had a chance to yell. McCabe clasped a palm over his mouth and hauled him to his feet. Graves' eyes were wide with terror, the pupils darting back and forth as if he was searching for help. "We're going to have a little chat, you and me. I'm going to take my hand away and you're not going to utter a peep. When I ask you a question, you'll answer in a normal tone. Any deviation and I'll break your neck. Do you believe me?"

Graves nodded furiously.

McCabe slowly pulled his hand away. When Graves opened his mouth, McCabe slapped him hard. "Last warning," he said pleasantly. Graves remained silent. McCabe liked the wild fear he saw on the weasel's face. But there was something else. A sort of calm rage, as if he knew something McCabe didn't. That, McCabe didn't like at all.

"How much did you tell the bosses?" McCabe asked. It had been Graves in the clearing, hiding under a burlap hood like the rest of the cowards. The problem was, Graves had been involved in the earlier conversations and Moore had sworn he was okay. McCabe had probed Moore as they'd walked to see Patrick's widow, but Moore had seemed to know nothing of Graves' betrayal.

"I only told them about the meeting. And only because—"

McCabe slapped him again, hard. Graves' teeth rattled and his head snapped back. A thin line of blood slid out of his left nostril. "Lying is only going to complicate your situation, Graves. Stick to the facts and we'll part ways. Lie to me again—"

"Okay, okay. Mr. Abbott caught wind the Mollies were coming. I swear I don't know where he heard that, it was long before you got here. He's been making Jackman give me the easy jobs and extra pay to keep an eye on the rest of the miners."

Abbott, McCabe thought, *shit*. Abbott was Jackman's boss and Walker's number one man. He was reputed to be a hard-driving, remorseless boss so cruel that some called him a psychopath. "I don't like to repeat myself, Graves," McCabe said, in that same steady, friendly tone. "But I'm going to, just this once. "How much did you tell the bosses?"

Graves sighed. "I told them about the meeting, and that you were the one organizing things. I told him Moore and Patrick Laughlin were taking on with you, but that's it. I didn't know so many miners were signed on."

McCabe studied him as he spoke. Most of the arrogance had seemed to slip out of Graves after the second slap. McCabe believed him.

McCabe smiled. "What do you propose we do now?" He liked to keep these guys guessing.

Graves stared. "I won't say anything else to Jackman or Mr. Abbott. Jackman's just a puppet, anyway. His heart ain't in being a boss. He's as scared of management as the miners are. So, maybe you rough me up a little and I'll tell Mr. Abbott I'm out. You know, act like you scared me off."

"*Act* like I scared you off?" McCabe said. His smile widened when Graves realized his blunder. Now he was properly scared.

"You mean, I didn't *actually* scare you?"

"I—That's not… I mean…"

McCabe shot a hand out and clutched Graves' scrawny neck. He really didn't like this part of the job, but some guys made it easy. He squeezed harder, watching Graves' face go red. Small veins burst in the whites of his eyes. Then he pissed himself. Finally, McCabe saw the light in his eyes extinguish. He waited, watching for something, some sign that the man had a soul, and that it was leaving his earthly skin. But, as always, there was nothing. He released Graves and let him slump to the floor. Just a little more work to do and he could go get some sleep.

CHAPTER SEVEN

Roan knew he wasn't supposed to go to the mines, but he was feeling better. And after the events of last night, he couldn't sit around in the house all day. As he approached the entrance, he saw a group of miners gathered around the elevator. It was too early to go down… *Strike,* he thought, and a shiver of dread shook him.

"You're not supposed to be here," Moore called from the crowd. The big man strode toward him.

"Is it—"

Moore cut him off with a sharp look. "It's Graves," he said.

Roan waited for an explanation, but Moore headed back into the sea of miners. Roan pushed his way through and froze at the scene in front of him.

It was Graves, all right. Strung up in the mine shaft by a

poorly tied noose, a paper pinned to his shirt. Roan edged closer to read it.

I'm sorry I'm a rat was scrawled in childlike writing.

"What in bloody hell," a voice boomed. Jackman shoved miners aside and stared at the slowly spinning body. He turned, red-faced, glaring through the angry slits of his eyes. "Graves didn't do this to himself. But I know who did."

A rumble of whispers went through the miners.

Jackman moved closer and inspected the swinging corpse. He mumbled something then turned again to face the miners. "Go on home," he said. "No work today, and that means no wages."

Angry voices rose in the mob. Moore stepped forward. "This is bullshit, Jackman. We deserve to work."

Jackman stepped up to Moore, seeming to loom over the bigger man. "Are you going to scale the fucking walls to get in and out of the mine? The fucking Mollies cut the elevator cable. So why don't you slink off to the shadows and thank McCabe for your lost wages?"

Moore's face went crimson and his whole body tensed. Heart thundering, Roan waited for the blows to fly, but Moore's shoulders slumped, and he turned his back on Jackman.

"That's right," Jackman crowed. "None of you are so tough in the light of day, eh?"

Nobody spoke. The air crackled with tension. Then Moore walked away.

Roan breathed out a sigh of relief and moved to catch up with him. Then he felt Jackman's gaze on him and slowed his pace, blending in with the masses. A wild thought struck him, and he slipped out of the crowd and went back to where Jackman stood.

"Who's going to fix the elevator?" Roan asked the foreman.

"Do you see anyone else around?" Jackman demanded.

"Will the night shift be able to work?" Roan's idea was forming into a plan. *It just might work.*

"It's half a day's ride to Berwick to get the supplies I need," Jackman grumbled. He looked at Roan. "Do me a favor, would ya? Spread the word that the night shift is off, as well. It'll be too late to start by the time I take care of—" Jackman jerked his chin toward Graves. "I'll have time to get the repairs done when I get back from Berwick, but it'll be well past dinner before the elevator's working again."

"I'll let the men know," Roan said, and turned to go.

"How's the skull?" Jackman called.

Roan turned, surprised at both the question and the compassionate tone Jackman had asked it with. "Still a bit sore, but…"—he shrugged— "…I'm not one to sit around when there's work to be done." He looked up at Graves. "Need a hand with him?"

Jackman shook his head. "Nah, go on and spread the word. Then get some rest. I'll need you tomorrow. Graves wasn't much of a miner, but he was a set of hands when we needed them."

Roan didn't know how to respond to that, so he remained silent.

"Go on, now," Jackman said. "I'll clean up this mess."

"I'll send Doc."

"Appreciate it, Roan."

Jackman was still staring at Graves, and Roan swore he saw

the boss's eyes bright with tears. He recalled the look of concern Jackman had given him when the drill bit had snapped. With all his bluster and angry words, the man might have a heart after all.

MOORE LOOKED HIM over warily. "Are you sure you want to do this?"

"Of course I'm sure," Roan replied, sounding surer than he felt. "Jackman's gone to Berwick for supplies. We'll get in and out before he's back. I have to know."

Moore studied him, then nodded. "Let's get to it, then."

The two men worked quickly, tying knots at roughly four-foot intervals in the long rope to use as hand and footholds. The intent was to secure the rope at the top of the shaft and climb down. They had lanterns, and would find out what was in Tunnel 17.

When the rope was tied off, they regarded each other gravely. "Last chance to back out," Moore said.

Roan shook his head. "I'll go first." Before Moore could argue, he took hold of the rope and began his descent. The climb was much more difficult than he thought, and a lightning bolt of panic ran through him at the thought of trying to climb *up* the same distance. *Too late now,* he thought. Ignoring the ache in his arms, he continued until he reached the main shaft. He called up to Moore, now two hundred feet above him, and set to lighting the lanterns. He'd never been in the mines in such utter darkness. The knowledge that the mines had closed in around him was suddenly sure. He knew if he reached out in any direction, he'd touch the cold, unrelenting stone. With shaky hands, he got the lanterns lit. The flames pushed the mine walls back but did nothing to alleviate the suffocating fear.

A few minutes later, a grunting and out-of-breath Moore dropped next to him. In the flickering light, he saw sweat pouring down the man's face, and that electric panic ran through him again. Moore was so much bigger, there was so much more weight to haul up that rope. He shook the thought away: Moore was also a lot stronger.

"Do you know where we're going?" he asked.

The big man nodded, still breathing too hard to speak. He pointed, took one of the lanterns, and started walking. Roan followed.

After a few minutes, Roan asked, "What do you think we're going to find?"

There was a long pause, the only sound their scuffling boots on the stony ground. "I honestly don't know," Moore said finally. "But I'm afraid it's going to be worse than anything my mind could conjure."

This gave Roan a chill. Moore was a stoic man. Levelheaded, and always calm. He was never one to get caught up in any of the superstitions so many miners believed in. To hear him talk like this… The realization that nobody else knew they were down there took Roan's breath away. If anything happened, they'd just be… gone, like they'd never existed. He gasped, sucking in great gulps of air. When Moore turned, he disguised his panic with a cough.

"There," Moore called, holding the lantern high, almost touching the mine's low ceiling. To his right, barely visible, was a small opening in the rocks. Moore went closer, climbing up and holding the lantern in front of him. "It's a small shaft. Looks to be a gate blocking it off…"

Then he was gone. Roan ran to the opening and scrambled up, peering over the rocks. Moore was inside, yanking at the metal bars that stretched across the tunnel. There was a chain and padlock, but Moore had found a tamping pole and was working the hinge on the other side of the gate.

"What are you doing?" Roan exclaimed as he climbed through the opening. "They'll know we were here."

"They'll know *someone* was here," Moore grunted.

The hinge snapped under the weight of the big man and the gate hung crooked, leaving enough room for them to pass through.

Using the tamping pole as a pry bar, Roan levered the gate back into position. It wouldn't open properly with the broken hinge, but it looked undamaged at a glance. They could rig the gate closed on the way out to cover their tracks. *If we get out.* The thought came unbidden and sent another cold jolt of dread through him.

They walked in silence through the tunnel, their lanterns sending eerie shadows dancing across the walls. Moore came to a sudden stop, holding up a hand. At first there was nothing, but just as Roan was about to ask him what he'd heard, a strange sound echoed down the tunnel. It was a grunt-like noise… but not quite. An injured man was Roan's first thought, but he quickly dismissed it.

Moore gave him a questioning look and he nodded. Then a guttural sound, closer to a growl, bounced off the walls ahead.

Every instinct was screaming at Roan to turn around and get out of there. Instead, he stepped ahead and walked with slow, exaggerated steps, deeper into the tunnel. He didn't turn to see if Moore was following; he knew he wouldn't give up that easily.

Roan stayed close to the wall as he navigated the tunnel. When he emerged on the other side of a sharp "S" curve, he stopped abruptly. This time, it wasn't a noise that halted his steps. He could see light ahead. He quickly extinguished his lantern and motioned for Moore to do the same.

The sounds were louder: a strange, almost animal sort of snuffling and growling. Roan edged closer, around another bend, then froze.

The tunnel ahead dead-ended, but light was being thrown from an opening on the right, about sixty feet ahead, just before the cave wall that signaled the end of the line. Something moved beyond the curve, throwing shadows on the wall. Someone was in the tunnel just around the corner. Or maybe it opened into a chamber, that made more sense.

He crept closer, sticking to the right-hand wall, giving him a better view of the shadows on the left side of the tunnel. Someone was walking around. He could see the shadow clearly, but it didn't look quite right. The person walked sort of hunched over, lumbering. He felt Moore grip his arm, but shook his hand off.

A voice echoed from the cavern, but it was distorted, so they couldn't make out the words. The figure moved faster, loping back and forth. Then, a scream erupted, multiplied tenfold by the echoes. The shadow bounded back and forth faster, like a horse galloping in a circle in its corral. Roan thought briefly of Plato's Allegory of the Cave. Then the growl escalated into a howl but was soon drowned out by screaming. Then, silence.

Roan stared at Moore, the man barely visible in the dim light, Still, Roan could see the wide eyes and the horrified visage and knew it matched his own. He motioned for Moore to go back the way they'd come. As he followed, taking aching care to remain silent, another sound rose from the chamber. The wet, slurping and sucking of an animal feeding.

CHAPTER EIGHT

Roan followed Moore back through the tunnels, certain every step would be his last. He imagined the footsteps of some great loping beast closing in on him. Smelled the hot, fetid breath on the back of his neck. Felt the ripping of flesh by the creature's teeth and claws.

Only when they had reached the gate did he dare look back. The tunnel behind him was empty. Quiet.

"Come on, Roan," Moore hissed, already on the other side of the gate. Roan slipped through, taking the time to hang the end of the gate on the broken hinge. The façade would fall apart as soon as someone unlocked the gate and tried to swing it open, but the damage would go unnoticed until then.

They reached the elevator shaft without incident. Roan knew this would be when disaster struck. Waiting for the elevator at the end of each shift was always the worst for him. Being so close to safety would be when the gods would smite him.

"What the hell was that?" Roan asked.

"I don't know," Moore said, between gasping breaths. "Start climbing. Plenty of time to talk when we're out of this godforsaken place."

Roan shook his head. "You go first—"

"No," Moore wheezed. "You'll be quicker, and I might need you to pull me up." Wincing, he rotated his shoulder.

"Okay," Roan said, and began climbing, hand over hand and using the knots for footholds to keep some of the weight off his arms and shoulders. It was harder than he'd expected, and he was sure Moore wouldn't be able to make it with a balky shoulder. He'd figure that out when he was up top.

It was slow-going, and Roan had no idea how long he'd been climbing or how much farther he had to go. Sweat trickled into his eyes, creating a salty sting that he could do nothing to relieve. He needed both hands on the rope at all times.

Finally, he saw a dim cutout above him, a lighter shade of black in the gloom. A few laborious pulls later and he could make out stars in the sky. He was almost there. As he climbed the last few feet, he was sure his grip would fail and he'd crash to the mine below. So close. Then, he reached the top. With a desperate heave and a sigh of relief, he collapsed to the ground. That's when he heard a loud click.

"Let's see who we've got here," a familiar voice cooed.

A match flared, then a lantern came to life. Jackman sat holding a shotgun cradled on his lap. The flickering lantern revealed his ghostly visage.

"Jackman," Roan breathed, still exhausted from the climb. "There's something—"

"Shut your mouth, Devlin," Jackman barked. "Not another word."

A distant cry echoed up the shaft. Jackman stood. "Who's with you, Devlin? Is it that Molly Maguire son of a bitch? McCabe?"

"It's John Moore," Roan said, sitting up. "We have to get him up."

Jackman's mouth twitched into a knife-blade smile, hideous in the orange glow. "Do we, now?"

"You don't understand—"

Roan was knocked onto his back, pain exploding in his head. Jackman had used the butt of the shotgun to silence him.

You've got a brain commotion. The medical journals are using the word 'concussion' now. Doc's words reverberated in his aching head. What would a second traumatic blow do to his commotion or concussion or whatever?

"There's something down there," he yelled, ignoring the shimmering pain. "We're getting him out of there, then you can do whatever you want." Roan stood shakily, tensing for another blow, but none came.

Jackman stood. "Let's get him up, then."

Roan and Jackman hauled Moore up on the rope. It was a lot quicker than waiting for Moore to climb, or Roan trying to pull him up alone. A couple of times, Roan stole a glance at Jackman's shotgun, but he was too afraid to let go of the rope to try for it. He spent the entire time waiting for Jackman to let go and shove him into the shaft, killing two birds with one stone.

When Moore's hands finally reached over the ledge, Jackman did let go of the rope, and retrieved his weapon.

Moore showed no sign of surprise at the sight of Jackman. "I didn't think ya had it in ya to pull me up that quickly!"

Roan didn't respond. It was up to Jackman to make the next move.

"You already knew about it," Moore said, glaring at Jackman.

Jackman shook his head. "I know something's down there," he said carefully. "Did you see it?"

"No," Moore said, "but we heard it. Heard what it did to someone. MacGreggor?"

Jackman shook his head again. "Bloke named Bingham." Jackman's face changed. "What did it sound like?"

"Are you fucking serious?" Roan exclaimed, stepping toward him. "Why don't you go down there and see for yourself?"

Jackman took a step back and raised the shotgun. "Stay right there—"

Moore grabbed the barrel of the gun and jerked it upward, swinging a vicious roundhouse to the side of Jackman's head with his other hand. Both barrels exploded as Moore yanked the gun free and tossed it aside. Jackman's knees buckled and he fell sideways to the ground.

Moore winced and grabbed his bad shoulder. "Ought to drag you down there and leave you for whatever demon you're keeping in that tunnel."

Jackman got to his hands and knees, then stood shakily.

"Please…"

"What's down there, Jackman?" Roan asked. "No more of your bullshit."

Jackman sighed, his gaze shifting between the two miners. "I swear I don't know for sure. Some… some sort of creature. I thought it was a bear or maybe a mountain lion, but…"

Moore stepped forward and grabbed the front of his shirt, shaking him. "What is it?" he boomed.

"It's a fucking monster!" Jackman screeched. "I don't know what else to call it. I've never seen it, and I hope I never do. But I heard some of the bigger bosses talking. Abbott was one of them. He said it crawled from Hell and they trapped it in the tunnel. They… they feed it."

Moore raised a hand to take another shot at Jackman, but Roan grabbed his arm. The big man released Jackman and stepped back, his face hardened with impotent rage.

"They said they'd kill my family," Jackman whispered. "They said they'd bring them down there."

"No more," Roan said.

Jackman nodded. "No more is right. I'll take my family and head—"

"No," Moore said. "I've got a better idea. Let's get this elevator fixed and then we can talk."

CHAPTER NINE

Elias Walker read the wire transfer, then crumpled up the paper and tossed it into the fire. He took a long, thoughtful puff of his cigar as he pondered his choices. The unrest in Serenity was bothersome. It had happened at just about every one of his mines, and it took a while to properly train the miners on how things worked. But Abbott's news was different. If the Molly Maguires got a foothold and influenced the miners, his profits would diminish. Word would spread to his other mines… No, he could not allow it.

Walker got to his feet and paced the spacious study. He stroked his beard absently, as he always did when deep in thought. He'd worked too hard to see Walker Brothers Mining suffer, even at one location. He grinned, contemplating the company name. The Walker brothers were no more, other than in name. Victor's untimely demise had been necessary. He and his sympathetic views on wages and the health of the miners. Not to mention half the profits. Now, Elias was free to manage things as he saw fit. Manage them properly.

He stopped pacing at the bar and poured himself a small glass of whiskey. Another tradition of his whenever he was about to come to an important decision. He would visit Serenity, Pennsylvania, himself. Make a gesture to the miners that would keep them content. He would bring enough men to eradicate the Molly Maguires while he was there. *A gesture of goodwill only goes so far. A show of force is what keeps miners in line.*

This train of thought brought him to the team he'd put in place. Abbott was the perfect foreman. Unflinchingly brutal, remorseless, and cruel. He'd take any order and carry it out without any thought, and certainly no regret. The mine bosses below him, including the crew chief, Jackman, were a different story. They were the eyes and ears for Abbott, and they needed to be just as fierce and loyal. Walker had his doubts about them. Now, he was down a mine boss because of a stupid accident. Abbott had dealt with it swiftly and mercilessly, as he should. Still, Walker had his concerns.

He decided he would have sit-downs with each of the bosses and come to his own conclusions. If any of them failed to pass muster, well, Abbott would do what was necessary. *Or maybe,* he thought, *I'll go down in the tunnels and do it myself.*

Pleased with his decision, he exited the study. He had a trip to plan.

CHAPTER TEN

McCabe gaped at the three men across the table, waiting for a punchline. Moore had found him at the saloon and told him to go to Roan Devlin's house for an important meeting. It was all very clandestine—not that he wasn't accustomed to that—but this was something else.

Moore, Devlin, and one of the mine foremen, of all people—a guy named Jackman—had spun a tale that was so outrageous and bizarre that McCabe almost believed it.

"Let me get this straight," he said, trying not to smile, "Abbott keeps some sort of creature—a monster—down in the mines. And he keeps it well-fed by making dinner out of any miners who step out of line. Is that about the size of it?"

"Roan Devlin," Sara said steadily. "I'm going to fetch Doc. That blow to the head—"

Moore slammed a meaty fist on the table. "It's no joking matter! I know what we heard down there."

Jackman spoke next. "Mrs. Devlin. Mr. McCabe. I don't know what's down there, but I know there's something. Miners go to Tunnel 17, and they don't come back. The bosses pay their families off, to leave town and keep their mouths shut."

Jackman's tone was so laden with guilt and pain that McCabe had to turn away. Then he said, "How do you know it's not just a matter of, well, someone, some *person* killing these miners?" He raised his hands in apology. "I'm not minimizing the horror of it by any means, but perhaps it's not as outlandish—"

"Damn it, McCabe," Roan exclaimed. "Do you think we concocted this madness? To what end?" He stood and paced the small room, running a hand through his hair, wincing as he touched the fresh bruise from Jackman's shotgun. The bandage on his ear was seeping red. "Are you going to help us or not?"

McCabe's face burned. "That is precisely why I came here in the first place, Mr. Devlin. Or did you forget I took a few lumps that night in the woods, too?" He watched the others exchange looks before he continued. "There's a way things need to be done. There's no law here. Walker and his soldiers *are* what passes for the law. If you go to the constable, you might be the next ones to be relegated to Tunnel 17." The look of fear on the other men's faces confirmed what he already knew. They needed him.

"What do we do, Mr. McCabe?" Jackman pleaded. "I've got a family…"

"First, you all need to carry on as if nothing's changed."

Moore opened his mouth to disagree, but McCabe silenced him with a look. "Mr. Jackman, you're going to report to Abbott that the damage done in the woods was enough to scare the miners out of any thoughts of striking. Moore, you and Roan need to show up for work, keep your heads down, and do your jobs."

"What will you be doing while we're all play-acting?" Moore demanded.

McCabe smiled. "I'll be lying low until my men arrive. I've wired my superiors, and they are assembling a formidable crew to assist us. I've also made a contact who has some very influential friends—"

"Who would that be?" Moore asked.

McCabe shook his head. "It's better you don't know, for now."

"You don't trust us," Jackman said. Then his face darkened. "You don't trust *me*."

"I promise you that's not the case," McCabe insisted. "Sometimes, the less you know, the better. He'll be sending some troops as well. I expect Abbott has done the same and Walker will be sending men of his own. If we're lucky, he'll show up himself, to rally his forces."

"Why would that be so lucky?" Roan asked.

McCabe grinned. "You kill a snake by cutting its head off, Mr. Devlin. If Walker shows his face here, well, the Molly Maguires will be more than willing to cut that snake's head off."

"You're starting a war," Sara exclaimed. "Roan, you'll get us all killed!"

"No, ma'am," McCabe said softly. "I'll know the minute Walker gets here. I have something in mind that might get this matter settled without any bloodshed."

Roan said, "What—"

"Not now," McCabe said. "I've got a little more reconnaissance, then I'll lay out the plan." He grinned wickedly. "I think you gentlemen are going to like what I have in mind."

CHAPTER ELEVEN

Roan arrived at the mine early the next morning, trying to pretend it was just another day. He felt as if everyone was staring. Like they all knew he'd snuck down to Tunnel 17 and then conspired with a Molly Maguire. Sweat soaked his shirt, even in the cool morning air. He was never going to be able to do this.

He nodded hellos to the other miners and tried to make small talk as they asked him about his injury. He did his best to respond as naturally as he could, but at times, he lost track of what they were asking, his mind drifting to all manner of terrible scenarios.

Moore showed up, nodded brusquely, and went to fetch his equipment. When Jackman came out of the office to join them, Roan nearly turned tail and ran home. Jackman caught his gaze and there was something in the man's cool demeanor that calmed Roan. Jackman had a lot more on the line with three kids at home. To Roan, Jackman's casual conduct was a testament to his desire to do the right thing. It would have been so much easier to pack up his family and slink off into the night. Or worse, to run to Abbot and tell him about Roan, Moore, and McCabe. The man's courage steeled Roan, and he joined the queue of miners at the elevator.

His resilience waned once the gate had swung shut and the car began its slow trundle downward. What if Jackman was playing it cool because he *had* run to Abbott last night? What if this was all a trap, and he and Moore would be sent to Tunnel 17 to get a firsthand—and final—look at whatever dwelled there?

Roan's breath quickened and he feigned a cough to cover it up. Mercifully, the elevator clanged to a stop and the gate was opened. Roan shoved his way through the men in front of him, ignoring their grumbling curses.

"Devlin," Jackman said, "have ya got the first-day jitters?"

The question brought a laugh from the miners and Jackman's amiable tone somehow set Roan at ease for the second time. Was he going to be this skittish all day?

Jackman handed out assignments and Roan was relieved to be paired with Moore. Then, his relief vanished when he thought it might be a ploy to pair them up and send them to Tunnel 17 for whatever reason Jackman dreamed up. A tight fist gripping his arm sent a jolt of sheer panic through him.

"Get a hold of yourself, Devlin," Moore hissed. "You look like a scared rabbit."

Roan managed a nod and grabbed his equipment. He tried to clear his thoughts and focus on the work.

The morning passed without incident. Moore's continuous chatter, interspersed with jokes and tall tales, helped get him through.

When the lunch bell rang, Roan sat with Moore, listlessly nibbling at the lunch Sara had packed. She'd begged him not to go down to the mines. She'd wanted to pack what they could carry and leave town on the noon coach, but he had been able to put on a confident façade and talk her into staying until this thing played out. If nothing changed, or their plan failed, Roan agreed to flee. Not that he'd have much choice in the matter.

As he ate, Roan kept his ears open. There was a lot of the usual banter, but he noticed a few of the men gathered in the far corner of the shaft speaking in hushed tones and looking around suspiciously.

"John, what are Donovan and Ellis up to?"

Moore gave them a long look. "I'm not sure. They were at the meeting that night, but they were the first to scatter into the wind when Abbott's men showed up. I don't trust the lot of them."

"Sara is friends with Donovan's sister, Rose," Roan said, getting to his feet. He had to stop being scared, had to go on the offensive. "I'm going to speak with them, see if I can find anything out."

Moore nodded. "Be careful."

Roan approached the group tentatively, though he did his best to look casual. "Boys," he said amiably. The men looked up, wary and perhaps fearful. Donovan, who seemed to be the ringleader of the group, said, "Devlin, how are you doing?" He gestured toward Roan's ear. "Healing up okay?"

"I might not look as pretty as I did before the accident," Roan joked. "Doc thinks a piece of my ear is still down here some-where." This got a few laughs. "Sara was asking for your sister," Roan went on. "Hasn't seen her in a dog's age and wanted to ask her over for supper. You'd be welcome, too, of course."

"Rose has been seeing a fella from over Gallop way. Seems like it might be serious." Donovan shrugged. "Nice enough guy. Runs a dairy farm. If things work out, maybe I'll get out of the mines and start milking cows."

Roan laughed along with the other men. "That sounds fine to me." Roan pointed to his ear. "After this… it makes you think. Could have blinded me. Or worse." The men nodded somberly. Their eyes shifted to each other furtively, but Roan noticed. He decided to take a chance, sitting down with the men. He lowered his voice to barely a whisper. "I know it went poorly the other night. I lost a good friend. It haunts me that I wasn't there—"

"Quiet," Ellis hissed. "You'll get the lot of us sent to 17 with that kind of talk."

The mention of the tunnel froze Roan for a moment. But it also reminded him of what was at stake. "I'm throwing in with them," he whispered. More looks between the other men, then a nod by Ellis.

"Come by the saloon after shift," Donovan said loudly. "We'll figure out when to get the women together for supper."

Roan stood just as the end-of-lunch bell rang. "See you there."

He went directly to fetch his gloves and tools, knowing the men would be watching. If he went and spoke to Moore, it would seem as though he was spying on them and reporting back. They knew Moore was in tight with McCabe.

Roan remained focused on his duties for the remainder of the shift. A huge sense of relief washed over him when the final bell rang. Unless someone grabbed him before getting on the elevator, he'd made it through the day.

The ride up was eternal, and he felt Moore studying him the whole way. When they finally reached topside, Roan returned his equipment and headed straight for the saloon, knowing Moore would catch up.

"So," Moore said once he had, "what's the word? Did you tell Donovan we're out?"

Roan stopped, a tight ball of worry in his gut. He'd been so intent on learning what he could from Donovan, he'd completely forgotten the plan. In fact, he'd been so nervous he'd done exactly the opposite. Was it his head injury, his *commotion*, or was he just an idiot? "John, I… I made a mistake."

"What do you mean?"

Roan's stomach burned. "I forgot what we'd discussed with… What we'd discussed last night. I told Donovan I wanted in."

Moore grabbed his shoulder and spun him around. "You did what?"

"I was so scared all morning… I—"

"What's going on here?" a voice boomed.

Roan looked past Moore to see Ellis, Donovan, and a couple of other miners forming a circle around them.

"Nothing—" Roan started, but Moore cut him off.

"What's it to you, Ellis?" Moore growled. "Last time I saw you, you was running scared out of the woods."

The circle tightened, Ellis and Donovan moving directly in front of Moore. "Boys, we're all on the same side here," Roan said.

"Are we?" Ellis clenched his hands into fists by his side.

"We are," Roan said, stepping between them. "Back off, Ellis. Let's go to the saloon like Donovan and I talked about."

THE SALOON WAS back to its loud, raucous self. It was as if MacGreggor and the other poor soul, Bingham, hadn't vanished after being sent to Tunnel 17. How quickly everyone had moved on. Roan and the others shouldered their way through the crowd, nodding and greeting other miners until they found a table in the back corner. Moore went to fetch them all beer as they settled in.

"What's wrong with Moore?" Ellis demanded. "Seems like he's got a bug up his ass."

"Just a misunderstanding," Roan replied, wishing he'd been the one to go order the drinks. He felt like the others were studying him, waiting for the wrong word or even the wrong facial expression. "Everyone is tense, Moore included. He's got reason to be, wouldn't you say?"

The others nodded. Donovan said, "I'm surprised Abbott didn't make a move on him already."

Moore returned with four mugs and took a seat. He looked at the others with a smirk on his face. "If I didn't know better, I'd think you were talking about me behind my back." His glaring gaze landed on Ellis.

"We were," Ellis replied calmly. "Now we're about to do it to your face."

Moore's expression softened. "Have at it."

"We'll get right to it, then," Donovan said. "Are you still…"—he looked around—"in?"

It was Moore's call whether or not to trust these two or stick with Jackman's plan. He shifted his gaze to Roan, lifted his mug, and said "Till the end!"

Cold hands gripped Roan's heart as he clinked mugs with the others to seal the deal. He remembered how Moore had trusted Graves. Look how that had turned out. They would have to get a moment with Jackman and let him know.

Happy to get up and stretch his legs, Roan went to fetch another round. He'd started to feel cornered sitting at the table as the saloon grew more crowded. He maneuvered through the throngs of jokers and storytellers, finally reaching the bar. He motioned for four beers and reached into his pocket. As he placed the coins on the bar, he noticed Townsend staring at the door. He also noticed the place had gone deathly quiet.

"Barkeep," a voice boomed. "Drinks on the house for the rest of the evening!"

A cheer went up through the crowd, along with clapping and whistling. Roan noticed the creased brow on Townsend, the man's lips a tight slash. Roan turned, standing on his toes to see over the taller men that blocked his view. Gooseflesh spread up his arms, circled his neck, and crept down his back. Elias Walker was making his way to the bar, shaking hands and slapping backs, a cold grin on his face.

"Son of a bitch," Townsend whispered.

Roan felt the blood drain from his face. There could be only one reason for Walker to have shown up: Abbott had told him about the Molly Maguires being in town.

Townsend gave him the four mugs, locking eyes with him for a long moment. Roan nodded, and shoved his way back to the table.

Abbott was a hard case, but Walker's reputation made Abbott seem like a saint. He was notoriously brutal and remorseless. There were rumors he'd killed his own brother to take his half of the family fortune.

"We may need to rethink things," Moore said, glaring in Walker's direction.

An idea occurred to Roan, probably hatched out of sheer panic. "Wait a minute." He turned to Ellis and Donovan. "Do you trust us?" he asked. "John and me, I mean." Roan caught Moore's questioning look but ignored it for the moment.

The two men exchanged a long look. Ellis gave a barely perceptible nod. Raucous laughter erupted from the other side of the bar.

"Aye," Donovan said. "Not that we've much choice," he added, with a sardonic laugh.

Roan motioned for the men to come closer and leaned over the table. "Moore and I have another partner. He's got Abbott's ear. The plan was to spread the word that Moore was out, and the rest of the miners were following his lead." Roan laughed bitterly. "I made a folly of that by talking to you two, but nobody else knows. Abbott will still get the word that the resistance has splintered after what happened to Patrick."

"Who—"

Moore cut Ellis off. "The less you know for now, the better. But Roan is right, we may be in the clear, but we must stick together on this."

Roan watched the two men carefully, noting the look that passed between them. He turned to Moore and raised an eyebrow. "There's something else," Roan whispered, stealing a glance toward where Walker was holding court. More laughter and cheering as Walker presumably charmed the masses. "We have an idea about Tunnel 17."

Donovan actually gasped. Ellis frowned at him before turning to Roan. "What are you on about, Devlin?"

Roan had to make a decision. Three keeping a secret was a tall order. Five, well, that was just asking for trouble. Still, he realized, they were backed into a corner with Walker's unexpected arrival. "Moore and I went down into the mines while Jackman was off to Berwick." This was good, Roan realized. Revealing this part of the story would act as subterfuge and keep Jackman's identity as their secret partner concealed. "We know what's down there. Well, we have an idea. And we have a plan on just what to do about it."

Ellis and Donovan both started to speak at the same time, but Moore cut them off again. "Not here, boys. We need to bring—" Moore stopped, again checking for curious ears, but everyone was focused on Walker. "We need to bring McCabe in; he's supposed to be wiring for reinforcements."

CHAPTER TWELVE

Jackman waited as the last of the miners exited the elevator and headed for the saloon. A few minutes later, the two foremen called the all-clear and headed in the same direction. Jackman waited another ten minutes to make sure there were no stragglers, then made his way to the shaft.

His shift at the mine that day had been endless, waiting for Abbott's hand to fall on his shoulder. *Come with me to 17, Jackman.* He could hear his high-pitched whisper, the voice that sent chills down the spine of every miner to hear it raised in anger.

Jackman had visited Abbott first thing in the morning, before shift. He'd told the boss that the strike had been averted and the men were scared. Patrick's death had sent a strong message. He'd been a good worker and was well-liked by the other miners and bosses. If that could happen to him, well, what of the rest? Abbott had listened to Jackman's tale, his cold blue eyes drilling into Jackman the entire time. Probing for holes in the story. For weaknesses. For lies.

Jackman had gone into the mine on shaky legs, afraid it might be his last trip down. He'd watched Moore and Devlin, but they seemed to be carrying on just fine. Until, that was, Devlin had gone to sit with Ellis and Donovan at lunch break. What the hell was that about? Jackman knew those two had been in the clearing that night. Was Devlin telling them the strike was off? Or was there another plan afoot?

Jackman had gone to the saloon after shift, intending to confront Moore and Devlin. Then, the unthinkable had happened. Walker had shown up. Jackman slipped out of the saloon before the owner had spotted him. If he had been seen conspiring with the miners, no matter how innocent the conversation was, it would have looked bad.

Jackman had gone home with a new plan. After a few hours of restless sleep, he'd returned to the mine to wait. Now, it was time.

Jackman stepped into the elevators and lowered himself down to the main shaft. He knew how to get to Tunnel 17, though he'd never actually gone before. Devlin had told him the gate had been left propped in place but that it was not secure.

It wasn't that he didn't believe Moore and Devlin, but Walker's arrival had changed things. He had to see for himself because their plan depended on Moore and Devlin's account being accurate. Up top, it was easy to believe they had gotten spooked, heard a man screaming, perhaps. Now that he was underground, feeling the depth and the darkness of the empty tunnels, his scuffling footsteps his only company, it was much easier to believe there was something down there with him.

Jackman reached the gate. It did seem to be properly in place but upon closer inspection, he saw where Moore had broken the hinge. He pulled the metal open enough to slip through. He paused, listening for something, anything to indicate what Moore and Devlin had told him was true. Nothing. With a sigh, he ventured deeper into the mine.

CHAPTER THIRTEEN

Elias Walker enjoyed the roisterous environment of the saloon; too many of his evenings were spent alone or in stuffy meeting halls discussing business. He had grown up in the mines and in the saloons that thrived in every mining town such as this.

There was one exception to his good spirits, that being the barkeep. Walker knew of him from his discussions with Abbott. Knew how Townsend refused to acquiesce to the demands of Walker Brothers Mining. How he'd threatened to bring in some hard cases from Philadelphia. To top it all off, Townsend had been giving him suspicious glances that bordered on hostile. Perhaps he would have to be dealt with.

He turned his attention back to the group of miners huddled around him. "Another round!" Walker boomed, glaring at Townsend. While waiting for the drinks, he regaled the men with another anecdote from his mining days, receiving roars of laughter in return.

Townsend brought over a tray of mugs and shot glasses. Walker took one of the mugs, held it up to Townsend, and drank deeply, his gaze never leaving the barkeep. When Townsend left, Walker passed out the drinks. "Gentlemen, thank you for your company this evening. I must make this my last drink and discuss some business with Mr. Abbott."

The rest of the men said their thanks and scattered about the saloon, leaving Abbott looking curiously at him.

"What do you have in mind, Mr. Walker?"

Walker held in a wince at the man's grating voice. It was a small price to pay for the diligence and loyalty Abbott provided, but *gods*, it was a terrible sound. "I'd like to see it," he whispered, eyes darting about the crowded saloon.

Abbott raised an eyebrow, a hideous grin crossing his face. "To what extent would you like to observe it?"

Walker drained his mug and uttered a wet burp. "To its *fullest* extent, if you please, Mr. Abbott. Is there anyone who has been shirking their duties? Someone not fit to be a Walker Brothers miner?"

Abbott took a long look at the faces in the saloon. Finally, he nodded. "Let's go have a chat with Mr. James Powell. He's hinted at a desire to be a foreman, but in reality, he's a slacker. He would jump at the chance of a private tour with the owner."

Walker made a grand gesture with one hand. *By all means, proceed.* He followed Abbott to a stout, moon-faced man.

Powell looked surprised to see Abbott and Walker approaching, but he quickly recovered, squaring his shoulders and puffing out his chest.

"Mr. Powell," Abbott said, "meet Elias Walker, owner of the mine that puts bread on your table and clothes on your back."

Walker stepped forward and pumped the man's clammy hand. "A pleasure, Mr. Powell. Mr. Abbott has been telling me all about you."

Powell's gaze shifted to Abbott, as if he were looking for validation. Finding none, he returned his bleary eyes to Walker. "My pleasure to do what I can for Walker Brothers."

Walker kept grinning, despite his immediate dislike for the

simpering bucket of lard in front of him. "May we have a word?" He turned and exited the saloon with Abbott, knowing Powell would follow. Once outside, away from prying ears and eyes, he said, "Mr. Abbott mentioned your interest in advancing up the ranks."

Powell nodded eagerly. "Yes, sir. Like I said, whatever I can do for the good of the mine."

"It brings me great joy to hear that," Walker said, his grin widening. "If that is the case, there's no time like the present to take the next step."

Powell appeared confused. "Sir?"

"Abbott and I are proposing a private tour of the mine. Abbott can explain the details of the, uh, position, while I perform an inspection of the mine."

Powell shifted his gaze back and forth between the pair. "You mean… now?"

"We certainly can't train you on your new duties while mining operations are taking place," Walker said.

Powell nodded. "I understand."

Walker noted the suspicion on the man's face but knew Powell's greed would supersede any concerns. "Shall we?" He started toward the mine, smiling when he heard two sets of footsteps fall in behind him.

When they reached the mine, Walker let Abbott take the lead.

"What's this?" Abbott squealed.

"Is there a problem?" Walker asked.

Abbott spun to face Powell. "Who was supervisor on night shift? It was Flanagan, wasn't it?"

Powell nodded. "Yes, sir."

Walker watched the exchange with growing delight: Abbott's face was alight with barely contained fury. Powell looked like he might faint or shit his pants. "Abbott, what's going on?" Walker said, enjoying seeing Powell flinch at his harsh tone.

"I just need to bring the elevator up, Mr. Walker," Abbott said through tight lips. "Apparently, Mr. Flanagan did not secure it properly after shift." He began the process of retrieving the elevator car. "I'll address this lack of attention with him tomorrow," Abbott said.

Powell shifted nervously. "If it's too much trouble—"

"Nonsense," said Walker. "Are you prepared to be a bigger part of Walker Brothers or not?" He glared at Powell, savoring the man's fear.

"Of c-course, Mr. Walker," Powell stammered.

Walker's wicked grin returned as Abbott secured the car and opened the door. "Then down we go," he chirped.
Walker stepped out of the elevator and gestured for Abbott to lead the way.

"Where are we going?" Powell asked.

"I'm sure you've heard the rumors, Mr. Powell," Abbott said. "The infamous Tunnel 17. There's a reason it's kept a secret from the miners, and to serve the mines properly, you need to see it."

Walker laughed. Abbott's voice might have sounded like a cat in heat, but he was devious. "Well said, Mr. Abbott. Lead on."

They began making their way through the tunnels, Abbott in front, followed by Powell, with Walker trailing behind. If Powell sniffed out the ruse and tried to run for the elevator,

Walker would be happy to get his hands dirty. It'd been too long.

"Tunnel 17," Powell breathed, almost reverently. "I wasn't sure if that was all just talk—"

"It's what makes the Walker mines unique," Walker said. He decided right there it was time to drop the "Brothers" from the moniker. It was all his.

Abbott paused at a metal gate and pulled a key from his pocket. He opened the padlock, slid off the chain, and pulled the gate to swing it open. Instead, the gate squealed and tipped drunkenly forward.

"What the hell?" Abbott squawked. He went to the far side of the gate and inspected something.

"Abbott, what in God's name is going on?" Walker demanded. Abbott's caterwauling was getting on his nerves. Perhaps he'd go topside by himself this evening and let them both serve the mines.

"Broken hinge," Abbott said.

Walker didn't like his measured tone. "Broken, how?" He held up his lantern.

"Brute force with a tamping rod, I believe."

"First the elevator, now this," Walker mused. "Are you sure you have a proper handle on things, Mr. Abbott?"

"Indeed, sir." To Abbott's credit, his gaze never wavered. "You have my word this will be dealt with."

"If you gentlemen need to deal with this," Powell said shakily, "we could—"

"Nonsense," Abbott cooed, "we're already here. Come, it's just ahead."

CHAPTER FOURTEEN

The tunnel dead-ended just ahead, but Jackman saw the flickering of a lantern coming from off to the right. *There must be another tunnel, or perhaps a chamber.* Was Tunnel 17 just a secret name for some manner of prison? *Or,* he thought, *a morgue.* Either way, there could be a guard posted around the clock. But wouldn't he have heard the elevator? Jackman crept forward, heart hammering as he edged closer to the tunnel. Then, he heard a noise that sent a fresh terror through him, nearly paralyzing him. It wasn't coming from the cavern ahead, it echoed from the tunnel behind him. It was the elevator car.

Jackman stood frozen. Should he go forward into Tunnel 17, and face whatever awaited him? Or try to get back through the gate and hide in one of the branches shooting from the main shaft? Either option held risk, with potentially deadly rewards. There was no way he could get back through the gate, set it in place, and find a hiding spot, all before the elevator returned. And whoever was coming down—surely it was Abbott—would already be on high alert because of the elevator not being up top, as it should have been after each shift.

He was trapped.

Jackman looked around wildly, his breath coming in short, panicked gasps. Then he saw something in the shimmering lantern light. Across from the entrance to what he presumed was Tunnel 17, there was an outcrop of rocks. Based on the depth of the shadows, he thought there might be enough room for him to crouch behind them, unseen. The only problem was he would be visible to whoever—or whatever—was in Tunnel 17.

The clanging of the elevator got him moving. Once they arrived at the main shaft, it would be only a matter of minutes before they'd reach the spot where Jackman stood. This must be where they were headed—why else would anyone venture down at this hour?

His mind made up, he crept along the right-hand wall toward Tunnel 17. He winced each time his boot scuffed a rock, and willed himself to be quieter. He reached the entrance just as the elevator clanked to a stop. Now, there was no sound to cover any noises he made. He peered around the corner, his mind conjuring every manner of horror that might come into view. Piles of dead miners. Men chained to the wall, starving and beaten. Some devilish creature that had been belched up from the depths of Hell. But he saw nothing apart from the lantern hanging on the far wall.

The chamber seemed gigantic, though it was hard to tell in the dim light. Then, something in there shifted. It was the slightest of noises, but it seemed magnified in the eerie underground acoustics. *Was that the rattle of chains?* Then another sound. This was different. A sort of wet, snuffling sound, like a horse chuffing. Then, the sound of the gate.

Without thinking, Jackman darted across the tunnel and dove behind the outcropping. Something grunted across the way, followed by the dragging of chains, until the echo of footsteps and raised voices drowned out whatever it was. Jackman crouched lower, trying desperately to get his breathing under control. He was sure his heartbeat was audible, echoing madly in the tunnel, a beacon to give away his hiding place.

More light flashed in the direction he'd come from. At least two men, maybe more. He squeezed himself deeper into the small crevice. The lights moved closer, almost upon him. He could see there were three men but couldn't make them out in the glare from their lanterns.

"What do you make of this?" a voice demanded.

Jackman didn't recognize it, but it was clearly someone in authority. Jackman couldn't mistake the high-pitched screech of the next man who spoke. *Abbott!*

"I'm not sure, sir," Abbott said. "I'll get to the bottom of it, of that you can be sure."

"See that you do," the other voice boomed.

Jackman had to stifle a gasp. *Walker?* Who else would Abbott refer to as *sir*?

"I think perhaps—" a third voice began, but Abbott cut him off.

"I don't pay you to think," Abbott shrieked.

The voice was familiar; it belonged to one of the miners, but Jackman couldn't place it.

"Now," the man Jackman believed to be Walker said, "let's show our guest why he's here."

"If you're going to be a leader," Abbott practically shrieked, "you're going to need to be intimately familiar with Tunnel 17."

Jackman craned his neck, trying to get a look at the third man. *Powell!* Then the three entered the tunnel.

CHAPTER FIFTEEN

The three men entered the chamber. Jackman watched the flickering lights until the men went deeper in and headed off to the right. He considered making a run for it, back through the gate, to the main shaft. Once he started the elevator up, he would be safe. *But what if you don't make it that far? What if they secured the gate and it slowed you down? What if they sent the car up as a precaution?*

It was too risky. One misstep, onc scrabble of a boot on the tunnel floor. That's all it would take. No, he would have to wait it out. His heart slammed against his ribcage and his breath came in short gasps, as if his body was trying to argue against his decision. He closed his eyes and took a deep, slow breath. When a scream shattered the silence of the tunnel, he nearly matched it with one of his own.

He dared a look, craning well beyond the outcrop to get a view. Shadows moved wildly inside the chamber, but he could see little else. The scream had been cut off abruptly. Jackman wondered if Abbott had covered Powell's mouth, or perhaps quieted him with a blow to the head. He didn't wonder for long. The next sound he heard wiped all other thoughts from his mind. The low growl caught his attention, turning quickly into vicious snarls and guttural howls.

The chamber entrance and its dancing shadows seemed to be drawing away, as if Jackman were watching through the wrong end of a telescope. A clanging sound rose above the animal noise, refocusing his mind. *Chains,* he realized. Voices rose, but he could not make out the words. He needed to see.

Instead of venturing closer to the chamber entrance, he climbed higher on the outcrop of rocks, hoping for a better angle. He was still unable to see the men and whatever else was in the chamber, but his higher view enabled him to distinguish the shadows on the cavern floor. He saw three of them, huddled close. He assumed Walker and Abbott were holding Powell between them. Then, a fourth shadow came into view, creeping toward the other three.

Jackman watched the shadow with disbelief. It walked upright but did not have the same shape or features as the other three. It was hunched over, its arms and legs disproportional to its torso, even taking into account the distortion of the shadow.

The other three figures moved in what Jackman deciphered as a struggle. Powell trying to escape. A muffled cry, then one shadow shrunk. Powell had been struck and knocked to the ground. Jackman gasped as two men, Abbott and Walker, came into view. They stood inside the chamber, staring in the direction they'd come from. Abbott moved over to the wall. He raised his arms, and Jackman heard a new sound. It was familiar, the squeal of a pulley in motion. The chains rattled, and wet, grunting sounds echoed through the tunnel. They escalated to gnarling as the rattling grew fervent.

Then a baying, wolf-like, but not from any wolf Jackman had ever heard. Screams threatened to drown out the howls—human screams.

"No! God, please, no!"

It had to be Powell, but mortal panic had turned the voice to an unrecognizable squawk. Then the howls stopped and there was only the screaming and the ripping of flesh and the snapping of bones. The screams subsided to cries, then moans. All that remained were the sloppy, sucking sounds of something feeding.

CHAPTER SIXTEEN

McCabe looked around the saloon, spotted Townsend delivering a tray of drinks, and shouldered his way through the crowd toward him. When Townsend spotted him, the barkeep gave a barely noticeable shake of his head and motioned to the small office behind the bar. McCabe nodded and met him there.

"What's the urgent business, Mr. Townsend?" McCabe had received a note sent by the barkeep. Very unusual, given the late hour.

"Walker's here," Townsend replied. "And he's brought a small army."

McCabe turned, peering out the door and searching the crowd for strangers. "How many?"

"A dozen that I'm sure of. Maybe more, if he didn't parade them all through the saloon."

"Where is he?" McCabe knew what Walker looked like, but couldn't spot him in the saloon.

Townsend shrugged. "Left a while ago with Abbott and some other bloke."

"One of his men?" McCabe pressed.

"No, a miner. Parson, maybe? Or Powell?"

McCabe frowned. It didn't make sense. Powell was just a working man, not a boss. Unless he was spying on the other miners for Abbott. The force that Walker brought spelled trouble, and McCabe's men weren't due in for a couple of days. "What about your men from Philadelphia?"

"A few were on this afternoon's coach but I told them to stay out of sight. The rest, not until the day after."

"Shit," McCabe said. "I didn't expect him this soon, if at all. Abbott must have panicked after the meeting in the clearing and sent word. I'll have to find Moore and Devlin, tell them we need to speak as soon as possible."

"They were both here when Walker showed up," Townsend said. "Talking in whispers with a couple of others."

McCabe considered this. "Who were the other men?"

"Couple of miners called Ellis and Donovan. Regulars. Been working the mine for a while now."

"What about Jackman?" Something wasn't adding up.

"The mine foreman?" Townsend shook his head. "Haven't seen him this evening."

McCabe paced the small room. He didn't like this. Everything was happening too fast, and he had no backup yet. He had to find the others. "Keep your eyes and ears open," he told Townsend. "I'm going to find the others and see if we can figure out how to get by until the rest of our men arrive."

Townsend said, "I'll see if I can get one of Walker's men alone and fill him with whiskey."

"Good idea. Be wary—those men are dangerous."

MCCABE RETURNED TO the saloon an hour later, frustrated and growing more nervous with each passing minute. He'd spoken to Moore and Devlin. They were both sure Ellis and Donovan could be trusted, but McCabe wasn't convinced. Devlin's blunder in speaking to them might have gotten back to Abbott somehow. And Jackman wasn't at home where he should have been, given that he had the morning shift the next day.

The saloon had emptied out considerably; only a few of the night-shift workers remained. McCabe spotted Townsend at the far end of the bar, laughing with a man he didn't recognize. Perhaps Townsend was having better luck. McCabe stood away from the two men but motioned for a drink.

Townsend brought over a mug of beer and said, "I've got some news. I'll fill you in shortly." Then he was back with the other man, pouring a generous glass of whiskey.

McCabe sipped his beer, glancing around the saloon. He didn't know as many of the night-shift workers so he couldn't determine if the remaining drinkers were miners or more of Walker's men. After a while, the man Townsend had been talking with stumbled away, weaving drunkenly through the saloon and out into the night.

"Not all of Walker's men are as loyal as the likes of Abbott," Townsend said, placing a full mug of beer in front of McCabe.

"I trust you've had better luck than me." He quickly filled the barkeep in on what he'd learned.

"I'm not so sure about Jackman," Townsend said. "The mine bosses are usually ruthless. Could he still be giving information to Abbott? Only pretending to be on the side of the miners?"

"I'm not sure myself," McCabe admitted. "There's something very strange going on in the mines—"

"You're not speaking of the mine devil?" Townsend said with a chuckle.

McCabe watched him carefully. "What have you heard?"

"Just the same nonsense you probably have. The stories have been going around since I've been in Serenity."

"But you think there's no truth behind it?" McCabe asked.

Townsend looked incredulous. "Of course not. The only devils in that mine are Abbott and the other bosses."

CHAPTER SEVENTEEN

Jackman waited for a long time after Abbott and Walker had left until he moved. Part of it was wanting to make sure they were really gone. He'd heard their muffled discussion about fixing the gate, followed shortly after by the sound of the elevator ascending. Still, he waited.

What if they sent the elevator up empty to lure him out of hiding? Or perhaps they were waiting up top for him. He told himself these were valid concerns, logical and reasonable. But the most primitive part of his brain knew the truth. He was afraid to move and draw the attention of whatever creature lived in Tunnel 17.

Jackman's rational brain tried to assert itself. *The chains,* his mind screamed, *the damn thing is bound in chains*. Otherwise, it would run free through the mines, at least as far as the gate. Yes, that sounded very sane. But the slurping sounds echoed in his head, and they told him not to move or he would hear those sounds again. Up close.

Jackman gasped, aware that he'd somehow started to doze off. The horror and the extreme tension of the evening had exhausted him. He had no idea what time it was. If the morning shift showed up and he was already down there, Abbott would know.

He got to his feet, shaking his limbs to get the sleep out of them. With a final glance toward the chamber they called Tunnel 17, he left his hiding place and stepped as quietly as he could toward the main shaft. No sound came from the chamber. Jackman pictured some horrific beast sleeping in the corner, sated with a belly full of flesh and bone. He moved quicker.

When he got to the gate, it was in the same state he'd originally found it, the broken hinge propped in place. Jackman pushed gently, still trying to be quiet, but the gate didn't move. A wave of panic crashed over him. Had they fixed the gate and trapped him in here? With…

He shoved harder, and a deafening screech of metal erupted in the cave, echoing madly down the tunnels. He scampered through. The hell with keeping quiet, he ran as fast as he could for the main shaft.

Jackman reached the elevator shaken and out of breath. He'd pictured some demon chasing him, all claws and fangs and hunger. He turned, but the tunnel behind him was empty. He knew he should fix the gate, but he couldn't bring himself to do it. He drew the elevator down, entered the car, and cranked himself slowly to the top. There was still a chance, a whispering voice told him, that Abbott and Walker were perched at the top of the shaft, waiting for him. But it was still better than meeting whatever dwelled below.

CHAPTER EIGHTEEN

Jackman stumbled through the saloon door, head swiveling wildly from side to side. His gaze landed on the group of men sitting around the two long tables that had been pushed together. They glared back, some of them reaching for their pistols. Jackman only recognized two, Townsend and McCabe.

McCabe stood, hand inside his jacket. "Mr. Jackman. What brings you here?"

"John Moore," he gasped. "Roan Devlin. I must speak with them."

McCabe motioned for the others to remain seated and stepped forward. "The hour is late, Mr. Jackman. What possible business could you have with the miners?"

Jackman lunged, taking hold of McCabe's lapels and pulling him close. Chairs scraped and guns cocked but Jackman ignored it all. "I know what's down there, Mr. McCabe." He looked around, then at his hands still gripping McCabe's coat. He released the man and held up his palms, stepping back. "I *know*," he repeated.

Townsend approached and handed Jackman a glass of whiskey. "Go fetch Moore and Devlin," he said to McCabe. Turning to Jackman he said, "Come. Have a seat, I'll introduce you to these gentlemen."

Jackman raised the glass to his lips, then stopped. He needed to keep a clear head. It was going to be difficult enough to convince the others without adding drunkenness into the equation. He handed the whiskey to Townsend and followed him to the table, sitting shakily in one of the empty seats. "Can I please have a glass of water?"

Townsend introduced the men he knew from Philadelphia. The others, McCabe's men—Mollies—introduced themselves. Townsend went back behind the bar and poured a glass of water.

Jackman drank greedily, wishing the glass was full of whiskey so he could erase the memory of those sounds. The men all pressed him for information about the mines, but he shook them off. "Wait for Moore and Devlin. I don't want to have to tell it twice." He drained the rest of the glass, then placed his elbows on the table and leaned his face into his hands.

He looked up when he heard the saloon door, suddenly sure it would be Abbott and Walker coming to get him. But it was McCabe, flanked by Devlin and Moore.

"What's happened?" Moore asked, covering the distance from the door to the table in four long strides.

Jackman sighed, suddenly bone tired. "Have a seat, fellas. I've got quite a tale to tell."

WHEN JACKMAN HAD finished talking, he slumped back in his chair, studying the other men's faces. They were looking around awkwardly, as if waiting for someone else to speak. Their expressions seemed to run the gamut. Fear, disbelief, mirth, confusion, shock, and anger.

John Moore stood, locking eyes with each man at the table, one by one. "Before anyone else says anything, I have to say a word. I was down there myself. I saw the gate and the tunnel. I heard some of what Mr. Jackman described. It was… unholy. Whatever they have down there…" He shook his head and sat down.

Roan stood. "It's true. Whatever doubts you have, you need to set them aside. There is a creature down there. Or a demon. And it's killing miners." He started to sit but then straightened. "And it's up to us to do something about it. Some of you are here to stand with us to make the mines safer, to fight for better wages, and that's both necessary and noble. But this…"—he shook his head—"this is different. This is…" Roan held up both hands, as if searching the air in front of him for the right word to pluck from it. "This is murder. It's evil." He sat down heavily and closed his eyes.

"Well?" Jackman prompted.

One of Townsend's Philadelphia men stood abruptly, tipping his chair over. "I don't know what you were thinking, Cal, but I'll be on tomorrow's coach. You might want to consider getting out of this town yourself." He turned to Roan. "I don't know if this is some kind of joke or if you're just mad, but I'll not hear any more of this nonsense." He nodded to the others and turned to leave. The others followed his lead.

"These are good, hard-working men," Townsend called after them. "I'll stand with them even if you're not man enough."

The first man, whom Jackman presumed was the leader, paused. He straightened his back and tightened his shoulders, then, without turning, he crossed the saloon and stepped out into the night. The others followed.

"It looks like it's just us," McCabe said. "John, how many—"

The scraping of another chair cut him off. To Jackman's horror, the Mollies were all on their feet now.

"The Molly Maguires vow to fight to improve the working conditions and wages for miners everywhere, by whatever means necessary. What you're talking about here, Thomas… it's outright madness. It won't reflect well on you that we've been called here on a wild goose chase." Then they were gone.

Moore pounded a fist on the table. "This has to end. I'll not set foot in the mines until that godless thing has been killed."

"It might be best if we're all on the coach tomorrow," Roan said.

Jackman studied the men at the table, panic descending on him like some giant bird of prey. Its talons found his shoulders, gripping for perch and causing them to tighten. Its beak explored the soft flesh of his throat, his wrists, then his chest, pecking faster and faster like a second heartbeat. "God help us," he sputtered, choking back his terror.

ROAN WAS TOO tired to think about the mines or the Mollies or anything else. He needed to get some rest before the next joyless trip down the elevator. The saloon door flew open, and everyone was on their feet, some with guns drawn from hidden clutches and holsters.

"Talbot," McCabe said, his shotgun disappearing into the folds of his duster. "What's the meaning of this?"

Daniel Talbot had bent over, hands on his knees as he struggled to catch his breath. He straightened, gulped in more air, then said, "Tomorrow."

Roan felt the hair on the back of his neck stiffen. He closed his eyes, wishing he'd left a few minutes earlier. The inevitability of whatever this man, Talbot, was about to say, fell on his shoulders like a heavy cloak.

Townsend handed Talbot a shot of whiskey and a beer. He downed the shot, gulped in a few more breaths, then took a sip of the beer.

"Walker is planning on making his move tomorrow," Talbot said. "At shift change, his men will surround the mine. Night shift will be up top waiting to go down. When day shift comes up, he'll have them all together. That's when it happens."

"That's when *what* happens?" McCabe asked, clearly confused.

Daniel gaped at him. "He's planning to cull the miners, Thomas. He's got lists from Abbott and some of the others. They've rated every miner based on work ethic, dependability, that sort of thing. But loyalty is their most important criteria. Anyone who attended the meeting the other night or is even suspected of consorting with the Mollies is put on the bad list."

"Goddamn him. All those miners out of work—"

"No," Talbot said, shaking his head madly from side to side. "Not out of work." He paused, eyes skittering around the room as if looking for a safe place to land his gaze. "I think they mean to put the miners in prison or relegate them to slavery." Talbot shrugged, suddenly looking perplexed. He downed the rest of his beer in desperate gulps. "I'm not sure what it is, exactly, but it sounded quite ominous."

Roan's legs buckled and he sat down hard.

"What are you on about, Talbot?" McCabe bellowed.

But Roan already knew. He opened his mouth to speak but he'd lost all ability. He was frozen in place, the sounds and lights and odors of the saloon dimming. *Diminishing*. He was numb, paralyzed with terror.

Talbot said, "Walker ordered Abbott to send all the men on the list to Tunnel 17."

Moore swore under his breath. McCabe brought both fists down on the table, rattling the glasses.

Talbot hadn't been there when they'd talked of Tunnel 17, he'd been off at the hotel mingling with Walker's men, looking for one with loose lips. By God, he'd found one. No, Talbot didn't know what Tunnel 17 was. But the rest of them did.

Roan thought of Sara and it snapped him out of his paralysis. "We have to…" *What?* his mind screamed. What could a handful of miners do against Walker's men?

"We have to get to the hotel and rally the rest of the Mollies," Talbot cried. "Thomas, this has to be on your order."

Roan closed his eyes.

"The Mollies won't be standing with us this time," McCabe said softly, almost wistfully.

"Why the hell not?" Talbot demanded.

McCabe recounted a short version of the earlier conversation. Roan watched Talbot closely, waiting for him to leap to his feet and take his leave, as the others had done. But he remained, listening intently to McCabe's bizarre tale.

"The others aren't having it," McCabe said. He nodded toward Townsend. "Same for the Philadelphia contingent. We're on our own."

"Well," Talbot sighed, "five's better than four, I reckon."

Moore leaned over and clapped the man on his shoulder. "That's the spirit, Talbot. But tell me, why are you willing to believe this madness when the others all abandoned us?"

Talbot took a while to answer, his gaze going distant as he looked into the past. "I grew up in Warren County," he began. "My grandpappy built a cabin by West Spring Creek. When I was twelve, my folks passed. Consumption got 'em both, just a month apart. My little sis, too. I went to live with Grandpa Russo; I had nowhere else to go. Granny had passed recently, too; I found out when I arrived. It was just me and this old man, a stranger. Both lost. He'd been married forty years when Granny passed. So, we found solace in each other out in those woods."

Talbot paused as Townsend brought fresh glasses of beer to the table. They were all rapt.

"Grandpa told me stories. Fanciful tales of witches and creatures that lived in the deep woods, that could only be killed with silver bullets." Talbot laughed. "I thought it was just stories, just his way of bonding with his grandson." He ran a hand through his hair and drank half his beer. "But I saw things out there. Things I won't speak of. Here or anywhere." He finished his beer in two mighty gulps. "I know there are things in this world that most wouldn't believe. Haints, witches, creatures that walk like men… all manner of hoodoo." He paused, his eyes clearing. "I'll stand with you."

Roan gaped at the man. A week ago, he would have thought him a drunk or a lunatic. Now, he was happy to have Talbot on their side. Roan turned to McCabe. "What can we do?"

It was Townsend who became the voice of reason. "Look alive, boys," he said with a grin. "We've got a long night ahead of us."

"What do you have in mind?" McCabe asked. Townsend's statement seemed to have calmed him.

Roan looked at Moore and saw the same was true. "Go on, Cal," he urged. "If you've got a plan, let's hear it."

CHAPTER NINETEEN

Roan returned to the saloon several hours later, exhausted, discouraged, and fearing for his life. The plan had been for him, Townsend, McCabe, Moore, and Talbot to visit each of the miners and rally them to stand against Walker and his men. It had been futile.

Roan dropped his weary frame into one of the seats and

waited for the others. He could barely keep his eyes open. One by one, the others returned, looking as defeated as Roan felt.

"Now what?" Moore asked.

Roan waited, expecting McCabe to reply, but he just stared at nothing. Moore looked from one man to the next, searching their faces for something. *Maybe he's looking for hope,* Roan thought, something he could cling to. Still, nobody answered.

Each and every house Roan visited had been in vain. He was greeted by angry miners or their scared wives. Walker's men had beaten them again, visiting the miners with a show of force and a promise of violence if there were any signs of revolt or strike. Walker knew the Mollies were there, but he also knew he had them vastly outnumbered. Not a single miner had agreed to stand against the bosses.

"I don't see that there's anything I can do but go to work," Roan said glumly. He was too tired to be scared. "Maybe the list is just another scare tactic."

Moore shrugged his big shoulders. "They can't very well send half the miners to Tunnel 17, can they?"

"Is that something you want to wager your life on?" McCabe asked.

"What's the alternative?" Moore thundered. "Mining is all I know. Am I supposed to just run away, tail between my legs?"

McCabe held his gaze. "Is that worse than Tunnel 17? Why fight a war you can't win, John? Live to fight another day."

Roan got to his feet. "I'm going to go home and sleep for a few hours." He clapped Moore on the back on his way by. "I guess I'll see you at the mine."

John stood. "I'll walk with you." He turned to McCabe and the others. "Thank you. Maybe it would have been better if Roan and I had kept our mouths shut about Tunnel 17, but what's done is done." He heaved a long sigh. "Walker is cunning. He'll think he's shaken us up enough to toe the line. Perhaps we will live to fight again."

They walked together in silence. Roan's mind kept returning to those wet, slurping noises in the tunnel. Such hungry sounds. Still, his fear was tempered by the resignation he felt. He'd take his chances in the mines. "If they try to send me to 17, I'll fight," he said quietly.

"Aye," Moore acknowledged. "As will I. To the death, if it comes to that. And not just for myself," he added. "If they try to send anyone to that godless tunnel, I'll fight until I can't fight anymore."

They reached Moore's house first. "Goodnight, John," Roan said. "You've been a good friend." He reached out a hand in the darkness for Moore to shake, but he surprised him by pulling him in for a crushing hug.

"This feels like a bad dream," Moore said wistfully. "Goodnight, Roan." Then he was gone.

Roan reached his house a few minutes later. He stood outside, staring at the dark silhouette of his house. His *home*. "To the death," he muttered, then went inside.

CHAPTER TWENTY

Roan sat up gasping, fragments of the nightmare dissipating like ripples on a pond. He was bathed in cooling sweat, his heart racing.

"Are you ill?" Sara asked groggily.

Am I? Roan wondered. "Go back to sleep," he whispered. "I'm just getting up for work." Sara moaned, and rolled over. Roan wanted nothing more than to slip in behind her and close his eyes. To forget the mines, the Mollies, the— He shook his head. He couldn't abandon his friends and coworkers, leaving them to face whatever waited in the mines. Whether it was Walker and his men or… the other thing, he would stand with them and fight.

He arrived at the mines a short time later, tired and scared. Looking at the faces of the men around him, he saw a lot of the same expressions: fear, exhaustion, or dull-eyed confusion. They exchanged greetings, but out of rote, not out of genuine cordiality. Any hint of cheer felt forced, another form of mask to hide their dread of taking that elevator.

Moore shuffled up to him a few minutes later. Sagging, dark circles hung under his friend's eyes. "Mornin', Roan." His voice was hoarse and husky, that of a man who hadn't slept.

"It is morning," Roan agreed tiredly. He looked at the lightening sky in the east. Brilliant red and orange stripes ran parallel to the horizon. "And in the morning, it will be stormy, for the sky is red and threatening. You know how to interpret the appearance of the sky, but you cannot interpret the signs of the times."

Moore followed his gaze. "Let's hope old Matthew has it wrong," he said.

The work bell rang, and the men fell in line with the elevator. Jackman was there, writing in the work log. "Going to be a busy day, boys," he called. "Looks like we're a few men down."

Roan turned, noticing that the line was thinner than usual. Several miners had either stayed home ill or disappeared into the night. A hot, oily ball formed in his gut. The urge to turn and run was nearly overpowering. Then the elevator's maw stood in front of him, and he was pushed into it on a wave of bodies.

The day wore on as Roan kept his head down and focused on the job. He didn't want to let his mind drift and possibly cause another injury. Or worse, give the bosses any reason to send him to Tunnel 17.

Jackman and Moore looked wary and afraid the whole time. At lunch, he sat with Moore, but they both picked at their food in a morose silence.

As the afternoon dragged by, Roan's anxiety grew. It felt like everything was closing in on him. The tons of rock between him and the surface seemed to weigh on him, making it hard to breathe. Lunatic thoughts bombarded his mind, each worse than the one before. *What if there's not enough oxygen? What if they cut the elevator and leave us down here?* Then, *What if they just open the gate between us and Tunnel 17 and let that thing run wild?*

This last one nearly did him in. His heart thundered in his chest, and he struggled to take a breath: his airway seemed to be closing. He raised a hand, signaling he needed to halt the drilling as his knees unhinged. He was down on all fours, gasping for air, when the shift bell rang.

Moore was by his side, pulling him to his feet. "Pull it together, man. Now is not the time to draw attention."

Roan closed his eyes and let Moore pull him toward the elevator. *Are we really going to get above ground?* Somehow, the thought of Walker's men waiting up there was less daunting than the confines of the mine. He stumbled in line with the others, slowly moving toward the elevator. Moore kept a firm grip on his upper arm to keep him from falling.

When they were on the elevator, Roan stood rigid, sure that the cable would snap just before they reached the top. When the car rattled to a stop, he couldn't believe it. He shoved his way through the crowd of miners ahead of him, ignoring their shouts and grumbles. He stepped out of the mine, blinking in the sudden brightness of day.

All of Roan's hysterical thoughts evaporated at the sight of what waited there. The night-shift workers were huddled in a tight circle, watching the shaft entrance. Their eyes were empty, resigned. Beyond the tightly packed gaggle of miners, two dozen hard-looking men stood in a vague semi-circle, holding rifles and shotguns. They wore dusters, and their faces were covered, not by hoods this time, but by kerchiefs over their lower faces, only their cold eyes showing.

Elias Walker stepped forward. He held an absurdly large revolver and wore the Devil's smile. "The time has come for a reckoning, gentlemen."

ROAN CALCULATED THE odds as Walker stepped through the circle of men. The miners outnumbered Walker's cronies two-to-one, but the only weapons they had besides their fists were a few shovels and pickaxes. It would be a quick and bloody mistake to go against them. Abbott stood holding a shotgun and wearing double revolvers on a gun belt. As intimidating as the situation was, he looked ludicrous.

"Walker Mines has a long tradition of employing the best miners and producing more coal than any other mine. This is accomplished through efficient drilling and mining, by employing hard-working, loyal men. Which brings me to why we're here today." Walker spoke the final line with an ominous undertone and a matching grin.

"Night shift, onto the elevator," Abbott screeched. "I'll be down shortly to continue this meeting."

When none of the miners moved, Walker's men brandished their weapons and started herding them toward the elevator. A few minutes later, they were gone. The odds had shifted even farther in Walker's favor, just a skeleton crew of day shifters remaining.

Roan snuck a glance at Moore. The big man was glaring at Walker, fists clenched by his side. "Steady, John," he whispered. Moore gave a slight nod that did nothing to alleviate Roan's fear that he might take a run at Walker.

"We've done your work, Mr. Walker," John exclaimed. "And

the thanks we get is an army of your boys carrying rifles." He gestured toward the men surrounding them.

Walker's grin held but his face reddened. He stepped towards Moore, flanked by two of his gun-toting minions. "And who've we here?"

"John Moore." He held Walker's gaze.

"Well, John Moore, perhaps you're aware of an infiltration of a band of scoundrels looking to cut me down. To turn my men against me?"

John stared at him but remained silent.

"I've not heard tell of such scoundrels," Roan said. "But I have heard of some good men about town who'd like to see better working conditions for the miners. Better wages, too." Murmurs rose from the crowd. Some in agreement, but others in dissent.

One voice rose above the rest. "Shut your mouth, Devlin, before you get us all killed."

"You won't all be killed," Moore responded, turning to scan the crowd for the speaker. "Only the ones who refuse to bow down to Mr. Walker, here."

More supportive grumbles from the miners.

"And those who do refuse," Roan added, his voice shaking with both fear and conviction, "will be relegated to Tunnel 17."

The rumbling in the crowd stopped. Walker moved in on Roan. Walker's face was beet-red, and his eyes held deadly promises. "And what do you know of Tunnel 17?"

Roan stiffened his shoulders and jutted his chin. "I know everything," he hissed.

Walker's jaw tightened.

One of the men flanking Walker cocked his rifle.

"Walker!" The voice came from somewhere behind the wall of men.

For a long moment, Walker continued to glare at Roan, eyes ablaze with contempt. Then shouts and the sound of more rifles cocking made him turn.

"What's the meaning of this?" Walker crowed, striding toward the voices.

Roan's shoulders sagged as he exhaled a tremulous breath. He felt Moore's firm grip on his shoulder. Voices grew angry as a circle of Walker's men surrounded him, now facing away from the miners. Then, a voice Roan recognized rose above the rest.

"Elias Walker, you'll not take any more of Serenity's men or their families!" A cheer rose behind the voice.

Roan blinked slowly, sure he must have been dreaming, then ran toward the sound of his wife's voice.

THE GANG HAD huddled protectively around their boss-man and Roan had to shoulder past one of the riflemen to see what was happening. And he could not believe it.

McCabe stood facing Walker, his duster flapping in the lazy afternoon breeze. Townsend, holding a Colt revolver, was at McCabe's side. Spread out around them, holding all manner of household tools as weapons and wearing angry scowls, were the women of Serenity.

"Sara," Roan cried and started toward her, only to be thrown back by one of Walker's men, who then trained his rifle on his chest.

"Thomas McCabe," Walker said mildly, that snake's grin reappearing. "This is what the Mollies have come to, is it?" He barked out a laugh, then pulled a cigar from his pocket and took his time lighting it.

"We know what you've got down in the mine," McCabe said. "What you've been doing to the men." He spread his arms wide, turning left then right. "We *all* know."

Walker's face hardened but that grin held fast. "Do ya now?" He nodded and puffed his cigar. "Might be that by nightfall, you'll know a lot more about it."

McCabe took a step forward, wearing a thin smile. Rifles cocked, almost in unison. "What are you going to do, Walker, have your men shoot innocent women?"

Walker shrugged. "They don't look so innocent to me, brandishing broom handles and shovels. In fact, I'd say they were here to disrupt mining operations, which, as you know, I have every right to prevent."

"Mr. Walker is correct," Abbott said, in that high, screechy voice of his. He cocked the shotgun. "Nothing stopping us from opening fire right now."

"Certainly not a conscience among ya to stop the bloodbath," Moore shouted. "Not after the Devil's work you've been doing down in the mines."

Walker glared at Moore, then held out a hand. "The list, if you please, Mr. Abbott."

Abbott leaned his shotgun against one leg and made a show of taking a paper from his pocket and unfolding it before handing it over.

Walker made an even bigger show of looking over the list. Then he nodded. "John Moore," he said. "According to Mr. Abbott, you've been conspiring with the Molly Maguires. That is an offense punishable by termination." He grinned wickedly. "But I think justice would be better served by assigning you to Tunnel 17."

The crowd on both sides—the miners and the wives—gasped.

Moore shook his head. "I'll die fighting right here before I let you and your minions take me down there."

Walker shrugged. "As you wish."

ABBOTT BENT TO retrieve the shotgun, but before he could level it at Moore, a cry rang out behind the mine boss and suddenly his head snapped forward. He stood, stunned, then his knees buckled and he fell forward. Blood flowed in a red river from his cracked head. Sara stood above him, wild-eyed, staring at the shovel that had cleaved Abbott's skull.

Walker turned, raising his rifle, but Moore and Roan were on him. Moore wrenched the rifle from his hands while Roan wrapped him in a bear hug, pinning his arms to his sides. He struggled briefly, then Moore had the barrel of the rifle jammed under his chin. Walker's men stood frozen, unable to act without an order from their boss. Roan breathed a sigh of relief. This was going to end peacefully, with the exception of Abbott.

Suddenly, the crack of a gunshot shattered the eerie silence, and the scene erupted into a melee. The women charged, broomsticks, rolling pins, and shovels raised. Screams and shouts rang out and the sound of wood striking flesh and bone drowned out everything. Until the gunshots began.

As soon as one man had either the courage or the stupidity to pull the trigger against the charging women, the mob followed suit.

Roan released his grip on Walker, leaving Moore to guard him, and joined the fracas. He lashed out wildly, swinging fists and feet alike, taking as many blows as he dished out.

The screams and the gunshots seemed to go on forever. Then the gunshots ended and the sound of blunt instruments dealing out pain reigned. Finally, all that remained was sobbing and moaning. Roan gasped for breath, wiping blood from his face, searching the battlefield for his wife.

He ran from body to body calling her name. *There!* He recognized her dress despite the blood and dirt that stained it. She was facedown, prone, and he feared the worst. He fell to his knees by her side and gently turned her over. Her eyes were open but sightless. Roan threw back his head and screamed at the sky.

CHAPTER TWENTY-ONE

Roan sat in the saloon glaring at Walker. Moore had tied him to a chair while they assessed damages. Walker's men were all dead. 17 miners had been killed, along with Daniel

Talbot, Cal Townsend, and eleven women. Dozens more were injured. McCabe had sustained a bullet wound to the shoulder and Jackman had been bludgeoned unconscious, but both would survive.

The night-shift miners had been brought up top and sent home, shocked expressions on their faces at what had transpired. Doc was busy, doing his best to tend to the injured. Roan had escaped with just cuts and bruises. Moore had been mostly untouched, a fact that irked him, but he'd kept Walker in custody.

Roan downed a shot of whiskey and reached for the bottle to pour another, but Moore grabbed his arm. "There's more work to be done," he said. "Then you can grieve."

Roan nodded. "Then let's get to it."

Moore left Walker's hands bound but freed him from the chair, dragging him to his feet.

"I'll see this town burn to the ground," Walker sneered. "And I'll listen to the sound of your screams as if they were music."

Moore grunted but said nothing. He pulled Walker toward the door. Walker continued his threats, telling them how many men were on the way and the torment and Hellfire they would bring with them. Once they were outside, and Walker realized where they were going, he lost his bluster.

"No," he said. "Y-you can't."

They reached the elevator and shoved him in. He tried to run, but Moore halted him with a vicious punch to the gut. He and Roan pushed the doubled-over Walker back into the elevator.

By the time they reached the bottom of the shaft, Walker was blubbering nonsensically. Roan slapped him in the face repeatedly until he shut up.

When they stepped off the elevator, Roan took Jackman's keys and went to the underground equipment cage. The gate opened with a screech and Roan gathered the supplies they would need to seal Tunnel 17 permanently. Explosives were something in which he and Moore were well-versed.

As he loaded the mine cart, he grabbed a pickaxe that had been left behind. Suddenly, the whole plan seemed like a very bad idea, especially the part about facing the thing in Tunnel 17.

They dragged Walker through the tunnels. Then he went rigid. "Wait," he panted. "I know how to fix this. I'll give you money, more than you've ever dreamed of. Ownership to half the mines in my brother's stead."

He rambled on as they approached the gate. Moore kicked it and the gate wrenched open with a metallic screech. Something deeper in the tunnel awakened and growled.

Roan looked at Moore. The big man paused for a second, then continued forward, dragging Walker with him. Walker was out of his mind with panic, as if finally realizing his captors meant business. This was not some scare tactic. He was going to be left with the beast.

Walker redoubled his efforts to break free, but he was no match for Moore. Even if he had been able to escape, what was he going to do? Did he think he could race back to the elevators, get up top, and somehow slink off into the night? Roan laughed at the thought, drawing a strange look from Moore.

They reached the tunnel entrance and stopped. Walker's entire body was quivering, to the point Roan feared he might be in the throes of a seizure. A stab of disappointment ran through him when he considered Walker might die of fright. *That would be too easy.* Given all the suffering and heartache this man had caused, no death would be gruesome enough. Talbot, Townsend, all the miners, and, of course, Sara. Poor, brave, sweet Sara. She'd been the one who'd rallied the miners' wives the night before. The women of Serenity deserved all the credit for saving the town. No, this was not about justice—this was vengeance, pure and simple.

"Your time has come, Walker," Moore said. At the sound of his voice, a snuffling growl emitted from the cavern, followed by the furious rattle of chains. It sounded like the creature was running wild. Moore grinned wickedly in the flickering lantern light. "The sound of voices is like ringing the dinner bell, eh, Walker?"

Walker was still quaking, but his eyes had gone distant. Something in his brain had shut down, rendering him just a husk. A living, breathing scarecrow.

"Let's end this," Roan said, and took Walker's arm.

AS THEY TURNED the corner into the cavern, Roan's heartbeat sped up. Sweat broke out on his forehead like a warm spring rain. Part of it was fear, there was no doubt of that, but there was a sort of morbid excitement, too. He was about to witness something few men had seen and lived to talk about.

They pulled Walker around the corner and into the lair of the beast. The chain rattled but the creature was hidden in the gloom. The flickering lantern light cast lunatic shadows dancing around them.

The cavern was huge, much bigger than Roan had suspected. Though the light didn't reach the far corners, he felt there were tunnels that went deeper into the ground. Had they brought the thing down from above? Or had this been where they'd found the creature and captured it? The latter seemed more likely, prompting another question: *Are there more?*

"How do we do this?" Moore asked. His gaze never left the dark corner where the chain clinked menacingly and the thing's low, guttural growl seemed to vibrate under their feet.

The beast leaped from the shadows in a blur of black-on-black commotion. Roan froze, not sure what he was seeing. He waited for the inevitable moment when the creature reached the end of its slack and flipped into the air like a roped dog, but it never came. Instead, the creature stopped, growling and slobbering.

Roan took an involuntary step back. He hadn't known which manner of demon he'd face down here, but it wasn't this. The thing crouched in front of him on all fours, head cocked, its snout in the air. Then, to his further shock, it rose on two legs. Though the proportions were skewed, and it was covered with wiry brown fur, it had a human-like appearance. It stood taller than Roan—taller than Moore, even. Its torso was thick and muscular, its arms long and powerful like those of a monkey. Then Roan looked at its eyes.

The creature shone with an intelligence he had never seen in any animal before. Hell, he didn't see it in most people. It was a cunning, sly intellect. It shook Roan more than the physically imposing size of the beast.

The creature stalked back and forth at the limits of its chain, keeping its eyes on the group of men. Walker began to whine, and slumped in their grasp as if boneless. The beast went down on all fours again, staring, great strings of drool spilling from its maw. It spread its jaws, revealing sharp, canine-looking teeth.

It was feeding time.

"Do we just shove him at the thing?" Moore asked tentatively.

Roan had never seen the big man shaken before. He tightened his grip on the pickaxe. Could that thing break its bonds? Roan studied the creature closer. Through its matted fur he could see bare patches. He held up the lantern and realized he was looking at scars. The creature had been injured. It reached the end of its chain and turned, stalking back the other way. Roan saw more scars, and something else. Fresher wounds, raw and bloody.

Roan turned and walked the perimeter of the cavern. John called anxiously after him, but he was single-minded, the horrible condition of the creature bringing distant memories to the surface. He found what he was looking for near the entrance, hanging above a crate of supplies: extra lanterns, another length of chain, and a few rusty mining tools. It was a heavy leather whip, with metal woven into the thick hide. He drew the lantern closer and saw the leather was stained with dried blood. Anger swelled as he reached out and took the whip.

When he walked back to where Moore stood holding Walker,

the creature went wild, loping back and forth. Then it returned to the far wall, threw its head back, and let loose an earsplitting howl. Moore uttered a gasp, but Roan recognized the mournful sound in the creature's baying. And he recognized the fear.

Roan was drawn back to the creature's eyes. Yes, there was an intelligence there, but something else. A sadness, the same despair he had seen in Buddy's all those years ago. He knew what he had to do.

"Roan Devlin," Moore said softly, "what are ya doing?"

Roan pulled Walker's quivering frame from Moore's grasp and threw the man to the dirty cave floor. He paused, wanting Walker to know exactly what was happening. When the man finally looked up at him, he raised the whip and brought it down with a vicious *CRACK!* on Walker's chest. The man uttered a high-pitched, feminine scream.

In the back of the cavern, the beast stopped howling, now watching Roan. Its eyes narrowed; it cocked its head to one side. Roan raised the whip and heard the whistle as it cut through the air. He heard the snap and Walker's screams as the leather strap brutalized him again and again. The coppery stink of blood and Walker's fear-sweat filled Roan's nostrils. He tossed the whip aside and kicked Walker, rolling him over twice until he was within the creature's grasp.

Slowly, down on all fours again, the thing advanced. Roan caught a new odor, something gamey and earthy. The creature stopped just a few feet from Walker's bloody form. Grabbing the pickaxe from the cart, Roan stepped around Walker.

"Roan," Moore gasped, taking hold of his arm.

Roan shook him off, and, without turning, said, "Prepare the charges, John, would ya?" Then he moved to the left, away from the creature, following its chain. As the beast fell upon Walker, Roan knelt and hammered at the chain. The metal-on-metal *clanks* echoed throughout the cavern but were soon drowned out by Walker's dying screams. As the chain snapped and the echoes died, the only sound remaining was the wet slurping of the beast, feeding.

"Dynamite is set," John said.

Roan nodded, then strode to the back of the cavern. It didn't take him long to find what he was looking for. Another tunnel, blocked off with a metal gate bolted into the cave wall, and stones piled haphazardly beyond it. Roan set to work with the pickaxe, first tearing the gate from its hinges, then heaving the stones aside until there was an opening large enough for a man. Or a man-like beast.

Air wafted by from the depths of the new tunnel. He didn't know if it went deeper into the mountain or eventually led to the outside world, but somehow, he knew it was where the creature had come from. Before he turned away, he wondered again if there were more of them.

ROAN RETURNED TO Moore's side, ignoring the big man's almost comical gawp. Roan forced himself to look at the creature. Its face was buried in Walker's throat and the sounds of it feeding were terrible.

"I think it's best we be gone before it finishes with him," Moore said.

Roan nodded, and without another word, walked out of the cavern. He turned the corner and spotted Moore's handiwork. The blast would collapse the tunnel, that was certain. Roan didn't know if the creature would survive, or if the cavern would cave in as well.

Moore approached, still looking dazed. "Why did you do that? You might have been its dessert."

Roan shrugged. "Walker and Abbott were the monsters," he said. "That thing was just in the wrong place at the wrong time."

Moore seemed to think about it, then nodded. "I'll light the fuse. Ready?"

Roan nodded, casting a final glance toward the cavern.

Moore lit the fuse; it was long enough to give them ample time to get to the main shaft and up in the elevator before it went off. It occurred to Roan that the creature could just as easily follow them as leave through the path he'd cleared, but there was nothing he could do about it now. He had a feeling the creature understood. It was free.

They navigated back to the main shaft and got up top with no issues. Wordlessly, they moved to a bench by the equipment shed and sat. Sometime later, the ground rumbled, and shortly after that, lazy tendrils of smoke wafted up the shaft.

A voice shattered the silence. "What have ya done?"

Roan turned to see Jackman standing aghast, staring at the

elevator shaft. He wore a blood-soaked bandage on his head.

"We did what had to be done," Moore said.

"By collapsing the mine?" Jackman said. "You've lost your minds."

Roan looked at Moore and they both laughed.

"Not the entire mine, just Tunnel 17," Moore said.

Jackman finally turned to them, understanding dawning. "You killed the beast?"

Moore was about to answer but Roan cut him off. "And sealed the tunnel at the same time." He felt Moore's gaze on him. When he turned, Moore gave a barely perceptible nod. Letting the creature live—or giving it the chance, at least—would be their secret.

Jackman moved to the bench and sat heavily next to Roan. "What's become of Walker?"

"He was a fitting last supper for the beast," Moore said, his voice touched with mirth.

"A bitter meal it must have been," Jackman countered. "Let's go have a drink."

"I'M SURPRISED CONSTABLE Rourke hasn't thrown the lot of us in jail," Moore said.

"That's not going to happen," Jackman said evenly.

"Why is that?" Roan asked.

Jackman offered a sardonic smile. "Let's just say he'd have a lot more to answer for than we would."

Moore gaped at him. "You mean he knew about—"

"No," Jackman said, cutting him off, "not that. But he knew enough and was getting paid plenty to look the other way. Fortunately, he was careless enough to sign an agreement with Abbott that would be damning if any real lawman—especially a judge—happened to see it."

Roan scoffed. "What kind of jackass puts his signature to an incriminating document like that?"

"Either the very greedy or the very idiotic," Moore said. "More likely both, in Rourke's case."

"What now?" Roan said. "For the mines, I mean?"

"How the hell should I know?" Jackman said.

"Devlin's right," Moore said. "Walker and Abbott are both dead. You're the man in charge now, I reckon."

Jackman seemed to consider, then shrugged and took a long pull on his beer. "I guess I'll show up tomorrow and tell folks there's no work because of the explosion in Tunnel 17. The next day, I'll show up and hand out assignments like always. When word gets back to Walker's people, we'll see."

They sat in silence for a few minutes, then Roan got to his feet with a groan. "I'm beat, gentlemen. Time for some kip."

"Can I count on you to inspect the mine tomorrow afternoon?" Jackman asked. "Both of you, that is. I'll need a couple of dependable foremen to help run the shifts."

Roan nodded. "It would be a pleasure."

"As long as you promise not to squeal the way Abbott did when he was calling orders," Moore quipped.

"It will be a different work environment now that I'm not

under Walker and Abbott's thumb, anymore," Jackman said. "That, I can promise you."

EPILOGUE: SIX MONTHS LATER

"Good morning," Jackman called to the men assembled at the elevator. Roan and Moore flanked him, already knowing the reason for the impromptu gathering. "I've received notice from mining headquarters and wanted to share some news with you."

Roan's eyes shifted to Moore to see if he'd caught Jackman's omission of the Walker name, but he was facing forward, watching the crowd.

Jackman continued, "I've accepted the permanent position of mining captain, and Mr. Devlin and Mr. Moore have also signed on as foremen." The crowd clapped and shouted approval, but Jackman quickly quieted them by holding up his hands. "There's more," he said. He smiled, and Roan knew he was happy for his men. "The new owners have agreed to a ten percent increase in wages, effective immediately—" He was cut off by applause and whoops of joy from the men. This time, it took much longer to quiet them. "In addition to the wage increase, the owners have also offered a bonus payment of two hundred dollars for each miner."

The roars of approval were deafening. Men were throwing hats in the air and yelling words of thanks to Jackman. Roan smiled a bittersweet smile, happy for everyone benefiting from the recent events, while still mourning those who had perished along the way.

Roan noticed Constable Rourke standing across the road and made his way over. Moore had been right; Rourke had gone along with everything the three men had concocted to explain the events in Serenity. The story was that the Molly Maguires had faced off against the mine owner, Walker, and his cronies. Then, the Mollies had slipped out of town. Conrad Banks, the owner of the hotel, was happy to make the records of the guests go missing. After all, his wife was part of the group who had really done in Walker's men.

"Hello, Constable," Roan said, and they shook hands. Moore joined them and exchanged pleasantries. Jackman was surrounded by happy miners singing his praises and it didn't look like he'd be joining them any time soon.

"I'm afraid I've got news," Rourke said.

Roan didn't care for the constable's expression. Whatever news he carried, Roan Devlin had no interest in hearing it. But he was part of Serenity now, for better or worse.

"Jonas Williams sent word from the valley." Rourke took in a deep breath and let it out slowly. "He's got a small farm in Southfork. Something got at some of his animals. His goats and cows."

"Got at?" Moore said.

"Killed 'em." Rourke shook his head and spat on the ground. "Mutilated them. Ate some. Ate a lot. Others just had their throats torn open."

Roan breathed an inward sigh of relief. He'd expected worse. He'd expected to hear that one of the townspeople had been found dead. "Wolves?"

"I heard one of the men talking about mountain lions in the foothills by Deerfield," Moore offered. He looked ill. Roan knew he looked the same himself.

"Jonas said he'd seen evidence of a mountain lion as well. But I have to ask, you're sure you killed that thing in the tunnel?" Rourke asked. "Positive?"

"I'd guess a few tons of rock fell in that cave," Moore said. His tone was matter-of-fact, but Roan saw the doubt in his eyes. "Nothing could survive that."

Roan put his head down. Despite the dire news, he was hiding a smirk. Moore had answered Rourke's question truthfully. "John's right about that," he added.

After a few moments, Rourke said, "Good enough. Thanks, men." He turned and strode back toward town.

When Rourke was out of earshot, Moore faced Devlin, his expression somber. "It's just cattle. *This time,* Roan."

"Maybe before Abbott corrupted that animal, gave it the taste of human blood, maybe it was *always* only cattle," Devlin said. "Wolves and mountain lions get after cattle, too. Maybe if some evil man chained them up in a cave and fed them human meat, they'd get a taste for it as well."

"I'm not looking for an argument," Moore said. "And I have no quarrel with your decision, as you well know. But what if it's not cattle next time? What if it's a farmer? Or a child?"

"It was probably a mountain lion," Devlin said. "That creature in the tunnel, John, it just wanted its freedom. No way it would go near humans again." He nodded, more to himself than to Moore. "Not a chance."

"Aye," Moore said, returning the nod. "If Jonas saw a mountain lion about, that has to be it."

They exchanged a long look. Roan almost told Moore about the furtive footsteps he'd been hearing around his property on the edge of town. About the strange footprints he'd spotted. About the rattling chain outside his window. And the snuffling noises that came nightly, like something guarding the house. But "Let's get a pint, shall we?" was all he said.

SARAH READ

Sarah Read is the Bram Stoker Award-winning author of *The Bone Weaver's Orchard*, *Out of Water*, *Root Rot & Other Grim Tales*, and *The Atropine Tree*. She lives in northern Wisconsin where she works as a public librarian, knits, and collects stationery and pretty rocks. Visit her at **authorsarahread.com**.

Cult of the Rat King

The Rat King says I'm lucky. Blessed. That now it's easy to pick; that everyone's chin-down these days, staring at their phones, oblivious. And I know it's easier for me, anyway, because I am a girl and have the blonde hair from my father's family. Not like my brother Leo, who favored Mama, who drew suspicious glances everywhere he went—before he disappeared. Vanished into "the system," which the Rat King says is just a bus with one stop, at the border. There's another system, though, where you end up without your hands, floating in the river. It depends on which system catches you. And there's a third system, but it didn't catch me—I caught it. Rather, I stole it. I'll explain.

The bald man on the train wore a long black coat, much too

large for him, so that the pockets hung at his sides, far from any flesh that might have sensed my tiny hand reaching in from behind. He stood in the aisle, one hand raised to the handle above him, the other holding his phone inches from his face, the finely woven fabric of his coat swaying with the movements of the train. The sounds coming from his phone promised some obscenity: a raunchiness best enjoyed alone, as I am sure he thought he was.

He never saw me, and I never saw his face, save a ghostly reflection of his profile in the window, strobed in the intermittent lights flashing past in the underground tunnel. I was there and gone in the space between two lights, the contents of his pocket transferred to the hidden seam in the lining of my coat.

Get away first, check your score later, the Rat King always said.

I flitted through moments of shadow down the train car to the back, where I sat on the low steps by the rear exit, ready for the next stop.

When the train lurched into the station, I was on the platform before the train fully stopped, pushed through a crowd of people waiting to board, and was halfway up the stairs before the other doors hissed open. I risked a glance back and saw that the bald man had not exited. Good. The doors slid shut, and the train carried him farther away from me, and from his own treasures, the train car now packed with a multitude of suspects, if he should notice his empty pockets.

Aboveground, I vanished into the chaos of an open-air market. Merchants at rickety tables called out late-day deals. The sun had already dipped low against the rooftops of the city.

I made my way through the dwindling crowd, past soaps and scarves, cheap jewelry and expensive baskets. I paused by a baker's table, my stomach twisting around its own emptiness. The woman was selling buns for cheap. They'd been baked that morning and had been sitting out all day, their value oxidizing.

Hunger made me foolish. I reached into the secret pocket in my jacket to check if my grab had included any money. There was only one coin there. It was too large to be currency, and its edge had been shaved away. Just a token of sorts—garbage. The rest of the take: a tooth flosser, a peppermint, an illegible handwritten receipt from an antiques store, and a prayer card. Nothing with which to buy bread. And nothing that would please the Rat King. Fear filled my belly, then, hunger forgotten. I'd have to pick again and hope for better fare.

I placed the items back into my pocket and scanned what was left of the crowd. This late on market day, they'd have already traded money for goods; I wasn't likely to score much cash. As I searched for a target, my eyes caught on a tall, dark figure standing still at the end of the lane. It didn't mull over half-empty tables or weave impatiently through dawdling shoppers. It stood, and it watched. I felt its eyes on me, though I was too far away to make out its face. It had the shape of a woman in a long black dress, a wide-brimmed hat shadowing its face. But it could have been a man, and my heart lurched at the thought that it might have been the man in the long coat. He had worn no hat, though. In any case, I was spotted, and there would be no picking here.

I slipped around the back of the market tents and made my

way through the hedge that bordered the square. Past the cathedral and the museum, I saw another crowd gathered. Here, everyone was in black. Long coats and gowns, fur, the glitter of wealth. They were all moving toward the opera house stairs. I ran my fingers through my blonde curls and pulled my coat closed over my dirty dress. It is harder to disappear into a crowd where one doesn't belong, but I tucked my head low and slipped past satin-gloved elbows, heading to the top of the stone steps.

I could not see if the figure in black had followed. I was in a forest of figures in black. But I was sure I'd be safe inside these walls. All theatres belong to the Rats.

In the theatre, no one sees the stagehands because they don't want to. It ruins the magic. And no one looks at the orchestra. They should be heard and not seen. Antonio had been a Rat, busking in the square with his nimble violin, drawing a crowd that dropped fistfuls of coins into his case, and they'd lost fistfuls more to me and my brother, making our way through the smiling audience. When an old man approached him one day and asked him to play in the orchestra, the Rat King wasn't even mad. He was proud. He'd even bought him his first suit.

Never lead a pursuit back to the hive, he whispered, when I'd described the figure following me. One of the Rat King's oldest laws.

Antonio settled me into a shadowed corner of the pit and I watched, in awe, the secret, unseen show of the musicians at work. I passed those hours in a trance, the music soothing my anxieties. I spent that night in the chamber hidden beneath the stage trapdoor, wrapped in a dusty velvet curtain.

In the morning, there was no shadow following me. The woman in the black hat was gone. But there was a woman in white. I caught sight of her twice as I traversed the square and headed down the wide lane where the market had been. I saw her again in the reflection of a store window, her face a blur against a backdrop of mannequins styled to perfection. She followed me across the city until well past noon, when I finally lost her by climbing aboard a school bus loading masses of children leaving the cinema. And though the children eyed me suspiciously, my being the strange girl in their midst, they knew, through some unspoken pact, not to out me to their chaperones.

The school where we disembarked was attached to a church well on the outskirts of the city. The children marched in an ordered line from the bus to the church, and it was easy to slip aside as we passed the narthex. It was a boon to be brought here. For all churches have crypts, and all crypts have catacombs, and all catacombs lead back to the hive.

I'D HAD THE coin in my pocket for nearly twenty-four hours by the time I made it back to the hive. I finally felt safe enough to examine it more closely, in the privacy of my own alcove. I sat on my worn blanket and pulled the handful of debris from the secret pocket in the seam of my coat.

It was a coin, or a pendant, with two holes punched in its center to make a sort of button, and the space between the holes was worn thin. It was gold on the surface, but the worn parts shone silver, highlighting the strange design stamped into it. An angry mouth stretched across its width, teeth bristling below a sharp nose. The buttonholes gaped where the eyes should have been, and a mess of etched texture resembling hair filled the rest of the space. On the back, an inscription spiraled from the edge to the center, growing smaller as it vanished at the middle like water down a drain. I could not discern the language.

I deemed the piece worthless, or at least not worth our time. Novelty buttons don't rate much when there are pocketfuls of airpods to move. Nothing stays in the hive long, not even us. Nothing can ever be found here, if anyone were to come looking, so the button went back in my pocket until I could drop it in an unsuspecting hat or tin or a busker's basket.

It is a rule that we turn all our finds in to the communal cauldron. The Rat King collects and manages our shared wealth. But he doesn't want garbage. I've seen Rats beaten for wasting his time, and his expectations for me were particularly high. I wanted to sleep after having spent my day evading my pursuer, but I needed a score. I'd been gone a long time, with nothing to show for it, and I dared not excuse myself by explaining that I'd been spotted, chased. He'd think I was losing my touch. Maybe I was.

So, after a change of clothes and a hot meal, I set back out into the city, where dusk had already fallen. I just needed one good pull, then I'd go home and rest.

But it wasn't to be.

The shadow was there again, too soon after I emerged from the basement of a laundromat. It was the indiscernible figure, all in black, this time without the hat. But I could tell from the way it moved that it was the same one from the market. Their long hair trailed behind them as they moved swiftly after me.

My fear turned to anger, then to curiosity laced with spite. Whoever they were, they weren't going to out-maneuver a girl born and raised in the hive. I arced my path, bending the route until our game became a circle and the shadow spun on its heel, searching for me, not knowing I was just behind it. And there I stayed, the prey become hunter, following the shadow.

I was close enough to hear their growl of frustration as they realized they'd lost me again. But they hadn't lost me. They had never had a Rat to teach them—no one had ever told them never to go home when followed. They led me right to their home, which was, it turns out, exactly where they wanted me.

THE HOUSE STOOD black against the sky, its stone walls soaked in shadow. This was the old city. Walls of rough-cut limestone, hauled from the quarry that now houses millions of old dead and hundreds of young living, or half-living.

The figure strode through an open gate set into a gap in an overgrown hedge, and vanished for a moment before it climbed the stairs and entered through the tall, narrow door.

Light bloomed in a low window.

While I admit I can be foolish, I was not foolish enough to go in through the front. I rounded the block to a wrought iron fence that enclosed a small garden at the back of the house. The back still caught the last rays of twilight and seemed less sinister. I made a subtle mark with the heel of my shoe on the stone pillar at the edge of the garden wall and left, waiting for full night— for the late hours when even the streetlamps are oppressed by the close dark.

When I returned, more windows were lit and shadows crossed the drapes at rapid intervals. I had hoped the house would settle, but instead it had grown lively. At first, I thought the figures were dancing, but as I watched, it became clear that it was the light behind them that danced. Firelight. The figures themselves were still, their outlines in the windows straight on, and it was unclear to me if they stared inward or out. There was no way they could see me through the dark and the curtain fabric. But I felt their eyes, heavy on me, as heavy as the coin tucked into my hem.

An ancient sycamore stood in the center of the back yard, its wide canopy stretching beyond the reach of the property. The wall was easy enough to climb, and from the top of it, I hopped like a squirrel into the safe harbor of the tree. I stayed in the tree and watched and waited—a staring contest through the dark across a garden that rustled with night birds and rabbits.

It wasn't until the sky glowed gold with morning that the figures began to disappear from the windows. They moved between glances, the left ones vanishing while I watched the right, and vice versa, until all the windows stood empty and the glare from the sun erased the view.

I hadn't moved. My legs, pressed up against the tree's bark, had taken on its texture, my hair the wild tassel of wind-blown leaves. An arbor garden nymph, still as a statue and afraid to make a sound.

The house moved before I did—its door swinging open. Three women in identical black gowns emerged, leaving the door open behind them. They wove through the garden and out the gate, their veiled faces never once looking up at me from under their elegant, broad hats. Nothing else stirred, and finally pain overcame my fear and I dropped from my perch, landing in a soft patch of ferns.

The garden pulled at my feet as I crossed it, as if it were holding me back.

The porch was made of white limestone, yellowed with age and pitted where centuries of footsteps had worn the stone away, one grain at a time. The door, hanging heavy on etched brass hinges, was made from thick timber, its carven features made soft by layers of paint.

I peered into the dark interior of the house, too afraid to cross the threshold.

The outside had promised opulence; inside, the furnishings were stark. Bare boards where lush carpets should have been, empty walls naked of art, and spare furniture—nowhere even to sit. There were no vases or flowers, no pictures or mementos. It was as if no one lived there at all. If I hadn't seen the figures filing out that morning, I would have supposed the shadows in the windows had been ghosts. The emptiness of the space filled me with unease. There was nothing to take, here. Nothing to find but trouble.

THEY WERE EVERYWHERE, these figures. Not one in pursuit, but many of them, spread across the city like a constellation, each within sight of the next, so I couldn't circle them again. Their lines of sight were a web woven over every route. I could not hide. All I could do was keep moving, slip out of reach, lead them in a dance that we all knew would end with me exhausted, outnumbered.

It was time to swallow my pride, ignore my fear of disappointing the Rat King, and get a message to the hive—a plea for help. Something I hadn't asked for since the day Leo went missing.

But there were no Rats to be found. Not in the square, or the churches; not in the market, or the museum. That also hadn't happened since Leo went missing. Because when the System is churning, the King calls the Rats home.

I HELD MY breath as the train shuddered through the station. There's a stretch, just past the reaching glow of the platform, where the interval lights are out—have been out for so long that the dark stretch of tunnel has created its own ecosystem.

In the chipped chrome handrail, I watched the reflection of the woman. Her face was lost in the darkness under her hat, but I felt her gaze on me—meeting mine in the funhouse arc of the chrome reflection.

I held my breath, legs tense—ready to move when the chance came—though I'd have to slip silently past her and hope she didn't notice. Hope she'd assume I'd head for the nearest exit— out the front of the car. That she'd make her pursuit to the wrong end of the train.

I closed my eyes to break the hypnotic hold of her gaze. When the platform glow vanished from my eyelids, I moved, smooth as water, silent as a knife, down the aisle. I crept slowly past the spot where I sensed her, leaving no furrow in the air, hoping her heavy robe would shield her from any sense of my heat.

She sat still and I was past—crouched behind the last row of chairs in the low stairwell, in the same place where I'd hidden from the bald man in the long coat. His coin weighed heavily in my hem pocket. In the dark, it was as if the hollow-eyed face on the coin hovered in front of me—wild, etched hair tangling with my own.

A dim glow began to fill the car as the train neared the light again—recurring fluorescence along the tunnel walls that flashed like a strobe.

I saw her shadow against the roof as she shot upright in her seat and darted forward to where I had been sitting. I glimpsed through the spindle legs of the chairs as she raced to the front of the car.

As she slid the accordion door open and leaned into the space between the cars, I took my chance and crawled out of the stair-well to the back of the train car, my heart in rhythm with the clacking of the railroad ties. I slipped out onto the cold interstitial platform, shutting the door quietly behind me.

I watched through the grimy window. She did not turn. She stepped out, and was gone. My breath briefly fogged the window, then I turned, and made my own way toward the back of the train—car by car, until I reached the end and settled on the swinging step, waiting for the train to stop.

ANYWHERE YOU ARE in the city, a graveyard is near, and where there is a graveyard, you'll find Rats. From the top of the platform stairs, I sniffed the air, seeking putrefaction. Not the rot of garbage or food or sewage, not the secret stink of the small deaths of pigeons, but the deeper, cherry-earth scent of the assembled rot of centuries. The smell of grass and cold marble, and the hay they sprinkle over fresh graves.

It was blocks before I caught a familiar sight, a familiar smell, and sped my pace—racing for the safe enclosure of a tomb and the protective reach of my found family. There were no more robed figures behind me. At least, none that I could see.

A scrawled mark on an old mausoleum signaled safety. I crouched behind a stone and surveyed the lawns, making sure my pursuer had not rediscovered my trail. The space appeared empty—this section was too ancient for living mourners, too forgotten for groundskeepers.

I slipped through the wrought iron door, flinching at the creak of the hinges.

A hand on my arm tore a shriek from my lips, then a hand

over my mouth stopped my breath.

"What color is the fur of the fox's ears?" A hot, rotten whisper in my ear. The hand loosened over my lips, setting free my shaky breath. It had been years since I'd visited this hive. But I remembered.

"The fox has lost her ears in battle," I whispered back into the cupped hand.

I was released. It was a Rat. This cemetery was well-guarded, much more so than our own. It is the Rat King's seat—his home base from which he controls every hive in the city. He makes his way across the satellites, remembers the name of every child, though I have never seen him sleep.

"Is the king in residence?" I asked, as the Rat pulled me toward a stairway carved beneath a coffin shelf.

The figure didn't answer, but passed me off to another Rat before vanishing back up the ladder to resume his post.

I was glad for my silent guide as we traveled through a labyrinth of interconnected tunnels, a honeycomb of graves, the remains laid respectfully in alcoves along the path, their dark gazes sentinel to our passage.

I tried to count the turns but was soon lost—until I noticed a pattern in the bones. We always turned to the side where there had been an alcove. We followed the bodies, like steppingstones through a river.

The tunnel ended with a carved wooden door, hanging lanterns glowing at either side. My guide rapped on the wood and stared at me while we waited.

"You're Leo's girl."

"He was my brother." My throat tightened at the sound of his name.

"He was a brother to us all."

"But mostly he was mine," I whispered.

The door began to open inward, its bulk unexpectedly silent. The guide gestured me inside and vanished back into the tunnels.

The Rat King sat at the back of the long hall on something like a throne, if a throne could be made of old cushions held together with silver tape.

"I've been looking for you," he said. "You didn't come home for a day and a night and a day. We thought you, too, were lost to us."

Too. Leo's name still hung in the air, buzzing around my head.

"Someone was after me. Following me," I said, taking a seat on one of the scattered floor cushions.

"Someone not one of ours?"

I shook my head. "A tall woman in a black robe with a wide hat. And a woman in white. There are others. They live in a big house behind a stone wall."

The Rat King smiled. "You followed your follower?"

"They lost me. But I didn't lose them."

"Well done."

"But... then another of them found me. I escaped again, but it feels like they're everywhere, and I don't know why..."

"You stole from one of them. Something valuable. But whatever it was... curiously, you didn't bring it to me." His smile had twisted into something more threatening.

I searched my thoughts.

"Think harder," he said.

I recalled having dumped my pockets, my socks, everything—and then I remembered: The coin in the hem of my jacket. I had forgotten all about it, again. I lifted the edge of my coat, felt for the round shape, and moved it along the seam to the hidden hole at the side. It fell into my palm with a cold weight.

"There it is." The Rat King grinned, his eyes drawn to the shine of the metal.

"They're looking for this? How do you know?"

"Because they told me. They came to me, angry, knowing it was one of mine who must have taken it."

I closed my fingers around the coin and lowered my hand so he wouldn't see it shaking. It was a crime to withhold treasure from the King—even by accident or oversight. With the shine concealed, his eyes found mine again.

"We are not supposed to take from them."

"But who are they? I didn't know—"

"Because it's not for you to know." Spit flew from his lips as he hissed at me.

The edge of the coin felt like a saw blade against my fingers.

"What should I do?" I opened my hand, held the coin out to him. He shook his head.

"What you do is up to you. They will follow you until they get it back. But you've eluded them for days. Longer than I would have thought possible."

I looked down at the coin, examining it more closely. The edge was, indeed, sharpened like a blade. The image at the center seemed to stare back at me, the red of my palm like flames behind its hollow eyes.

I couldn't run forever. They had come too close, already, and it was as much luck as ability that had spared me. They had underestimated me, but they were unlikely to for much longer.

I slipped the coin back into my hem, worried the sharp edge might cut the fabric.

"You've decided. Good. Don't tell me your plan. If they come back, it's better that I don't know. But you may present your plan to the Oracle, if you wish."

I shook my head.

"Still my stubborn atheist, I see. You know, Leo was devout."

Yes, Leo had made the trek here to the King's seat weekly, consulting the Oracle about everything from fate to fortune to the weather. It hadn't saved him.

"Well, if you're not going to seek spiritual counsel, you'd better go. You can't stay here. They'll follow."

I stepped off the cushion, the stone chilling my feet. The door opened behind me, pulled by a small child dressed in grave rags.

I nodded a nervous goodbye to the Rat King and backed out. There was no guide to meet me, but I followed the clues I had spotted earlier.

The tunnels seemed longer on the way out, as if the rules had changed and the map shifted behind me. But soon I found the stone wall with the wooden ladder, and the mausoleum sentinel above. I felt the coin bounce against my thigh as I climbed, heavy and cold, and its edge seemed sharp even through the wool of my coat.

The guard said nothing as I made my way past, and when the

door closed behind me, I knew it would not open again, even if I were to knock. Perhaps ever.

If there was nowhere to go where they wouldn't follow, nowhere far enough to hide, and all they wanted was the damn coin back—it seemed I had one choice.

Night had fallen while I was in the grave, and there would be no more trains running back to the quarter where the gated house stood, so I buried my hands in my pockets and began to walk. Not quickly, and not in the shadows, but with purpose. If they were to find me now, they would only speed things along.

But there were no shadows in the alleys, no footsteps close behind. Either I had lost them more thoroughly than the Rat King thought possible, or—more likely—they knew I was coming. And were waiting.

WHATEVER GATHERING HAD lit the house the previous night was over, and the structure stood dark and silent behind the garden wall. It was past midnight and the ache in my bones made me bold. I didn't care what awaited me, as long as it was inside, somewhere warm.

I scaled the ivy-coated gate and dropped down into their garden, not pausing to check my surroundings before striding up the steps.

I raised my hand to knock, but thought better of it. Instead, I tried the handle, and found it unlocked. The door pushed in on silent hinges, revealing an entryway with a single flickering candle on a narrow table. I picked it up and lit my way to a parlor, opulently fitted with many chairs and plush sofas, each seat occupied by a figure in black.

I stopped and let the candlelight play through the sets of eyes all turned toward me.

The coin seemed to grow heavier. I felt my jacket twitch as if the metal sought escape from its woolen prison.

The candle guttered as my breathing quickened. I set it down on a nearby surface, then slid my coat from my shoulders. No one said a word, but their eyes traced my fingers as I worked the coin free of its concealment.

I held it out in my palm and felt the weight of their gazes in my hand, dragging my arm to the floor.

"I didn't know," I said to the silent room. My voice echoed off the windows and pale plaster. Still, the figures did not move.

"It seemed like just an ordinary coin."

At that, the candle flame strained, as if someone had silently laughed.

"Well? Take it back if you want it."

No movement. Heat rose in my face, pulsed in my frozen fingers. For days and nights they had followed threateningly, all for this stupid coin, and now they would not even take it back?

I moved my scowl from face to face. "Fine, then. If you don't want it…" I closed my hand over the disk and made to put it in my pocket.

Every figure stood at once, chair legs stuttering across floorboards.

I smirked, though the smirk faded as I took in the glowing

rage reflected back at me.

A figure stepped forward, separating from the rest. The woman in white. I hadn't seen her, white against the white curtains.

"Set it there—on the table." She gestured to a low glass surface in the center of the room, the center of the crowd.

I stared into her face, searching for the trap. I didn't want to approach them, to surround myself with them.

I had kept my back to the open doorway—to the entrance, the garden, freedom. I didn't intend to close off my escape route. I held the coin out again.

"No. Take it if you want it."

"We can't take it. No one can take the coin from another. Set it down, and we will pick it up."

"I took it," I said. "Easily enough. And besides—you're not taking it; I'm giving it to you."

The still figures grew restless, shifting feet and murmuring. But none of them reached for the coin.

"Fine." I flicked the coin. Candlelight played across its faces as it soared, end over end through the room. I didn't wait for it to land. I spun on my heel and dashed back out, down the unlit entryway. The keyhole, a wink of moonlight, like a tether pulling me to freedom.

A shuffle erupted in the room behind me. Furniture overturned, glass shattered, and graveled voices bellowed as my fingers closed around the hooked door handle.

I pulled, and it stuck fast, a bolt rattling inside the mechanism. I panted, a high whine rising in my throat as my fingers played over the metal, searching for a button or lever to release the latch. There was nothing. Only a key could release this. I was as locked in as the world was locked out.

I turned. The dim light from the parlor shook with the commotion of the room. Beyond the parlor was a tall, white door, narrow and tucked away, as if not wanting to be noticed. I raced for it, slipping past the entrance to the parlor, where screams erupted.

It opened into a kitchen. It was modern in an incongruent way that suggested an ancient character beneath its stainless veneer.

Cupboards lined one wall—too obvious a place to hide. The windows all held small panes set in a sturdy thatch of wood, and the only other door led to a stuffed pantry. The options for escape were none, the options for hiding few—and poor. I pulled a cast iron pan from the rack overhead and smashed out the narrow window closest to the sink. Glass and wood splintered onto the countertops and to the ground below. I could have crawled out, but not without cutting myself to ribbons and maybe bleeding to death in the garden. But all I needed was for them to think I had gone that way. I chose my spot—the least likely to be searched, I thought—and squeezed myself into the wide, industrial oven, pulling the door closed behind me.

My heavy breathing echoed around me in the enclosed space. I could smell my own fear, sour and sharp.

Footsteps filled the house like an anthill coming alive, a stampede, an army called to arms. I heard a man bellowing orders from down the hallway, directing his troops. Cupboards slammed and rattled all around me, boots crunching in the piles of broken glass.

One barked orders at the others, directing them from room to room. The house was enormous, reaching far beyond what I had seen of it. Behind those other doors must have been other halls, stairs leading to other floors. I tried to make a mental map from the inventory called out by the angry man in the hall.

Eventually, the rooms cleared, the voices carried outside, and the house fell still.

I didn't move. I wouldn't. Not until I felt sure that they supposed me long gone. I lay, cramped, huddled in my metal cubby, rebreathing ashy air, my heartbeat flooding my ears.

Then a soft shape moved across the shaded oven window. A grind of screeching metal sounded in my small space, and the walls around me came aglow.

I shoved at the glass door, but it had been locked, its lever slid over by the woman whose face hovered on the other side of the glass—the woman in white, who would not take the coin from my hand.

I glared at her as dry heat circled my body. My skin prickled as sweat poured from me and evaporated. She watched impassively as I pounded at the oven door, banging my elbows, even my head—any part of me I could fit against the glass, kicking at the back wall, feeling the rubber of my shoes melt and stick.

It hurt to breathe. My tongue felt like a dry bag of sand in my mouth.

My arms grew weaker, as the fight cooked out of me. I pressed my hand to the glass and felt my skin blister and split there, the juice from my wound hissing as it bubbled a trail down the window.

There was no air left to breathe, only heat, and the smoke from my burning clothes and skin.

Then the light went out. The latch groaned and the door tipped open, letting in sweet, cold air that set my skin ablaze with pain.

I screamed as the woman's hands closed on my arms and dragged me from the metal rack, threads of my flesh left behind on the grate.

I lay on the floor, twitching and scalding as other figures joined the woman standing over me.

"Should we call the others back?" a man asked.

"No," the woman said. "Take her below. Let's question her alone, first." Many hands seized me, fingers rough against my hot skin. I'd scream again, but the heat had seared my throat raw, and even the whimpers that crept from me made my head swim with pain, each breath agonizing.

They carried me through the hall and down a narrow staircase. Each step jostled me, tugging at my wounds and sending fresh waves of pain through me.

The coolness of the damp stone felt almost soothing as I fell upon it. A cold sweat coated my body, seeping like acid into my split skin.

A man nudged me with his boot. "Sit up."

I pressed my shaking arms to the floor and tried to lift myself. Hands grabbed me again and pulled me up, tossing me back against the rough stone wall. I pressed my cramped back against the rock behind me. A hand closed over my neck, tilting my face upward.

"How did you get the coin?"

The man's eyes burrowed into mine. His head was bald, and he wore a long black coat—one where the pockets were set too far back, gaping. Inviting. It was the man I had stolen the coin from. He tightened his grip.

"I'm just a pickpocket," I choked out past his fist. "I thought I was taking loose change."

He let go and shook his head. Then he roared in my face, "That was my one chance and you stole it from me!"

His hot breath reminded me of the oven, his spit hitting my face in a spray that smelled of putrefaction. I tried to shrink back into the stones behind me, but the wall was as unforgiving as my captors.

He struck me with the swiftness of a cobra and my head bounced off the stones, knocking me sideways, back to the cool relief of the floor.

The group argued amongst themselves, but I no longer cared. In that moment, I cared only about the sting where my lip had split and the striking burn on my hand, the stars dancing in my vision, and how long I would have to wait before sleep claimed me. Sleep, or death.

My plan had not worked. I had delivered the coin, but had not escaped the consequences of the theft. I should have ditched it in the street, should have thrown it into their garden and run. I should have consulted the Oracle. Or at least received his blessing.

The argument above me turned to thunder, and I was sure,

then, that a rain of blows would fall and end my short, pointless life.

The first kick arced into my stomach, driving all the air from my lungs. I curled in over the ache, and a boot met my head, granting my wish for sleep.

IN JULY, THE heat is a misery—like an oven.

Still, the tourists flock to the city, fill its open squares, crowd its fountains and cathedrals. They wear wide hats purchased from vendors on roadside blankets, and drop coins in foreign currency into the buskers' baskets. Some are vigilant, wary of their strange surroundings, aware of their vulnerability. And some are too charmed, distracted, easy. It is a skill to be able to tell them apart, and none was more skilled than Leo.

The heat that day had flattened my curls, my cheeks no longer a blushed rose, but sunburned. Leo did not seem to mind the heat so much, though his shirt stuck to the dampness of his back. Sweat dripped down Antonio's face, running across his pursed eyelids as the sharp notes of his violin cut the air.

The crowd had formed a ring around him, some dancing, some clapping in rhythm, or out of it. They reached into pockets, bags, billfolds, pulled out folded stacks of cash, peeled away a note to put into Antonio's violin case, and tucked the stacks away, oblivious to the way the paper-thin layers peeled away while their eyes were drawn.

Leo and I made our way through the crowd, pocketing a take

that only a summer harvest could bring. It was these hot months that would see us through the cold ones, unlike that first winter after our parents died.

It was a fever that had taken them both, and a miracle we were spared, the Rat King had said from the shadows on our doorstep.

My throat had burned from crying, but I'd asked, "Are you the one our parents left us to?"

He had smiled sadly, kindly. "No. I'm here to keep you safe from the ones your parents left you to." And he took us into the hive.

Leo had been angry. He wanted to honor our parents' wishes and meet our new guardians, to decide for himself whether he would go with them or stay a Rat. He fought the King with sharp words and sharper teeth, but the old man locked him in the chapel with the Oracle for three days, and Leo emerged a different person. He said he'd been shown the answers to his questions. But he never shared those answers with me.

He shared his bread, though, and his strength, his kindness—and together we survived our first winter in the understreets, and by the richness of summer, we were thriving.

Leo made the Rat King proud, pouring more into the cauldron than a dozen Rats combined. His efforts fed us all, and I suspect it was his will that bent the King to buy Antonio that suit, and let him go.

Leo never got to see Antonio in the suit.

If it hadn't been so hot, perhaps the man would not have reached for his handkerchief at just the right time. Or the wrong time. His reaching hand would not have brushed Leo's as it left the man's pocket, his nylon wallet pinched in Leo's fingers.

The man shouted.

Leo whistled. Antonio heard, and began to play faster, louder, covering up the commotion spreading through the crowd like a coin tossed into a fountain. The crowd was hypnotized by his flying fingers, his sawing bow, the toss of his damp hair against his brow.

While they all watched Antonio, I watched Leo, running through the crowd with the man after him.

Find the nearest church. It was our plan, always, if we were to be separated. *All churches have crypts, and all crypts have catacombs, and all catacombs lead to the hive.*

I backed out of the crowd, and forced a smile across my face. I was just another tourist girl, see? Enjoying the music with my parents…

I tore my eyes away from Leo and watched Antonio, just as the other tourists were doing.

I would not have done that, if I had known.

I would have watched him, every step he beat away, if I had known.

His feet pounding across the stones, carrying him away, away, away.

FOOTSTEPS POUNDING. BOOTS stomping, echoing in the hall above, and a man's voice booming like a church bell.

"She's here," the woman in white called out as the loud man hammered down the stairs, followed by half a dozen others. The wood of the basement stairs creaked in protest.

I croaked in response. "Leo?"

The woman in white snapped her gaze to me. "Shut up," she whispered. "Don't say anything else."

All the figures assembled, as they had in the parlor, but I had nowhere to run this time, and no will left to do so. My head swam, then pounded.

"She said she thought it was pocket change," the bald man said.

"You questioned her without me?" The loud man squared up to the bald man and pursed his lips. He was shorter, but broader in the shoulders, his face set with lines that mapped a lifetime of anger.

"You'll get used to it," he said. "I hold the coin now." He turned away, and the bald man shot a look at his back that should have drawn blood.

They were all mad for a sliver of metal that couldn't even buy an apple at the market.

I curled my knees to my chest and willed my mind to give up, to send me back to that summer square, but the loud man's voice cut through the fog like a river of needles.

"Bring her upstairs."

The woman hesitated, but the bald man grabbed me, hoisting me up by his hip and sending a shock of pain through my body that forced me to break my silence. My wail spilled out of me like a thick soup.

"That's right, little bird, start singing," he said as he carried me up the stairs, through the house and back to the parlor where the sumptuous decorations had all been tipped up, destroyed in the scramble to retrieve the tossed coin.

He dropped me on a chair that was missing its seat cushion. Springs jabbed at the back of my legs as I scooted back from the figures standing in front of me.

Women in black stood to either side of the sliding parlor doors, blocking any chance of escape. The loud man stepped forward and all eyes snapped to him.

"I'm sure you have a lot of questions," he said. "So do I. Let's help each other out."

I traced the lines of his face with my eyes. The Rat King had taught us all to read our queries—to look for signs of weakness or danger. There were both, here. He was angry, and he wanted everyone to know it—but mostly he was scared, and it was written across his face.

"I'll go first," he said. "We are a... private group with special interest in the city. Whoever holds this coin rules the group. And the group rules the city." He held the coin out in his palm as I had only moments before. Hours? Days? How long had I been dreaming of summer? My vision blurred, snapped back into focus by the volume of his voice.

"It cannot be taken from the person who holds it. It can only be abandoned and claimed by a new, rightful King. So, what we all really want to know is, how did you get it?"

My throat still burned from the heat of the oven and the crushing grip of the bald man's hands. My burnt and split lips stuck together, glued by their own leaking wounds. But the loud man's eyes bore down on me—his fear so much worse than the bald man's rage. And so much more dangerous.

"I'm just a pickpocket," I whispered. "I picked it out of his pocket."

The loud man laughed. Loudly.

"You didn't even know what it was? Didn't even know that you ruled this city for almost a week?"

The others did not laugh.

He sighed and dabbed at an eye. "You should not have been able to do that." He held the coin out again, this time toward the bald man. "There you go, Matthew. Take it if you can."

The bald man in the long, loose coat, Matthew, stared at it and shook his head. "John, no."

"Try! I want her to see."

Matthew's hand shook as he reached for the coin, his whole body shaking as he drew nearer. He flinched back as the coin twitched, but not fast enough, and the small disk spun like a sawblade, cutting into the meaty pads of his fingers. Blood cut an arc through the air as the coin stilled and settled back into the other man's palm.

Matthew panted and wrapped his wounded hand in his shirt, where the blood soaked in and gave the black fabric an oily sheen.

"The coin knows who it belongs to. If you had really stolen it, it would have cut you to ribbons. The last person who tried to take it lost his hands." John flipped the coin in the air and caught it in a pinched grip, then leaned forward over me, holding the blade edge near my eye. "So. What you're telling me can't be true. I don't like liars." He straightened and faced Matthew, the blade coin still raised in his pinched fingers.

"You must have given this to her. By accident, I assume? Did you drop it in her beggar's cup, or was it mistakenly traded for... services rendered?"

Matthew's face twisted, angry lines cutting deep. The woman in white looked as if she wanted to disappear. And the longer I sat, regaining my strength, the more I wanted to burn the place down with all of them inside.

"I stole it," I said, my voice louder, stronger. "I'm one of the Rat King's best thieves, and I don't know why he's so scared of you, but I'm not." It was as if the fire of the oven had filled my belly, and the words came out hot.

"Show me, then," he said. He reached down and dropped the coin into his pocket, then turned his back to me. "Gloria, go get some bandages. Matthew is bleeding all over, and this young urchin is about to lose her hand."

Matthew and the woman exchanged a look and I moved in that instant. The man's pockets were tighter than Matthew's, and the heat of his leg made the acid rise in my scalded throat, but I closed my blistered fingers around the coin and had it tucked into my sleeve before the others broke their gaze. No one had even seen me move.

Gloria left the room, her soft steps retreating up the narrow staircase off the entryway.

"Go ahead, little one. I promise we won't let you bleed out before Gloria gets back with the bandages."

"And what will you do if I succeed?" The coin hung heavy in my cuff, its metal cold against my skin.

"You won't."

"I did, once. And if I do it again?"

John laughed again. "Well, then you'd be king of the city again."

I couldn't help but laugh along, this time. Matthew narrowed his eyes at me over John's shoulder. Of all of them, he was the only one who knew I was telling the truth—that I had stolen the coin from him fair and square. And I could tell he was beginning to suspect I'd done it again.

"First, I want you to get me some water," I said. "With ice."

John seemed more amused than angry. "I'll get you some water, sure. While Gloria bandages your hand. Hell, I'll bring you the whole river, cup by cup if you want. But first, show me how you took the untakeable coin from the former King Matthew over here."

"I can't."

"I know you can't, that's my fucking point."

"I mean, I can't show you. If you see me do it, I haven't done it right."

"That sounds like an excuse to me," he said, smirking. "So, if you won't tell me, and you can't show me, I've got to find another way." He raised his hand to strike me, but I was faster. I pulled the coin from my sleeve and held it, as he had, like a knife.

His hand shot into his pocket as his face paled. He spun to Matthew. "You were watching her—you saw. What did she do?" Spit flew from his lips as he shouted.

Matthew shook his head. "She never even moved."

John raised his hand again and struck Matthew. Twice. And

again. I let him. The bruises on my neck throbbed in time with the blows.

Matthew fell to the floor just as Gloria returned with the bandages.

I stood from the chair. "Perfect timing. Matthew's going to need those."

"John!" She screamed and hurried over to Matthew, shoving John away from Matthew's prone form. John turned back to me as Gloria knelt to Matthew.

"I said I wanted some water." I lifted my chin, tried to will my tired legs from shaking. I walked the coin across my knuckles.

John laughed again. "A fake, I presume? You had one cast while the coin was in your possession?" He reached into his pocket again, denial turning his face an ugly shade of green.

"Why don't you try to take it from me?" I held his gaze. I did not expect him to actually try. He lunged, wrapping his hand around mine, screaming as he tore himself away, blood slicking his arm from palm to elbow.

Gloria almost smiled. "I guess the coin has chosen her, John. Are you really surprised, considering?"

"That's impossible," he growled through gritted teeth. "Call up the security footage. I want to see her take it."

That startled me, though it shouldn't have. Of course there were cameras. There are cameras everywhere these days—I'd been filmed stealing before. If one is fast and subtle enough, it looks like nothing more than a passing brush, a gesture, something entirely deniable. The cameras here were no doubt better than those at the metro stations and city squares, but I was confident they wouldn't show much more than me shifting slightly in my seat.

"John…" Gloria reached for his shoulder, but he knocked her hand away. "You have to honor it. Even if you don't want to. Just like Matthew did when you picked it up."

"Where does the Rat even find these brats? Sewer dwellers. Flushed, discarded infants. We should wipe them all out—should have done so decades ago. Fuck them, and fuck our agreement."

Heat rose in my face again, reigniting the burns there.

Gloria stood and leaned in toward John. "You don't know who she is, do you?" She whispered something in his ear that made his eyes draw wide. His anger evaporated as hope crossed his face.

"What did you say?" I asked Gloria. She knew who I was? How could she, when I didn't know, myself?

"Well. I can't take the coin from you, child. But perhaps I can buy it from you. Everyone has a price." John's demeanor had changed. He cradled his bleeding arm as he leaned in toward me, like a friend. His shift in tone left me feeling queasy, as though I were standing on quicksand.

"I don't need money." I stood from the lumpy chair and began to back slowly toward the door.

"I'm not talking about money, foolish girl. Give me the coin, and I'll give you your brother."

FROM THE DEPTH of the crypt, the church bells sounded as if they were ringing in another world. Still, dust trickled from the seams between the stones overhead. Ten chimes. Night had fallen, and neither Antonio nor Leo had come to the church. How far had Leo run? Far enough that the closest church was a different one, I supposed. I had waited, hoping to reunite here before making our way back to the hive. But as the hour was growing late, I knew I must make it back alone.

All catacombs lead to the hive, but that doesn't mean the way is straight, or easy. I passed piles of bones, paths slick with lime, crumbling passages threatening collapse, and pools of indiscernible depth. This was a route not often taken, and spider webs and threaded tree roots had drawn barriers across the tunnels. By the time I reached the hive, my hair and dress were torn, my skin reddened from the caustic mineral coating of those forgotten passages.

Leo was not there. He was not in our alcove, nor Antonio's. He wasn't at the cauldron, or seated at the long boards where we dined.

"Have you seen Leo?" I asked the Rat whose alcove was near ours. He shook his head, his gaze darting away too quickly.

"Is Leo here?" A girl nearly too grown for the hive plucked a strand of spiderweb from my hair, but she hadn't seen Leo.

Finally, I made my way to the King's chamber. A boy with a spear, more decorative than deadly, stood guarding the entrance.

"Is the King available?"

"There was a messenger. An emergency aboveground. He didn't say when he'd be back."

My heart hammered. An emergency? In my gut, I already knew. The emergency was Leo.

"I'll wait for him." The boy let me pass.

I waited on a cushion in the hall for the King to return. Not eating, not sleeping. I don't even know how many days passed there in the dark, but then the chapel door opened and Antonio stepped out.

I tried to jump to my feet, but my stiff legs collapsed, and I hit the floor hard. Antonio lifted me up, pulled me into an embrace.

"Tonio, where is he?"

"He was caught." He held me tighter as I began to shake.

"Where are they keeping him? Where is the King? We have to get him out. I'll get him out myself, I'll—" I tore myself out of Antonio's arms and made to leave, but he grabbed my wrist and pulled me gently back.

"The King will be here in a minute. He wasn't far behind me."

"Where were you?" I looked him over, and saw he was dressed… differently. Nicely. His clothes were clean and new, tailored, like the suits tourists wore to fine dining. His violin was slung across his back in its usual battered case.

"I was auditioning for the orchestra. A man in that crowd was a conductor, and he liked my playing." A smile spread across his face, despite the concern still writ across his brow. "The King said I could go, and he got me this." He spread his arms and looked down at himself, shaking his head in wonder.

"You're leaving?"

His smile wilted, but didn't vanish altogether. "Not leaving the city. I'll be playing at the opera house. You can visit me whenever you want."

I nodded, but my throat was tight, holding back the tears that threatened to overwhelm me. First my parents, now Leo, and Antonio. Everyone was leaving. And I had nowhere to go.

The heavy, carved door to the hall swung open on creaking hinges, and the Rat King stepped through. He looked unsurprised to see me waiting for him.

"Don't you have a job to get to, Antonio?" he said as he crossed the room to his lumpy throne of cushions.

Antonio squeezed my hand and kissed my forehead, then he slipped out through the door just as a small Rat pulled it closed.

I waited until the King had settled himself on the throne. I approached him, fists clenched, both wanting and fearing answers.

"Where is he?"

The King sighed. "I'm so sorry, my dear girl. I tried, but there was nothing I could do. The System has him, now."

I forced myself to breathe. In. Out. In again. "Which system?"

The King half-smiled. "Clever girl. You remember your lessons."

"*Which one?*" My voice rang off the stone walls. Trails of dust sprinkled to the floor in soft whispers.

The Rat King's face folded into a frown. "The bad one," he said, no cushion of mercy or tenderness in his voice, now.

The bad one. Not a prison, then, where there might be some hope of process, or justice. Or escape.

The King must have seen the light die in my eyes. "There is

nothing you can do but make peace with it."

I felt tears coming, and there was no holding them back, this time. "There will be no peace," I said.

I swear I heard him chuckle as I spun away and stalked toward the door.

"You should consult the Thieves' Oracle, child. He will help lead you to peace."

I did not answer, and I did not wait for the young Rat to open the door. I flung the large panels open myself, with enough force that the wood struck the stone wall with a sound like a gunshot.

I FELT AS if I had been plunged back into the oven, the air dark and unbreathable.

"What do you know about my brother?" I was breathing fire, I was sure of it, but their faces didn't melt, their hair didn't combust, no matter how much I willed it.

Gloria took a step back at the menace in my voice, but John grinned and stepped closer.

"You really don't know who we are. Nothing happens in this city without our learning about it, little girl. You may hold the king coin, but you don't have our real legacy—our knowledge, compiled for centuries."

"I don't care about your legacy. I asked you a question."

"The coin first. Then I'll tell you."

"I'm not interested in a trade. I'm ordering you to tell me what you know about my brother."

John's smug smile faltered, the battle in his mind writ clean across his face. I thought back to the times I'd seen the Rat King discipline errant Rats—how he had brought them to heel under the weight of his gaze. I tried to channel that authority. What would he do? What would he say? He would have his guards toss the troublemaker in the river. Or lock them in with the Oracle.

"Are you going to obey or not?"

He squared his shoulders. "Perhaps the coin can be taken, but its authority cannot. I'm the one who received the coin when it was last given. I am still the king, here, and you are just a thieving child, a Rat, not even worth drowning in your sewers. And so was your brother."

My heart hammered. *Was?*

"How is it that you could know who I am and who my brother is, and I don't? Not even the Rat King knows, and he has more eyes and spies than you do. And better ones."

John smirked, and Matthew and Gloria exchanged a glance.

"The old man always was a liar," John said.

My blood ran cold, sweat stinging the burns on my brow.

"Of course the Rat King knows. He's the one who told us."

My feet were moving before I could think. The hall, the entryway, the stairwell—all were filled with figures in black.

Someone grabbed my arm, and I spun to strike them, but Gloria's pleading eyes met mine in an expression that begged my stillness.

"I won't stop you. But we're coming with you. We have an agreement with the Rat King, and this situation complicates it."

I didn't want her with me, this woman who had chased me

across the city, who had nearly burned me alive, and who was keeping secrets from me even now.

"Of course you won't stop me. You can't. Isn't that obvious by now?"

Her face paled and her hand fell away from my arm.

The figures in black parted as I passed through, and as I crossed the threshold, they fell in line behind me.

WE WERE A graveyard processional, a funeral march, and the dirge in my head was filled with drums. War drums. We must have looked odd—a girl, grim-faced, in rags, followed by a dozen figures in black, all marching in the cemetery.

I did not freeze on the march this time. My skin radiated heat, both pulsing from the burns and fueled by my own rage. I led them straight to the crypt entrance of the hive, heedless of rules or consequence.

I entered the mausoleum and shoved the guard aside. I did not hear what he said as he fell back, heels-over-head, across the stone slab. He crouched to spring back up, but thought better of it as the figures in black trailed in after me.

We descended the ladder, and I led them through the catacombs, the guide Rat left cowering in an alcove beside a skeletal body. I turned toward each body we passed, always chasing death.

I rounded the corner to the Rat King's door and faced a cluster of guards—all children—nearly a dozen of them filling the narrow stone hall.

One, a girl taller than the others, stepped forward. I recognized her, the way one of her eyes drooped from a punch she'd received from a security guard at the museum as she'd tried to nick the golden arrow from a statue of Eros. They'd let her go, in the end, with a bruised face—and a Roman pearl bracelet hidden in her hair.

The Rat King had it delivered back to the museum. But she hadn't been punished. She was something of a hero to the younger Rats. And now she stood in my way.

"You're to go in alone," she said. "These lot stay out here."

I tried to match her height but couldn't quite. "Why should I obey?"

The girl took a deep breath, and the Rat King's voice came from her mouth. "Because that bit of shine doesn't work down here in the deadlands. We have different laws, here."

It was not the first time I'd heard him throw his voice. I'd heard him speak through Leo once, and it had scared me so badly I'd slept outside the hive that night. I wasn't scared this time. "All these stupid laws are just made up, anyway. I'm bringing my second. The rest will wait here."

I motioned Gloria forward. The tall girl seemed to accept this, and she opened the doors. The large chamber was full, as if all the young Rats in the city had been called home. Children lined the walls, standing in corners, and huddled in tiers on the steps leading up to the throne where the Rat King sat.

"So, you figured it out, I see. Good for you. That went quite a bit better than I predicted, though by the marks on your neck, it did not come so easily for you."

I swallowed against the tight rasp of my bruised throat.

"Where is Leo? They told me you know. Where is he, and… and who am I?" It was difficult to maintain a tone of authority while asking such a simple question.

The Rat King rested his chin in his hand. "The story I told you was true. He was taken. Caught in a grab. He was not so skilled a pickpocket as you."

"Who took him? Where is he now? You implied he was killed, but these people speak of him as if he's alive."

He ignored my questions, keeping his posture relaxed, almost bored, as my anxiety whipped up a frenzy in my stomach.

"Do you know why we call our domain the deadlands, child?"

I wasn't going to tolerate his deflection. "Answer the question."

"It's not just because we live in cemeteries. Not because we sleep among the dead. We *are* the dead. The lost and forgotten of society, the discarded remains of better lives. Wasted potential."

"So, he's alive?" My voice shook.

"He is among the dead."

I pulled the coin from my pocket and danced it over my knuckles as I scanned the many faces of the room, searching for something familiar. I could hear Gloria shifting nervously from foot to foot behind me.

"So… he's here?" I stopped the coin and squeezed it in my palm, savoring the sting of the sharp edge.

"How long has it been since you visited the chapel—prayed to our Thieves' Oracle for guidance?"

I raised my jaw in defiance. I had lost faith after Leo disappeared. The Rat King knew that—knew I cared nothing for his made-up religion as I cared nothing for his made-up rules. "The last time I spoke to that old man was about Leo. He knew nothing. He wouldn't help me."

The Rat King gestured to the chapel door off to the side of the throne room. It was more cave than church. More tomb than cathedral. "Perhaps you should ask again."

I looked to Gloria. Perhaps they, too, had their strange religions and customs—ones I'd have to learn if I intended to keep the coin. If.

She nodded.

I ground my teeth in frustration.

Rat children scattered as I stalked across the room to the chapel, cutting a path through the crowd like a plow in a field.

The door was not ornate—not carved or decorated in any way. But it was locked. The cold iron lever didn't give. I looked over my shoulder to the Rat King, but he only smiled.

Of course. Only a thief may visit the thieves' chapel—speak to the Thieves' Oracle.

I pulled a pin from the hair at the nape of my neck and picked the lock. I entered alone, closing the door behind me. I was not surprised to hear the lock click back into place, or the scrape of wood against wood as a beam was drawn across the door. Being locked in with the Oracle was common for those who challenged the King's authority.

Deprived of the light from the throne room, the chapel stood in total darkness. The soft sound of running water guided me to the back of the room, where a natural spring fed a fountain over a bottomless well, where thieves could leave their wishes and take their blessings.

I searched my memory, going years back, for the layout of the chapel. Beyond the fountain would be the carpeted aisle leading to the altar. I found it with my feet and followed it.

When my toes hit a low stair, I climbed to the dais and felt for the altar, ran my hands along the cloth to narrow candles and a dish of scented matchsticks.

I lit one candle, and the room filled with disproportionate light. It bathed the rough stone walls and glanced from a rose patterned stained-glass window set high up by the ceiling—an ancient window, stolen by the Rat King himself, from an abbey restoration site. The honey-sweet scent of warm beeswax drove off the smell of damp stone.

Behind the altar stood the Oracle in his grayed white robe— the antithesis of the black-clad cultists who had followed me here. His orbless eyes were bound in a red ribbon, his arms held aloft, truncated in a mass of scars and twisted flesh. His hands were missing.

But his face was smooth, his hair jet black and curling gently over the ribbon that bound his eyes. This was not the old man who had drained my faith, my hope, years ago. My face heated, heart hammered, throat tightening in anxious realization.

"Leo?"

It was him. Though he had been mangled, I knew him.

I ran into his outstretched arms. I clung to his shoulders, burying my forehead against his cold neck.

His breath shuddered, but he did not close his embrace.

"Leo, I didn't know you were here. The Rat King lied to me—I would have come." Tears came, then. A flood of them. All the ones I'd held in for three years, pouring out at once. They ran into the cuts on my face, the burns on my lips, soaking the bloody collar of my dress.

Leo said nothing, but the red ribbon dampened, the fabric darkening to the color of fresh blood.

I heard a splash behind me and turned to see the Rat King drop an offering into the fountain.

"Who did this to him?" I shouted down the aisle.

The Rat King sauntered up the carpet and settled on a rough stone pew. "He did it to himself."

"No. I don't care who he robbed or what he took—tell me who hurt him! Who took his hands and eyes?"

"He did it to himself," the Rat King repeated. "He tried to take the coin."

I spun back to Leo. "What? You knew about it?"

"He knew," the Rat King answered for him. "But he didn't know enough. He thought he could take it if its bearer was dead. But it doesn't work that way."

"Who did he try to take it from? Which one of them?"

"From your father."

The chapel seemed to spin. I had few memories of my parents. Our parents. And no stories of them, either. The Rat King had simply told us they were dead. The same way he'd said Leo was dead.

"When you took us…"

"I took you in when your father took possession of the king

coin. It was your mother's request—to protect you. Those in the King Coin Cult live short lives. It proved to be a wise decision."

"How long? How long were they alive, ruling the city while we robbed pockets for enough coins to buy stale bread?"

"Only three years. I was surprised, actually, that they lived that long. The cult is loyal to the coin—to power. Not the person who wields it. You'd do well to remember that."

My knees shook, threatening to give out, to drop me to the stone steps.

"How did they die?" I whispered, so quietly, I wasn't sure he'd even heard the question.

"Violence, of course. Betrayal. When Leo fled from the square that day, he was caught by the cult. The man he had tried to rob was one of their business partners. They didn't take kindly to that. So of course, they brought him before the king, for justice. And of course, your father refused to punish him, and the cult soon found out why."

I pulled my eyes away from the Rat King and turned back to Leo. His lips trembled. I wanted to hold him again, to pull him down from that dais and wrap him in a warm blanket until he stopped shaking.

The Rat King pulled at a loose thread on the bandage that wrapped one of his swollen knees. "There is a loophole whereby the cult can kill its king. It's been used a few times. As I said, the cult lacks loyalty to the individual. And they all crave power. While the king may not be killed directly by a member, there are numerous indirect methods that may be employed. In your parents' case, they simply cut the break line on their car. Not terribly creative. But they knew they would try to flee with their son, and they did. When the car wrecked, your parents were killed. Leo was only injured. Before the paramedics arrived, Leo tried to take the king coin. It maimed him terribly, as you see. The doctors assumed the injuries were from the crash."

The Rat King struggled to his feet and brushed the stone dust from his legs. "When he was released from the hospital, I took him in. What became of the coin next, I cannot say, exactly. I know they've been through a few kings, since. But that is what happened to your parents, and to your brother. He tried to take power. Instead, he gave everything. And became the Oracle. If only you'd kept your faith, little one. But it seems royalty runs in your blood."

Rage boiled in me. The coin ripped from the wool of my sleeve and sizzled in the blisters of my palm. I raced down the dais stairs and drew the coin in a hot swipe down either side of the Rat King's face. Blood ran in thin sheets from the wounds.

"I should take your tongue for all the lies you've told me," I screamed into his bleeding face.

His eyes fluttered in shock, but he composed himself. He smiled, causing the wounds to gape and gush. "What a tyrant. Is that the kind of king you'll be?"

"I don't want to be the damn king!"

"It seems to have chosen you. I'm not sure you have a say." The Rat King's smile broadened as blood ran over his mouth, painting his brown teeth red.

I turned back to the dais, to Leo, his arms shaking as he held them open.

"Leo. You wanted it. You can have it—it's yours." I held the coin out to him, though he couldn't see it, or take it. I held it before his face, and he strained his neck, pulling away from it, moaning. His mouth gaped in terror from the king coin's eyeless face. The coin grew hot in my hand as Leo twisted himself away, breaking his Oracle composure and falling backward, head striking the stone floor behind him.

I drew the coin back into my palm. Leo pushed himself up on his elbows, his shoulders slouched and heaving. I braced an arm behind his back and helped him to stand. He pushed me away, flinging his arms out, resuming his penitent pose.

"Leo…" My heart felt as twisted as the scarred skin of his wrists.

"You could give it to me," the Rat King said. "Or rather, discard it, so that I might pick it up. I could rule the upper city as I do the lower."

"I'm sick of rules. And I don't like rulers. And I *hate* liars." I strode down the carpeted aisle.

The spring at the chapel's entrance burbled into its bottomless well. I held the coin out over the black water.

"No!" the Rat King screamed. "That isn't the answer. Please. The only thing worse than order is chaos." He held a hand out, pleading, as he shuffled up the carpet toward me on weak legs.

"That kind of talk is why I don't like kings. I don't need a coin to rule my own fate. I'll take what I need, when I need it. I don't need a kingdom, or a king." The coin grew hot in my fingers, its metal glowing faintly in the dim candlelight. It began to rotate slowly in my grip, the tiny sawblade coming to life.

"Set it down on the stones, child. You'll end up just like your brother. It doesn't like being threatened." The old man sped up.

"Neither do I."

I let go.

He rushed at me.

But he was not as fast as the falling coin, the falling legacy, the falling empire, sinking into the dark abyss of the cavern spring. The hot metal hissed as it hit the water, its glow fading to the cold, and the endless dark.

The blessing of the fountain, it was said, would be in proportion to the offering. My shoulders felt lighter already, as if the blessing was freedom itself. I hadn't known how heavy the coin was until I let go, watching it sink in the dark water like a star shooting across the night sky.

The Rat King fell to his knees on the carpet, panting, ten feet behind me. He'd screamed, though I'd hardly heard it. Its echo still carried around the stones.

"They'll kill you," he whispered, his voice barely audible over the gentle splash of the fountain.

Behind him, Leo smiled. The red dye of the ribbon ran down his face in the tears streaming from beneath it, mirroring the blood that continued to pour from the Rat King's wounds.

"Only if they catch me," I said.

I left them both weeping in the chapel.

The door had been left unlocked after the Rat King had followed me in. I exited into the throne room, where the Rats and Gloria stood, silent, tensely waiting. I slid the wooden beam across the chapel door behind me.

"We're done here," I said to Gloria, and we crossed the wide room to the door, which the young Rats opened for us.

In the tunnel, the tall Rat girl stood guard against the line of figures in black, the cult shadows, who looked like assembled mourners for the bodies that lined the alcoves.

I stalked past them, keeping my eyes straight ahead, and they fell in line behind me.

"Did he tell you?" Gloria asked, when we were far from the earshot of the Rats.

"He only tells lies."

We were silent all the way back to the gated house, where John and Matthew sat in the wreckage of the parlor, glaring at us as we entered. I matched his glare, then stooped to a pile of shattered glass and pulled a broken tumbler from the shards. I handed it to John.

"The whole river. Cup by cup. Just like you promised."

He took the cup in a shaking hand, the pad of his thumb grazing its broken edge. The etched pattern turned pink in the dim light.

"You can stop when the river is empty," I said.

He slouched out the door, shoulders heavy but eyes like coals.

Matthew stood. Gloria stepped forward to meet him. A lamp lay overturned at their feet, its light flickering an irregular strobe.

"I want that fixed," I said. "Tonight."

Matthew nodded and left the room.

Gloria turned to me. "You don't have to stay," she said. "Make us promise not to follow you, ditch the coin somewhere and we'll go find it and leave you alone forever."

I studied her for deception. Her face was wrinkled with anxiety, but she couldn't have been more than thirty-five, maybe forty. There was nothing hidden in her face. Of all of them, she had been honest. Cruel, but forthcoming. She truly thought I still had the coin.

"I'll consider that," I said.

Mattthew returned with a black aluminum box. He set it down beside the stuttering lamp, pulled the cord from the wall, and tipped the lid open. Inside was a line of tools, their metal dulled with use. I smiled. I had assumed it was him, and as his hands wrapped familiarly around the handles, I knew I was right.

Had I known, a week ago, that I had stood in the train car with the man who had killed my parents, tried to kill Leo, and would later beat me and squeeze the breath from my neck, I'd have pickpocketed the very eyes from his sockets, his heart from his chest.

I stepped closer to watch him work, and as he bent over the twisting wires of the lamp, I slipped the claw hammer from the case. And as he cut the wires, severed the light from its source, I swung it up and down again, sinking it into his skull with a crack that was echoed by the sound of Gloria's knees hitting the hard floor.

Matthew did not even scream, but Gloria did. Matthew slumped off the end of the hammer and fell forward over the broken lamp.

Glora sprang up and reached for me, but pulled her hands

back as I spun toward her.

"Did you help him do it?" I asked. "Were you part of that plan?"

She was shaking her head before I'd even finished the question.

I turned my gaze, then, on the cluster of women in black behind her. They lined the hallway from the parlor to the door.

"How loyal are you all? How well do you obey?"

They did not move or answer, but stood like ghosts. Automata. It chilled me and filled me with hot rage at the same time. Even the Rats had more freedom than these fools.

"Come here," I called to them.

They stepped in unison, filing into the room. Their swaying black robes looked like smoke on water.

Gloria, stark in her white clothes streaked with the rust of drying blood—Matthew's and mine—shook in front of me.

"Break her limbs," I said.

They seized her. Gloria's heavy breathing hissed through her clenched teeth, her eyes ablaze. She said nothing, did not beg or reason or bargain. She knew better than to haggle with a thief.

She did scream, though, when the bones broke. The crisp, wet snap of fracture echoed off the broken glass surrounding us.

They lowered her, heaving, to the floor, her twisted limbs splayed as though she were a shattered spider.

Then they stood, attentive, watching me, obeying me.

"Pick up a shard of broken glass."

They did.

"Cut your own throats."

They did.

The grain of the floorboards drank up the blood, the stain spreading and seeping in, until the floor was saturated and the seams ran like the river.

The River. One cup at a time.

I turned my back on the mess, on Gloria weeping on the floor, the strands of her hair lifting on the red current.

I walked down the empty hall to the kitchen. The oven door still hung open, jaw agape, dark throat pregnant with glowing promise. It came alive with the twist of a knob. The tight burns on my skin sang with painful memory.

I freed the gas flow from each of the burners.

In the pantry were decadent blended oils, and I spread them over every surface, lit every decorative taper I could find.

The heat of the room warmed my back as I turned away.

As I passed the parlor door, Gloria screamed. I ignored her. When I laid my hand on the doorknob, she screamed again—a name. A name I'd forgotten, if I had ever known it. A name I'd searched for for years and never found until now. Until it was too late and I didn't even need it anymore.

I did not answer.

No names. No mercy. And no kings. Just let it all burn.

JOHN STOOD ON a quay near the water's edge, clenching the broken cup in his bloody fist. I crept up beside him on silent Rat's feet, but he did not startle to see me there. He kept his gaze on the water.

"So you're going to rule us, little tyrant queen?" I didn't need to see his face to know there was a sneer that crossed it.

"There's nothing left to rule."

He looked at me then. "What do you mean?"

"They're all dead."

His eyes traced to the glow on the horizon, and his face fell. Grief wound up into anger.

"We don't all stay in one house, you stupid girl. We're everywhere. In hospitals and government, in schools and churches. That was your own seat you destroyed. You just killed your own officers and bodyguards. There's no one left to protect you, now."

"Protect me from who?"

He smiled then, eyes alight with a kind of madness. "From the rest of us."

"Because you think a coin holds power."

"The coin *is* power." His voice shook with reverence.

"No, it isn't."

"Stupid girl."

"The coin is meaningless. I ditched it hours ago, but they slit their own throats for me, anyway."

He spun to me, then, and the glass in his fist shattered. "What have you done?" His whisper carried raw over the rush of water at our feet.

"And here you are, holding your cup, for no better reason than because I told you to."

"Where is the coin?"

I smiled out over the dark river. "It's in the water."

The splash was quieter than I'd expected. He was a large man, but the swift water carried him like a twig, out past the buoys, to the channels where cargo ships and tourist ferries mapped the river to the sea.

Hospitals, government, schools, churches. There was a lot of work still to be done.

I pulled the coin from my pocket and ran it over my knuckles. It danced across my hand, its empty eyes dark against the flash of metal, its razor edge a cold kiss against the heat of my skin.

Coins and kings, names and thieves. It's all the System. And I stole it. I didn't mean to. But now that I have it, it's mine to break.

"We are as a people inherently and historically opposed to secret societies, to secret oaths and to secret proceedings."

President John F. Kennedy

AFTERWORD

Thank you, dear reader, for coming along on this twisted journey with us. It's been lovely having you by our side.

Did you have a favourite tale? With such a diverse selection of voices—what a stellar line-up!—you'd certainly have your work cut out trying to pick. For me, it's akin to my having to choose a favourite crotchgoblin, so I shan't even go there—but I must give hat-tips and head-nods (Ed nods?) to some rather delectable techniques and turns of phrase that get me where I live. I promise I'll try to be brief (honestly, I could get proper waxy about some of these lyrics).

In *Cult of Least Resistance,* Cindy O'Quinn's signature subtleties are at play, with blink-and-miss-it minimalism and the quiet, folk horror of a character-driven narrative.

"I was approaching familiar territory. I'd been here before, after all."

Our chatty protagonist *knows* something… but what? That we, as readers, reach the revelation along with Charlie Hartless is pudding-proof of Cindy's skills. *Resistance*—simultaneously condensed and epic and replete with implicit horror, nuanced foreshadowing and intensely Flanaganesque monologues—is a novella that feels like a novel and plays out like a Hammer Horror.

Next up, Errick Nunnally, an author who had me hooked from the get-go. I mean, come ON: he opens with a murdered Nazi—what's not to love? In *Agent Josephine Baker Against the Island of Horrors*, a tale perfect for the more discerning, intelligent reader, we learn that "…she'd bathe the entire world in blood to protect them." And we believe it. She *would*.

Errick has that rare gift of combining evocative, often devastating imagery—"she swam through cotton…"—with an apparently effortless ability not only to tune in to our worst fears, but to normalise the peculiar. Ultimately, we find ourselves embarking on a mysterious, intriguing ride where one queen fixes another's crown.

Mercedes M. Yardley's *The Witches of Paradise* is a fine (*so* fine) example of literary lusciousness delicately woven; this is anthropomorphism at its finest. Mercedes' words take me places; they take me away. Away from myself and right to the heart of the story, where:

"It pulled tight against her throat, a noose made of itself…"

Miss Murder, that I consider you a goddess is no secret. Can you blame me? I quote: "He looked like a man who had come home from the war, but the war had found a home in him instead."

AMIRITE? Nuff said.

In *Vengeful Spirits,* Michael Burke depicts a darkness that looms "like an open throat."

With foraging dogs and characters creeping forward on "silent rodent feet," Mike's tale is chock-a-block with fragrant and lyrical imagery that fills the senses. The "earthy rhythms" and the "fast beats of jazz" not only provide a soundtrack to the disturbing visuals, but also hark back to Errick's Josephine Baker, no less. (Gotta love an inadvertent tie-in or two—our fabulous authors are certainly on the same page when it comes to evoking the senses.) *Spirits* is a sumptuous piece that showcases Mike's unique voice and unbounded creativity.

When it comes to building giant worlds within oppressive settings, Tom Deady comes into his own—and what could be more claustrophobic than *Tunnel 17's* nineteenth-century mine-shaft? Add mystery and monsters into the mix and you're onto a winner! I can smell this story. I can taste the grime.

There are timeless (and timely!) observations, too:

"Lessen her burden and she'll do her job."

…not to mention some scrumptious wordage: "He had a scrawny, rat-like face that no beard seemed to want anything to do with."

Characters, schmaracters. These are *people*.

We close with Sarah Read's last-but-by-no-means-least *Cult of the Rat King*, a piece woven from threads of blood, topped with a sprinkling of grit, and underscored by a healthy injection of fantastic realism (or, indeed, realistic fantasy!) Sarah's grasp of the dark side of human nature reveals itself through an inventive, overground underworld, where a network of avaricious players vie for position.

Rat King explores the matrix of a new, old humanity via "Coins and kings, names and thieves.' With a timeless palette of odd monarchs and 'orribly unfortunate Rats, Sarah's vivid, earthy canvas fills me up with its "mess of etched texture." If you wish to worship at Sarah's church, please do heed her advice: "…all churches have crypts, and all crypts have catacombs, and all catacombs lead back to the hive."

What a ride.

A note on dialogue: the more eagle-eyed reader might have perceived the occasional "error," where we've perhaps used "were" in place of "was," or vice versa, et cetera. These are no oversights, Dear Pedanticus, but rather, quite deliberate choices. Consider, if you will, a first-person narrator. They're speaking to us; thus, their recounting of events can be considered dialogue of a sort, and for the purposes of this book, it is treated as such. Thumb-rule: if it sounds right to the ear, it stays. And this entire book sounds so, so right, despite being so, so wrong in all the best ways: the not-rightness of the situations depicted, of the characters—nay, the *people* leaping from every page. The wrongness of the dark side of humanity, of nature, of trees and hair and rats and … of life. Of pure, honest-to-badness real life.

But none of this matters—my opinion, I mean. Who cares, right? Don't listen to me—listen to the book. If you are lucky enough to have had it whisper to you via the wind in your hair, then our work here is done. If this book has spoken to the very core of you in seascapes, rats and kings, then any picture I may attempt to paint in summation is little more than irrelevant waffle, is it not?

On that note, I'm reminded of Ben Jonson's Shakey-related musings (translated):

> This Figure, that thou here seest put,
> It was for gentle Shakespeare cut;
> Wherein the Graver had a strife
> with Nature, to outdo the life:
> O, could he but have drawn his wit
> As well in brass, as he hath hit
> His face; the Print would then surpass
> All that was ever writ in brass.
> But since he cannot, Reader, look
> Not on his Picture, but his Book.

It is no secret that however lyrically their editor may wax, these stories, and the authors who created them, speak for themselves. To paraphrase[1] Sarah's delicious final line: now that you have it, this book is yours, dear reader. A gift from our six incredible authors, to you.

---

[1] Nick wholesale, then bastardise.

Linda Hartley is a weirdo. She is also an author, poet, screenwriter, and editor of more than eleventy million award-winning books, with penchants for wordplay and hyperbole and an intense dislike of writing about herself in the third person. You can find her self-indulgent ramblings here: **https://liberatetutemet.com** and/or hit her up at: **SplatterpunkFranklyn@gmail.com**.

COVER ARTIST LYNNE HANSEN

Lynne Hansen is a horror artist who specializes in book covers. She loves creating art that tells a story and that helps connect publishers, authors, and readers. Her art has appeared on the cover of the legendary Weird Tales magazine, and she was selected by Bram Stoker's great-grandnephew to create the cover for the 125th Anniversary Edition of Dracula. Her clients include Valancourt Books, Cemetery Dance Publications, Thunderstorm Books and Raw Dog Screaming Press. She has illustrated works by New York Times bestselling authors including Jonathan Maberry, Brian Keene, and Christopher Golden. Her art has been commissioned and collected throughout the United States and overseas. For more information, visit **LynneHansenArt.com**.

Deliciously.
Dark.
Fiction.

WINTER
IN THE
CITY
R.B. WOOD & ANNA KOON

BLACK FIRE
CONCERTO
MIKE ALLEN

120
MURDERS

PORTRAITS
OF
DECAY
J.R. BLANES

SPR
IN

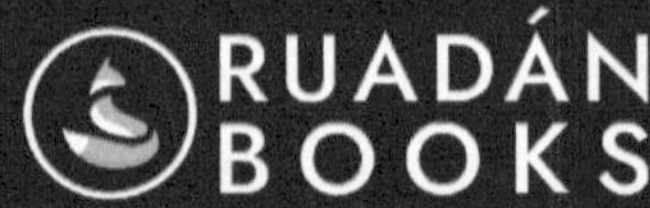

RUADÁN
BOOKS
ruadanbooks.com